D0944323

THE
UNIVERSITY OF WINNIPEG
PORTAGE & BALMORAL
WINNIPEG, MAN.   R3B 2E9
CANADA

HERITAGE PERILOUS

PR
6011
·A745 H4
1974

Heritage Perilous

by

Jeffery Farnol

This reprinted edition published by

DIPLOMA PRESS LTD.

40 Broadway, London, SW1

Published in this edition 1974.
First published by SAMPSON LOW
in 1946

MADE AND PRINTED IN GREAT BRITAIN BY
WILLMER BROTHERS LIMITED, BIRKENHEAD

To

ARTHUR CATLING

(The Unconquered)

Whose brave, glad spirit is an inspiration
more especially to his friend

Eastbourne   JEFFERY FARNOL
1946

CONTENTS

BOOK NUMBER ONE

The Sailorman

BOOK NUMBER TWO

THE ARISTOCRAT

BOOK NUMBER ONE

THE SAILORMAN

CHAPTER I

INTRODUCES THE INHERITOR

SAM stared down at the blunt toes of his big, clumsy shoes and shook his big, rather clumsy head that appeared set rather awkwardly on his powerful shoulders as, crouched ungracefully in the elbow-chair, he pondered this amazing thing that had befallen, while the keen-faced lawyer, silver-rimmed spectacles on sharp nose, viewed him with a certain supercilious perplexity.

"Money, eh?" enquired Sam, at last. "A lot of it, eh, sir?"

Mr. Joliffe having smoothed his trim wig, coughed and waxed eloquent:

"Indeed, a vast heritage! An e-normous fortune! Quite stu-pendous! Your father, the late Earl of Wrybourne was an immensely wealthy person——"

"And a dev'lish scoundrel!" growled Sam, with gesture so fierce and sudden that Mr. Joliffe started and clutched his toppling spectacles; then, having readjusted them, gazed at the speaker with even closer scrutiny. This tall, muscular fellow whose shabby garments smacked of the sea, and whose sun-tanned face, grim by nature, was rendered even more so by the line of a newly healed scar that ran from left eyebrow to vanish in the thick-curling chestnut hair.

"Ha!" exclaimed Sam, fiercely. "Earl or no, I hate to think he was my father. Are you sure o' this, sir?"

"Beyond all possible doubt——"

"Then curse him for that too!"

"May I venture to enquire why—what you know or may have heard——"

"Ay," replied Sam, clenching his hands to quivering fists, "I know he compelled my mother to slave or starve. . . . She did both!"

Mr. Joliffe coughed gently behind two fingers and was about to speak when Sam continued:

"All this dam' money! And now! when it's too late! Things always did go dev'lish contrary with me——"

"Contrary?" echoed Mr. Joliffe, clutching at his spectacles again.

"Contrary, ay!" nodded Sam. "This money and so on will come pretty handy, I suppose, but—not as it might ha' done, for, d'ye see,—she's dead! This mother o' mine . . . and not so long ago! This money might have helped her to ride out the storm and weather Old Man Death,—but no, it comes too late! She'd worked so precious hard all her life—she forgot to leave off. . . . Worked? Ay, she did so—and mostly for me, my schooling,—to feed, clothe and keep me decent—ah, she was a noble mother!" The deep, gentle voice hushed on the word and Mr. Joliffe peered through his glasses and over them at the speaker's bronzed, scarred features, beneath tousled shock of hair, thick brows knit above long-lashed, grey eyes, arrogant jut of nose and chin with close-lipped, shapely mouth between; finally he coughed again and enquired:

"You are, or were, a sailor, a privateer's man, I understand?"

"Ay, sir, first mate of the *Fortune*, privateer. And mighty fortunate she's been, thanks to her commander, Captain Ned Harlow."

"You have apparently been in action recently?"

"Off and on," answered Sam, touching his scar with sinewy finger. "I got this when we boarded and took the *Citoyenne* frigate off Toulon. Ay, I've been at sea a pretty goodish time and afore that, tried my hand at many things. For Lord love me—even as a boy I couldn't bear to see that mother o' mine slaving her life away—stitching, washing and scrubbing for other folk, so I cut school and turned general handy-man and finally shipped myself to sea in the *Albatross* whaler, became a chief harpooner and made good money, took to privateering and made a good deal more, prize-money, d'ye see—most of which I saved and brought home to mother, too late, of course . . . seeing she'd been dead and buried a month or more. No word of complaint in any of her letters . . . such cheery letters—— Oh, but damme," he broke off, "you don't want to hear all this! So get on, sir, and talk business."

"Con-found business!" exclaimed Mr. Joliffe, to his own surprise, and moved despite himself by the deep, passionate sincerity of these softly-uttered, slow-spoken words. "Pray continue! Tell me more of yourself and your heroic—mother."

"Thankee, Mr. Joliffe! 'Heroic' is the word, for she was indeed such a grand soul—ay, brave to the end . . . smiling away tears! A lady born and a lady always, d'ye see—up to her poor elbows in soapsuds or on her weary knees scrubbing floors, there was always about her a gentle dignity and graciousness . . . God's very woman and angel of mercy to all in affliction. And she died . . . worn out . . . for lack of what money can buy,—so to-day she is in her grave and I am rich! Ah, but any good that is in me, and there's little enough, comes from her." Again the deep, solemn voice was hushed and when Mr. Joliffe next spoke it was with look almost apprehensive.

"And did she never mention . . . never refer to the Earl of Wrybourne?"

"Not a word! She was too proud, God bless her. I knew she was highly born and of course that she was a widow, but she never spoke of her people and I never enquired. . . . But now, sir, what more o' this heritage? A while ago you said something about a handle,—a title, pray let's have it again, let's know exactly who I am and what I possess,—money and so on."

Instead of answering, Mr. Joliffe sat dumb, indeed he seemed strangely ill at ease,—he shifted in his chair, took off his spectacles, wiped, put them on again and stared down at littered desk, up at dingy ceiling, round upon book-lined walls,—anywhere but at his questioner; finally he coughed again and, with gaze still averted, spoke:

"I fear what I have to say will prove somewhat of a—hum—a shock to you."

"Oh well, sir," Sam replied, grim-smiling, "a man gets pretty well used to shocks of all sorts at sea, 'specially aboard a privateer, ay—and one commanded by such a dare-devil as Captain Edward Harlow,—so out with it, sir."

"Then," said Mr. Joliffe, taking up a quill pen and staring at it, "I am . . . compelled to inform you that . . . this brave and gracious lady who so wrought and slaved to your welfare, was . . . not your mother."

"Not——?" Sam leapt afoot, his tall form towering above the lawyer almost threateningly, so that Mr. Joliffe leaned back in his chair to gaze up into the contorted face above him with eyes of understanding wherefore their gaze did not waver as he continued, gently:

"Your mother, the Lady Monica Devine, an orphan and lady in her own right, was a wealthy heiress who eloped from school and married the Earl, your father, lived with him six months or thereabout, and fled his brutality in fear of her life. She found harbourage with her widowed cousin Ruth Felton in the village of Alciston, Sussex. There you were born and there, shortly after, your mother, the Countess of Wrybourne, died. Upon this sad event, Mrs. Felton, this good and noble lady adopted you, poor though she was, and brought you up as her own child. Thus instead of Samuel Felton you are Japhet Eustace Scrope, Earl of Wrybourne."

"And what," demanded Sam, deep-breathing, "what of my —real mother's fortune?"

"Reverted naturally to her husband the noble Earl, your father,—every acre, every stick and stone, to the uttermost farthing! Your mother would have been quite destitute but for her cousin Mrs. Felton's generosity."

"Then," said Sam, in a harsh whisper, "may the Earl my father be everlastingly damned! I grieve he is dead and beyond my reach."

"Indeed," sighed Mr. Joliffe, laying down the quill pen and shaking his trim head at it, "some men are . . . much better . . . dead!"

"But—but how," stammered Sam, hoarsely, "how am I . . . how are you assured of . . . of all this?"

"Be pleased to sit down, my lord, and——"

"Don't call me—that!"

"But, my lord, I must, since indeed lord you are henceforth and Earl of Wrybourne. Yes, my lord, as I said before, instead of Samuel Felton, mariner, you are most truly, Japhet Scrope lord and Earl of——"

"Belay!" growled Sam. "Sounds a lot of tom-foolery to me."

"However, my lord, pray be seated, compose yourself and permit me to explain fully as I may. . . . Thus, then, when the late Earl, your father——"

"Call him the Earl—and be cursed to his fatherhood!"

"Certainly, my lord. When the Earl died, thirteen months and—hum—five days since,—by the way he was killed by his horse, the animal threw him, breaking his neck——"

"A cheer for the horse!" growled Sam.

"Hum—ha!" murmured Mr. Joliffe, caressing smooth-shaven chin. "The horse is, I believe, and has ever been regarded as a highly intelligent animal! However, my lord the Earl being dead, instant enquiry was made for his wife without result until I called in the aid of a certain perspicacious Bow Street officer well beknown to me, one Jasper Shrig by whose efforts your—hum—unfortunate mother was traced, evidence of your birth established and yourself—well—here you are, my lord, thanks to the unfailing Shrig. You'll remember him, of course."

"Ay," nodded Sam, "an odd, rum sort of customer,—talked of murderers and murder-ees."

"I'll warrant he did and of vindictiveness also. . . . Now as to proofs of identity, they are here for your perusal,—certificates of your parents' marriage and your birth, by which it seems you are aged twenty-eight and seem, if I may say so, much older than your years, by which I opine a seaman's life is far other than a—hum—bed of roses?"

"More especially, sir, in time o' war," answered Sam, frowning at the documents Mr. Joliffe had set before him. Having glanced through these proofs of his identity and apparently limitless wealth, Sam passed fingers through and through his thick, chestnut hair until it stood on end, then sinking back in his chair, shook his head in helpless manner, saying:

"Sir, I'm taken all aback . . . shivering in the wind's eye . . . falling off and on like a rudderless ship, ay damme I am!"

"It is, as I told you, a vast heritage, my lord!"

"Too vast!" groaned Sam. "And seems quite utterly preposterous! I'm a sailorman and content so to be——"

"Ah but," quoth Mr. Joliffe, finger upraised portentously, "you are also a great landowner with huge rent-roll from estates in three several counties, hence your responsibilities are correspondingly great, especially in regard to your tenantry."

"Lord love me!" groaned Sam.

"Amen!" murmured Mr. Joliffe, his eyes twinkling. "And thus, m'lord, with your permission, I should like, indeed I will venture to proffer a few—hum—suggestions, if I may——"

"Ay, pray do, heave ahead, sir, I shall be grateful."

"I thank you for the assurance, my lord."

"Well?" enquired Sam. But again Mr. Joliffe sat mute,—for the eyes of his questioner, wide-set, well-opened, black-lashed, were unexpectedly shrewd, strangely compelling and lit up his rugged features, softening their grimness so wonderfully that the lawyer, this student of faces, could but gaze in surprised and ever-growing interest and once again, seemed vaguely disquieted.

"You were going to make me some suggestions," Sam reminded him.

"I was . . . I am . . . and yet——" Mr. Joliffe paused as if deliberating pro and con. . . .

"And yet?" Sam prompted. Mr. Joliffe resettled his spectacles and looking keenly into the bronzed, battle-scarred face before him, read there so much of fearless truth and inherent honesty that when next he spoke it was in warmer, more intimate tone and with a certain grave anxiety:

"My lord, henceforth the world is yours, all the glory and all the folly of it. You are become a master of life, a mighty power for much good or great evil. This heritage of yours, this vast wealth must and will make or mar you, prove you a man capable of much or merest weakling able only to his own eventual destruction. You are indeed a dangerously wealthy young man!"

"Dangerously?" murmured Sam.

"Yes," sighed Mr. Joliffe, "and in more senses than one! Great wealth is always a very mixed blessing, if blessing indeed it be, and a lure to rogues and harpies of every sort."

"Ay, true enough!" nodded Sam. "I've run athwart 'em, men and women in every port half round the world, so I've learned enough to keep 'em in my lee, give 'em a wide berth, d'ye see—steer clear of 'em, if you know what I mean, sir."

"Ah but," said Mr. Joliffe, leaning nearer, "there is an even greater danger threatens you, closer . . . more insistent, a . . . cold and deadly menace that, given opportunity, may strike unseen . . . swiftly and without . . . mercy!" Now as he listened Sam was amazed to hear Mr. Joliffe's voice sink to a hissing whisper, to see his brows knit above fierce or anxious eyes while the hand that had grasped his sleeve was shaking.

"Sir," questioned Sam, laying his own large, vital hand upon these clutching fingers, "what is this menace?"

"Your paternal uncle, Lord Julian Scrope."

"Uncle, eh?" murmured Sam. "Never knew I had one, but since I have—what about him?"

"He is your father's only brother and would have succeeded to this great heritage but for you, my lord!"

"Ah, I see!" nodded Sam. "I suppose he wishes you'd never discovered me,—finds me damnably in his way?"

"Pre-cisely!" exclaimed Mr. Joliffe, with quick, sharp nod. "He would yet succeed were you to die—suddenly!"

"Um!" mused Sam. "Then he might perhaps desire . . . my removal—or . . . even consider the how of it, eh sir?" Mr. Joliffe, re-settling his glasses, did not speak but his look was so eloquent that Sam nodded in turn, saying:

"So! He's that sort of cove, is he?" Here ensued a brief silence wherein Sam stared down at his shoe again while Mr. Joliffe, fumbling in pocket of his embroidered satin waistcoat, drew thence a gold snuff-box, tapped, opened and proffered it to Sam.

"Thankee, no, sir," he answered, "I take mine in a pipe."

"Then pray smoke if you will, my lord." But instead of so doing, Sam leaned back and with those grey eyes of his now eloquent and wistful, said:

"Mr. Joliffe, ever since I went seafaring to help that mother of mine, for I shall always think of her as my real mother, I've spent my life mostly aboard ship, whaling or fighting the mounseers, d'ye see. So to-day I'm a stranger. In all this big London ay and England too, I've no friend to trust or advise me except my old messmate and Captain, Ned Harlow. Now if you, sir, could manage to feel yourself friend enough to bear a hand with help and advice I should be . . . well . . . mighty grateful. And if you can so contrive, then please to let go all this 'my lordship' foolery, at least when we're alone, and call me—just Sam. So now, sir, what's the word?"

Mr. Joliffe snuffed with gusto, closed and fobbed his box, dusted himself with snowy handkerchief and glancing up—smiled.

"Sam," quoth he, in tone altered as his look, "I am a bachelor, with few interests outside business and fewer cares, reasonably selfish and fond of comfort as a cat! To-day, in this last half-hour, I am distinctly uncomfortable, have actually forgotten myself and am in a state of extraordinary disquiet, not to say perturbation, and all by reason of—you!"

"Why so, Mr. Joliffe?"

"Because though you are a belted earl and peer of the realm, you remain so essentially—just Sam!"

"Why d'ye see, I'm not a changeable kind of cove."

"Exactly! You remain the Sam who came into this stuffy

office like a fresh sea-breeze, and this heartened me. Then, instead of gloating upon your sudden great good fortune, you gloomed, and this surprised, and won my interest. But your grief was because your devoted mother could have no joy of it—and this touched me sensibly! And now, Sam, knowing poor Humanity as I do, its shams and hypocrisies, its crookedness and double-dealing, I prove you so . . . so very much the reverse and opposite of all this . . . with the best of your life before you, that I cannot bear to think you may risk losing it unwarned by me. And I begin by advising you that blind Fate, or devilish spiteful Fortune, has raised and armed two enemies who must destroy you or—themselves go down to irretrievable ruin!" Here Mr. Joliffe fumbled again for his snuff-box.

"Lord!" murmured Sam. "Two of 'em? Sounds interesting."

"Eh?" exclaimed Mr. Joliffe, pinch of snuff suddenly arrested within an inch of his nose, "did you say 'interesting'?"

"Yes, sir. I mean to say—two of 'em! I guess my uncle for one but who's t'other?"

"His only son, your cousin Ralph."

"Oh?" enquired Sam. "Ah! What like is he?"

"About your own age and size, but a regular Buck, a dashing Corinthian and perfect terror by all accounts."

"How a terror, sir?"

"He is esteemed a fistic expert."

"Ah!" sighed Sam, his eye brightening. "You mean a fibber, a bruiser, a fancy article, eh sir?"

"Just so. I am informed by Shrig how the Honourable Ralph is famous, or infamous, as a two-fisted smasher through all the countryside."

"Which countryside, sir?"

"Sussex. He is a quarrelsome hothead to be avoided and especially by you, Sam!"

"Ay but d'ye see, I've also done a trifle of fibbing afloat and ashore and if so be we chance to meet and he feel inclined——"

"No, no!" cried Mr. Joliffe so vehemently that his pinch of snuff was scattered broadcast. "You must not meet and certainly—oh, certainly not be drawn into quarrel! No, this would be their opening . . . give them their chance——"

"For what, sir?"

"Listen, Sam, and draw your own conclusions . . . I know your uncle, my lord Julian, only too well, having been compelled to deal with him in business. We Joliffes have been lawyers and agents to the Scrope family for generations. Thus I have known Lord Julian all his life and understand him as few possibly can,—and the more I have learned of his inner self the more appalled have I been! For, Sam, I do assure you he is beyond Nature, an anomaly, a—creature without a conscience—absolutely!"

"He sounds pretty inhuman!" murmured Sam.

"Listen and be warned! Lord Julian is a law unto himself, beneath handsome person and courtly manners he masks a beast of insatiate appetites and a boundless will—and with none of those moral restraints imposed by civilization! Highly esteemed in Society and privileged courtier, he is famous as a sportsman, known for reckless gambler, heartless libertine, unerring pistol-shot and notorious duellist with two deaths to his account already!"

"Lord!" exclaimed Sam again. "Lord love me!"

"Amen!" said Mr. Joliffe, with fervour. "So, this is the man who confidently expected and would have inherited this great fortune but for you, Sam, but for you! And I know how very desperately he is circumstanced, how deep he is in the clutches of the moneylenders—without this heritage he is ruined beyond redemption, he and his son! So now you are warned, Sam, are you warned?"

"Ay, I am indeed! And pray know me vastly grateful, friend."

"Then you will take all due, all needful precautions?"

"That will I. Now, pray, sir, what does he know, what has he heard of me?"

"Nothing beyond the fact of your being the legal heir and lately from abroad."

"Does he know I'm a seaman?"

"He does not! And shall learn nothing more of you—at least from me."

"Good! Then should I venture athwart his hawse it shall be under false colours, braces manned to bear up and go about, ay and with guns run out and double-shotted."

"All of which means precisely what, Sam?"

"That should we chance to meet, he shall not know who I am, yet should he suspect my true identity I'll duck and dodge

but be ready to give more than I take.   Besides I shan't be
quite alone, for d'ye see I'm due to meet my Captain and
friend, Ned Harlow, three days hence at the White Hart in
Lewes. And, Mr. Joliffe, blow foul or fair there's none like Ned!"

"You esteem him very highly?"

"Sir, he's my friend!   Ay and saved my life besides, and
what's more a finer seaman never trod plank and a fighting
captain few can match!   To see him take his ship into action
is pure joy for d'ye see he follows Nelson's own maxim
'engage the enemy more closely'.   It's keep the weather-gauge
and board and Ned himself generally first on the enemy's
deck.   Sixteen prizes we took on our last cruise, for says he
to me as we laid the *Intrepide* frigate aboard, 'It shall be
competence for life, shipmate, or Davy Jones'."

"A regular fire-eater, eh, Sam?"

"Ay, sir.   Yet mild-spoken and meek-seeming as the most
parson-y parson!   Seldom put out, never swears—much, never
at a loss and choke-ful o' book-learning.   Shakespeare, poetry,
the classics, Homer, Virgil, Horace and reads 'em in the
original too—learned himself Greek and Latin to do it."

"Your captain is truly an original, Sam."

"Ay b'George, sir, that's the word!"

"Consequently, Sam, I'm relieved and glad to know you
will be companied by such a man, especially as it seems you
intend for Sussex."

"Why oddly enough, sir, this was Ned's idea, he has friends
living there and, 'twixt you and me, I'm sadly afraid he
means to live there too, being so flush o' prize-money he talks
of buying a farm which, seeing he's such prime sailor-man is
great pity."

"Howbeit, Sam, for reasons aforementioned Sussex holds
danger for you.   Wherefore I shall take such measures for
your protection as I deem proper——"

"Lord, sir!   I do hope you won't."

"I know, Sam, I know.   But then I am also aware and
too uncomfortably certain of the malign cunning and utter
ruthlessness of the evils opposing us.   And I say 'us' because
to more or less degree I intend sharing these perils."

"But, sir,—it's very handsome of you, but—why should
you?"

"Sam, look around you, these musty tomes, this stuffy
office and myself like a human spider spinning webs to catch

malevolent villainy . . . pitting my wits against their devilish cunning and usually, I am glad to say, with the happiest results. Here I work plotting their destruction, unknown, unheard, unseen. . . . But sometimes if the case is sufficiently remarkable, I take occasion to witness the criminal's arrest and—hum—final exodus."

"Exodus? You mean—by hanging?"

"I do. Precisely! I have witnessed the execution of several cold-blooded scoundrels with my natural horror tempered by a very lively satisfaction, knowing the world a cleaner, better place for their removal. You have never seen a hanging?"

"No! I've seen too many hearty fellows die by steel or bullet but never by rope and hope I never shall."

"Indeed 'tis a sordid, a dreadful yet, I fear, most necessary business, not as a deterrent but to be rid of social evil."

"Yet evil persists, sir."

"Alas,—and always must, Sam, until the curse of Cain is lifted, ignorance banished and Humanity turns to and seeks for the hidden good rather than the too blatant evil."

"Ay, but when shall this be, sir?"

"When Mankind has grown wiser by suffering. There are only two ways in life's journey, Sam, up or down, the right or wrong and we are free to choose, more or less, and this alone lifts us above the brutes whose only guide is instinct. Talking of evil naturally brings me back to your uncle, Lord Julian. And I now take occasion to assure you, strictly betwixt ourselves, that I am setting in motion such latent forces as shall render him powerless to harm you—or anyone else! But this will need time, six months or more. So I must ask you to be patient and make no effort to assume your title and lofty rank in Society until you may do so with perfect safety. Meanwhile, of course, you are at liberty to draw what monies you require, to buy any properties you fancy or sell such of your own as you will. Only, and again, I beg you to have patience."

"That will I, sir. For, d'ye see, I've no mind to this title, and as for society, why damme, sir, I should be like fish out o' water, ay helpless as hulk in a driftway."

"Ah but," chuckled Mr. Joliffe, "you will be one of the wealthiest bachelors in England and able to choose the proudest beauty in town or out! Mothers with marriageable daughters will haunt you——"

"Lord love me!" groaned Sam. "I'd liefer turn farmer along o' Ned."

"Which reminds me,—where in Sussex do you and your captain propose to stay?"

"With friends of his, I understand, though where, I've no idea."

"The chiefest of your many estates, Wrybourne Feveril, is in Sussex, Sam, and 'tis but natural you should wish to see the glory of it, but——"

"Ay ay, sir, I'll be wary, trust me."

"Are you lodged here in town?"

"At the Turk's Head on Snow Hill, sir."

"Sam if, as I hope, we are to be friends, pray know that my name is Ebeneezer—'Ben' to my intimates—and that I have a house amid trees in Streatham village where I shall be happy to entertain you so long as you will. What do you say?"

"With all my heart, Ben."

"Good!" said Mr. Joliffe, consulting his watch. "In five minutes my carriage will be at the door, we'll drive to Snow Hill for your baggage, then home and on the way I will give you more particulars of your blue-blooded, extremely arrogant, most discreditable family."

It was as they descended the outer steps towards Mr. Joliffe's waiting carriage that Sam was aware of one who chanced to pass by, and this such a very commonplace, ordinary seeming person, indeed so entirely unremarkable that Sam would never have noticed him had not their eyes happened to meet,—a swift, casual glance instantly forgotten as Sam took his seat in the carriage. But no sooner had the vehicle rolled away than this unremarkable person did an odd, not to say remarkable thing,—halting suddenly, he took out a small pocket memorandum wherein he scribbled hastily, whispering as he did so:

"Six foot tall, or thereabout. Aged about thirty. Tough and determined-looking. Tanned complexion. Scar on left side of brow. So,—there y'are m'lud Earl, but—for how long? I wonder." Then pocketing his notebook, this so ordinary person set off at no ordinary speed.

CHAPTER II

JAPHET EUSTACE SCROPE, fifth Earl of Wrybourne set forth on his travels not in pride of state with gleaming coach, footmen and outriders like the aristocrat Fortune had determined he should be, but as the man he was, that is to say, with no pageantry of hoofs, wheels and servants attendant, but alone and upon his own sturdy legs. Moreover, as if to defy Fortune's so compelling decree, he had rigged his muscular person in most sailorly fashion. Thus upon his thick newly-cropped hair a glazed hat was cocked at devil-may-care angle, about brawny throat was a blue neckerchief brightly patterned with large, yellow anchors, its loose ends fluttering gaily; round his lithe middle a broad belt with vast, gleaming buckle, supported nether garments of dashing, nautical cut; in one powerful hand he grasped a knotted, bludgeon-like stick, in the other a trim bundle tied neatly in large, spotted handkerchief of the kind made notable by that great fistic champion Jem Belcher. Thus equipped, vigorous of movement, cheery of visage, alert for instant action and ready to engage all comers as the Navy itself, this new Earl of Wrybourne strode on to front grim Destiny and perilous Circumstance like the English sailorman he was.

CHAPTER III

IN pleasant chamber of the White Hart Inn overlooking the
busy street sat Captain Edward Harlow. Richly though
sombrely clad, he seemed more like studious landsman than
the hardy captain of a battle-scarred privateering vessel whose
many daring exploits had won renown in the narrow seas and
beyond,—for Captain Ned's comely head was bent over an
open book, his clean-shaven, shapely lips forming soundlessly
the noble lines he was reading.

It was thus Sam found him as pausing upon the threshold,
he enquired:

"What is it this time, Ned, Virgil or Horace?"

"Neither, shipmate. Shut the door, sit down, listen and
tell me." And forthwith he read aloud:

> " 'This royal throne of kings, this sceptr'd isle,
> This earth of majesty, this seat of Mars,
> This other Eden, demi-paradise;
> This fortress built by Nature for herself—
> Against infection and the hand of war:
> This happy breed of men, this little world;
> This precious stone set in the silver sea
> Which serves it in the office of a wall,
> Or as a moat defensive to a house,
> Against the envy of less happier lands;
> This blessèd plot, this earth, this realm—
> —This England.' "

"Shakespeare, an't it, Ned?"

"Ay,—who else could frame our England in words so apt and
deathless true? Ha, Sam, the oftener and further I voyage,
the happier and prouder am I of this right blessed old island!"

"So am I, Ned, but it goes without saying—for I've no
words for it."

"However you've bled for it, Sam, and that's far better. . . .
But what luck with your lawyers?"

"Pon my soul, Ned, I don't know! For it seems I'm confoundedly rich, ay, money enough to build and fit a ship o' my own—a fleet! Ha, but, along with all this wealth I've relatives who are, or will be, after my blood! For d'ye see, messmate, but for me they would have come in for this heritage and without it they're in shoal water with rocks alee and certain to founder." Captain Ned closed his battered volume on a finger and leaning back regarded Sam with a pair of the mildest-seeming blue eyes which widened beneath lifting brows as they took in the various items of his companion's attire.

"Eh—Sam," he exclaimed, "why this too-nautical rig? Scupper me, if you don't show like the Navies, Royal and Merchant, all rolled into one!"

"Ay, I do, Ned, I do indeed! Nobody could possibly mistake me for anything but a slap-up sailorman, a regular Jack-ashore."

"Only a jack afloat,—he'd certainly damn you as too sailorly to be true!"

"Ah but," quoth Sam, tossing the glazed hat upon the nearest chair, "I'm rigged for the eye of shore-biding folk—especially two! No landsman spying yon hat and this neckerchief only could possibly mistake me for a blue-blooded aristocrat, eh Ned?" The Captain closed his book, laid it aside and looked Sam over with closer regard.

"Shipmate," said he, "I've never known that tough figurehead of yours affected by liquor or sun, and yet now I'm . . . wondering——"

"Same here, Ned! It all sounds too curst ridiculous for belief,—so let's cut it adrift,—tell me instead, when does your widow clap you aboard and grapple you in wedlock for better or worse, my poor, old lad—when?" Captain Ned winced, his athletic form appeared to wilt and he uttered sound like a stifled groan ere he answered:

"Sam, I . . . don't know. I . . . I haven't seen her—yet!"

"Oh?" said Sam. "Why?"

"I waited for you to . . . to stand by and bear a hand as messmate should."

"Well, here I am, Ned, ready and willing to do all I may. Though women are craft I steer clear of as you know—ever since that French mamselle so very nearly——"

"All I want is your advice, Sam. For here am I with hard

Duty hauling me one way and . . . tender inclination the other. For though pledged to the widow I'm . . . well . . . yearning to be free."

"And rightly so, Ned, for this means you're clean out of love with her. Agreed?"

"Ay, that is so!" groaned the Captain. "But then—she has my word."

"However, since you're not in love this alters the case, for without love d'ye see——"

"Ah, but I am in love, Sam, deeply! Heart and soul!"

"Why then this alters the case back again, though you're steering a plaguey erratic course, Ned. Still, if you're in so deep, why not marry your widow and be done with it?"

"Because . . . Sam . . . messmate, I . . . love another!"

"Not another widow, Ned?"

"No, damme!" groaned the Captain, "Never again! No more widows for me!"

"Well then, don't marry this widow."

"Ah, but Sam, duty compels!"

"Oh!" murmured Sam. "Ah? Then the widow it must be after all—I suppose. Though lookee, Ned, wedlock without love is all lock! Ay and consequently means breakers in your lee and a foul anchorage. Love, d'ye see, Ned, is wedlock's sheet anchor, that gone, marriage is wrecked soon or late."

"Ah, Sam, that is what dreads me! And yet she has waited years for me to make enough money, and now that I have . . . well . . . how can I go about, sheer off and leave her desolate, how?"

"Sounds a foulish course, Ned. But what of the one not a widow? Does she wait too—and know you love her?"

"I . . . yes . . . I fancy she guessed it, for I never dared tell her. No indeed, I've kept a fairish offing for fear I might speak—and myself no free man! So there's the case, Sam,—what is your counsel?"

" 'Tis plaguey awkward situation, Ned."

"It confounds me, Sam. This is why I ask your advice,—seeing you are my mate and friend of years besides. So out with it."

"Well first, is your widow mercenary?"

"N-no, I should say 'prudent'."

"Does she love you deeply, heart and soul?"

"Y-es, I . . . suppose so."

"Can't you be sure and certain, Ned?"

"Hardly, Sam. She is not . . . not a very . . .demonstrative person."

"Oh!" murmured Sam, pondering deeply. "Ah!"

"Well, shipmate, what's the word?"

"Cut her adrift, Ned, your widow and——"

"Impossible! Not to be thought on! For as I told you——"

"Ay ay, duty compels, I know! But Ned, such duty will surely compel the three of you to misery all your days,—it will so! Your properest course is to be now as desperate bold ashore as you are afloat. Up now and bear away for the widow, speak her fair, gently though firm. If she rages, comfort her with cash. If she weeps console her with more. Come now, tacks and sheets, let's stand away at once."

So, together they rose, took hats and sticks and together descended to the street where all was stir and bustle for it was market-day; nor had they far to go, for presently the Captain halted before a small, neat dwelling.

"Sam," said he, dabbing moist brow with dainty handkerchief, "you'll remember that night we boarded and cut out the *Serapis* under the batteries at Brest?"

"Shall I ever forget it, Ned! B'gad 'twas touch and go with us!"

"It was, messmate,—yet I never felt then as I do now. Look at me,—damme, I'm all of a quake!"

"Well, to it, Ned, to it! Cutlasses out and boarders away!"

"You'll keep an offing but stand by, Sam."

"Ay, I'll bear away for a sight o' the castle yonder, you'll find me thereabout. Now 'bold' is the word and good luck, old fellow!"

"Well, here's for it!" So saying, Captain Ned breathed deep, squared his shoulders and striding forward knocked upon the door of this small, neat house.

CHAPTER IV

OF NOTHING IN PARTICULAR

MEANWHILE Sam stood gazing up at this Castle of Lewes, stately in its ruin, massive gateway, scowling battlement and mighty keep, this hoary monument of an age remote and well-nigh forgotten, its lofty walls rising up and up in rugged grandeur against an azure sky; this part of old England whose very stones might be so eloquent for those blessed with ears to hear, crying out of battle, siege and storm, of cheers for victory, of the cries and groans of martyrs amid the vicious crackle of searing flame,—and of a virile nation's upward struggle through blood and suffering and anguished tears, to that freedom which is England's glory and makes its hallowed earth the secure haven for all those fleeing from tyranny and oppression:

> "This fortress built by Nature for defence
> Against invasion and the ills of war:
> This mighty isle set in the silver sea
> To fling back foes and shelter all distressed."

Sam was thus misquoting, and such were his thoughts when he became aware of one beside him, a person, this, so ordinary and altogether unremarkable that Sam merely glanced towards him then gave all his attention to the old castle again, until a perfectly expressionless voice remarked:

"A noble spectacle, friend!"

"Ay ay!" answered Sam, carelessly, but meeting the glance of the speaker's small, colourless eyes, he set the glazed hat to lower more jaunty angle over his scarred brow, with light tap on the crown.

"You are a mariner, I see."

"You were blind else, my hearty."

"Yet greatly interested in ancient ruins!"

"Why lookee, I'm wondering how yon old place 'ud look arter say a couple o' broadsides from a seventy-four."

"Ah, you have served in a battleship, my friend?"

"Off an' on, sir. But gimme the little craft for action."

"I see. And you are but new-landed, I fancy?"

"Ay ay, that's me! And loaded to the hatches wi' rhino, my hearty!" Here Sam winked, slapped his pockets and made a sudden gesture with his sailorly legs like the beginning of a hornpipe.

"So now you are on your way home, I suppose?"

"Mate, you suppose true! Foller in my wake, ay, keep astarn o' me and you shall see sich welcome for jolly jack as'll warm the very cockles o' y'r 'eart."

"Is your home far from here?"

"Depends on what you'd call far."

"Is it a mile?"

"Ay and more."

"Where then?"

"D'ye know Brighthelmstone?"

"I've heard of it."

"Well, it ain't theer."

"Eh, not?"

"No, my home lays 'twixt and 'tween here and theer——"

At this moment came a familiar hail:

"Ahoy, Sam!"

"Snoggers!" he exclaimed. "Sink and burn me if theer ain't my Cap'n!" Saying which, Sam turned hastily and left the man in the shadow of this great castle showing the more insignificant by contrast. . . . But the Captain's step was light, his blue eyes shone and he flourished his stick triumphantly.

"Sam, oh Sam," he exclaimed joyfully, "Lord be thanked —she refused me, d'ye hear, refused me! And what d'you say to that?"

"Congratulations! And what now?"

"A bottle, Sam, a bottle! And of the best, for this is an occasion! It seems she couldn't wait any longer and so, ha, messmate,—the day after to-morrow she's being married to a town barber-surgeon and I—shake hands, Sam, I'm free! So a bottle it is and then we'll bear away together for—never mind, but we will! And this night, Sam, you shall eat of the best, and sleep 'twixt sheets white as lilies and sweet with lavender! Ah, you shall taste such cookery and see such beauty as bless this old world too seldom."

CHAPTER V

OF ARGUMENT BY THE WAY, WHICH ENDS WITH A SCREAM

THE white road winding upwards between shady hedge-rows, led round a sharp corner to show them suddenly a wide, fair prospect of richly green, undulating country stretching away, lush meadow, glittering stream, darkling coppice and bowery hamlet, away to a line of noble hills rising afar in gentle majesty.

Here Captain Ned, who had walked some while in musing silence, paused to feast his sight and say:

"Ha, Sam, here is Will Shakespeare's 'demi-paradise'. Ay, 'this land of such dear souls, this dear, dear land, dear for her reputation through the world!' And all unchanged since his day, thank God! 'Let us be backed by God and with the seas . . . in them and in ourselves our safety lies . . . England is safe if true within herself'. Ah, Will knew and said it all, eh, Sam?" Finding him silent, the Captain turned to see his companion's sombre gaze was backward towards Lewes town already vague with distance.

"Messmate," he demanded, "why must you peer astern of us so often?"

"Spies, Ned,—one at least. Ay, they're after me already it seems."

"Eh? What? Who are?"

"My relations, I fancy. This bloody-minded nunks o' mine . . . this accursed heritage!"

"How, Sam, then was that dog-watch yarn you spun me of a fortune left you—was it true fact?"

"Ay, true as death, Ned! So to-day I'm being dogged and spied on, or so I think. For, d'ye see yonder by the old castle a strange fellow brings to alongside and tries to pump me, but got only foolery for his pains, because, Ned, I'd glimpsed this same fellow in London by the lawyer's office . . . and now I'm wondering if he's away to warn my relations how I'm on the road to 'em."

"What like is he?"

"B'gad, Ned, it's hard to say, for he's so exactly like

everybody else that he may be anybody, nobody, or somebody more than he seems——"

"Easy, shipmate, easy!" quoth the Captain, in frowning
perplexity; Sam chuckled.

"I mean," he explained with white-toothed grin, "this insignificant, ordinary-seeming fellow may be one to reckon
with, so I'm keeping my weather-eye lifting for squalls."

"Ah!" said Captain Ned, also glancing back whence they
had come. "You think he is standing after us, a stern-chase,
hey?"

"However, there's no sign of him, so let's carry on. Tell
me now," said Sam as they went on down the hill, "are
you still minded, quite determined to . . . quit the sea,
Ned?"

"Yes, I am indeed. I mean to try my hand at farming—
in a snug, comfortable way . . . a farmstead, not too small,
bowered in trees, in a garden not too large with a row of beehives, and a few acres with cows, say eight, an orchard and
a paddock with an easy-going nag to jog around on . . .
in a word, Sam, Home, ay, with a capital aitch! A quiet
anchorage at last, a peaceful haven . . . to pass the rest of
my days."

"How so, Ned? D'you mean in sowing and mowing—
hayricks and so on, eh?"

"Naturally! Then besides I shall always have my books."

"And beehives, Ned."

"Why yes, so I said——"

"And cows, Ned."

"Ay, I mentioned 'em too."

"And a nag,—but what beside, messmate? An't you
leaving out the one most important and necessary item?"

"Eh, what tack are you off on now, Sam?"

"Woman, Ned! A wife! I've heard no home is complete
without one. Though I've heard also that when woman comes
in at door, peace flies out up the chimney. And for my part
I'm pretty sure 'tis only too dam' true."

"You would, Sam, being such confirmed, ay, and confounded, woman-hater."

"Not woman-hater, Ned, merely a female evader, plying
well to windward o' their feminine bewitchments."

"Yet what of that Spanish dame in Rio who knifed
you?"

"All quite natural, Ned, for d'ye see a don was throttling her, I floored him and she knifed me because he happened to be her newest husband, which was only to be expected, she being a woman—and dago besides."

"Someday, Sam, you'll meet a real woman,—I hope!" After this, they went in silence, Sam trudging heavily, head bowed in frowning thought, Captain Ned striding blithely, shoulders squared, blue eyes fixed yearningly on the distance before them until:

"Listen!" said he, suddenly. "Hear the song of that lark and be glad you're alive—and in England!"

"Ay, but," growled Sam, hardly troubling to lift his frowning gaze, "yon's only a bird! Yet away there is ocean calling . . . calling day and night: 'Oh sons o' mine, come ye, dare me,—trust me and I'll give ye life and maybe death. Ah, but while ye breathe, no living may compare with the joys and dangers of me, the glad freedom of my rushing winds, the hiss and surge of my ever-restless, hungry billows! So come ye mariners of England that are my children all, dare me, trust me as ye have done through the ages!' Can't you hear it, Ned, don't you hear?"

"Sam," exclaimed the Captain, halting suddenly to stare his amazement, "now God bless my soul! What's this you're quoting?"

"My thoughts, Ned, put into words this time because I'm troubled——"

"You've been reading poetry, Sam."

"Not I. Can't abide the stuff."

"Yet you were talking it, or very nearly."

"No, what I said had never a jingle or rhyme."

"There is such thing as blank verse, Sam. So keep a bright look-out or you'll be turning poet or some such."

"However," answered Sam, shaking his head, "what I said was for my grief, ay, and Old England's too, that we must lose prime sailor, such ship-master and leader o' men as yourself, Ned. I've seen you in tempest and battle, how our lads would jump, instant t' your command or follow the gleam o' your cutlass no matter the odds, follow you to victory, ay, and death often enough, just because you were—you! And now . . . that you should turn farmer! You of all men——"

"Hell and damnation!" exclaimed the Captain, his usual placidity ruffled at last. "Why the devil shouldn't I?"

"Because you are yourself, Ned, while yonder at sea lie Old England's foes waiting and watching their chance to foul this island, dammem! Ha, and Nelson dead and Buonaparte across the Channel, back in triumph and making ready to spring——"

"Well, let him, the sooner the better. For:

> " 'Come the three corners of the world in arms
> And we shall shock them. Naught can make us rue
> If England to itself do rest but true.'

"So says our Will. And true she will be, says I. And as for me, like you I've shed my blood and will again if need be. . . . But to-day . . . I'm nigh forty years old and have sailed the seas since a lad. I've roughed it afloat and ashore doing my duty how best I may, and so will I ever."

"This I know, messmate, this I surely know."

"Why then I have as surely earned a right to peace at last, home and maybe a . . . a happiness I scarce dare think on. However, if England must be fought for, I'll do it on English soil. Ha—and there it is!"

"What?" enquired Sam, in startled accents. "Where?"

"Yonder, Sam, behind those trees to starboard,—the Old Dun Cow which suggesting milk shall supply something stronger. How say you, shipmate?"

"Ay, ay, Captain, with all my heart!" But as they approached this quiet, tree-shaded inn, from somewhere nearby rose a sudden, gasping scream.

CHAPTER VI

OF FISTS,—AND—THE BLACK-HAIRED, GOLDEN-EYED ANDROMEDA

"EH—a woman?" quoth Sam, glancing about.

"Ay. The inn-yard, I fancy."

So thither went they and beheld,—a rough-clad man on hands and knees, dripping blood from battered nose, two young dandies who laughed and a woman struggling vainly in the arms of a third, a tall, powerful young fellow whose dashing air and foppish attire from buckled hat to be-tasselled hessian boots, proclaimed him, in sporting parlance, for a "bang-up tippy", a "go" and regular "buck"; the woman whose shabby, rumpled garments betrayed too much of her young shapeliness, was silent now, striving desperately against the large, white hands that became ever more aggressive and masterful until—the jaunty hat was whisked from his astonished head and he became suddenly aware of painfully intrusive fingers that twisting themselves in his ornate cravat, wrenched and twisted, drawing him irresistibly towards a bronzed, lowering face lit by grey eyes fiercely wide.

"S-so, my buck?" hissed Sam, and flung him away so violently that he reeled backwards and would have fallen but for the wall that checked and propped him. At this so sudden and unexpected assault ensued a moment of amazed silence; then with encouraging shout, forward strode the two dandies, one of whom flourished a modish cane, which slim elegance was instantly beaten to earth by Captain Ned's bludgeon-like stick.

"Sirs," quoth he pleasantly, glancing from one to other, "fair play if you please, or I shall be happy to engage you singly or together. And, messmate, if you must, do not hit too hard!"

Sam, about to reply, closed lips firmly instead, for the Buck, square chin tucked well in, powerful fists up, was advancing against him, poised gracefully on toes of his gleaming hessians, and with all the easy assurance of a finished boxer.

So they fronted each other, eye to eye, gallant Buck all arrogant confidence by reason of past victories in academy and ring,—and rugged sailorman, lithe, grim, and hardened by exposure, who had fought many a time and not for glory but life itself.

The Buck feinted gracefully, leapt nimbly and smote viciously; the sailor ducked as nimbly, countered heavily, was away and in again with hard-driving left. So the battle was joined. And now for some while there followed such dexterous foot and fist-work seldom witnessed; grace of powerful bodies in swift, lithe action that as time passed became only the more furiously purposeful. . . . The Buck, a gay and joyous fighter, sailed in, both fists going with more or less effect; the sailor using powerful left, stung and checked him, yet watching for chance to use his ever-menacing right, meeting determined attack with light though punishing defence.

Thus as time passed the Buck grew more cautious, the Sailor more aggressive; both now were bleeding, both seemed tiring, especially the Sailor whose feet seemed heavier and blows less accurate, so that it became a matter of skill backed now by sheer strength, grim fortitude and experience.

The two dandies, both lovers of the Game, had been first thralled beyond speech, then plaintively anxious, were now jubilant and vociferous:

"Go it, old fellow," cried Number One, "you've got him! Ha demme, what su-perb fibbing, eh, Bob?"

"Mag-nificent!" gasped Number Two. " 'Pon honour . . . never saw th' equal . . . no, not even Jackson himself! Ha, Ralph . . . he's groggy! Level him! Measure him for a finisher!" So they encouraged their champion while Captain Ned, keenly watchful, poised himself for swift action, waiting for the expected moment which came with dramatic suddenness,—stamp of foot, thudding impact of unerring right fist . . . the Buck's head jerked violently up and back. . . . Then Captain Ned leapt, caught the falling body and lowered it gently to earth; the gleaming hessians kicked feebly once or twice and were still, and for a moment none seemed to move or breathe; then:

"Sam," quoth the Captain, chidingly, "why must you hit so hard? Had I not caught him he would certainly ha' cracked his skull on the cobbles. You always use needless force!"

B

"Ay . . . I do," panted Sam meekly, as he wiped blood from his torn cheek. "Always . . . forget my . . . strength, damme! How is he, Ned?"

"He requires a good souse of water," replied the Captain, "Come, sirs," said he, beckoning the two apparently stupefied fine gentlemen, "stir yourselves and carry your friend indoors——"

"Why so we will," cried Number One, "ha but, by God, sir, if he is anyway seriously hurt you shall hear of it, I promise you! You shall be hounded to prison, the pair of you, by George! For let me tell you his father——"

"All right, Bob, he's coming to! See, he's stirring! How are y'now, Ralph, m'dear fellow? Can y' walk? Help me with him, Bob, can't you?" So together they lifted their feebly-moving hero and half led, half carried him into the house.

"Lord!" exclaimed Sam, looking after them, "I believe I've floored one o' the family!"

"Eh, what family?"

"A . . . most discreditable one. However, he's a pretty tidy article,—nearly levelled me twice!"

"So I noticed. And he cut your face."

"Ay, he wears a ring on his left like a knuckle-duster, consequently I'm a sore, he got in one or two ribroasters. Wherefore, Ned, my present need is ale and——" He paused and turned at sound of hoofs and wheels and thus beheld a plump, sleek-coated pony harnessed to a weather-beaten, four-wheeled cart wherein sat, or was enthroned,—The Woman.

Her gloveless hands grasped the reins, her small, close bonnet, weather-beaten almost as the cart, shaded a face shadowed already by a vague sadness, such face as drew and held Sam's gaze and the Captain's, too,—oval, sunburned, framed in hair black as midnight lit by strange, golden eyes beneath low-arching brows; and when she spoke it was in voice matching the tender beauty of the lips that uttered these words:

"Sir, I hope he did not hurt you very much . . . and I'm trying to . . . find words to thank you properly . . . as I would. But oh, I'm glad, very glad you hit him so nice and hard . . . that brutish satyr."

"Lady," murmured Sam, looking up into these strange,

golden eyes, "I . . . it was a pleasure!" At this she smiled,
though very wistfully, saying:

"Well, please know that I am truly . . . deeply grateful!"

"Please . . . one moment," pleaded Sam, as she made to
drive away, "do you chance to know the name of yon . . .
fine gentleman?"

"Oh yes, he is well known, quite notorious hereabouts, his
name is—Scrope, the Honourable Ralph Scrope . . . yes,
that beast is called 'honourable'. And he hurt poor John
Dobbs, John is the ostler here who sometimes looks after our
pony Joshua, this is Joshua. John did his best to defend
me but that beast was too strong for him. I've been bathing
his poor, bruised face—I mean John's, of course. And now
I'll thank you again and go——"

"First," said Sam, a little awkwardly, "may I know . . .
will you . . . favour me with your name?"

"Why y-es," she answered almost unwillingly, "though I
expect you, a sailor, will think it quite ridiculous, but I was
christened Andromeda . . . Good-bye!" Then poking Joshua
with the whip she drove out and away.

"An-dromeda!" murmured Sam, gazing after her.

"Ah!" said the Captain, gazing at Sam, "and your phiz
might show a trifle less grim if you washed away the gore,
Sam,—though I ought to call you Perseus now."

"Oh?" enquired Sam, "Why?"

"Because, according to the Classics, he also saved his
Andromeda from a monster."

"Ah?" murmured Sam, "let's hear."

"Not 'till you are washed and I have been close engaged
with a tankard, shipmate."

CHAPTER VII

THE afternoon was hot and airless, the road dusty, but Captain Ned held on at the same brisk, seemingly tireless pace, his blue gaze ever upon the distance ahead until at last, Sam, removing the glazed hat to wipe perspiring brow, enquired:

"Are we in any particular hurry, Ned?"

"No, Sam, no, only when I walk, I—walk."

"Well now, let's bring to among the trees yonder and sit to smoke a sociable pipe."

So presently seated within this leafy shade they puffed in companionly silence and content until at last the Captain enquired, drowsily:

"You've never fancied any particular woman, have you, Sam?"

"Twice!" he answered. "But—never again. Not I!"

"Sam," quoth the Captain, viewing his Chief Officer's stalwart form and grimly confident visage with twinkling eyes, "you are a fair navigator, a prime officer afloat, but first-rate jackass and juggins ashore!"

"Oh?" enquired Sam, pondering this. "Ah! Why?"

"Because, my over-confident numbskull, this man and woman business, this mutual attraction, call it love, disease or madness, takes a fellow before he's aware, and if 'tis the real thing, brings him up with a round turn, has him in irons, ay, helpless as dismasted hulk rolling to every sea. Or, conversely, so inspires him that daring all he stands away fair weather or foul, heedless of tempest, fire, fury and hell itself —so he may come to his heart's desire."

"Sounds a pretty desperate business, Ned."

"Why so it is, shipmate. And should you ever catch this disease, you'll take it badly, Sam, badly! So—watch out!"

"I will, Ned, I will indeed, for d'ye see I——"

At this moment with rustle and flurry of leaves, out from thicket nearby stepped a pony, sleekly plump and well groomed; which animal having paused to survey these two humans with leisured, dispassionate gaze, snorted gently and stooped graceful head to crop the richly succulent grass with slow-crunching gusto.

"A brown cob!" said Sam.

"A bay pony!" quoth the Captain.

"Looks familiar, eh, Ned?"

"Joshua!" called a voice at no great distance, whereat the pony cocked his ears and both men sat up to gaze expectantly in the one direction, for this voice though raised, was sweet-toned and clear. Then the leaves parted again and Sam was looking into a pair of golden eyes set between black lashes and was so instantly and perfectly aware of her beauty that he wondered how it had failed to impress him before; he noticed also that she was older than he had then supposed. At sight of them she stood suddenly arrested, yet with no least sign of awkwardness or confusion.

"Miss Andromeda," said Sam rising, hat in hand, as did the Captain, "I am glad to see . . . to meet you again."

"Oh?" said she, in her very lovely voice (thought Sam), but with glance direct and almost challenging, "Why?"

"First to tell you that instead of ridiculous I think your name is a . . . well . . . a very . . . lovely name. I do indeed! And secondly to make known to you my friend Captain Edward Harlow of the *Fortune* privateer."

Andromeda curtseyed gracefully, Captain Ned bowed gallantly, saying:

"And may I, Miss Andromeda, present to your notice my First Officer, Sam Felton, who should be called 'Perseus', don't you think?"

"Perseus?" she repeated, wrinkling her dark brows, "Ah yes, of course! Perseus rescued his Andromeda from a vile monster, didn't he. So, Mr. Felton, this Andromeda thanks her Perseus again . . . and very truly. And now, I'm wondering if you——"

"Meda! Meda child, where are you?" Uttering this petulant summons, a little, plump, rosy-cheeked gentleman tripped into view, such breath-taking vision of silk-stockinged, belaced and embroidered elegance as should have been gracing a London drawing-room rather than these rustic solitudes; now even as Sam, so thinking, gazed,—this plumply cherubic face underwent a sudden and terrible alteration—the eyes glared, between parted lips was gleam of clenched teeth, the white lock of hair above scowling brows seemed to rise like a hackle.

"Ch-ild," he demanded, hissing the word ferociously, "are these scoundrels molesting you?" And with motion incredibly fast, his right hand had armed itself with a small though deadly-looking pistol.

"No, Uncle dear," she answered in her smooth, soft voice and seeming wholly unperturbed, "no, these are the good friends who were my protection at the inn, as I told you. So put away your pistol, like a pet——" The little gentleman dropped the weapon as if it had stung him and leapt forward, both hands outstretched, crying:

"Oh, friends, oh, gentlemen both, I beseech on you the benediction of Almighty God! Defenders of helpless Purity, avengers of offended Innocence, smiters of impious Iniquity accept my profound gratitude. For this my Andromeda, this beloved child is the one sweet bond that chains me to this loathed living! Your hands, sirs, your hands! Now would I bathe them with tears of my gratitude ineffable, but my tears were all shed long and long ago! I am no more than withered wisp, a human husk. This my niece is my truest consolation, without her—I perish! Meda love, the fire burns, kettle singeth, go brew tea! These our friends shall drink with us and eat. Nay, I protest you must and shall. For, sirs," said the little gentleman, taking an arm of each and leading them whither Andromeda led, "you will be conferring a notable favour. In me you behold one Arthur Verinder, a son of sorrow, sore smit by the hammer of a merciless fate, since when I have existed in a world of woe. But I am also a child of the Muses,—Clio, Euterpe, Thalia and Melpomene. I paint, I play, I sing, I dance and in each find some faint respite and relief. . . . Ah, we arrive,—be welcome, sirs, to our vagrant home and hospitality!"

They had reached a grassy clearing shut in by dense thickets and great trees where stood a large, varnished caravan with, close beside it, a roomy though weather-worn tent. Here also blazed a fire of crackling sticks above which a blackened kettle steamed and sang merrily; Andromeda with crooked stick and handful of grass was trying to lift this when Sam, stepping forward, did it for her.

"Oh wait!" she cried, "you'll burn yourself!"

"I have!" he admitted, setting down the kettle very hastily.

"Let me look!"

"It's nothing——"

"Show me!" Out to him came her hand, which Sam noticed instantly was roughened by hard work yet beautifully shaped and, like her golden eyes, so compelling, that he obeyed.

"Blistered, of course!" said she, shaking her head.

"Oh, well—a dab o' grease," he suggested.

"No, water first. Come with me to the brook. Uncle Arthur," she called, "you must brew the tea."

"I cannot!" he wailed, fretfully. "I cannot, Meda. You know very well I——"

"Allow me, sir!" said Captain Ned. So, while this was doing, Andromeda led her submissive patient to a brook that rippled pleasantly nearby and there kneeling side by side, while Sam laved his throbbing fingers in this sweet coolness, she drew a handkerchief from her bosom, and having soaked and folded it:

"Now," said she, holding out this dripping bandage; and Sam, mutely obedient, watched her tie up his hurt.

"There!" sighed she, sitting back on her heels, "that should relieve the smart a little."

"It has," he answered. And now, struck again by wistful sadness of her face as she gazed down at the sparkling water of the brook, he questioned her in his forthright manner:

"Pray, Miss Andromeda, why are you troubled,—is it— your uncle?"

Without raising her eyes she answered, almost whispering:

"He was such a man . . . once . . . so greatly gifted! To-day he is such a child and . . . so wayward. Years ago he had a shock and ever since he has been as you see, a—little queer. He has a horror of roof and walls . . . had they shut him up he would have pined to death. . . . So we roam the countryside vagrant as the wind. . . . This is why he carries the pistol, though it is never loaded, I take great care of that. . . ."

"And you've devoted yourself to his welfare, tending, working for him?"

"Mr. Felton, I love him . . . I am all he has in the world. And then besides——"

"An-dromeda! Tea waits and the bread and butter to cut! Come, we famish!" cried a querulous voice. "Attend this moment, we need you, Meda!"

"Coming, dear!" she called in answer and, rising with effortless grace, went back where her uncle, throned in padded, wicker arm-chair watched Captain Ned buttering and slicing a crusty loaf with sailorly dexterity.

"Gentlemen and good friends," said Mr. Verinder, his bright-hovering, bird-like glance on the growing stack of thin-cut bread and butter, "here with God's own firmament for canopy and His verdant sward for our table, His kindly sun to bless us, we make you welcome to our simple fare—Meda, my love, have we no jams or jellies to honour our guests? I seem to remember a conserve of wild strawberries you concocted for me some while ago, and richly delicate I deemed it! Have we no meats or savouries? Have we not?"

"Yes, dear, we've a ham and tongue with——"

"Let them appear eftsoons, child!"

"Allow me to help you," said Sam. "Please!" he added as she hesitated. So she brought him to the caravan and following her up its three steps, Sam was amazed to see it so spacious, richly furnished and carpeted, with a luxurious bed at the one end in a sort of curtained alcove with beside this a small, collapsible table whereon lay gold-backed brushes and comb with other toilet articles and bottles of cut glass.

"At least," said he, glancing round upon this unexpected splendour, "you are housed like a princess here, Miss Andromeda."

"Not here," she answered, opening a beautifully carved locker, "this is Uncle Arthur's——"

"Eh?" exclaimed Sam. "Meaning you live—sleep—in that dingy tent thing?"

"Of course! Uncle would perish in the tent and I should stifle here! And the tent is not dingy, it's my home and I love it, especially in summer when the stars peep at me and with the moon to light me."

"Ay, but how when it blows, storms and rains?"

"I always set up my tent in the most sheltered places and——"

"D'you mean you pitch it alone? Doesn't your uncle bear a hand?"

"Dear me no. He would only get all tangled up in the guy-ropes—he did once and nearly strangled himself, poor dear! But you see I'm used to it now and it is quite simple and soon done."

"How d'you manage in winter when it sleets and snows?"

"Oh, I have plenty of blankets. And besides I don't mind—Oh, there is Uncle calling me! Will you please carry this large dish?"

"Ay, ay, and the little one too. Anything else?"

"No, I can manage."

Thus laden, back they went and with this goodly fare set out on snowy cloth spread upon the grass, a hearty and joyous repast they made.

"I am a soul," quoth Mr. Verinder, selecting a well-buttered slice of bread and forking thereon a pinkly-delicate slice of ham, "I am a soul, good my friends, that fain would soar to the infinitudes yet pent, alas, in prison fleshly! My pinions ethereal clipped by accursed Circumstance! For sixty and two years my spirit has striven to win free of this earthly envelope —body is the clog that cumbers and circumscribes my natural genius. Ah, but for body I should be a very demi-god to sing with the everlasting spheres,—to paint Perfection that is deathless,—to strike forth melodies that should echo eternally the joys and sorrows of God's creation."

"Ay, sir," nodded Sam, helping Andromeda to some of her own wild-strawberry jam, "but can you do any o' the ordinary, commonplace things o' life, trivial and yet so necessary, like f'r instance, washing up these tea-things, chopping wood for the fire or scrubbing your own shirts?"

Mr. Verinder recoiled so violently that his wicker chair squeaked aloud, and when he spoke it was in tone of shocked disdain:

"Young man, such things do nowise interest me and therefore have for me no actuality!"

"Yet, sir, you use cups and saucers and wear shirts!"

"Alas I do!" he sighed, now plaintively reproachful. "Base humanity so compelling I confess I do, but as the wind blows and flowers spring, by no volition or care of mine. Thus, young sir, even as the sun shines and stars wink, my shirts are washed I know not how, yet am duly grateful therefore. As to cups and saucers, their cleaning I have attempted and broken them ere now. Wood also I have chopped, or made the endeavour, to mine own injury, since when I have left the axe, that crude and cruel implement, to hands more able——"

"Your niece's, sir?"

"Why of course!" said Andromeda, in her gently serene voice. "I am quite expert with the axe—or bill-hook, yes and hammers too. Uncle Arthur's hands were made and meant for nobler use."

"Oh?" murmured Sam, pondering this. "Ah! What, pray?"

"The painting of glorious pictures! The making of divine music,—could you but hear him play his great harp! But it is away being mended because last week I . . . oh, I let it fall. . . ."

"Careless of you, Andromeda, criminally careless! However, I say no more. . . . And we yet have our small harp, child, a sweet though feeble thing in comparison, yet it shall serve!"

"Oh, Uncle!" she exclaimed breathlessly. "Oh, will you play, my pet, will you?"

"We will attempt it, child, though alas,—without inspiration! This moment, Meda, we feel like abysmal creature writhing 'neath the heel of our own unworthiness. Yet in honour of these our guests we shall attempt. You shall sing and perchance I also! Go fetch the instrument, child." Away sped Andromeda and presently returned bearing the harp, a smallish though beautifully made instrument. With this upon his knee Mr. Verinder sat mute and still, his bright eyes upturned to the blue, cloudless heaven; then slowly he lifted hands and touched the strings, waking them to soft, sweet whisper of sound, then struck a full chord that melted to a rippling ecstasy such as only a master's fingers might evoke, a melody that rose and fell with deep suggestion of laughter and tears, a glory of sound rising to a fervour that held his audience spellbound till—with sudden, harsh discord, he cried, as in swift agony:

"Oh—ineptitude! Oh, accursed, clogging flesh that bars me from achievement of the dreamed Perfection. . . . Take it, Meda! Take it lest I rend the strings that but for these earthly fingers might now wake to glory the very melody of God! Take it—away!" And he spurned the instrument from him so furiously that it would have fallen had she not been ready to catch it.

"You see, good friends?" he cried, looking round on them with tear-filled eyes. "You see how it is with me? I dream perfection so absolute that myself being mere base human

may never attain . . . thus is my soul stultified by base body!
Play you, my Andromeda, you my comfort and consolation,
play now and soothe my so bitter grief—play!"

So Andromeda played, and though her music was tenderly
soothing and the movements of her sun-tanned arm and hand
so wonderfully graceful that Sam could look no other where,
her performance lacked the power and glorious resonance of
her Uncle's passionate mastery. Now presently her slender
fingers wove from the quivering strings a sweetly plaintive
air and she began to sing in full, rich contralto; and after a
little while, her Uncle joined in with rich and flexible baritone,
and these the words they sang together:

"Grieve not, dear love, although we oft do part
But know that Nature doth us gently sever,
Thereby to train us up with tender art
To brook that day when we must part forever.

"For Nature doubting we should be surprised
By that sad day whose dread doth chiefly fear us,
Doth keep us daily schooled and exercised
Lest that the grief thereof should overbear us.
Then grieve not, dear love, although we oft do part."

The duet ended in a sigh with soft throb of harp like a stifled
sob, and for a moment none spoke; then:
"That," murmured Sam, "was almost . . . too beautiful!"
Scarcely had he spoken than Mr. Verinder reached out a hand
plump, dimpled, delicately white and clasped Sam's sinewy
fingers, saying:
"Oh, my friend, Nature, I perceive, has blessed you with
ears that do truly hear,—for this song is as truly beautiful,
the words are anonymous, the music was composed by my
young friend Eustace Jennings, a youth dowered with genius,
—and it was perfectly played—God bless you, Meda love!
And as perfectly sung, God bless us both! Dear my young
sailor-friend, what didst say thy name was?"
"Sam Felton, sir. Pray call me Sam!"
"No, no! Alas,—ha, poor young man to be cursed with
such patronymic, so flat, so utterly toneless, sodden as a
swamp! No, no, I shall call you Felton, there sings in Felton
a fugitive chime. Well, Felton, my dear, since God has blessed

you with hearing, has He also dowered you with sight, an
eye to see latent beauty in the mere obvious,—a tree, a
stock, a stone?"

"Well, sir," answered Sam, rubbing his square, shaven
chin, "I have seen a . . . a glory of ocean at sunset and day-
break, likewise something grand in raging tempest and breaking seas. Then in the sparkle o' the little brook yonder there
is——"

"Ha—the brook!" cried Mr. Verinder, leaping in his chair,
"I painted it this very morning . . . apeep amid shadows, glad
with sun like the smile of God in woeful world. Child, ha,
Meda, go bring hither my canvas and take heed for 'tis wet.
Ah, but you," said he, turning on the Captain as Andromeda
hastened to do his bidding, "you, sir Captain—Harlow is the
name, I think? You are very pensive, your thoughts are not
with us, I fear?"

"The fact is, sir," said Captain Ned, "time is getting on,
and so should we," here he drew out and consulted his watch
at sight of which, Mr. Verinder groaned:

"A timepiece,—hateful thing! Put it away, sir, put it
away! 'Time was made for slaves!' Time is a tyrant without
mercy or reason! That we should fail to hold your interest
is a grief and—ah, Meda," he cried passionately as she
approached carrying her awkward burden, "be careful!
Merciful heavens, have a care! No, no, Felton, do not touch
my picture, wait—wait, she will manage best alone——"
But, unheeding this fretful clamour, Sam hastened forward
and had relieved Andromeda of the large painted canvas
almost before she knew, and now bearing it rather carelessly enquired:

"Where will you have it, sir?"

"There—against that tree," answered Mr. Verinder with
sullen petulance. "Turn it to your left, more—more—
another inch! So! Now stand back,—look and tell me all
you see, how much or—how little. Look and speak!"

A delicate harmony of greens—stately trees with leaves that
seemed astir in gentle wind, blooming thickets and velvet
sward; fugitive shadows leading the eye to a verdant gloom
pierced by vivid sun-ray reflected back from glimpse of radiant
water.

"Well . . . well? What of it, friends?" The words came in a
gasping, broken whisper.

"Wonderful!" murmured Sam.

"Uncle, it is beautiful, as I told you!"

"Yes," said the Captain, "wonderful, beautiful and—much beside!"

Gazing upon his handiwork, Mr. Verinder leaned down slowly from his chair and as slowly gathered a handful of grass; then uttering a wailing, heartbroken cry, he leapt and scrubbed that artfully blended glory of colour into a hideous, formless smudge.

"There!" he cried, passionately, hurling the ruined picture one way and handful of clotted grass, the other, "So perish all unworthiness! This that I meant for vision of the hidden God-head smiling love upon His Creation, was no more than tawdry picture of trees and bubbling water, a mess of paint! Oh God . . . God of Mercy, when—when shall I attain— achieve the dreamed perfection, when oh—when?" And with this desolate, wailing cry, Mr. Verinder went bounding to hide himself within the splendour of his caravan.

"Poor . . . fellow!" murmured Sam.

"Ay," nodded the Captain, "yonder is tragedy!"

"And yet," sighed Andromeda, kneeling to collect her crockery, "very soon he will be playing his flute or violin."

"So?" enquired the Captain, kneeling also (as did Sam) to help her, "is your wonderful uncle master of these also?"

"Oh yes, there is hardly an instrument that he cannot play, though some better than others."

"A truly astonishing person!" said the Captain, as he and Sam, laden with crockery, followed Andromeda to the brook, for the washing-up. And with these two deft-handed sailor-men to help, this business was soon done; yet there a while they lingered to talk.

"Yes," said Captain Ned, "your uncle, Miss Andromeda, as painter or musician is equally great."

"He was a genius—once!" she murmured, her golden eyes uplift and radiant. "First, spoiled by too much money, then . . . shocked by bitter, terrible grief and loss!"

"A woman, of course," said the Captain.

"Yes, she . . . was found dead in the Black Pool at Wrex-ford old mill . . . a dark and deathly place even now— especially of an evening!"

"Pray how did it happen?" enquired Captain Ned.

"I don't know . . . I never heard."

"But . . . you suspect?"

Dumbly, slowly she bowed her head. . . . And now, all at once, sweet and rich as pipe of thrush or blackbird, merry as song of mounting lark, came the clear notes of a flute trilling in a very ecstasy of gladness.

"There!" sighed Andromeda, with her slow, wistful smile, "he has forgotten. . . . Nature is not always cruel. . . ." Even as she spoke the fluting ceased and instead of this lovely sound a querulous voice cried:

"An-dromeda!" Slowly she arose and glancing from Sam to the Captain and back again, gave them each a hand, saying as she did so:

"Thank you for your help—and company! And now . . . Good-bye!" With the word, she turned and left them, walking with unhurried grace but not one backward glance.

Quoth Sam after some while of musing silence, as they came out upon the dusty road:

"The old buffer's mad, of course!"

"More or less, Sam, but only in the one direction. Nor-nor-east, say."

"Ay," growled Sam, "knows which side his bread is buttered . . . and makes a slave of—her! Did you notice her hands?"

"Ay, I did, messmate! Hands roughened by devotion, glorified by service. Yes, I noticed her hands, Sam, and her clothes."

"What of 'em, Ned?"

"Glorified by her and 'spite their shabbiness."

"Shabby, ay!" growled Sam again, "nigh threadbare, yet how can they be any otherwise and she always at work for that dam' selfish, pinkly plump——"

"Cherub, Sam! He seems no more than child-man and yet, ah, by old Davy Jones, he is so greatly more,—a veritable master!"

"Ay—but what of—her?"

"Well, my Perseus, your Andromeda might be a rare beauty if she would, but she cares nothing for her appearance and never will—no, not till LOVE, spelt in capitals, Sam, wakes her selfless, sleeping womanhood!"

"Oh!" quoth Sam and strode on in such gloomy abstraction and for so long that the Captain nudged him at last and enquired:

UNIVERSITY OF WINNIPEG
PORTAGE & BALMORAL
WINNIPEG
DISCARDED

"What d'you think of her, Mister Mate?" And Sam replied in most sombrely ponderous manner:

"That she is the . . . saddest woman creature I ever saw, ay, and the bravest . . . except one. For d'ye see, Ned, her little hands are as hard with patient service, and as rough, almost, as the hands of . . . my devoted . . . mother."

CHAPTER VIII

HOW THEY CAME TO WILLOWMEAD

IT was an evening lit by glowing sunset when they came to the parting of the ways, for here three roads converged; and here Sam paused to mop brow, glance about and enquire:

"What course d'ye give me, Captain, how do we steer, sir?"

"Larboard, Master, full and by."

"Ay, ay, sir, full and by it is. But, if I may make so bold, where do we bring-to for the night?"

"In snug harbour, Sam, a right good anchorage, messmate! Now—hard a-starboard!" So saying, Captain Ned turned sharp right down a pleasant, tree-shaded lane, along which they had not gone very far when Sam halted again and suddenly; for before them was an age-mellowed, thatched farm-house not too small, set within a flowery garden not too large, beyond which was a paddock wherein a plump steed nibbled; here also stood a row of bee-hives and beyond these an orchard with beyond this again, a lush meadow where several corpulent cows chewed in somnolent beatitude. Beholding all this, Sam drew a deep breath and spoke:

"Ned," he began,—but at this moment the cottage door opened and a woman appeared, a tall, handsome creature in shady sun-bonnet and sprigged gown and who, espying the travellers stood suddenly arrested, then, with both hands outstretched in welcome, she came hurrying and her face the more lovely for the look it now wore.

"Edward!" she cried, breathlessly. "Oh, Ned!" And striding forward, the Captain took those welcoming hands and said in voice quite new to Sam:

"Katherine . . . Oh, my Kate . . . at last!" He drew her close, her shapely body yielding to his arms, and seemed about to kiss her, checked the impulse, saying instead:

"Katherine, I've brought my First Officer along, this is the Sam I've told you about, Sam Felton, he improves on acquaintance! Sam,—Mistress Katherine Ford."

"Mr. Felton," said she with smile of hearty greeting, "indeed you are very welcome."

"Miss Ford," he answered, taking off the glazed hat as their hands met, "I'm very grateful and as greatly relieved."

"Relieved?" she enquired. "Good gracious,—why?"

"To find all things so vastly better than expected."

"What did you expect?"

"A cottage, a garden, beehives, a horse, cows and—a woman."

"Well, I am a woman."

"Ay," nodded Sam, "such woman as might spoil the best sailorman that ever trod deck."

"Oh, but how spoil him, pray?"

"By turning him into a landsman, Miss Ford." She laughed, flushing consciously as she met the Captain's adoring gaze.

"Well, now come indoors . . . we've a barrel of ale, home brewed, and cider besides perry and small beer,—come!"

"First," said Sam, "by your leave, Miss Ford, I'll bear away for a look at those beehives and the cows." So saying, off he went, leaving them together; scarcely was he out of sight than they were in each other's arms.

"Oh, Ned," she whispered, clinging to him, the sun-bonnet crushed against his breast, "are you . . . free? Have you come home . . . home to me at last?"

"Yes," he answered, "yes, thank God, I'm home at last . . . here in your arms, Kate, your heart on mine . . . nevermore to let you go. . . ."

Meanwhile Sam having looked at the beehives from a respectful distance, and surveyed the cows who blinked at him with drowsy graciousness, wandered on and thus presently found himself back in the shady lane. Here he paused and stood, somewhat at a loss, looking at nothing in particular, for remembering the sudden, deep tenderness in his Captain's voice, the look of inexpressible joy in Katherine's face, he felt himself stranger in a world unknown, with sense of greater loneliness than he had ever found leisure to experience in all his busy and hazardous life.

It was a narrow lane this, with steep, grassy banks where ferns sprouted and wild flowers bloomed; here sinking down rather wearily, Sam began to ponder his altered circumstances and then muse upon his immediate future until these ruminations were interrupted by a child's voice upraised in song, a sweet though timeless chant that had to do with someone called "Bluebell" and a personage named Jane.

Presently the singer herself appeared carrying a very large doll, and stood instantly mute, staring at Sam who gazed as dumbly on her; and when this silence had endured for perhaps half a minute, he smiled and she, beholding his face thus transfigured, smiled also and spoke:

"I'm granny's Jane, who's are you?"

"Oh, I'm nobody's Sam," he answered, "I'm all alone."

"Alone?" she repeated. "Haven't you got any granny to hear you say your prayers an' tuck you up in bed with a kiss, haven't you?"

"No," he answered, gravely, "not any longer, because my dear mother is dead."

"Ooh—so's mine!" exclaimed this small person, brightly. "That's why I've got a granny instead, and a auntie too! Have you?"

"Not one."

"Then you must be awful' lonely—so you shall be a uncle for me. I've only got one and have my child a bit to comfort you while I talk to you, and her name's Batilda."

"Eh, Matilda?"

"No, Ba-tilda, and when she's not naughty nobody could be gooder and she's good now and'll comfort you,—take her!" Obediently Sam folded the doll in his great arms as the child seated herself beside him.

"Now if I'm your uncle, you must be my niece,—and your name's Jane, is it?"

"Yes, an' 'Charmian' too an' I b'long to my granny what has a donkey named Robert. And your name's Sam and I like it b'cause it's nice and quick."

"And I like 'Jane' because it means you."

"And I like everybody 'cept Mr. Tangy."

"Who's he, Jane?"

"Well, he is the man who always makes my granny pay too much rent, she always says so because she's a lorn widow's body this thirty weary years and money is hard come by. I've heard her say so lots 'n' lots of times. And now I think I hear her calling me."

"Then I suppose you'd better go, my dear."

"Oh no! If I only wait patiently she'll come to me, she always does."

"Oho?" murmured Sam. "Aha!"

"Yes!" nodded Jane. "So 'course I always wait . . . why are you smiling at me for?"

"Thoughts, my dear."

"Well, I like you even more when you smile 'cause it makes your face nicer."

"It's not much of a face, eh, little Jane?"

"Well, no it's not," she answered, gazing up at him in wide-eyed scrutiny. "And you've been hurting it, but I like it—in places." Now at this, Sam chuckled and felt so strangely glad that minded to kiss her, he laughed instead.

"Jane, come you . . . to me!" cried a voice resonant, commanding, albeit somewhat short-winded; Sam held out the doll, saying:

"I think you'd better go, little Jane."

"Very well!" she sighed. "Only you must come too an' carry my Batilda."

So up they rose, but had gone only a little way when round a bend in this winding lane strode an aged though formidable dame; she wore a black dress that rustled to her every vigorous stride, she bore a ponderous stick, and she glared on the universe beneath a large poke bonnet, tied on somewhat askew.

"So—oh!" she exclaimed, halting suddenly with a thump of stick upon the earth before her and scowling portentously. "There you are—hey, mistress, hey?"

"Yes, here's me, Granny, an' this is a man called Sam what I've found for my uncle an' he needs a granny too because he's a lonely lorn body like you."

"Ho—indeed!" exclaimed this intimidating old lady, surveying Sam with such keen and terrible eye that he almost cowered. "Have I not told you over and over again never to talk with strangers—and especially men, Ma'm Disobedience?"

"Yes, Granny, only Sam looked so all alone an' I like him though he hasn't got much of a face—he told me so, and my Batilda likes him too."

"And, indeed," said Sam, taking off the glazed hat, "I'm a little better than I look, marm, and well beknown to Captain Edward Harlow."

"So don't you think, Granny, that we ought to take him home and tuck him up in bed with a 'kiss me good-night' like a nice granny should, don't you?"

"No, I do—not! And you," she demanded, frowning upon Sam again, "how am I to know the Captain is your friend?"

"By stepping so far as Miss Ford's house."

"Ha! So you know Kate Ford?"

"Yes, marm, since about half-an-hour ago."

"So the Captain is there again, is he! A rolling stone like all sailormen and no fit mate for any sensible woman,—rickety-racketsome rovers as they are,—and you're another by your looks?"

"Yes, marm, though I fancy our roving days are over,—at least Captain Ned's are, I'm afraid, which is marvellous great pity!"

"What then, is he leaving his seafaring ways at last?"

"He shall tell you himself if you trouble to go far as the farmhouse, marm."

"I will, seeing I'm on my way there now to borrow a goffer-ing-iron and a pinch o' tea. So lend me your arm, young man, these hills, drattem,—make me know my age."

"And you're so awful old, aren't you, Granny?"

"No older than I feel, child."

"And you feel such lots, don't you, Granny? Lots an' lots 'cause you're such a poor, old, lorn, widow's body this thirty year, aren't you, Granny dear?"

"Hoity-toity, chatterbox! Cuddle your dolly and hush!" quoth the old lady, clutching Sam's ready arm in surprisingly powerful grip, saying as she did so: "Now not too fast, young man, remember I'm not so young as I was."

"He's a nice big Uncle Sam, isn't he, Granny?"

"He is, child——"

"Bigger'n Uncle Captain Ned, isn't he?"

"Oh, kiss your dolly and be silent, Jane!"

"But how can I when Sam's nursing her? And she isn't a dolly now 'cause she's growed herself into my child an' I told you her name's Batilda——"

"Now did you ever hear such a pert little magpie?"

"No," answered Sam, "but now that I do it does me a power o' good."

"Ha! You are fond of children?"

"Well, yes I . . . I suppose so, marm."

"What d'you mean by 'suppose so'?"

"Why d'ye see, I've never seen or heard any at close quarters till now."

"No children of your own, then?"

"Lord—no!"

"Married?"

"No, marm, certainly not and no will that way."

"Which comes of your roisterous roving!"

"Not so, marm, for women and——"

"Hush, not before the child! And don't tell me of your wanton wanderings from port to port and most of them foreign, of course, sinfully shamefully foreign, eh, young man, eh?"

"More or less, marm, but——"

"No, no, young man, your 'buts' will butter no parsnips with me—No, no! For as a respectable Englishwoman and great-grandmother at that, I do—not—hold with foreigners, especially females, with their jargon, their foreign ways and lawless goings on—no! Just look what they did to their poor, dear Queen Antoinette in that wicked Paris with their nasty guillotine and tumbrils and things! Think what they would do to us if they could! Thank God for our Lord Nelson to 'frustrate their knavish tricks'! say I——"

"He was a 'roving sailor' also, marm."

"And also the preserver of England, and that means the whole wide world too, God bless him! And now that he is dead, having ascended through the smoke of battle and blood of Trafalgar, he is risen with his one arm and poor blind eye to be a bright angel of——"

"Ooh, but Granny, can a bright angel be a real angel with only one arm and a blind——"

"He can, Jane, he has! I think our merciful Creator has cherished and healed his poor, maimed body,—if not, then the wounds he suffered for England and the right, will only make his heavenly glory shine the brighter."

"But, Granny——"

"Be hushed, child, and suffer your elders to speak! Young man, there's a look about you strikes a familiar note, and I'm wondering how and why! Be pleased to inform me—your name."

"Felton, madam, Sam Felton and humbly at your service."

"Ha!" she exclaimed, glancing at him with her keen old eyes. "You spoke that as if you really meant it."

"Because I do—indeed!" he answered.

"Well, I am Anne Leet who used to have servants at her beck and call, male and female, forty-six and a half of 'em,—

the half was Joe Tangy the boot-boy. But this was when I ruled the Great House, years ago."

"Where is that, marm?"

"Mr. Felton, when the Great House is mentioned hereabouts it can only mean one and that is Wrybourne Feveril, of course."

"Oh!" murmured Sam, thoughtfully. "Ah?"

"Yes, indeed, young man, you would say 'Oh' and 'Ah' if you could see it,—all the glory of it! Throned on its three terraces,—gable and chimney and noble frontage! And then its panelled chambers, painted ceilings, great carved mantels, and splendid hall, the gardens English and Dutch, the deer park! Ah, you ought to see it for yourself!"

"I should like to—with you to show it to me, Mrs. Leet, —could you?"

"Why yes, to be sure. Mr. Perkins the butler is still there and Thomas the first footman. I've shown hundreds of visitors over, before now, the splendid furniture and famous pictures, Lely, Holbein, Reynolds—and many other famous painters. . . . And here we are—already!" she exclaimed as Sam opened the garden gate. "This Willowmead is a pretty farm-house, I always think, eh, Mr. Felton."

"Ay, it is, marm, being neither too large nor yet too small."

"And cosy as it looks. Come your ways in,—no need to knock!" So saying she led the way into a spacious chamber half parlour, half kitchen, its walls adorned by one or two dim pictures and many brightly burnished pots and pans of glowing copper and shining pewter, its wide generous hearth where spicy logs smouldered, flanked by roomy, cushioned settles, its massive, age-blackened rafters hung with bunches of sweet herbs and one or two noble, smoked hams.

Beyond the open, many-paned lattice was a garden where flowers bloomed, growing how they would, to blend their many-hued sweetness in a very glory of colour and fragrance, —a place this of leafy nooks and shady corners where birds chirped or piped melodiously,—an unpretentious and therefore lovable garden and all the more so because of the two who walked there seeing only each other and talking murmurously as they approached until suddenly, as by mutual consent, they turned to clasp and kiss one another. . . .

"Gemini!" exclaimed the aged dame, her keen eyes widening on these unseeing happy ones. "Goodness me!" Then rapping the window frame with her ponderous staff, she called in ringing tones:

"Aho—Ned, Kate—what do I see?"

And turning to smile on her questioner, Katherine answered:

"Happiness, Anne! My love has come home to me—at last."

"True enough, Grannyanne," said the Captain, advancing with hand outstretched, "the banns go up at once . . . Kate will be my wife soon as possible! Yes, I've quit the sea, Granny, from now on, I'm Kate's farmer and man of all work."

"Ha, well, Ned," said Mrs. Leet, shaking hands with vigorous heartiness, "you've served your country at sea against the moosoos and done mighty well, I hear. But now you're safe home with your Kate my prayer is may the Lord bless ye to each other and send you sturdy children to be your joy and serve Old England after you! And now, Kate, I've dragged my poor old bones here, with this young man's help, to ask the loan of a goffering iron and a pinch or so of tea."

"Why yes, Granny, and you'll bide for supper, of course."

"No, Katie, no thankee,—here's my little Jane should be in bed——"

"An' I found this Sam all alone, Auntie Kate, to be a nuncle for me, isn't he nice an' big! An' he's carried my Batilda all the way 'cause she likes him an' so do I!"

"Bless the child!" laughed Kate as she entered the house, seeming to bring something of the glad sunshine with her. "Come and kiss me, Jane."

Up reached the childish arms and down to them stooped the graceful woman.

"Now," said Jane when they had embraced, "now Auntie Kate, I want you to be Sam's auntie too, 'cause he's so all alone that he hasn't got any aunties or even a single granny. An' you see he's been hurting his poor face, an' he says it's not much of a face but I like it in parts, don't you?"

"Yes," answered Katherine, her shapely lips made lovelier by the smile that curved them, "yes, I do."

"Well then, won't you be his auntie too, an' tuck him up at night an' kiss——"

"Goodness—gracious—me!" gasped Mrs. Leet. "Hoity-toity! Come you home at once——"

"No, Granny, no—please!" Katherine pleaded in laugh-shaken tones. "Pray let her sleep here to-night with me. And besides, Granny, you must stay and sup with us, I insist—for by the happiest chance I have something in the oven, my dear, that I hope may be worthy of this—oh, this most wonderful occasion—a favourite dish of yours, too! Now Jane, let's go to the cook-house and see what Nancy and I can find for you."

Speaking, Katherine opened a certain door,—and lo! Upon the ambient air stole such mouth-watering, hunger-begetting, palate-wooing savour of luscious, cunningly seasoned baking meats that Mrs. Leet sighed, handed her staff to Sam and removing her enormous bonnet, gave it to Captain Ned; then throned upon nearest settle, she spread her voluminous skirts, folded her hands, and drawing a long breath through her rather hawk-like nose, sighed again, saying:

"Ah, Ned, Captain Ned I hope you are duly aware what extreme fortunate man you are to have won to wife such beauty, so much gentle loveliness as Kate,—a wife who can not only bewitch the eye, but also gratify the stomach——"

"Eh? Stomach?" repeated Captain Ned.

"Of course!" nodded Mrs. Leet. "For a wife's beauties, alas, fade with time,—look at me,—but a good cook improves with age! And our Kate is most excellent housewife and cook. Now, for instance, my nose is informing me, and it is never wrong, that we are shortly destined to enjoy a hare, jugged, in thick gravy enriched by port-wine and seasoned with force-meat balls. . . . Ah, Captain Ned, I say again you are an exceedingly fortunate man!"

CHAPTER IX

THE jugged hare had become a joyous memory and one that was to endure; little Jane, having been kissed "Goodnight" had climbed the "wooden hills" and kneeling by Auntie Kate had said her brief though vociferous prayers and thereafter had been tucked up with her Batilda in Auntie Kate's big bed with its dainty curtains; and now her elders, sitting in comfort of soft candlelight and cosy fireglow, for the night was chilly, began to converse, thus:

MRS. LEET (*Producing knitting from capacious reticule*): Betsy Pardoe's sow farrowed yesterday, eleven and all doing well!

CAPT. NED (*Taking out pipe and tobacco*): Ah, of course, we must have pigs, Kate! May we smoke?

KATE: Let me fill your pipe. . . . There are tapers on the mantel-shelf.

SAM (*Beginning to fill his own pipe*): Miss Ford, I——

KATE: No, please call me Kate or Katherine and I shall call you "Sam", because though we only met to-night, you are no stranger. Ned has often told me about you,—oh yes, and how you saved the second harpooner from drowning when that great whale upset the boat in his dying flurry. And afterwards when you went to fight the French and boarded the corvette off Toulon was it? how you drove off the enemies who would have killed him—my Ned——

SAM (*Busy with pipe*): But I'll warrant he never told you how he dragged me from death aboard the *Citoyenne* frigate when they'd downed me with a musket-butt, kept the mounseers at bay and with only his cutlass until our lads charged to our rescue.

KATE (*Looking up at her Captain with adoring eyes*): No, Sam, he never mentioned that!

SAM: Nor yet when I rammed my head against a froggies' boarding-pike and should have been trampled but for him, or the time when our main-top-mast was shot away and I, going aloft to clear it, got fouled by the wreckage and should have gone overboard but that he——

49

CAPT. NED (*Stooping to light taper at the fire*): Belay now, Sam, let's be done with the past and talk of the future——

KATE: No, Sam, go on—tell me more about my sailorman——

CAPT. NED: Who is turning farmer, Kate, your farmer! Ay, and I'm hoping Sam will swallow the anchor likewise and turn landsman too. How about it, messmate?

SAM: (*Smiling into Kate's happy face as she holds the lighted taper to his pipe*): Why as to that, Ned, I'm nowise sure—yet.

NED: However, you'll stand by long enough to bear a hand on—the day! My best man, eh, Sam?

SAM: (*Puffing*): Ay, with all my heart!

MRS. LEET (*Clicking her knitting-pins indignantly*): That Tangy wretch called on me to-day! Sat on his horse at my gate and shouted me, he did! I was hoeing weeds and felt like hoeing him—clouting his nasty arrogant head.

KATE: Yes, Mr. Tangy can make himself very unpleasant. Was it your rent, Granny?

MRS. LEET: Of course! It always is! And because I ventured to complain again of my roof leaking. A hard master makes a harder man!

NED: This Tangy is Lord Wrybourne's bailiff, isn't he?

MRS. LEET: That he is,—and many's the time I've boxed his impudent young ears when he was a bit of a boy—and foot-boy at that! Ah, but now, Kate, now my Earl is dead, and good riddance,—I'm wondering and so are others, what the new earl will be.

KATE: Yes, everyone is talking of that. Yesterday when I drove to Lewes market, old Farmer Bagshaw told me our new earl was abroad, living in foreign parts, and——

MRS. LEET (*With ferocious contempt*): Foreign! Then, Kate, so much the worse for us and the rest of his tenantry! For, now mark my words, he will have turned foreign in his ways,—and I'd rather put up with a hard English landlord than a bad foreign one!

KATE: But, Granny, being the old earl's son he is English really, and you remember his mother, don't you?

MRS. LEET: To be sure I did—and before!

SAM (*Forgetting to smoke*): How so, marm? Pray what might you mean by "before"?

MRS. LEET: I mean, young man, before she was a mother. Ah, before the Earl married, and so suddenly too,—I was in charge of the Great House which I always thought much too good, all too noble and splendid for such a base wretch!

SAM: What wretch, marm?

MRS. LEET: The Earl, of course, with his drinking and nameless abandonments! How such a sweet, gentle creature could ever have married him I don't know and can't think! However, she did—ah, but—poor child,—from the very day, the first hour he brought her home, she began to be afraid of him, to pine and languish, and he to neglect and then abuse her, frightening the poor, sweet soul till she'd fly to me for protection!

SAM (*Polishing pipe-bowl absently on broad palm*): And did you . . . protect her?

MRS. LEET: I think so, I hope so! It comforts me now to know I truly did my best . . .

SAM: And was . . . she . . . comforted?

MRS. LEET: Ah—no! That is the dreadful part of it! So things went on for nigh six awful months, getting from bad to worse until one evening she came running to me, breathless, white as a sheet and all of a tremble. "Oh, Anne!" she gasps, clinging to me, "he's going to whip me!" "Oh, no!" says I, clasping her, "he shan't do that, my lady." "Ah, but he will," she sobbed, "he will, he's got a whip and he's after me—now—ah, listen!" "My lady," says I, reaching for the fire-irons, "get you behind my easy-chair," but before she could we heard the jingle of his spurs and in he came, dressed for hunting and, sure enough, a whip in his hand! Yes,—in he rushed but checked suddenly, for there was I, fire-shovel in one hand, tongs in the other. "My lord," says I, "this is my room, so out you go or take these!" But he only laughed at me and made a step forward——

Here Mrs. Leet having roused her audience to pitch of breathless suspense, went on with her knitting until stayed by Sam's large though very gentle hand and voice in subdued but eager question:

"And what did you do?"

"Threw the shovel at him," she replied, with ferocious nod, "then the tongs, and when he saw me snatch up the poker, he laughed again but went. So I slammered the door and locked it."

"Yes," enquired Sam, "yes and what then?"

"That night was a grand party for other wretches abandoned as himself, fine gentlemen and ladies too—leastways males and females! And so it was we found chance to run away, my lady and I. And when we'd left the Great House far behind and we both breathless with running, 'Where now, my dear lady'? says I. 'To my cousin Felton at Alciston, she will shelter me if only for to-night and he can never find me there,' says my poor lady. So to her cousin Felton we came and kindly welcome they made her, Mrs. Felton and her good husband. And there her baby was born, this same new Earl, though his sorrowful, too-sweet, much too-gentle mother didn't live long enough to enjoy him properly, she faded like a flower and died with a smile on her lovely face and her poor, motherless head upon this bosom, these arms of mine close about her . . ." The long, steel knitting-pins clashed and were stilled, the bright, fierce old eyes were gentled and dimmed by sudden, kindly tears.

"Ah, Granny dear," sighed Katherine, " 'tis very piteous, dreadful story! You never told me this before."

"No reason to," quoth Mrs. Leet, her knitting-pins clicking busily again. "And I don't know why I spoke of it now. . . . Though it's odd your name should be Felton too, eh, young man?"

"Yes . . . I suppose so," answered Sam; and then after musing hesitation: "Marm," said he, very diffidently and staring hard at his pipe which had gone out long since, "I should like you for . . . my Granny too, if . . . if you will so honour me . . . and . . . if so, pray call me 'Sam', will you?"

"Sam!" snapped the old lady, instantly, clicking away at her knitting but viewing him with her sharp, steady eyes, "and I'll 'Granny' you so long as you're in sight or sound of me— if only because my little Jane put you in her prayers this night, which means a great deal, for the eyes of children, especially girl-children are quick to see and—heed! And my small, great-granddaughter is no fool! Besides you're a friend and shipmate of our Captain Ned, and this means a great deal also—eh, Kate?"

"Yes, Granny. And, Sam, this is why we are hoping, Ned and I, that we may persuade you to settle down with us. You shall have the gable-room, it's all ready for you now! Because Ned and I,—if we can only buy this farm, are hoping we may learn you to love the land, this rich, good, kindly earth better

than you ever did the treacherous sea. Ah, if only we could
buy this dear place, this home to be our very own for ever!
But Lord Wrybourne is so hatefully rich I'm afraid he will
never sell."

"Oh?" murmured Sam, pondering this. "Ah! So this
house and so forth belongs to the Earl, does it?"

"Of course, Sam! All the land hereabout is his—far as
you can see, and beyond."

"Shame!" growled Sam. "What's he ever done to own so
much, worked for it? Not a hand's turn! Fought for it?
Never a stroke, I'll warrant, not he——"

"Oh, but, Sam, his ancestors did, in some wars and battles
long ago and some King gave it as reward. The Scropes have
been here for hundreds of years——"

"Then it's about time they were cleared out,—for a precious
fine lot they seem to have been!"

"Very true, Sam!" nodded Granny. "All too true! But
lords of the soil they were, are, and will be, good or bad,—
and that's England, and the wonder of it. But now, seeing
it is past ten o'clock, your Granny is going to ask—no, demand
the loan of that big arm of yours so far as her cottage."

"And here it is, Granny, at your service whenso you need
it," answered Sam, rising to help the old lady to her feet,
while Katherine brought her large bonnet and Captain Ned,
her stick.

"And when," she demanded, as Katherine tied her bonnet-
strings, "when does your Aunt Deborah return?"

"To-morrow, Granny, thank goodness! Sam, you'll love
her, for she's the dearest, smallest, gentlest Aunt that ever was,
I do believe."

"Ah!" nodded Granny. " 'Tis pity she never was wed,
some man lost notable good wife in Deb. Well, good night,
my dears both, the Lord bless and keep ye!" Then grasping
her ponderous stick in one fist and Sam in the other, forth
she led him into a night where stars were paling to herald a
rising moon.

"Talking of wives and marriage," said Granny, as they
turned into the lane, "yon shall be a good, true mating, I pray
God—present joy with the future gladness of children! When
shall you do likewise, Sam?"

"Eh? Me? Oh no, Granny, for d'ye see, I'm not the marrying sort . . . no airs or graces to catch a woman's eye——"

"Tush and nonsense, Sam! You're a born lover, and consequently will become a respectably married husband—let's hope."

. "Lord, Granny, you seem uncomfortably sure and certain of it!"

"I am! With those black-fringed, wide-spaced eyes, that aggressive nose, that mouth and chin you will be tempestuous, all fire and fury as a lover, take heed you're not too serenely placid as a husband!"

"But, Granny, I've no inclination that way or——"

"Pish and a fiddlestick! You have and you are,—it's all in the cut o' your jib, Sam."

"Cut o' my—marm, I mean Granny, you're a wonder! You talk now like——"

"Ay, ay, like my own father, Sam, for he was a seaman too and sailed round the world with Lord Anson aboard the *Centurion* and was wounded beside him afterwards in battle,—there's honour for you! Someday, if you don't run off and leave us too soon, I'll show you his fighting-sword and one presented to him, with other things I treasure. But now yonder is my cottage with its dratted leaky roof! Yet before we part, I'll tell you something of that too-beautiful sweetness named Katherine and the danger that threatens her."

"Danger?" enquired Sam, halting suddenly, "what danger, Granny?"

"Oh, Beauty's usual menace, a man of course,—but this such an arrogant, calmly assured, most determined villain who beneath a courteous respect and specious promises masks brutish lust,—an infamous fine gentleman notorious for his gallantries, Lord Julian Scrope, no less!"

"Ah!" murmured Sam. "It would be!"

"So you know of him?"

"Ay, enough,—but—does Kate?"

"She does, Sam, and avoids him all she may. Ah, but my lord troubles himself to ride this way all too frequently."

"Oh!" quoth Sam. "Ah? About how old is he?"

"Forty or thereabouts, the dangerous age and a very dangerous man!"

"And what are his—um—days of call?"

"Whenever wickedness prompts him, and so my new anxiety is lest Captain Ned antagonize him, because, as I tell you, my lord is such a cold, deadly-dangerous wretch."

"Ay, but then," murmured Sam, "so is Ned! And, for that matter, under certain circumstances, I'm no pet lamb."

"Oh well," she sighed, as Sam opened her cottage gate, "maybe I'm over-anxious. Good night,—bring me my little Jane in the morning and I'll show you some of my treasures, my father's sword of honour, with other curious oddments. Now, good night and God keep you all, ay—the three of you!"

On his way back, Sam pondered whether or no to warn Captain Ned of this lurking threat to his peace and future happiness; finally and for obvious reasons, he decided to say nothing, but since this foul menace was his own uncle, to make it a family affair should violence become necessary. Thus, later on, as they lit their candles for bed, Sam remarked, casually:

"On second thoughts, Kate and Ned, because I know you meant it, I'll accept your hospitality right gladly and bide here at Willowmead till some foul wind sends me adrift."

"Small fear of that, Sam, with such tried seaman as yourself."

"Thankee, Ned, but the best of us are apt to be taken aback sometime or other."

"However," said Katherine, "you're staying for the present! And we'll teach you to reap and mow, to stack and thatch and lay a hedge, eh, Ned? And, ah, Sam, the more you learn and longer you remain the harder you'll find it ever to go away! And now," said she, as they followed her up the wide, old stair, "tread softly lest you wake our Jane."

CHAPTER X

INTRODUCES MR. JENNINGS

THE Honourable Ralph, dismounting in stable-yard, scowled at the bow-legged old groom who hobbled forward to take his hard-ridden steed.

"What the devil are you staring at?"

"Nought! Never nothing at all, Master Ralph."

"Then don't look as if you were."

"Been a bit fierce like wi' your 'Lassie', ain't you, sir?" said the old groom, running gentle, experienced hand along the mare's drooping crest. "Eh, sir?"

"Yes, yes, I have, damme! I wasn't thinking,—that is, I was thinking too devilish hard of other things. Look to her, Tom, a good rub down and—no, let Will. Ho, Will, come and take the mare!" At which summons a young groom appeared who chewed a straw, knuckled an eyebrow and led the distressed animal away.

"Come now, Tom," said the Hon. Ralph as soon as they were alone, "out with it! Is my chivvy, my phiz,—is my face much damaged . . . very noticeably, eh, Tom?"

"Well," replied the old groom, surveying the speaker's usually almost too-handsome visage, its beauty of outline now marred by sundry lumps and abrasions, "a bit—odd-like it be, sir."

"Eh, curse it! How so, Tom?"

"Lop-sided, Master Ralph! A bit more of it one side than t'other."

"Oh, damn!" muttered Ralph, feeling the left and more damaged side of his face with tenderly exploring fingers. "Tell me, is it so dev'lish noticeable, Tom?"

"Rather so, Master Ralph. But only o' the one side, t'other 'un be all as it should ought for to be—almost."

"Hell!" snarled Ralph. "Is the Governor in?"

"Ay! And 'e wants ee—very pertickler, sir——"

"Does he, b'gad! What for? Damnation, what's up now?"

"Dunno, sir, only 'e's sent that Mr. Jennin's along yere

twice, to say as 'ow you was to go to m'lord in the libree the moment as you rode in yere, Master Ralph."

"Not me, Tom, damme no! He mustn't see me like this! Here's where I lie low, ay—I'll sleep in your cottage to-night and your Martha shall doctor this damaged phiz o' mine and get me a change of linen."

"Ay, your shirt be very tore and bloody, sir. Looks like lions and tigers 'ad been maulin' of ee,—wild beasts wi' claws and sich."

"And 'egad, Tom, this was a beast and wild enough—on two legs and a left, Tom, a left pepperer there was no getting past and—no avoiding! Ha, but I'll seek him out and have another go, by George, I will. And next time——"

"Better luck, let's 'ope, sir! Now off with ee, Martha'll put ee to rights and—no, too late, Master Ralph!"

"Eh? What d'ye mean, what the devil——"

"Devil, ah,—Mr. Jennin's, sir! He's seen ee and comin' for ee, Master Ralph."

"Ha, that pallid wriggler! How I loathe the fellow."

"Same yere, sir!" muttered old Tom as they watched my lord's gentleman pick his way daintily and with quite unnecessary care across the clean-swept stable-yard. "Look at 'im!" growled the old groom. "Picks up they pretty trotters of his like any delicate miss! 'E ought for to be in petticuts!"

"You're right, Tom! But whichever and however he's a wriggling worm, the Governor's pet, consequently a power and he knows it, damn him!"

Mr. Jennings was indeed a delicate and dainty creature, his air, attire and every graceful movement proclaimed the fact,—he also wriggled, that is to say, whenever he bowed to or addressed anyone he did so with a graciously insinuating sideways twist and when he spoke it was in a flute-like tenor softly modulated, while his sloping shoulders performed this slow, quite graceful writhing movement; as they were doing now:

"Oh, my Ralph, dear fellow," he fluted, "my lord your Father presents his compliments and begs the favour of your presence in the library, immediately, dear boy, this mom——"

"Cut it, Jennings! What he really said was: 'bid that dam' son o' mine to me at once',—eh?"

"Oh, Ralph, your knowledge of him confounds my poor diplomacy," sighed Mr. Jennings with a writhe. "Yes, my

C

lord's message was phrased a little more bluntly. But, as you are aware, your noble sire has been much perturbed of late! A bolt, Master Ralph, a bolt from the blue, dear sir! So unexpected! So direly sudden! So preposterously——"

"Ah, to be sure!" nodded Ralph. "This new heir, damn him! Yet here's no reason why the Governor should vent his spleen on me——"

"Spleen?" repeated Mr. Jennings, in gently-shocked accents and writhing graceful reproof. "Ah no, indeed no! Never that. My lord is never anything but his own superb and stately self——"

"Except when foxed or——"

"Foxed?" Mr. Jennings' delicate eyebrows registered innocent enquiry. "Foxed, Master Ralph——"

"Don't call me 'Master' Ralph, as if I were a dam' boy——"

"Very well,—though I cannot forget you are three years my junior. But pray what do you mean by—foxed?"

"Oh—drunk, then!"

"D-drunk?" fluted Mr. Jennings recoiling in graceful horror. "Oh, dearest boy! I really must venture protest, for I cannot hear, I must not hear such——"

"Dammit, Eustace, you know better than I, how he's taken to brandy o' late, guzzles it like water,—and when he's been at it long enough the devil himself couldn't match him for——"

"No—no!" piped Mr. Jennings. "Your lordly father may be all you say—and even more, but I must not hear you say so, my dear Ralph, you really must not! For your own sake I beseech—ah!" The flute-like voice rose to a sweet, soft scream.

"What the devil now?" demanded Ralph, starting.

"Blood!" gasped Mr. Jennings, backing away on slim, elegant feet. "There's blood on you! Oh, how dreadful! And your poor beautiful face—now so horrible! So bruised, so battered, so marred! Ah, my poor, dearest Ralph, what dire mischance has befallen you, what oh—what?"

"Two dev'lish hard fists, if you must know," answered Ralph, sullenly. "And this blood ain't all mine, we clinched once or twice and I tapped his claret pretty well, I'm glad to say. And anyhow there's no real harm done—except to my shirt. So I'll go in and change before tackling the Governor——"

"No, no, you must not! You cannot! Oh Ralph, I dare not wait upon my lord with such message,—you must to him at once! If he knows you are home and not instantly in his presence, I dread to think what may eventuate! For he is in such mood——"

"Ha, a mood, eh? A brandy mood, I'll warrant! He'll be all mocking devil or ferocious brute——"

"Hush, dear boy, do pray remember that devil or brute, his lordship though a lord is also a man and therefore formed in God's own image! So are you and so am I——"

"You!" exclaimed Ralph, contemptuously, "I can't understand how the Governor puts up with you."

"My dear Ralph, I am happy to assure you that my lord is bound to me, as I to him with bonds nothing can ever break. Now I suggest you hurry to him."

"Oh well, if I must, I must!" Saying which, the Hon. Ralph removed jaunty hat, ran fingers through his luxuriant, jet-black curls, squared his stalwart shoulders and strode away to the ancient Manor House which, like all things hereabout, showed signs of neglect. . . . Reaching a certain gloomy door he gave a perfunctory tap thereon, opened it, closed it behind him and thus stood to front this superb creation and highly-polished gentleman of quality, his father.

CHAPTER XI

LORD JULIAN SCROPE was seated at a writing-table
whereon among other things stood a decanter and glass
together with an open letter and it was down at this that his
heavy-lidded gaze was directed; and thus he remained without
speech or movement and for so long that Ralph shuffled
nervously, then contrived to jingle a spur, then recoiled a step,
for his father, without raising head, was looking up at him—
and in those wide, dark eyes a glow he knew only too well, yet
when my lord spoke it was in tone very pleasantly casual:

"What is your age, Ralph?"

"Twenty-six, sir."

"Then you are old enough to—Dear me!" he exclaimed,
gently. "You show bloody as a slaughter-house or the last
scene of *Hamlet*! You have not been killing anyone, I suppose,—this new earl, for instance? But no, this would be too
much to expect of you, or hope for! Your tattered and gory
person, a repellent spectacle, is merely evidence of your dis-
tressing addiction to vulgar fisticuffs, of course. In my youth,
instead of brutal fists, a gentleman's weapons were delicate
small-sword or hair-triggers."

"They are yet, sir, if one's honour be involved."

"Are you well in practice with such tools, Ralph?"

"Naturally, sir,—though not so much with swords, the
'sharps' are becoming démodé, but with 'pops'-pistols, sir,
these new saw-handles, I'm very well,—though not so deadly
accurate as yourself, of course. Still, I fancy I could get my
man, should honour compel."

"Honour!" repeated Lord Julian, "The little flame that
shows off our gentility, so soon extinguished and therefore
to be nurtured so tenderly and shielded at hazard of our
blue blood! Ah but—there is that which I esteem even more
precious . . . more compelling . . . to be guarded and preserved
at all and every cost, Ralph!"

"And pray what is that, sir?"

"Existence, my son! Freedom to live and do how we will! To be lords and masters of Circumstance! For this we must dare and venture all. This is, my son, an axiomatic fact we must accept."

"Yes sir, though I've no idea just what you——"

"Ralph, you are twenty-six, a man, my only son and, to the best of my belief, the child of my own begetting. Hence, I deem it time you were better informed and made a little more aware of how we stand in regard to—let us still call it Circumstance. You may sit down—that chair—here beside me—so! Now," continued Lord Julian, tapping the open letter upon the table before him with one long, white finger, "pray, how should you describe this?"

"A letter, sir, I suppose."

"Your supposition is correct, it is a letter, and yet—so much, so very much more! For here, Ralph my son, is our ruin, shame of beggary, death sudden and sharp or one more lingering—in a debtors' prison."

"Oh, but . . . but, sir," stammered Ralph, "how . . . how is this? Are you telling me we are so . . . so utterly destitute?"

"I am! This house, the furniture, the horses in their stables, the very clothes on our backs, all can be seized by our creditor."

"Good—God! Sir, how . . . how comes this?"

"Ralph, your question is one you should be well able to answer. . . . Inform him, Eustace."

Thus summoned, Mr. Jennings, who had entered unheard and unseen by Ralph, now writhed into his sight, piping in melodious tenor:

"The new Earl, my dear Ralph! Who other could or should possibly cause your noble Father such harrowing disquietude?"

"But," said Ralph, turning his back on the speaker, "but indeed, Father, I . . . I know this house was ours, yes and all the country for miles around . . . two or three villages . . . farms! Then how, how in God's name——"

"Ralph, while your Uncle Japhet and my brother the late Earl lived—unmarried, our future was perfectly assured and we lived as became our station,—though on borrowed money! When brother Japhet married but—died so suddenly, I as the natural and legal heir, anticipated the fact, took old Time by the forelock and spent largely until, and like thunder-clap, came news of——"

"Ha—yes, sir, yes," cried Ralph, "of course, I remember now,—this accursed new heir turned up from nowhere and claimed everything!"

"No, my son,—this heir of whose birth and existence none had ever heard or even suspected, was deliberately sought for, diligently enquired after, and—on the mere, bare possibility that there might be a child of my brother's hasty marriage! And all those many months and weeks of ceaseless effort and unremitting labour were inspired by one whose only aim was and is—my injury, and, yes, Ralph, our ruin and utter destruction, yours and mine!"

"Then curse the fellow! Who . . . who is he, sir?"

"That lawyer person—Joliffe. A rat or rather, a mole-like creature who has burrowed and delved without let or respite until—from Heaven knows where, he has unearthed this unknown, unheard-of young man, proved his legitimacy, claimed and thus despoiled us of this heritage that, I hold, should be most justly ours by ties of blood and long tradition. Eh, Eustace?"

"Oh, my lord, yes!" piped Mr. Jennings. "Yes, most emphatically,—yours by every right, justice and equity,—or even otherwise! Oh, beyond all possibility of doubt! For this new-found heir, besides being an absolute stranger here-abouts, was born all unknown to the Earl his father, which was an impertinence, by a run-away mother, among strangers and in place unknown—which, certainly was most incon-siderate to your noble father!"

"Egad, sir," cried Ralph, "this all sounds so dev'lish odd . . . something might and must be done . . . can't we fight the fellow . . . in the courts . . . law and so on?"

"Oh, yes," sighed my lord, "we can fight the fellow, we certainly shall fight the fellow, because we must fight or perish! But—not in any court of law. Joliffe has proved young Japhet's legitimacy beyond all chance of doubt or cavil and is far too able a lawyer to have left us any smallest loophole—and you may be sure I have had the best legal opinion, con-sulted the highest authorities. So, to-day, my son, thanks to Mr. Joliffe, we are worse than paupers! We stand upon the very brink of destruction . . . the abyss of absolute ruin."

"But . . . but, sir . . . Father, surely . . . oh, surely some-thing can be done, something—anything to——"

"Four months hence—and a few odd days, my son, we, you

and I, must to the sordid oblivion of a debtors' prison, without hope of delivery! Four months hence, we pass out of our world to a lingering and most discomfortable death. But, Ralph, I do not intend so to die, no indeed! If anyone is to be destroyed, if anyone must perish as victim of damned Circumstance, it shall not be us! Eh, Eustace?"

"Ah no, my lord!" fluted Mr. Jennings with agonized writhe, "no, no a thousand times! The mere thought is horror and smites me to the heart! He must be found, he must! Oh indeed, indeed he must—and induced to nobly sacrifice all for the honour of his family—this side of it, of course!"

"He shall be found!" murmured Lord Julian.

"Who?" Ralph demanded.

"Eustace, tell my son. He knows, of course, yet pray inform him."

"Why then, Master Ralph," whispered Mr. Jennings, writhing so near that Ralph jerked back his chair, "if you will insist on plain and brutal fact, whom should my lord mean but this—ah—this detested interloper, your cousin Japhet, the new Earl of Wrybourne——"

"Yes, yes, but where is he?" enquired Ralph, turning to his father, "where on earth is he, sir?"

"Where?" echoed my lord, gently, yet as he uttered the word, his long, white, cruel-looking fingers clenched slowly, crumpling the letter they held. "Where else but in Joliffe's tender care. Thus much we do know, and shall learn more,— Eustace?"

"Oh, indubitably, my lord, and undoubtedly soon! The man Jupp is a cunning fellow, a perfect bloodhound of a creature never at fault for long. Our dear Mr. Joliffe may be astute, he may be shrewd—nay even crafty, but—there are others! Oh yes, there are others! If Joliffe is a mole, our Jupp is a perfect worm! Your cousin, Ralph, your cousin Japhet—this utterly preposterous heir that could not, should not, and—must not be, will, I am happy to know, be run to earth before long!"

"Yes, and—what then?" enquired Ralph, and turning to ask this of his father, saw Lord Julian's thin but shapely lips curl to such smile that he quailed and, glancing from that smiling mouth to the clutching hand that crumpled the letter so remorselessly, Ralph turned away and made as if to rise, then checked and sat very still as my lord said:

"Son Ralph, the Earl your uncle died of a fall from his horse . . . some such way must be found for the Earl your cousin."

"Sir, what . . . what are you . . . suggesting?"

"I am not suggesting, Ralph, I inform. I would also remind you of those time-honoured saws, namely: Desperate ills need desperate remedies, and, Necessity knows—no law!"

"Good . . . God!" exclaimed Ralph, in broken whisper, and sank back as if all strength failed him, while his stately father regarded him with an aloof though curious interest, saying as he did so:

"Eustace, my poor boy shows faint, pray administer water . . . a sip of brandy. . . . Ah no, he revives, he is better! Dear me, Ralph, you appeared about to sink and swoon in manner quite feminine! Ha, yes, now grit those white teeth of yours, set that dimpled yet masculine chin—excellent! Yet it seems that although son of mine, you are very much the child of your lamented mother."

"Thank God . . . she's dead!" muttered Ralph.

"Amen!" sighed his father. "For indeed these are days of desperate ill to be fronted only by men of as desperate and resolute mind—and purpose! Men who for that purpose, must, and will, hazard all——"

"What is—that purpose?" demanded Ralph, hoarsely.

"To live, my son! Ah, yes, to live, honoured of course, respected—perhaps, but—in that pride of estate and leisured ease the which is ours by right of birth, education and long ancestry."

"But what . . . what of the heir who being legally so as you say, is therefore the rightful inheritor, what of him and——"

"My . . . dear . . . boy," drawled his father, "think rather of yourself and then . . . of me! Shall we allow Circumstance to shame and then exterminate us,—for me the twitch of a trigger and oblivion,—for you the slow rot and slower death of a hopeless debtors' prison,—shall we? Emphatically no! Instead, my son, Circumstance itself shall be—eradicated, and we enjoy, to the full at last, that lofty station in life to which we were predestined! And to this vital and most necessary purpose, we all—our Eustace included, have our several parts to play."

"And what is . . . mine, sir?"

"Marriage, Ralph,—the Hawkins widow, of course!"

"But I detest the woman!"

"Which proves your admirable taste, my son,—for she is truly a pathetically uncomely creature. But then as all the world knows, her late spouse endowed her with more than a sufficiency of worldly goods, the figure is somewhere near a million, eh, Eustace?"

"More. Oh, far more, my lord, and all of it well invested, —a vast sum in the funds!"

"Then also, my son, this 'Golden Widow' dotes on you already! At mere sight of your stalwart form and handsome features, she flushes, palpitates, and so breathless, poor soul, she can scarce articulate,—this I have observed for myself and I am never wrong as regards—The Sex. And you are quite ridiculously handsome, my boy, and though so disgustingly bloody—could she behold you now she would be ready to swoon with womanly pity or kiss your bruises for——"

"No, sir, no!" cried Ralph, sitting up and squaring his shoulders. "You know very well that——"

"That you have but to speak, my son, and she will be in your arms, or you in hers."

"Never, sir! For as you are aware, I am in love with——"

"Thus, Ralph, so soon as it is known my son is to espouse the 'Golden Widow', we can defy damned Circumstance, form our plans at leisure and bide our time——"

"Sir, you . . . you know I love Cecily Croft——"

"Ah yes, the farmer's buxom daughter! Yes, a fine, handsome creature, Ralph. Well, you may continue to love her as well—or better when married to your widow——"

"Nothing of the kind, sir! You mistake, for, sir, I do most truly love and respect Cecily, and I'll never wed any other——"

"Fool!" said my lord, and though the word was softly uttered, he now and for the first time, allowed a frown to crease and trouble the arrogant placidity of his darkly handsome features. "Dunderhead! Sentimental dolt! Beggars have no choice! Have you ever heard of—Jasper Gaunt?"

"Yes, sir, I fancy so, a money-lender, isn't he?"

"A . . . money-lender!" repeated my lord, in tone of weary scorn. "Eustace, pray describe this lender of money fully yet briefly as possible,—inform my innocent offspring."

"Oh, my very dear Ralph—Oh, my dearest boy!" The words were a piping wail. Mr. Jennings writhed as in acutest agony. "Jasper Gaunt is the very mammon of all unrighteousness,—a heartless monster, a merciless bloodsucker whose victims high and low are everywhere and many in their graves! Suicide is, in his shadow, for whoso falls into his clutches is forever doomed, yes—ah, yes—to a perpetual damnation, never—Oh, never more to win free——"

"Admirably expressed, Eustace! Now, son of mine, pray oblige your father by hearing this! Have I your attention?"

"Yes, sir."

"Then listen to this that must be the inspiration to our instant counter action."

So saying, Lord Julian with leisured, graceful movement of his well-cared-for hands, smoothed out the crumpled letter and read aloud:

Kirby Street,
June 1, 1807.

To Lord Julian Scrope: My Lord,

Having lately become possessed of all and every of your many liabilities, accounts long over due, I beg to give notice they must be met and liquidated in toto. June the 30th proximo being the extremest limit of time that can be allowed.

I am, my lord, your lordship's most faithful

Jasper Gaunt.

"So, my son, here is our sentence of ruin and damnation! Eh, Eustace?"

"Beyond all doubting, my lord, ruin in this life and damnation hereafter—as you so truly say."

"Someday," sighed my lord, laying down the letter, "yes, someday Mr. Jasper Gaunt will be . . . very properly . . . murdered, and would I might be there to see. A foolish wish, of course, yet extremely natural! However, there is the compelling fact, my son,—unless you wed your 'Golden Widow' and we . . . achieve our Heritage of Wrybourne, you and I—and Eustace of course,—our course is run!"

Up starting from his chair, Ralph crossed unsteadily to the door, but there his father's commanding voice and gesture stayed him:

"Where away, my boy?"

And speaking the words between hard-shut teeth, Ralph answered:

"To Cecily!"

"Ah, yes!" murmured his lordship, smiling at his son's drooping, disconsolate figure, "wisely chosen! Thus shall we make Circumstance a stepping-stone—up and back to our so rightful place. Adieu and God bless you, my son."

CHAPTER XII

TELLS, WITH ADMIRABLE BREVITY, HOW UNCLE AND NEPHEW MET

WILLOWMEAD, small for a farm yet very much too large for a cottage, lay drowsing in the afternoon heat; birds chirped sleepily beneath the deep-thatched eaves, the roomy old house was hushed save for distant voices where Nancy and her four maids were busied in kitchen and dairy, for Katherine and her Ned had driven away in the gig on a shopping expedition while Sam, seated by the open window, was writing this letter:

Willowmead,
Sussex.
June 8, 1807.

To E. Joliffe, Esqr.

SIR AND DEAR BEN,

This being a strictly business letter written to a friend in spirit of friendship, I am, Sir, trying, my dear Ben, to combine the two. And first to business. You, Sir, being agent for the Wrybourne Estates, I therefore and herewith give you notice that I desire to sell the farm known as Willowmead, and all appertaining thereto from trucks to keelson, lock, stock and barrel and at as reasonably low a price as possible, because the purchaser will be my friend and shipmate, Captain Edward Harlow. So much for business, Mr. Joliffe, sir. But now, Ben, you must know there is a marriage in the offing between friend Ned and a very beautiful lady Mistress Katherine Ford,—wherefore I want your advice as to some gift, a wedding present worthy such a pair. Here I revert again to business—re the Scropes, father and son. The more I hear of them, the more your estimate of them is proved correct. Cousin Ralph I have met in a regular set to with naked mauleys and though a pretty fancy performer he could not last and I finished him with a right hand leveller that knocked him completely out of time, to my satisfaction and yours too, I hope, Ben, when I tell you he is totally unaware he was floored by his cousin. Lord Julian I have not seen as yet though I have heard enough, as for instance that he casts a goatish eye on a certain lady Miss Katherine herself no less, and Ned when properly roused is such very terrible fellow that my present care is to keep him in ignorance and thus prevent him from taking action. So I mean to keep it in "the family" should violence become unavoidable and if so my lord Julian shall know and experience me only as a rough tween-decks tar, free of speech and fist as British mariner usually is. And here I come to a question I have thought over a great deal lately, this Ben —I feel myself to be little better than a dam' intruder in this Wrybourne Heritage so would it not be more just and better for all concerned if I should divide the estates with these Scropes father and son to save them from the disaster you mentioned? Lord knows here is more money etc. than I can ever use or want. How say you, Ben? Or, as per business,—Sir, I desire your considered opinion, legal and human, on this matter. As for me, friend Ben, here am I in snug berth and sweetly peaceful haven, this dear old farmhouse set amid beautiful country the more so because from the home meadow I can glimpse and smell the sea. Truly a lovely land is Sussex and breeds lovely folk. I have already acquired a sweet, small niece named Jane and a somewhat formidable though gentle-hearted Granny, and as for Ned's Katherine, words fail me. And here glancing over what I have written it seems there are words too many, especially for such busy man of law and weaver of webs as yourself. So here I end, dear Ben,

Yours in friendship most sincerely,

SAM.

Sam was reaching for the sand-box to dust and dry his flourished signature when he became aware of approaching footsteps upon the flagged path outside, and knowing that whoever came must pass this window to reach the front door, he listened and waited expectant . . .

Footsteps slow and deliberate; assured feet these (thought Sam) that trod with such irritating deliberation, pausing now and then as if their owner had stayed to look around him or listen for some expected or familiar sound, then came on again more slowly, planting themselves masterfully and with small, soft jingle of spurred heels.

Sam put down the sand-shaker and leaned forward as into his line of vision strolled a tall, stately personage whose every garment was a work of art and worn with a languid grace; the elegantly-booted feet halted, and Sam, knowing at once and instinctively who this dominating person must be, spoke in gruffest and most offensive challenge:

"Belay there! If your name's Lord Scrope bear up and tack about,—smartly now!"

My lord Julian, used to and expectant of that somewhat slavish deference ever accorded to his dignity and rank, especially in his own county, opened his eyes rather wider than usual while the hand grasping his heavy riding-whip, gripped and half-raised it in sudden, instinctive menace, yet his voice was pleasingly modulated when he troubled to speak:

"Drunk, of course . . . and so early in the day! However, if your legs will serve you so far, you may go and inform Mistress Kate that Lord Julian Scrope desires her presence——"

"Avast!" growled Sam, leaning out from the window with threatening gesture, "drunk I mebbe, and then again mebbe I ain't. 'Owsever, I'm sober enough to know dirt when I sees it, ay and a land-shark afore I'm bit. As for the lady you mentions so free, I'm warning ye as she's agoin' to be spliced to my Cap'n. So, m'lud, you clap your desires under hatches or heave 'em overboard and sheer off."

"Ah?" murmured his lordship never stirring and surveying Sam's scowling visage feature by feature. "You are not so drunk as I deemed, no—you are endeavouring to be insolent——"

"Lord," snarled Sam, leaning farther out of the window and looking his grimmest, "I'm tellin' ye to sheer off and give Willermead a wide berth from now on! I'm likewise warnin' ye as there be summat yereabouts as ain't 'ealthy for your sort and that's me! And what's more, I'm sayin' as 'ow if ye don't tack about and show me your starn right smart, I know a cove as'll take and heave ye out into the lane yonder, and that's me again."

With languid gesture Lord Julian lifted the quizzing-glass that dangled on broad ribbon upon his breast and peering through it at Sam, murmured as if to himself:

"A sailor by his looks . . . and if not drunk, he is perhaps a little mad . . , a touch of the sun . . . or that ugly scar . . . a recent wound, I fancy. However, an extremely obnoxious fellow I am quite sure——"

"Do ye go?" demanded Sam, making to climb out through the window. "D'ye march on y'r own legs or do I heave ye out into the——"

My lord's seeming languor changed to instant and ferocious action, the heavy riding-crop whizzed—a blow so sudden, so vicious and truly aimed that Sam, smitten upon his scarcely-healed wound, dropped to his knees and for a moment remained thus, dazed and half-blinded by gush of blood; then somehow, anyhow, he was up and out of the window—to be met by another blow as calmly and truly aimed, but as he fell this second time, his long arm shot out instinctively, his fingers grasped slim riding-boot—jerked, twisted, and my lord went down backwards, to lie half stunned. Then Sam arose and grasping Lord Julian by the collar, dragged him along the path, out through the gate and so into that shady lane where a splendid horse stood tethered.

"So . . . there y'are, lord!" panted Sam, wiping blood from his eyes. "I've spattered ye a bit wi' my good blood. . . . Y'r coat's tore, and you ain't s' dam' dignified as you was. . . . So this'll do . . . till next time. But if y'ever do venter back 'ere to Willersmead wi' y'r desires and that like, it'll be worse for ye, lord,—ay, ay it'll be one on us . . . or both . . . for good and all!"

CHAPTER XIII

TELLS HOW AUNT DEBORAH MINISTERED

HOUSEWARDS went Sam but being much shaken and in no little pain, turned aside where stood a rustic seat, and sinking there made some attempt to staunch his bleeding while he waited for the sick faintness to pass. And it was now that a gentle, cooing voice came to him:

"Oh, paladin! Are you Roland, Oliver or Saint George for Merrie England? The Dragon has gone, thank heaven—and you, of course! But, oh, did you—do you know who he really is—do you?" Glancing up, Sam beheld a small, gracious lady whose coquettish plumed bonnet framed a small, pretty face and smooth and unwrinkled though remorseless Time or Circumstance had turned her ringlets of glossy hair to shining silver.

"Oh, my gracious!" she exclaimed, clasping small, mittened hands, "he's all blood . . . wounded and going to swoon——"

"Not I, marm, no I'll just . . . close my eyes 'gainst the sun-glare. . . ." And, sinking back, Sam lay upon the border of unconsciousness until roused by a blessed refreshment, he opened swimming eyes to find the lady sponging his wound with hand very deft and light, cooing murmurously as she did so:

"Goodness gracious me! A ghastly gash,—most murderous. The villain! Do I hurt you,—do I?"

"No, marm, there's healing in your touch."

"My word! What a courtly mariner,—such very gallant jack-tar! Are you able to walk now, out of this hot sun, can you?"

"Why of course," answered Sam and rising too hastily, staggered and would have sunk down again but that she propped and stayed him, saying in most determined manner:

"No, no! I must get you out of this heat . . . there now, lean on me, lean I say, this moment! Though not over-large I'm prodigiously powerful—for my size. Yes, that's it . . . your arm over my shoulder—now walk, slowly—be careful!" With rueful and shaky laugh Sam obeyed and thus she brought him into the fragrant coolness of the spacious kitchen.

"On the settle!" she commanded. "Full length! This cushion under your poor head—so! Now while I comfort and cherish your ghastly wounds, my bold Dragon-dragger, if you can talk—talk and tell me why you did it and if you know who our terrible Dragon really is. Do you know and did you?"

"Yes, marm, he called himself Lord Julian Scrope."

"Well—so he is! And you dared! You actually dragged him—like a sack of something very nasty, which he truly is, of course,—and you hauled him away by his lordly collar, his stately limbs sprawling! Oh sweet, sweet spectacle! Ah, what grandly brave, heroically bold defenders our gallant stalwart sailors are—for you are a sailor, of course?"

"At your service, marm."

"No, no, I am at yours, with this sponge and on my knees too! And while I am, let me tell you of our Dragon—that stately Wickedness! If you only knew how we have feared and dreaded him,—his politely persistent, pernicious persecution,—there's alliteration for you! His lofty arrogance and the determined evil of him! Kate's horrified loathing of him—Kate's my niece and a beauty—and my anxiety for her! He so serenely, hatefully assured and masterful and we so helpless! With no man to our protection! But now, ah now,—to have seen him felled in his sinful pride and dragged away and kicking and helpless—Oh glory! So now Paladin, my heroic and hardy sailor-man, this night you shall be in my prayers, so how shall I name you?"

"Sam," he answered, glancing up at her rather shyly over the sponge, "Sam Felton——"

"Ah, then you must be—you are—Captain Ned's friend, he has often mentioned you,—his first officer."

"And you, marm, at a guess, are Aunt Deborah."

"Yes, of course I am. Now lift your head that I may set this bandage."

"Is that needful, marm? I'm hoping the others won't notice anything of——"

"It is, and they will!"

"Couldn't it be hidden under my hair, marm?"

"It could—not! Good gracious no! It is quite a bad wound,—the cruel monster must have struck you terribly hard—— Oh, quite murderously!"

"He happened to strike where I rammed my head against something a lot harder a while since at sea."

"Oh, just what, pray?"

"A French musket-butt, or some such, marm."

"Ah,—in a battle?"

"Yes, marm. But what's bothering me is this, d'ye see, I don't want anyone, especially Ned, to know how I got this— no, nor anything about Lord Julian Scrope."

"Because you think there would be more trouble betwixt him and the Dragon?"

"Marm, if Ned ever knew this lord had ever tried to . . . molest his Kate, t'would mean sure death for one or other of them. So, marm, d'ye see, I want to keep, yes, b'George, I must keep this business strictly between our two selves and if I must wear this bandage we must think of some other way to account for it. But the question is how and what, marm?"

"Perfectly simple!" said she, securing the bandage in question and bestowing a soft pat on his curly head, "and in place of 'marm-ing' me so very persistently, don't you think I should sound a great deal better as 'Aunt Deborah' or even 'Deb'?"

"I do indeed," he answered, heartily, "yes, marm!"

"Well, nephew Sam, say it—this moment, sir."

"Then pray, Aunt Deborah, will you show me how to account for this bandage."

"Can you walk without tottering or tumbling?"

"To be sure I can."

"Come then," said she, and leading him across this wide kitchen to a tall dresser stored with crockery, pointed to a large dish on lofty shelf, saying:

"Tall nephew, reach that down for me. Now bring it to the fireplace. Now—drop it."

"But, Aunt Deb, 'twill surely break."

"Of course it will, so—drop it!" Sam obeyed and the dish splintered upon the hearthstone. "Well, nephew, there is your explanation, you see—or don't you?"

"I'm afraid I don't," said Sam, rubbing his chin perplexedly, "unless——"

"Return to the settle, nephew Sam, sit—no, lie down again and while I sweep up these fragments I will explain,—are you listening?"

"I am indeed."

"Then," said she, busied with the broom, and quite gracefully, "what happened was this: I asked you to reach me the dish, which you did, so that's true. You dropped it—so that's true again! The nasty thing struck you upon your poor, wounded brow,—which it did not, but there is the explanation of your hurt, two truths and only one very small, perfectly white fib. Does that meet the case?"

"It does and very cleverly."

"Then, nephew, express your thanks."

"Aunt Deborah, I am very truly grateful."

"And now being such a very sailorly mariner you'll be yearning for rum or grog in a noggin? But no, spirits would only heat your wound, you shall drink tea and so will I. And we will toast the muffins I brought and soak them with butter. So if you will take the bellows and blow up the fire, I'll put on the kettle and brew tea; real Soochong that never paid a farthing duty, this is Sussex remember,—dear, naughty, lovely old Sussex by the sea."

CHAPTER XIV

GIVES SOME DESCRIPTION OF THE GREAT HOUSE OF WRYBOURNE FEVERIL

IT was in the radiant sunshine of an early afternoon that Sam for the first time beheld the Great House, this "seat of his nobility", Wrybourne Feveril.

"Pull up!" said Mrs. Leet, sitting beside him in Kate's gig borrowed for the occasion, "I always think this the best of all the distant views, so pull up, Sam, stop, or perhaps I should say 'back your tops'ls and heave to'. There!" sighed she, with wide-armed sweep of mittened hand, "there's stateliness for you! There's glory of stone, tile and brick, ay and carved oak besides! There's true beauty framed in a grandeur mellowed by Time . . . reaching back and back through the ages, for they say the foundations are Roman. And there are two Norman towers, the rest is early Tudor. Yes, there is the Great House, Sam, a home for kings, and indeed kings and queens have slept there,—ah yes and villains too! For the Scropes are a breed unworthy such great and noble heritage! Well, what d'you think of it?"

"Vast!" he replied. "Too hugely big for comfort and impossible as a home."

"Fiddle-de-dee and nonsense, Sam! Folk have lived there since the dim ages. According to tradition it was first a Roman fortress, then a Saxon stronghold, next a Norman castle, then a noble mansion, and now—well—the stately glory you behold."

"However," quoth Sam, shaking his bandaged head (though gently) "it's not my idea of homely comfort, nothing cosy or home-y about it, Grannyanne."

"Oh, but there is!" she retorted vehemently, "I mean—there are all sorts and kinds of cosy nooks and corners, with lovely home-y rooms too besides the big state apartments, the huge hall and galleries. The Great House has everything to suit all tastes and moods. Ah yes, Wrybourne Feveril is a place of wonders! Drive on and I'll show you—some, at least. Heave ahead, Sam."

So he touched up Jabez, the sleekly powerful horse and away they sped across richly-wooded, undulating park where graceful deer stood to watch them gentle-eyed; ah, but the great house itself was watching them and very differently (or so thought Sam). This huge thing of carved wood, grey stone and ruddy brick which persisting through the ages must therefor know so much of living and dying, so little of good, so much of evil, yet proud and arrogant ever,—which even now was glaring down on him with all its many latticed windows so haughtily that Sam instantly scowled in return as he watched this home of his hateful ancestry grow upon his sight. Nearer and nearer it rose and spread before and above him, lofty gable and twisted chimney, soaring tower, battlement and turret, chilling him with its sheer immensity.

"Sam," demanded Mrs. Leet, "why d'you frown so?"

"Because, Grannyanne, your Great House is too much so."

"Too much what, pray?"

"Great and—splendid. Aha, and yonder in the splendid doorway of all this magnificence is a person, no—a person-age as stately as the place itself."

"Oh no," said Mrs. Leet, waving a hand to this imposing creature, "that is no more than Henry James Perkins the butler, though he was merely the fifth footman in my time."

"However, he's all butler now!" quoth Sam, as the person-age wafted airily in response. "Such awesome dignity, Grannyanne!"

"He always was, even as a footman and it's grown on him, it seems. Well, Perkins," she called as the gig came to a standstill, "you look as well as I feel. The years have been kind to us, James."

Mr. Perkins descended the broad, marble steps with dignity as a butler should, then bowed as few butlers could, for he did it with a certain restrained majesty of look and gesture, and when he spoke it was in throaty voice schooled to chaste and genteel murmur:

"Mrs. Leet, pray be welcome! And as to looks, indeed you bloom, marm, you bloom. Allow me to assist you to terrier firmer, marm."

"Thankee, James," said she, performing this somewhat intricate manoeuvre with surprising agility, which done, she enquired, "Now, James, what of the horse and gig?"

From the snowy frills at his bosom Mr. Perkins extracted

a large silver whistle attached to him by broad, black ribbon and blew a mellow though resounding note, in answer to which call presently appeared a footman ornate as to livery and large as to ears, shoulders and calves to whom, with dignified gesture towards the vehicle, Mr. Perkins issued the command:

"To the stables, William, grooms. Begone!"

"Sam," said Mrs. Leet, as William led horse and trap away, "Mr. Perkins! James, here is my grandson—by adoption, Mr. Felton."

"Honoured, sir!" quoth the butler, performing his bow again. "Any friend or relation of Mrs. Leet is persony greater with myself! For Mrs. L. marm, to us of the—ahem—old reggime you were, are and ever will be part and, as it were, parcel, marm, of this 'the Great House', the time-honoured faybrick called Wrybourne Feveril, this most truly historic and——"

"Thankee, James! So now since there's so much I want my grandson to see here, let's begin."

"So be it, marm. Though first may I venture to enquire if you can tell or inform me aught of our new lord whose present whereabouts, like himself, is a profound mystery and hence a source of carking anxiety to boot. So if you have the least scrap or tittle of news——"

"Nothing, James. All I know is that he has been resident abroad, hobnobbing with foreigners,—Lord frustrate their knavish tricks,—and therefore will be full of foreign fads and faddles, all shrugs and scrapes and will probably speak broken English!"

"Oh, this is sad news, marm, heavy tidings and highly woeful to contemplate. Yet, even so, our new Lord can hardly be more—ahem—more——"

"Villainous, James?"

"Marm, I was about to say 'trying'."

"Ay, to be sure, James, he was ever trying and succeeding in some devilry or other——"

"A-ham!" quoth Mr. Perkins and led the way (almost hastily) into the great echoing hall dim lit by small narrow windows set high in ancient walls hung with pennons and banderols dingy and faded by Time, yet bright with glittering array of antique weapons, while ranked below stood effigies in burnished armour of different periods.

"Ha-hum!" quoth Mr. Perkins again, "I observe you are interested in our armour, Mr. Felton."

"Yes," answered Sam, "you keep 'em very bright."

"We do, sir, we do. I have them all dooly and reverentially cared for, since each helped, as it were, to erect and maintain the glory of this do-main of Wrybourne Feveril. Fif-teen suits, sir, cap'a pee! Here you behold the pan-o-plee wore by Sir Amyot at Agincourt,—this next Sir John Scrope used at Cressy, he was boon companion to Sir Walter Manny and Sir John Chandos and was honoured by King Edward himself . . . helm and breastplate bear marks of combative violence you'll pray notice. . . . And so on through the ages, sir, to that mag-nificent soot that adorned the person of Sir James Scrope at the Field of the Cloth of Gold, sir, then yonder we have the splendid harness worn by Sir Japhet Scrope at Naseby, Newberry, Marston Moor and other fee-rocious encounters——"

"Well now," said Mrs. Leet, "now, James, we'll to the galleries, and there, Sam, you shall see pictures of the wearers. Give me your arm."

Through echoing chambers cold and stately she led him, through rooms snug and cosily furnished, along deeply-carpeted, richly-panelled corridors and so to a vast gallery, its splendour of carved woodwork and painted ceiling lighted by many long windows that showed row upon row of portraits, noble lords and gracious dames who scowled, smiled, simpered or merely stared from backgrounds dim or glowing; bearded and shaven ferocities in heavy armour, gloomy gentlemen in ruffs, gallants who smirked or gazed, pensively passionate, between curled lovelocks and—a grim-faced nobleman in black half-armour who leaned negligently upon a large cannon with a distant though furious sea-battle in progress just above his right shoulder. Now before this portrait Mrs. Leet halted suddenly, exclaiming:

"Ha! Yes, of course, now I remember! Sam, look at this one! Well, what do you say?"

"That he's no beauty, Grannyanne, and by the ships a seaman, I suppose."

"He was indeed!" quoth Mr. Perkins. "Sir, you behold the likeness of my Lord Japhet Scrope, Vice Admiral of the Blue, wounded in the three days' battle with the Dutch off Beachy Head. He was also, you will notice——"

"Yes, yes, James," said Mrs. Leet, "but what else do you notice?"

"I notice, Mrs. Anne, marm, no more than I have beheld hundreds of times when showing visitors around and——"

"Then you, Sam, what do you notice?"

"That he looks a pretty grim sort of customer——"

"So do you, Sam, when you scowl as he has been doing all these years! James, don't you see the strange likeness? Look, man, here and there!"

"Ah-ham!" exclaimed Mr. Perkins, glancing from Sam to the portrait and back again. "Ye-e-s," he admitted, "I do remark a vague, a faintish seemularity, Mrs. Anne."

"Vague, d'you say, James? Put Sam in that same black armour, it's out there in the hall, and they would be as like as two peas!"

"Lord!" exclaimed Sam. "If I'm really like that old cut-throat I hope I'm better than I show."

"Sam, the Admiral was a very brave gentleman and one of the few good ones—for a Scrope!"

"In-deed yes!" quoth Mr. Perkins. "The Admiral restored the old Norman chapel and built the public almshouses——"

"And what of this lady?" enquired Sam, turning towards a portrait that seemed mostly eyes, ringlets and bosom.

"The Lady Araminta,—a baggage, Sam! A bold, heartless vixen! The less said of her the better."

"Ah, but," added Mr. Perkins, "a famous beauty and toast, Mrs. Anne! Gentlemen fought doo-els very frequently on her account——"

"More fools they, James!"

"But, oh ponder, marm, consider the wicked age she lived in, Mrs. Anne——"

"She did her best to make it worse, James! And now the tapestries; they are truly famous, Sam, though their subjects, one or two, are inclined to be a little so-so. And thereafter, James, tea if you please in Queen Elizabeth's small parlour."

"Mrs. Anne, I was myself about to suggest same. I go, proceeding this moment to order it."

And away past these rows of long-dead Scropes paced Mr. Perkins, himself more imposing than any of them.

"Strange!" exclaimed Mrs. Leet, glancing back towards the pictured Admiral. "Among all the many hundreds of visitors I have shown through these galleries in my time, I have never

known it happen before. Never did anyone of them resemble
in the slightest degree any of these pictured Scropes. And now
. . . to-day . . . at last . . . you, Sam, and the Admiral! And
he was a sailorman, too! Don't you think it strange and
surprising?"

"Well, no, Granny, for if you go on comparing faces long
enough, you'll be sure to find someone like somebody else
some time or other, it stands to reason."

"Hum—yes, perhaps . . . and yet, Sam, he was a sailor, too"

"Yet looks more like a pirate, Granny! But tell me, did
Queen Elizabeth really stay here?"

"To be sure she did, and frequently. You shall see the bed
she slept in, the goblet she drank from—ale, Sam, and quite
a large goblet! I'll show you the fine embroidered shoes she
wore and silk stockings out of Spain, great rarities in those
days. Then there's a bow she used for shooting deer, poor
things,—the glove she gave Sir Julian who wore it on his
helmet at a tournament. Oh, there are lots more glories and
wonders for you to behold, Sam!"

"And yet, if you please, Grannyanne, I would much rather
see the room that was your own, I mean that one where you
once hove fire-irons at a lordly brutish villain."

"Then of course you shall, Sam, 'tis much the same now
as it was then, not very splendid,—but you can see the very
marks upon the door and panelling. . . . Ah, but thank goodness,—yonder comes our pompous James to say tea awaits
us!"

"Well," sighed Mrs. Leet, as they turned into the leafy,
home lane, "thank you for the drive, Sam, it has done me a
power o' good."

"And thank you, Granny, for showing me the wonders of
Wrybourne Feveril."

"Ay, the Great House!" she sighed. "A rare treasure-house,
a jewel of antiquity that has grown with and is part of this
Old England of ours. . . . How should you like to live there,
Sam?"

"I shouldn't!" he answered, frowning.

"Ha!" she exclaimed, glancing up at him with her shrewd,
old eyes. "Yes, it is odd how strangely you resemble my lord
the Admiral when you scowl, Sam. And he was one of the
good ones!"

"And that is truly much more odd, Granny, for the Scropes, past and present, run to pretty foul villainy of all sorts and kinds."

"Still, there have been good ones, a few, here and there, Sam, they happened every fifty years or so. Maybe this new Earl will turn out a good one, by some happy chance. I'm hoping so with all my heart, for a very particular reason."

"Oh?" murmured Sam. "Pray why?"

"Because a good Earl might be induced to grant our Kate and Ned their own hearts' desire and allow them to buy the freehold of Willowmead! And besides," she continued, seeing Sam lost in silent contemplation of the long, winding lane before them, "he might even be persuaded to allow my cottage roof to be mended,—it leaks shamefully. I've a great idea of writing Mr. Joliffe direct about it."

"Oh?" enquired Sam. "Ah, so you know of Mr. Joliffe?"

"Why, of course! I've writ him many a letter on business of the Great House, and many's the cup o' tea he's drank with me in my sitting-room there. Mr. Joliffe has been lawyer to the family all his life, like his father before him, he and I are old friends. . . . Oh, but you're driving past my cottage!"

"Ay, Granny, I am. According to orders——"

"Whose, I'd like to know?"

"Kate's. For d'ye see, I was commanded to bring you back to supper——"

"Oh, but, Sam, I——"

"Stuffed breast o' veal, Granny! Not to mention such oddments as—a vast, cold ham, beef roast—cold, and beef boiled —spiced! Also Ned will brew grog, though he calls it 'punch', for you specially, Grannyanne, to hearten you after this long drive. And orders being orders, d'ye see,—here we are!" So saying he pulled up in the farm-yard fragrant and spicy with scent of ricks and stables, where presently came Ned and Kate to welcome them.

CHAPTER XV

DESCRIBES CERTAIN WILLOWMEAD FOLK

IT was a glad, golden morning and Sam, wandering into the cool, trim dairy, paused to marvel at the swift dexterity of Nancy this buxom, though ineffably demure creature, skimming rich, yellow cream from wide pans of milk; then turned to watch Kate, in apron and print gown, her lovely round arms bare, performing that everyday miracle—the making of yellow, luscious butter. In the midst of this homely occupation she glanced up at his gravely intent face and enquired:

"Have you never seen butter made before, Sam?"

"Never. And now that I do, I'm wondering how it happens and why."

"I'm wondering too," she sighed. "I could scarcely sleep last night for wondering!"

"Not about butter, of course, Kate?"

"No, about Ned . . . travelling all that great way to London . . . and the roads so unsafe! The Mail was stopped only last week by highwaymen and the guard wounded, poor man!"

"Ay, but Ned is Ned and safe in London by now, I'll warrant."

"Dear Sam!" she murmured. "What a comfort you are! But if he is there safe, I'm wondering if he has seen Mr. Joliffe, the lawyer yet. And if he has I'm wondering still. . . . Oh, Sam, how I'm wondering what the outcome will be."

"The best, Kate, depend on 't. Ned deserves the very best of life if ever a man did, for he's earned it, also he has been mighty fortunate, seeing he has you."

"'Deed yes, Sam, to be sure he has me for ever, but——"

"And b'Jingo, Kate, you're a prize rich enough to content any man breathing."

"But I'm not rich, Sam, I can hardly make the farm pay and should have failed long ago but for my good Ben Toop and his dear old father. I'm quite poor——"

"Ay, but rich in all that makes a woman lovely and that's the only riches worth having."

"Why—Sam! You'll make me blush! Such compliments and—from you!"

"Not compliments, Kate, I can't manage 'em, being no lady's man, d'ye see, I speak straight forrard and mean what I say, every word. And what I'm meaning now is—that when Ned takes such prize as you and tows her safely into the Harbour of Matrimony he is far richer than those Maya folk in South America, Aztec and Inca, who mined and used gold by the ton as we do iron. So, although personally I keep well to windward of wedlock, I'm saying that, blow foul or fair, Ned is mighty fortunate to have you alongside . . ." At this moment the grandfather clock that had ticked on the wide old stair time out of mind, uttered its mellow chime.

"Eleven o'clock!" sighed Kate. "At this very moment Ned should be with lawyer Joliffe! He will have asked if we can buy Willowmead . . . not that I dare suppose it possible . . . but . . . if he only could. . . . Oh, Sam, the thought almost . . . chokes me with joy . . . but it seems too wonderful ever to come true."

"I don't see why, Kate."

"Then . . . Oh, Sam, do you think there is the least possible chance, do you?"

"I can't see why not."

"But the Earls of Wrybourne are all so terribly rich. The old lord would never part with an acre to anyone and this new lord may be the same."

"Too true!" nodded Sam. "And yet again he may not. No, he may be an altogether different sort of fellow, in fact I believe he is."

"Do you, Sam, do you? Oh, if he only is! But what makes you believe so?"

"Why, Kate, d'ye see, it so happens," answered Sam, cautiously, "I've heard that he's been, well, knocking about the world, hither and yon, the seven seas, port to port and consequently seen so much of the world in general that this particular bit of it may not seem so almighty precious to him as it was to his hoggish ancestors. It stands to reason."

"Does it?" she questioned wistfully, lovely head drooping. "I wish I could be as certain of this as you seem to be,—why are you so sure, Sam?"

"Lord knows!" he answered, avoiding her glance. "Of course, there's few things sure or certain in this world, Kate, yet I believe in looking on the bright side . . . hoping for the best and—well—while there's life there's hope, d'ye see?"

"Yes, Sam, I'm hoping now and praying, in thought, that you may be right."

"Good!" he nodded. "Then you may depend upon it that I am right. So smile, Kate, God bless you, smile! Ah, good again! Now I'll bear away for the orchard to smoke a pipe or so and listen to the birds, I never heard them sing as they do here at Willowmead——"

"Wait, Sam! Before you go do please tell me all you know or have ever heard about our new lord. Have you in all your wanderings ever met him or seen him perhaps—— Oh, have you?"

Sam turned to gaze out through open doorway across the sunny garden, saying after momentary hesitation:

"Now God love you, Kate, how should I? Earls and lords don't usually ship aboard whalers or privateers or join company with seafaring men the like o' me, it goes without saying . . . stands to reason, Kate, d'ye see?"

"Yes,—yes, of course!" she sighed, "I was only . . . hoping and wondering again."

"Ay, ay, that's the word—hope! Hope hard, Kate, so will I and who knows but our wish may come safe to harbour all a-tauto alow and aloft." So saying, he smiled and stepped out into the sunshine. Now on his way to the orchard he met a man, a stalwart, blue-eyed, comely fellow (though just at present grimly woeful of aspect) and busily sharpening a scythe with a certain neat deftness of movement that Sam was quick to heed.

"Good morning," said he, pausing. "You are Tom, I think?"

"Ay, sir. Tom Toop, at your service."

"And you've been a sailor, Tom."

"Lor-dee, sir, 'ow should ye know that?"

"By your smart and general handiness, Tom. Royal Navy, eh?"

"Yessir, afore I larned enough to quit."

"Don't tell me the sea didn't agree with you."

" 'Twern't the sea, sir, 'twere my brother Willum as got took off by a cross-bar-shot alongside o' me just arter Lord Nelson were struck down."

"Ah, so you saw, you were there, Tom?"

"Ay, sir, sarving a quarter-deck starboard carronade. Poor Will were beyond speech, him being nigh cut in two,—but says Lord Nelson as Cap'n Hardy stooped to lift him, 'They've done for me this time, at last', says he. Well, sir, there was brother Willum and Lord Nelson done for, so when us *Victory* men got paid off, I bore away for home soundings and yere I've been ever since. Ye see, sir, there was a right tidy lass yere-abouts and waiting for one or t'other on us, though which she favoured Willum and me never could nowise decide. So arter he was took off, I bore down, laid her alongside,—but—" here Tom sighed deeply, his cheery visage glooming, "only to larn as 'twere poor Willum as she favoured arter all!"

"Dam' hard luck, Tom. And you say she lives hereabouts?"

"She do, sir. And she be in dairy at this yere instant."

"Eh? You mean——?"

"Nancy, sir."

"And a tight, handsome craft she is, Tom."

"Ay, no question, sir, though she ain't—complete."

"Eh? Not——?"

"No, sir, can't nowise be, seeing as how."

"As how what, Tom?"

"As how part of her be missing, sir."

"Oh!" murmured Sam, pondering this. "Ah? What, Tom?"

"Her heart, sir, 'tis laying fathoms deep along o' poor Will."

"Did she tell you so?"

"Constant, sir."

"Ha!" murmured Sam. "Well, what d'you think?"

"Sir, I dunno what, so I'd be obleeged for your opinion."

"Then I'm pretty sure her heart is in the right and proper place and waiting for the right man to take it! And who better than a Nelson and Trafalgar man?"

"Meaning . . . me, sir?"

"Of course. You'll mind Lord Nelson's fighting signal: 'Engage the enemy more closely', eh Tom?"

"Ay, ay, sir,—but a mounseer's broadside is easier for to face."

"Then get the weather-gauge and board, man, board!"

Tom rubbed his well-shaven chin with the whetstone and glancing askance on Sam, smiled though very ruefully, saying:

"Sir, I tried it once but was repelled wi' loss, ay, the casu-allities was pretty heavy."

"Took it amiss, did she?"

"Well, sir, if a rap across my figurehead be amiss, she did. And, what's more, she ain't took heed o' me by look nor word since."

"So?" exclaimed Sam, also rubbing shaven chin but with thumb and forefinger. "Why then, since the Navy never accepts defeat, the only means left is surprise, a dashing boat action, a cutting-out attack and damn the shore batteries!"

"E'cod sir, I never thought o' that . . . muffled oars . . . surprise . . . neck or nothing . . . close quarters!"

"Think it over, old 'Victory and Nelson' man."

"I will, sir, ay, I will, and thankee. But, sir, if I may make s'bold, will ee,—would you, sir, be s'good to speak her a word on my behalf—should opportoonity offer?"

"Ay, Tom, I will so." Then Sam rambled on his way while Tom started mowing, but now his lips, no longer grim-set, were puckered to a soft, melodious whistling.

CHAPTER XVI

REACHING the orchard at last, this green remoteness pleasantly shaded by aged trees, apple and pear, Sam lay down beneath one of the largest, broad back to rugged bole and began to fill his pipe.

But so quiet was it and the warm air so conducive to sleep that presently Sam closed his eyes slumberously and, after some while, opened them drowsily—then sat up suddenly broad awake; for here in this peaceful seclusion where it seemed, a moment before, no man save himself had been, a man was now standing and within a yard of him. A shortish, broad-shouldered youngish man trimly clad in blue spencer, cords and top boots; a round-faced, keen-eyed, powerful-looking fellow who grasped a shaggy-napped hat in one fist and a remarkably knotted stick in the other.

Now meeting Sam's astonished gaze, this sudden visitor beamed, lifted the knobbly stick to his right eyebrow, saying in voice hoarse though soft:

"Ax parding, sir, for this here in-troosion, but I'm begging the favour of a vord or say—a couple, say—three or four."

"Lord!" exclaimed Sam, blinking. "Where in the world did you spring from?"

"The immejit vi-cinity, sir."

"Ha!" quoth Sam, picking up his fallen pipe. "And you're Mr. Shrig, the Bow Street officer."

"That werry i-dentical, sir. And, sir, my wisitation is on a werry personal and private matter."

"Oh?" enquired Sam. "Ah! What, pray?"

"Vich, sir, seeing as how you're a-sitting there so nice and-see-clooded as no creeping crawlers can unseen hear nor yet hark, I'll tell you frank and free as 'tis a matter o' life and death."

"Ah?" murmured Sam again. "Whose?"

"Your werry own, sir."

"Yes," nodded Sam, "that is rather personal. Bring-to, Mr. Shrig, beside me, if you don't mind the grass, and let's hear."

Down sat Mr. Shrig with surprising nimbleness and nodding at Sam's pipe took out his own, a short, blackened, villainous-looking clay, enquiring as he did so:

"No objections, sir, I hope?"

"Of course not," answered Sam, proffering his tobacco-box whereat Mr. Shrig beamed but shook his head, saying:

"Much obleeged, sir, but I prefers my own." And when both pipes were aglow and drawing well, Sam leaned back against his tree; thus having puffed once or twice in silent content, Mr. Shrig removed his pipe an inch or so from his lips and spoke:

"Talking o' bandages, sir——"

"Eh? Bandages?" Sam repeated. "But we're not."

"Hows'ever, Mr. F. sir, I'm glad to see as your damaged tibby is now getting along vithout same."

"Yes,—though it wasn't much, just a bit of an accident, d'ye see——"

"Ar—in shape of a vip, sir, a pretty heavy 'un as vips go."

"Ay, but how should you know?"

"Observation, Mr. F., and evidence received, sir. I likewise know as your ass-aylant vich, naming no names I'll call Number Vun, downed you wi' two ex-tremely wicious strokes! Yet, arter said strokes you downed Number Vun and throwed him out into the lane."

"So then you saw——"

"No, sir, no, I were denied that pleasure, but I had eyes as see for me."

"Ha, a spy?"

"A ass-istant, sir—viskers and a red vaistcoat, answering to the name o' Dan'l."

"Dammit! Mr. Shrig, I strongly object to being spied upon!"

"And werry natral too, sir!" answered Mr. Shrig, puffing serenely. "But then I object jest as strongly to seeing you a bleedin' corpse afore your time! 'Twouldn't do, sir, and myself in charge o' the case! So you mustn't go getting yourself shot, nor yet stabbed, p'izened nor drownded, 'twould be bad for the both on us."

"It would!" Sam agreed fervently, yet with flashing grin. "Especially me, so I'll do my best to keep alive—if only for your sake."

"Sir," retorted Mr. Shrig with reproachful shake of head, "you take this here ugly business altogether too cool and calm.

D

Murder ain't never to be sneezed at—no, sir. Being The Capital Act it should ought to be treated accordingly."

"Oh?" murmured Sam, watching the blue smoke wreathes of his pipe ascend into the still air. "Ah? How, Shrig?"

"Respectful, sir! Ar, with a respect bordering on h-awe." Here Mr. Shrig, having puffed vehemently to keep his pipe going, continued: "Sir, or, seeing as there's nobody to peek nor hark, should I ought to say 'my lord'——?"

"No!" answered Sam. "Certainly not!"

"Werry good, sir, then allow me to inform you as how, ever since the moment I run you to earth and diskivered your true i-dentity, you have been and are, a werry large fly in my ointment, risking your precious life to no purpose and my constant ang-ziety."

"You think my life in such peril, eh, Shrig?"

"I do, sir! Ar and so does Mr. Joliffe! So why don't you think the same and act according?"

"Well," answered Sam, musingly, "I'm pretty sure, of course, that if my noble nunks could blast me by mere word or wish, I should be dead this moment! Yes, considering I must be his ruin I can well understand his burning desire to be rid o' me at any or every cost,—ay, even at risk of his lordly, confounded neck! A most determined, desperately cool gentleman, Shrig."

"As any cowcumber, sir! And besides," here Mr. Shrig leaned nearer to whisper harshly: "if ever I see a true, hell-fire Capital Cove, 'tis him, Number Vun! I'm glad you've took notice and hope as you'll go werry cautious henceforrard."

"Ay, I will so! But then, d'ye see, for chance to come at me he must first of all find me . . . and he has no least idea where I am or what I look like,—ay, before he can act he must find me out and make sure of my identity——"

"Ar! And so soon as he does, how then, sir?"

"Eh? Soon? Are you so sure he will?"

"Sir, I am so werry sure and cartain of it that I'm a-sitting here at this pre-cise moment to tell you sich is so."

"Oh!" exclaimed Sam, forgetting to smoke. "B'gad, are you? Pray explain."

"Sir, how much d'you know con-carning a Mr. Tobias Jupp?"

"Nothing at all, I never hear the name. But tell——"

"Vich don't sap-rise me none, sir, though he knows a on-common lot about you!"

"Oh?" exclaimed Sam, again. "How?"

"By creeping, sir, crawling, and likewise peeping and pry-ing. He spoke to you in Lewes, by the old castle."

"Ay to be sure! You mean that remarkably unremarkable fellow."

"That werry same. A most ex-tryordinary ordinary cove is Tobias, that's his partickler line o' business, a werry downy bird is Tobias! Having been a lawyer he's full of it and up to all the moves, but then, sir, 'twixt you and me, so am I. There-fore, so soon as Tobias J. left London and took arter you, me the Gimblet and Dan'l took arter Tobias, in my gig, to keep our peepers or, as you might say, ogles on both o' you."

"So that's how you saw me in Lewes, eh, Shrig?"

"Ar, and that's how I'm seeing you here, sir. But while we sits here puffing our steamers so werry sociable,—in a old, ruinated mill werry picture-esque and not so far hence, blind-folded, gagged, tied up precious secure and com-pletely flum-moxed, Tobias Jupp aforesaid is lying at this pre-cise moment, pondering how it all happened and oo dropped on him so sudden and onexpected!" Here Mr. Shrig, glancing askance on his hearer, emitted a soft, throaty chuckle.

"Aha!" murmured Sam, leaning nearer in his turn and lowering his voice. "Grassed him, levelled the fellow, did you, b'George?"

"Mr. F. sir, I did,—full length, face down'ards, and afore he knowed oo or what, I'd got same tied up helpless as a ninfant and blind as a kitten noo born, sir."

"Shrig," quoth Sam, with that sudden, white-toothed smile which so lighted and transfigured his grim features, "give me your hand."

"Honoured, sir."

"Lord love me!" chuckled Sam as their hands met. "Assault and battery—and you a limb of the law!"

"Sir," answered Mr. Shrig, gravely, "there's times like this here, when I'm all Law,—arms, legs, body and soul! Ar, and I perform according with fist, brain, boot or bludgeon if tackling (as in dooty bound) Wiciousness afore it can act, Murder as creeps unseen and crawls unheard upon its onsus-pecting wictim. So there lays Tobias in the old mill and here, Mr. F. sir, is the reason thereof." And from the breast of his trim, blue, bright-buttoned coat, Mr. Shrig drew a pocket-book which he opened, saying as he did so:

"This here little reader belongs to Tobias, you shall see it in a minute, sir, but listen first to what he's wrote down here." And now leaning still nearer, Mr. Shrig read aloud, though very softly:

" 'Six foot tall about and powerful build. Darkish hair, chestnut. Bold features of sat-ter-nine cast. Strides long and vith rolling gait. Looks formidable. N.B. Now dressed as a sailor and bears newly-healed scar above left eyebrow. Impossible to mistake and therefore easy to i-dentify!' A remarkable true and acc'rate description, eh, sir?"

"Yes!" nodded Sam, grimly. "Yes, damme, I'm easy to recognize! Whoever reads that will know me at a glance——"

"Ar,—like a flash o' lightning, sir! Now, hark again." And in the same hushed accents Mr. Shrig read this:

" 'To whom it may con-cern. Gentlemen, at no little bodily risk, trouble, labour and ex-pense, the information required is now in the writer's possession. But owing to unforeseen risk and labour aforesaid, cannot be handed over except the sum, already stipulated, be doubled. The writer may be heard of at the Stag's Head, Wrexford, but for three days only, by reason of risk aforementioned.' And now, sir," said Mr. Shrig, passing letter and pocket-book, "take a look at 'em yourself."

"Evidently a cunning rascal!" said Sam as he returned these, after reading.

" 'Cunning' is the vord, sir. Our Mr. T. J. is a slimy article as has dodged The Law frequent—so far."

"But you have him safe and sound for the present, have you?"

"As the Bank of England, sir! Tobias can't see nor speak nor yet stir a finger."

"And what now, friend Shrig?"

"All depends on you, Mr. F. sir."

"How so?"

"Sir, just so soon as Tobias J. passes on this here information to—us knows oo, vich same he'll do soon or late, Windictiveness (ar and with a werry large Wee) will be afoot—up and arter you, sir. Wiciousness'll be in the werry air you breathe! Murder'll creep and crawl, seeking chance to commit The Fact,—to strike you dead, sir, sudden, sharp and final!" Here Sam, finding his pipe had gone out, shook his head at it and began to polish it thoughtfully upon his broad palm, while Mr. Shrig continued:

"But sir, you have now two courses o' pro-ceedure as I can offer——"

"Two, eh?" questioned Sam, still polishing his pipe-bowl. "Only two, Shrig?"

"Two, sir, and no more!"

"Not a large selection, but let's hear."

"First, sir, you can skip and run,—vay-cate or, as you might say, hop this here rustical perch, me keeping Tobias werry close and see-cure for a day or so till you can get safe onto some ship and sail off—ar, and keep sailing till Mr. Joliffe sends you the office as how he's laid—you know oo by his willainous heels and you may come home in perfect safety. That's your first course, sir, the most commonsense, safest and therefore ad-wiseable."

"Ah!" murmured Sam. "Yes, to be sure. And what's your course Number Two?"

"To stay as y'are, sir, taking a chance but trusting to me. Risking your precious life as a dee-coy drawing on Wiciousness to attempt The Act, thereby giving me the opportoonity to trap Wiciousness, tackle Murder and end same prompt—for good and all. So there 'tis, sir, the ch'ice is yourn! . . . How d'ye say, Mr. Felton, sir?"

"That the sooner we make a start the better."

"Eh, 'start', sir? Meaning as you'll—go?"

"No, damme! I'm flying the signal for 'close action, enemy sighted'. So we'll bear down on 'em together, Shrig."

"To-gether?" he repeated, his bright eyes seeming rounder than usual. "Meaning as you'll—take a chance?"

"Just so!" nodded Sam. "For, d'ye see, I like Sussex and the folk hereabout. And, for another thing, when trouble shows in the offing, instead o' bearing up and standing away from it, I believe in Lord Nelson's maxim 'engage the enemy more closely'. So, friend Shrig, we'll engage 'em together, bring 'em to action yardarm to yardarm, ay, we'll fight it out broadside for broadside, dare all and hope for the best."

"Sir," quoth Mr. Shrig, beaming, "you are a gen'leman, ay, and a man, my lord, as 'tis a rare pleasure to vork for——"

"Not 'for' but 'with', Shrig, 'with'! . . . And since we are going to fight this action like shipmates, we'll ha' done with any 'lording' or 'mistering'. For in spite o' what Fortune means me to be, Nature made me an ordinary sort of fellow, a seafaring cove and my name is Sam."

For a space Mr. Shrig looked at Sam and slowly his lips curved to a smile, yet when he spoke, his tone was grave:

"Sir, if so be a gen'leman so honours me wi' his baptismal monnicker, like as now, then I regards that same as my 'pal' —vich is a gipsy vord meaning 'brother'—ar and more than brother! So now, sir, I begs to regard you as 'my pal Sam', sir, and herevith proffers you my daddle." Saying which, Mr. Shrig reached forth his hand which Sam grasped and shook heartily.

"And now, sir and pal, if you have the time and incli-nation, my gig's handy, I could take you a little drive and tell you, ar —and show you summat as I fancy'll prove inter-esting and werry suggestive. And, Sam pal, my name to you henceforth is Jarsper. So how about it?"

"Ay, ay, Jasper, I'm with you, so heave ahead, shipmate."

CHAPTER XVII

IN the lane stood a vehicle mounted upon a pair of the tallest wheels Sam had ever seen, drawn by a slim-legged, speedy-looking horse and driven by a meek-seeming individual remarkable for a red waistcoat and woebegone visage, which was rendered even more so by a pair of drooping, hay-like whiskers of the kind sometimes known as "weepers". This person Mr. Shrig forthwith addressed, saying:

"Dan'l, you know this gen'leman." Dan'l nodded and touched whipstock to straw-coloured eyebrow in silent greeting. "But," continued Mr. Shrig, "but what you don't know is—Mr. F. is also my pal!" Dan'l instantly bared his tow-coloured head, gave his hat a peculiar spin and replaced it, all in as many moments, saying in feeble, die-away voice:

"Greetin's, sir! D'you drive, Gov, or me?"

"You, Dan'l. And go easy for I'm a-going to use my chaffer, —a council of vor, pal Sam, sir, a talk on vays and means, sir. So it'll be the back seat for you and me,—arter you, pal."

Up they mounted, and seated side by side, away they drove at leisured, ambling pace.

But now as they rolled smoothly through the warm kindly air of this bowery, peaceful countryside, they talked of the sure and certain approach of murderous evil, thus:

MR. SHRIG: Pal Sam, sir, it now be-hooves us to—are you harking, Dan'l?

DAN'L: Yus, Gov.

MR. SHRIG: Werry good! It be-hooves us to consider the methods warious by vich willainy may attempt The Act upon you.

SAM: Meaning my murder, Jasper? I suppose there are many ways it could be done.

MR. SHRIG: Oceans! So let's take 'em in doo order. And first, by shooting, eh, Dan'l? Shooting's pretty common.

DAN'L: Yus, Gov, it are. Though knives is commoner and razors is frequent.

MR. SHRIG: Ar, in back streets, cellars, dives and rookeries,

Dan'l. But this is the country all coverts and rabbit varrens, so I put shooting first. F'instance, pal and sir,—you take a evening stroll to see the sun set or moon rise—a shot from the leafage and there y'are, dead as mutton and nobody to heed, for if said shot is heard 'twill be put down to poachers. Second,—stabbing, pal. Say you pause by a stile or gate to hear the birds a-varbling as the shadders fall,—ah, but there comes a shadder as creeps soundless, a knife upraised behind you—and down you go, said knife in your back and only the birds to see the how and who of it and they can't talk nor tell. Thirdly,—throttling, Sam pal, strangu-lation, sir. But you're sich a tough, powerful fighting-cove you'd take a deal o' throttling, so we'll pass that and come to: Fourthly,—drownding. 'Spose you're standing to admire a rippling brook or silent, lonesome pool,—the crack of a bludgeon on your on-suspecting tibby,—and in you go to a reg'lar vatery grave. There's a pool as us'll pass werry soon——

DAN'L: Wrexford Old Mill dam.

MR. SHRIG: Ar, and a bee-u-tiful place for it, as by Natur' formed for The Act. Fifthly, pal Sam, there's—p'izen— in your food or drink vith death in every swaller and gulp!

SAM: That would be worst of all, Jasper.

MR. SHRIG: It is, pal, or it ain't, according to the p'izen used or a-dopted. Sixthly, there's—accidents, Sam and sir, a trip-line to throw you headlong, say downstairs, say down a old mine-shaft, cliff or quarry or other deadfall. Seventhly——

SAM: Belay, Jasper, avast! B'George, you've said enough!

MR. SHRIG: Eh? Enough to make you think better of it, hop the perch and toddle . . . take ship and go a-sailing, 'stead o' chancing death by such bloody wiolence, eh, sir?

SAM: I've chanced it pretty often afore now. And violent death isn't always so horrid or bloody as you describe, Jasper. I've seen too much of it aboard ship and I know.

MR. SHRIG: Then you ain't a-going to fly the coop or, as you might say, e-lope?

SAM: No. I'm scheming how we can force the enemy to action. For, d'ye see, I've no mind to hang i' the wind or ply off and on. The sooner we can get to close quarters the better.

MR. SHRIG (*Heaving sigh*): Ah, pal Sam, dog bite me if I didn't think—no matter! But as to a-bringing of 'em to action——

SAM: That's it, Jasper! I want 'em face to face, none o' this hole and corner business or——

MR. SHRIG (*With sudden anxiety*): Hold hard, sir! Lord love you, hold precious hard! The vord for us, and 'specially you, is—caution! Ar, and wrote in capitals! To act too soon or anyways previous vould be our con-flammeration, and p'raps your death. So, pal, and I say this werry earnest indeed,—you must leave the how and when and where of it to me! You must continny to lay low, do nothing and make no move till my plans is laid and trap dooly baited! You——

SAM: When will that be, Jasper?

MR. SHRIG: Pal, ekker alone replies. But, sir, you must gimme your solemn oath, ar a word of honour into the bargain not to stir foot nor finger till I give you the office, or my case is ruinated and yourself stiff and cold in death——

SAM: But, dammit, man, where do I come in?

MR. SHRIG: Sir, you'll come in, like I say, as a poor, bleeding corpse if you move afore I'm ready.

SAM: Well, I'd risk even that for chance of right prompt action.

MR. SHRIG: 'Twould be more than risk, sir. 'Twould be sure and sartin fact. So gimme your oath not to——

SAM (*Impatiently*): Oh, very well!

MR. SHRIG: Good! You have took a load off my throbber.

DAN'L (*With sideways jerk of mournful head*): The old mill, Jarsper.

MR. SHRIG: Then pull up, Dan'l. Now gimme the reins and cut along to see if Toby J. is safe and snug.

DAN'L (*Reining up beside a stile and descending from lofty driving-seat*): Must I feed him, Gov?

MR. SHRIG: You give him brea'fast, didn't you?

DAN'L: Ar, a lump o' cheese, two slices o' bread and a mug o' water.

MR. SHRIG: Then he'll do till supper-time. Cut along now—and take care he don't spy your chiv, Dan'l, nor hear you speak, the less he knows, the better for all con-sarned.

DAN'L: Righto, Jarsper.

MR. SHRIG: Then cut along.

"Ay, Gov," said Dan'l, in his softly doleful voice and turning, leapt the stile with surprising agility and was gone. Left thus alone, the two sat mute a while, Mr. Shrig's quick, bright glance roving to and fro and round about, Sam gazing down across hedgerow and spinney where in the valley below lay a pool very still and dark for it was bowered in tangled thickets and shaded by tall trees, amid which dense leafage showed a crumbling ruin.

"Ar!" exclaimed Mr. Shrig, with a sigh that had a certain gloating ecstasy in it. "The old ruinated mill,—there's a sight pal and sir! 'Tis on Wrybourne land, three mile over yonder lays the Dower House, they call it the Manor, and in the Manor lives—us knows oo, Number Vun, and that there old mill belongs to him. Look at it, pal,—there's a picter for a painting cove to set about, eh?"

"Yes," replied Sam, adding on impulse, "and a very hateful one!"

"Eh, hateful?"

"Very! It's so . . . dam' desolate . . . and worse!"

"How so, pal Sam?"

"There's something evil about it."

"Now burn my neck if there ain't! 'Evil', says you, 'werry much so', says I, for, I've got Tobias J. tied up there and Toby's a pretty evil article. But the old mill, you'll allow, is picturesky. I never see any place properer and more bee-u-tifully fit for The Act! No murderer could resist it,—so nice and lonesome, so fur from any hope or chance of ass-istance, ar and a pool so handy, all ready and vating to receive or drownd all as remains of Murder's poor, bleeding wictim! Nobody'll wenture nigh the place at night, and few b'day—vich ain't to be expected, con-sidering!"

"What, Jasper?"

"As how a murder and two sooicides has befell there already. And 'tis there, as I should like to end this here case and bring Willainy to its just and proper doom, by means o' you, pal Sam, sir."

"Eh? Me?" enquired Sam, starting. "Oh? Very good! How?"

"Pal," sighed Mr. Shrig, shaking his head rather mournfully, "up to the present ekker alone responds 'how indeed'? But, sir, you are my cheese for the trap, lime for my twig and vorm for my hook as I shall use wi' all doo care, hoping for the best. For, if agreeable to you, I shall, this werry night and soon as 'tis black dark, turn loose Tobias Jupp, expecting and also hoping as he'll do and per-form his heenious part and set Murder a-crawling on your dewoted heels."

"Oh?" murmured Sam, pondering this, chin in hand. "Ah! And what am I to do?"

"Bide snug at Villersmead, lay low, ar precious low and leave it all to me—and Dan'l. For——"

"Not I!" quoth Sam, clenching his fists. "No, damme! I mean to take my part and fight this action along o' you. D'ye think I'll cower and skulk and be inactive——"

"Ay, I do, sir, and laying inactive for ever still,—in a vooden overcoat, elm, sir, and silver fittings—if you don't! Sir, if you go out looking for Murder—Murder'll find you, ar—sure as death!"

"I'll take my chance o' that as I have before."

"Ar, but that was at sea, in a clean fight, man to man,—but this'll be Murder as crawls and you the dee-fenceless wictim."

"You seem dev'lish sure of it."

"Nat'rally, sir. For in this here Wale o' Sorrow and Iniquity, there's murder-ers and murder-ees, born for each other and so to be. Therefore wictim never can and never did escape, dodge, nor yet e-lood his murderer or there'd be neither vun nor t'other. And there y'are!"

"However," Sam retorted, squaring shoulders and jaw, "if my life is attempted——"

"As 'twill surely be, sir."

"Then I shall stand to my guns and go down fighting, if I must——"

"Vich, sir, down indeed you'll surely go."

"Jasper, you're a confounded misery!"

"Werry true, sir, and you so eager to play ducks and drakes wi' your precious life and——"

"Oh, but I'm not——"

"And also seeing as how Mr. Joliffe made me ree-sponsible for your safety—'Though', says he to me, 'you'll find him a handful, Shrig'! says he. And dog bite my neck if you ain't! So here's myself, and for the last time, axing you—no, pleading of you to lay low, leave all to me and not try nor yet at-tempt the impossible."

"Ay, but—what is 'the impossible', Jasper man? If Old England hadn't attempted—ay and done it pretty often through battle and storm ever since King Alfred invented The Navy, then History would have a very different tale to tell. And what d'you say to that, Shrig?"

"Sir, all I can ree-spond is—your own tale'll be told pretty soon—but by others, seeing as your tongue, or as you might say 'chaffer' 'll be for ever dumb as any eyster! And talking of Holy Writ, the Bible——"

"Eh? But we've never mentioned it——"

"Hows'ever, you read it now and then, I hope, sir?"

"Why yes, but what the——"

"Then you may remember as a gent, a law officer name o' P. Pilate vashed his hands on a certain o-ccasion?"

"Yes, but——"

"Sir, though I ain't got no vater, I'm a-doing the werry same at this i-dentical moment! I'm soaking my daddles as a sign that I'm done wi' this here case and am off to London, prompt, to report same to Mr. Joliffe."

"Ha!" exclaimed Sam, rather bitterly. "Leaving me to tackle this foul business alone, eh?"

"No, sir, leaving your sorrowful friends to la-ment over your unfort'nate remains."

"Is that so!" Sam demanded, scornfully.

"Ar!" nodded Mr. Shrig, dejectedly. "So it is! But you'll make a werry handsome corpse,—arter they've cleaned you up and laid you out."

"Well, that's something!" said Sam.

"It is, sir. But arter I've took your murderer and seen him dooly scragged, topped, hung and jibbeted,—though that can't do you no manner o' good, I shall grieve for a pal as got himself cut off so reckless, so young, and all to no purpose,—a wictim as need never have been."

Here ensued a silence wherein Mr. Shrig sighed mournfully, shook his head dismally and turned to watch for the return of Dan'l; then, hearing a chuckle, he glanced round and meeting Sam's flashing smile, instantly beamed in response, saying:

"So, pal Sam, you was only flamming me, a flam, eh?"

"No, Jasper, I meant every word, for d'ye see, I can't imagine myself any sort of victim. But since you got me into this ugly business by discovering my true identity, dammit,— I'm going to leave you to get me out of it the best you can and in your own way."

"And," quoth Mr. Shrig, drawing a bulbous pocket-book from the breast of his trim, blue coat, "you couldn't do better nor say fairer. So now, being pals and ass-ociated in this here case, I'll ax you," here he opened the book and consulted a certain page, "talking o' the old mill yonder, did you ever hear tell of a Lady Barbara Stowe?"

"Never!" answered Sam, glancing again at that dark and stilly pool. "Who is she?"

"Vich aren't to be expected o' you, pal Sam, seeing as she ain't, con-sidering as twenty-two year ago she was found a-floating there."

"Eh? That dev'lish pool . . . drowned, Jasper?"

"Werry com-pletely, pal, and nobody knows the oo, the how or why—yet! Then four year and six months ago Susan Marsh also gets drowned there, but she'd been crossed in love, poor lass, so us can pass her case as feller-de-see. Two year ago Thomas Jeffs a Preeventive officer is found dangling from a beam."

"Another suicide, Jasper?"

"Hardly so, pal, seeing as according to evidence, said Thomas had received nineteen stabs."

"Were his murderers ever caught?"

"Never a soul, pal, no! And talking o' souls, can you tell me anything con-cerning a Mr. Eus-tiss Jennings?"

"No, I can't."

"Yet I hoped as you might, pr'aps."

"How on earth could I? I'm as strange hereabouts as you are."

"Hows'ever, I know as he's a neighbour o' yourn, lives yonder at the Manor, along o'—Number Vun."

"Well, I never heard of the fellow. What's he like?"

"A werry dainty, soft-spoke gen'leman as I took to on sight and so amazing, that I've got him down here in my little reader as—Number Two."

"Oh?" questioned Sam, "why?"

Before Mr. Shrig could reply, the man Dan'l reappeared, vaulted nimbly over the stile, nodded feebly and said, in his die-away voice:

"All's bowmon, Jarsper."

"Good!" exclaimed Mr. Shrig, thrusting away his "little reader". "Tobias is nice and snug then?"

"Yes, Gov, 'e grunted and jigged a bit when he felt me move the 'ay."

"Hay?" enquired Sam.

"Ar," beamed Mr. Shrig, "I've got Toby J. covered up agin chance obserwation though same aren't likely in sich bee-ooti-fully lonesome spot. How much further, Dan'l?" he enquired as that unexpectedly agile person swung up to the lofty driving-seat.

"Next gate, top o' the 'ill, Gov."

"Sam pal, you have never yet seen nor heered tell of Bracton spinney and the chalk pit, eh?"

"No, I haven't."

"Then if youm so minded, you shall see same, ar, and hear the dee-ductions as I have drawed therefrom, making things, as seem pretty ugly now, ass-oom a aspect even and ever more hijjeous. How about it, Sam pal, are y' game?"

"Ay, ay, Jasper, I'm with you."

"Then drive on, Dan'l."

CHAPTER XVIII

CONCERNING A MURDER, THE HOW OF IT

AN age-worn gate with beyond a narrow glade or ride that curved away through dense woodland where rabbits scurried and birds piped amid a hush of leaves, for the day was hot and very still. Reaching this gate Mr. Shrig paused to lean there, yet with a tense alertness in every line of his powerful body; motionless he stood, head bowed as though listening intently while under close-knit brows his bright eyes shot quick, roving glances above and all around, until Sam demanded, impatiently:

"Why are we hove-to, Jasper, what are you waiting for?"

"To look, pal, to heark and ax questions—the grass, the leaves, ar, every indiwidual bush and tree—as I have done afore now, and someday they're agoing to answer."

"Answer what?"

"The truth, the whole truth and nothing but. For Natur' can't lie, leastways not to me it don't!"

"Jasper, you've set me all aback, shivering in the wind's eye! Speak plain, Shrig man, plain."

"Werry good!" he answered and opening the gate paced on beside Sam at leisured amble and explained thus:

"The reasons as I questions Natur' hereabouts is for the follering—are you listening?"

"Ay, be sure I am."

"Then, pal Sam, sir, along this here track so leafily re-mote, upon a fair summer's eve, your dad the late Earl o' Wrybourne rode to his sudden death. So the first question I asks is: Verefore should his lordship come a-wisiting in such desolate soli-tood? And, Nature vispers: 'Jarsper S., my lord being a Scrope, the answer is in the Femi-nine Gender'! So here he comes galloping so gay and free,—and yonder, for good and all, he ends—look!" They had turned a sudden, sharp bend in the track; and here Mr. Shrig halted to point with knobbly stick, saying:

"What d'ye see, pal?"

"A stretch of grass," Sam replied, "and a broken fence."

"Ah! And now, pal, treading werry cautious, come and look beyond said fence . . . now, what d'ye see?"

"An abyss," answered Sam, peering down and beyond these broken palings. "And mighty steep too."

"Ab-biss?" repeated Mr. Shrig. "This is a new un to me as I'll make a note on later,—ab-biss. But this here same abbiss is a werry ancient chalk-pit and a sheer drop, two hundred foot and more. And through yon fence, down into this here ab-biss aforesaid tumbled the late Earl, hoss and all, to lie stone dead, corpses both, at the bottom. And Sam, sir, nobody grieved except for the hoss as was a mare and a good un, nobody mourned the earl, quite the contrairy! For when a werry rich man hops the mortal perch, there's always some folks as re-j'ices in or out'ardly, vich, arter all, is only nat'ral. So now my next and second question is: Oo benefits? And Natur' answers werry plain: Us knows oo! And my next question is: How should my lord's mare come to shy at the vun and only place where certain death must en-soo? Also, from information received, said mare being a creeter never known to shy,—so how came she so to do? A sudden fright . . . a stumble . . . a headlong plunge to final o-blivion. So I ax how could such fright, stumble and fall be con-trived? And, Sam pal, Natur' vispers and werry soft indeed: 'A trip-line! a rope tied low 'twixt two trees——' "

"Good God!" exclaimed Sam, speaking himself in harsh whisper, "Jasper, are you suggesting . . . murder?" Instead of replying, Mr. Shrig beckoned and Sam followed—away from that fatal spot to a small clearing beside the track and here Mr. Shrig seated himself upon a fallen tree, saying in the same hushed tones:

"My lord and pal, you being a sailorman too, know the blessed conso-lation of tobacker smoke drawed gentle through a pipe be it vood or clay, so sit down and smoke along o' Jarsper and let's talk open and free. Also," he continued, easing a large silver watch out of his fob, "in about ten minutes,—say fifteen, I'm expecting a country cove, a poacher as chanced hereabouts on that fatal eve and is therefore a vitness-by-ear! Name o' Barnes baptismal Ezra, a simple sort o' cove but nat'ral born slinker."

"You mean he heard something, Jasper?"

"Ar! And if he hadn't been such a werry furtive slinker

he might ha' seen. But that 'ud be too much to hope or ex-pect——"

"Ay, ay, but what did he hear, man, what?"

"The mare's hoofs coming at a gallop,—then said hoofs checked to stumbling stagger, then the crash o' the breaking fence, and then—ha, then—the scream o' the Earl as he pitched down . . . and down . . . to his finish . . . screaming in mid air . . . screaming vords, pal, till they ended for evermore in the final bump."

"Rather . . . horrible, Jasper."

"Ar!"

"Well—what were the words?"

"Pal, all as ekker alone can respond is—vot indeed? For Ezra Barnes didn't hear, or don't remember, but arter he'd took courage to go down and take a peep at the re-mains, the Earl and his poor mare lay mangled corpses, werry mangled indeed, vich you'll agree was a fairish ugly end."

"Yes," growled Sam, "a bad end for a worse man! For d'ye see——" he paused as his keen, sailorly eyes glimpsed something that moved amid the nearby thickets, an indeterminate object that presently resolved itself into a weather-beaten moleskin cap crowning a bewhiskered visage that peered furtively through the dense leafage; Mr. Shrig's roving glance had seen also, for he hailed cheerily:

"Greetin's, friend Barnes! Step forrard and earn five shillings, seven and six,—say ten." Thus admonished, Mr. Barnes sidled through the leafage, shambled into the open and thumbed his cap, saying:

"Ten shillin', maister, roight! Wot'll oi say?"

"The truth, Ezra lad, the gospel truth, friend! As f'rinstance,—about a year ago on a sunny evening you are doing a bit o' poaching, setting snares in' the spinny here-about and you hears summat, eh?"

"Ay, hoss-huffs, maister."

"So what did you do, Ezra?"

"Lays me flat in' the bracken, maister."

"And werry nat'ral too! Then—what did ye see?"

"Th' Earl, maister, ay, Oi sees m'lord ride by."

"Was he going fast or slow?"

"Fast,—full gallop loike 'e allus did."

"Could ye see his face?"

"Ay, I did, maister."

"How did it look, angry or pleased, smiling or scowling, hey?"

"More smiling loike, Oi'd say."

"So! And then, Ezra lad, and then?"

"Then, maister, I heered the mare's huffs check, then a shout, then the crack o' the fence a-goin', and then—th' Earl shrieked,—turned me ice-cold, it did!"

"And you're sartin-sure 'twasn't a wooman's scream; eh, Ezra, ye're sure?"

"Ay, Oi be mortal sure. No woman ever could cry so wild and 'oarse like. 'Orrorsome, it were and freezed me good blood like!"

"Then what did you, Ezra?"

"Dropped me snares and run! Ah, but that gashly cry followered me till it ended sudden like in a gert thump— down there in old chalk-pit."

"Ar! And how then, lad?"

"Then, maister, Oi lays me down, sick and faint like, for Oi knowed as that gert thump meant death."

"Hows'ever, you took a peep to make sure, eh?"

"Sure-ly, maister. After a bit down Oi crep' and—there they was, in their blood, arl broke up like. . . . Ah, blood——"

"Plenty of it, eh, Ezra?"

"Plenty, maister? Lordy, Oi never seen s'much in arl me days, no not even when I 'elped Sim Brooke to slaughter 'is prize 'og!"

"Ha! So that's all as you can remember of it, eh, lad?"

"No, maister. 'Cause arter you axed me of it t'other day, I moinded, arter you'd gone, 'ow I'd forgot to tell ee o' the face."

"Eh?" exclaimed Mr. Shrig, nearly dropping his precious clay pipe, "face? Oo's face?"

"Dunno, maister, only 'twere a face as peeped down from upalong. For whiles I'm lookin' at the Earl, and him so on-common dead, I 'ears a sound above, and sees a face a-peepin' down at me through the broke fence——"

"Wot sort o' face? Male or fee-male?"

"Couldn't say, maister, only 'twere smallish face . . . longish 'air and nary a whisker."

"Should ye know it again, Ezra, eh?"

"Nay, maister, Oi got but a glimp' loike, 'twere gone in a flash."

"Ho!" sighed Mr. Shrig, mournfully. "Only a glimp'!
And this here face seemed like it were taking a peep down at
you and his lordship's re-mains, eh?"

"Ay, maister."

"Took a peep it did and wanished at sight o' you, eh?"

"Ay, maister, so then Oi didn't boide f'no more but crep'
off—along 'ome, Oi did."

"But didn't meet anybody or glimp' anything on your road,
eh?"

"Nary soul nor thing, sir. So that be arl as Oi can tell
ee . . . so now . . . you says summat about ten shillin'."

"Ar, I did so!" nodded Mr. Shrig, thrusting hand into
pocket of his neat cord breeches. "But afore I pay you same,
tell me this, Ezra: As you crep' off homewards did you
happen to—hear anything,—say a rustling in the bushes, a
shout, a cry or even a visper? Think now and think precious
hard,—did you ketch any sich sound?"

"No, maister, none o' they loike, arl as I 'eered was only
the sound of a axe."

"Ha!" exclaimed Mr. Shrig again, his whole form stiffening suddenly. "Only . . . the sound of . . . a naxe, hey!
Come, that's better, Ezra, that's oceans better! Now did
this axe sound near and plain or faint and far off?"

"A bit faint and fur loike, maister."

"Still, you could hear it pretty distinct, eh, Ezra?"

"Ay, Oi could and did,—chop, it went, chop, chip, and
chop again."

"Good!" nodded Mr. Shrig, beaming. "Sounded like
somebody chopping in a precious great hurry, did it?"

"Ay, so it did, maister, the strokes sounded very quick
loike, they did."

"And did this same chopping come from afore you or from
be-hind?"

"Back along, maister."

"Good!" exclaimed Mr. Shrig again, his eyes brighter than
the plate buttons of his smart coat.

"And that be arl as I can moind or tell ee——"

"And here's your ten shillings, Ezra! Take 'em and good
luck t'ye."

"Thankee, maister, Oi'm sure! Good day, gen'lemen!"
So saying, Mr. Barnes touched moleskin cap with scrawny
finger and edging himself back amid the denser undergrowth,

vanished like the furtive creature he was. And when all sound of him had died away, Mr. Shrig sighed happily, tapped out his cherished though fragmentary pipe very tenderly and beaming on Sam, murmured in hushed accents:

"A naxe!"

"Well, what of it, Jasper?"

"Sir and Sam, said impli-ment answers a most wexatious, con-flummerating question—I hope!"

"Oh?" questioned Sam, as they rose, "ah! Pray what, Jasper?"

"A tree, pal! A tree as should ought to be, yet ain't! A tree as must be if the dee-ducktions as I've drawed is co-rrect and according to The Fact."

"Afraid I don't get your meaning, Jasper."

"Pal, I didn't ex-pect as you could. Hows'ever come along o' Jarsper and let's take a obserwation."

So back they went to halt again where the track made the sudden bend to skirt the ancient chalk-pit; and now, turning his back to broken fence and the green abyss beyond, Mr. Shrig pointed with his stick, saying: "Here 'pon our left is trees and 'specially this un beside the track,—this un as has growed itself year by year, day arter day for—The Purpose!"

"Eh? Purpose? You mean——?"

"The Deed, pal Sam! Murder, sir! The Capital Act!"

"But, Jasper, I don't see——"

"No more did I and no more I don't now spy that tree as should be standing opposite this un but ain't. Therefore, pal, seeing as there's none other near enough for suspected fee-lonious purpose, all I can do is hope and—seek." As he spoke, Mr. Shrig turned aside and began searching where tall bracken grew thick and grass lush, questing to and fro much like hound on the scent, though never far from the track itself, while Sam, puffing his pipe, watched with puzzled frown.

"Jasper," said he, at last, "say what you're after and I'll be glad to bear a hand."

"No need," replied Mr. Shrig, straightening broad back, "I've found it! Ar, by goles, and in the right and proper place too! Come and take a peep." Stepping forward, Sam looked down where Mr. Shrig's stick had put aside bracken and undergrowth to show the hacked stump of a small tree.

"Look!" murmured Mr. Shrig, gazing down upon this jagged object as if he loved it, "how much does this here tell you, Sam pal?"

"That whoever felled this was either in desperate haste or quite unused to such work."

"Both, ar—he was both! The party as chopped down this little tree, chopped wild—look at the cuts,—chipped and chopped to destroy evidence. The hands as used axe so werry orkard was the same as tied the trip-line so neat—'twixt this same little tree and the big un yonder, fixed it fast and true enough to tumble the Earl to his doom."

"The hands," murmured Sam, frowning thoughtfully down at this jagged stump, "of someone—unused to the axe! A terribly suggestive thought!"

"Werry much so!"

"And you are convinced here was—murder?"

"I am, pal Sam, for that's what this place, or the woice o' Natur' is telling me. . . . If only it had befell a veek ago, or even a month, I'd ha' been werry sure. But time vorks changes, trees grow, ditter grass and bushes, so the woice o' Natur' is hushed thereby. Hence, from con-cloosions drawed I can only suspect and—hope werry hard."

"For what, Jasper?"

"Proof, pal, proof! For by The Law of England the goriest willain is innocent as frisking lamb or babe noo-born till proof, with a Capital Pee, shows him guilty! So I can suspect and, in my mind, be sure o' guilt till I'm black in the phiz for no proof—no guilt and all is labour in wain. Ar, Guilt can cock a snook at me and toddle off to more willainy, leaving your pal J.S. helpless as a poor bird vith broken ving. Lord love you, but for proof there'd be many a murderer jigging in a rope collar at this i-dentical minute! Proof is a stumbling block and the ruination o' my business—sometimes. So I can only vork, as in dooty bound and hope, as is my natur'."

Then, together and as by common consent, they turned and left that place of death and sinister brooding solitude where now (or so it seemed to Sam) no leaf stirred, no rabbit frisked, and no bird sang; the blessed sun shone bright and warm as ever, yet Sam felt suddenly chilled by sense of lurking, implacable evil, a hateful menace that filled the woodland all about him and was to haunt him day and

night, following his every step with a dreadful patience until
—at last . . .

"Jasper," he demanded, "why so dam' silent and speechless? What are you thinking?" And instantly Mr. Shrig
replied, and very wistfully:

"Foam, Sam pal! Froth atop of a pewter pint pot, wi'
summat cool and moist and nutty below, eh?"

"Ah-h!" quoth Sam, lengthening his stride, "the sooner
the better, messmate!"

CHAPTER XIX

CONCERNING THE SUBTLETIES OF A SCYTHE

THE jaunty glazed hat, the too-ornate neckerchief and sailorly jacket were adorning a gate-post of the five acre meadow, for Sam, bare-armed, intent of eye and square of jaw, was performing on that so ancient and subtle implement, the scythe, and doing it very badly.

Thus after some while of violent hacking and slashing and all to distressingly small effect, he had paused to mop perspiring brow and survey the meagre result of his powerful efforts in rueful surprise when, hearing a hoarse chuckle behind him, he glanced round and beheld a small, old man perched precariously upon the gate, a wizened, frail-seeming old fellow in wide-eaved hat and neat smock frock, who chuckled, laughed, choked and finally enquired:

"Young man, wot be ee a-doin' of, I wonder?"

"Well," replied Sam, shaking his head, "I thought I was mowing, but——"

"But you ain't!" quoth the old man, with beaming nod. "No, that you ain't, no'ow. You'm jest mickin' and muckin' about, ah no question! That theer thing as you'm mis-usin' of so shameful, bean't a axe, nor yet a swop-'ook, bill or saw, 'tis a scythe, that's wot it be."

"So I believe," answered Sam, meekly. "But the dam' thing must be blunt."

"Young man, dam' thing be sharp as razor! I see and 'eered my Tom a-whettin' of it jest afore 'e were called away by Mistus Kate."

"However, it won't cut——"

"Ay, but 'twill—if ee uses un proper and like as a scythe should ought for to be used."

"Oh?" murmured Sam, wistfully. "Ah! Then it seems I haven't the right trick of it, eh?"

"That you ain't, no, nor like to 'ave neether, the crool way as you 'andles un."

"Well," said Sam, taking a fresh grip, "I'll have another go and hope for the——"

"Wait!" screeched the old man, "I can't abear for to watch ee slish and slash so 'orrid wild and fierce! Bide a bit and I'll show ee 'ow, for I be Toop—Silas Toop—that's oo I be, and no man could larn ee better! I'll show ee."

"I'd be grateful," said Sam.

"Oh?" demanded Mr. Toop. "'Ow grateful?"

"Very grateful."

"Would your gratitood run to a pint—or say, a couple?"

"Yes, indeed, and——"

"Very good! Ketch 'old o' me stick and I'll come down."

"Shall I help you, Mr. Toop?"

"No you shan't, young man. I clumb gates and stiles 'igher than thus un, long afore you was born, and I bean't so doddlish as I can't yet." So saying, the aged man very deliberately and with the utmost care, descended safely to earth, smoothed his smock, resettled his hat upon silvery hair, moistened his palms and said:

"Gimme that scythe!" Sam obeyed,—and lo! As these old hands took and gripped, the small form seemed to dilate, the bowed back to straighten, eyes brightened, age and feebleness seemed forgotten as, leaning forward, Mr. Toop began to mow, cutting a wide, clean swath with such effortless skill and unconscious grace of movement that Sam exclaimed, impulsively:

"Marvellous!"

"No, it ain't!" snapped the Aged One, when at last he paused. "'Tis jest bein' used and knowin' 'ow."

"But," said Sam, admiringly, "you don't even puff and blow!"

"Not likely!" retorted Mr. Toop, with lofty scorn, "I were champeen mower in my young days, ah and old days tu! Mow arl day, I could, faster, cleaner, straighter than any on 'em, I could! Lookee, here's the way on it,—keep p'int up a bit, heel down a bit, swing un smooth and steady, don't ee hurry un, give un time for to cut! Don't ee drag nor slash nor yet chop, no jiggin' nor jaggin'!"

"I see!" said Sam, deeply interested.

"Ay, but 'tis one thing tu see and another thing tu do!"

"Well, let me have another go."

"Ay, ay, there y'are! Mind now,—p'int up a bit . . . foller y'r p'int, swingin' steady and slow, easy now! Ay, that be a mite better! Don't ee force un,—no driggin' nor draggin', nor slishin' nor slashin'! Ef ee du mind wot I says and keep at it every day for a week or so you'll mebbe use a scythe pretty good someday—mebbe. And now in the matter o' your gratitood——"

"Here, Mr. Toop, behold it!"

"Gorramitey!" exclaimed the old fellow, goggling at the coins upon his horny palm. "Yere be a sight more'n I expected! I rackon yu must be the gen'tleman sailor friend as come home a long o' Cap'n Ned 'Arlow."

" 'Home'!" repeated Sam, glancing away to a certain thatched roof peeping above distant tree-tops. "By George —yes, home it is . . . and growing more so every day!"

"Well then, sir, seein' as youm so powerful grateful, I'll come 'long frequent and larn ee arl as I can. And now, afore I goo, I'll show ee 'ow tu keep a edge on scythe so sharp as razor. Gimme the stone as lays yonder. So! Now lookee, lay stone pretty flat for to gi'e un a good, longish edge, then stroke un easy like back and forth, first o' one side, then t'other, kind and gentle, so and so! Now I'll leave ee to it, young sir, wi' my thanks and best respex till I see ee again, for I've worked yere at Willowmead for sixty odd year and my Tom do work yere now."

"Yes, I've met your Tom——"

"Ay mebbe, but you 'aren't never met my Willum and never will no'ow and nowhen for Willum were snatched up to Glory Everlastin' by a cannon ball along o' Lord Nelson, God bless 'em,—on the *Vict'ry*. Well, good arternoon, sir!" So saying, Mr. Toop touched his hat, nodded and hobbled away.

And now, heedful of the old man's words and example, and being so patiently determined in all things, Sam truly began to mow,—watching the gleam and listening to the whisper of the long keen scythe-blade as he swung it rhythmically back and forth, cutting smoothly, cleaning with every leisured stroke.

Thus, heartened by achievement and taking joy in his labour as a man should, Sam worked on through the long afternoon heedless of time, heat, fatigue and all else except the work in hand, until evening began to fall.

Meanwhile . . .

CHAPTER XX

HOW SAM LOST HIS PIPE

SELDOM or never in all its many years had the cosy old farmhouse of Willowmead held more joy or echoed to happier voices than upon this same midsummer evening, for Captain Ned was safe home again and had returned in triumph with a certain document that he now spread out upon the table before his glad-eyed, momentarily speechless Kate. A large, formidable-looking document this, beautifully inscribed on fair parchment, couched in terms quite incomprehensibly legal yet with many repetitions of such phrases as: "Parties of the First Part" and "Parties of the Second Part" . . . "As aforesaid", "In perpetuity", "As above mentioned", "Tenements and messuages", etc. etc.

"Oh, my goodness!" sighed Kate, flushed of cheek and radiant of eye, glancing from this to Ned's happy face, and round about the spacious parlour where Aunt Deb sat crocheting on one side of the wide hearth while Mrs. Leet knitted on the other.

"Does this mean . . . oh, is Willowmead ours, Ned, really and truly—for ever and ever?"

"Ay," he answered, stooping to touch her bright hair with his lips, "every stick and stone of it, Kate, ours to have and to hold——"

"Till death do you part!" added Mrs. Leet. "And then——"

"Lord, Anne!" exclaimed Aunt Deborah, "what horrid suggestion! So odious!"

"And then," continued Mrs. Leet, imperturbably, " 'twill be for the heirs o' your bodies which will——"

"Dear me, Anne!" cried Aunt Deb, "what a suggestion! So extremely—previous!"

"Which will be," continued Mrs. Leet, "perfectly right, proper, hoped for and expected."

"Oh, Anne! And they aren't even wedded yet!"

"Meanwhile," pursued Mrs. Leet, serenely, "I suggest pigs, pigs pay——"

"Being so—well—prolific!" added Aunt Deb.

"And cows!" quoth Mrs. Leet, "a herd——"

"With plenty of sheep!" nodded Aunt Deb.   "We ought to have flocks of nice, woolly sheep——"

"Certainly—not!" quoth Mrs. Leet, clicking her knitting-pins. "This should be a dairy farm pure and simple, Deborah!"

"With sheep, Anne, sheep and lambs to flock and frisk! How say you, Ned?"

"Yes to both!" he laughed. "But where's Sam? Sam must see this portentous document and hear the news,—where on earth is he?"

"In the five acre meadow," replied Aunt Deb, "performing powerfully and perspiring profusely upon a scythe, poor dear—— Gracious me—there's alliteration!"

"Sam? A scythe?" exclaimed Ned and Kate together.

"Now you're both doing it and so will I—so I tell you again Sam's swinging a scythe as sailor should, so strongly that his bronzed brow is beaded with the energetic efforts of his excessive exertions."

"Why then," laughed Ned, "let's give him a hail before he sinks, swoons and languishes o' labour. Come, Kate!"

"Yes," nodded Aunt Deb, "go fetch him, my dears, he has probably mowed the whole meadow by now."

Thus it was that Sam, now master of this very difficult and therefore fascinating implement, had paused to re-sharpen his blade and glance back with no little satisfaction at the result of his persistent and determined labour, when his ears were gladdened by a clear, resonant, long-familiar hail:

"Ahoy—Sam! Sam, old hearty, stand by!"

And turning, he beheld Ned and Kate hastening towards him through the radiant sunset glow.

"Old fellow——" began the Captain.

"Oh, Ned dear," cried Kate, and both speaking together again; and then:

"Sam, the expedition succeeded!"

"Oh, Sam, Willowmead is ours, for ever and ever!"

"And the heirs of our——"

"Hush, Ned! Oh, Sam dear, when you tried to comfort my doubts and bade me hope, I couldn't though I tried, because it seemed so impossible. But now——"

"Now, old shipmate, you are standing on our own particular bit of Old England!"

"Yes," said Kate, taking him by one arm, "and mowing our very own meadow, Sam——"

"In proof whereof," said the Captain, taking him by the other arm, "yonder in our own farmstead, signed, sealed and attested is a—no—the document, Sam, large as a mizzen—tops'l—almost! Come and see."

"Hurrah!" quoth Sam, heartily.

"Oh, but," said Kate, as they turned housewards, "your hat and coat,—where are they?"

"Athwart the field on the gate-post yonder."

"My gracious!" exclaimed Kate, as they crossed the meadow, "Sam, what a lot you have mowed! I'd no idea you could use a scythe."

"Nor had I," he answered, "until old Mr.——" He paused and stood gazing in mute surprise . . . for the glazed hat, the gaudy neckerchief and smart, too-nautical jacket had given place to a grimy, shapeless old cap and bedraggled something that had once been a coat.

"Soho!" he murmured, glancing about instinctively. "Piracy, b'Jingo!"

"Oh!" gasped Kate, "do you mean . . . someone has stolen your clothes?"

"Ay!" he nodded, surveying these unlovely things askance, "Though I suppose exchange is no robbery. However, my things are gone——"

"So much the better!" chuckled Ned, "I can't imagine where or why you got 'em, Sam! That jacket all jauntiness and buttons! That ghastly scarf and the hat,—like the dashing, jolly jack-tar in that silly opera *Black-eyed Susan*!"

"Ay," nodded Sam, "that's where I got the idea."

"Well, they're a good riddance!" quoth the Captain.

"So they are, Ned. Yes, I'm well rid of 'em,—ah but—" Sam shook his head woefully.

"Ah," said Kate, "was there money in the pockets?"

"Only a guinea or so, but I shall grieve for my good old pipe."

"Then I'll buy you another," said the Captain. "But now, confound it all, sheet home, man, and bear away for our farmhouse, Kate's and mine, and we'll drink to it, ay—to

the future and to each other, love and long life, Kate!
Friendship and prosperity, old fellow—come!"

And so, with happy Kate on one arm, his friend and
captain on the other, Sam went to this cosy, old farmhouse
where lights began to beam as the evening shadows fell.

CHAPTER XXI

DESCRIBES A "FAIRY AUNT"

THE Five Acre was mowed smooth as a lawn and Sam perched upon a gate was viewing this green expanse with prideful content; birds in the leafy hedgerows round about him twittered drowsily, from the shady orchard nearby thrush and blackbird piped melodiously yet no sweeter than the clear, childish voice carolling this old song:

> "In Scarlitt Town where I was borned
> There was a fair maid dwellin'
> Made all the lads sigh well-a-day
> Her name was Bar-bree Alling."

With this song on her lips, the sun bright in her hair and Batilda tucked lovingly beneath her arm, Jane came seeking her uncle, saying as she stood on tip-toes to be kissed:

"Auntie Kate said I'd find you here, so now I've come to take you a walk."

"Ay, ay, Sweetheart," said he, slipping long arm about her, "whereaway this time?"

"To the—Deep Dark!" she whispered, small finger to rosy lip.

"Oho?" he laughed. "That sounds nice and mysterious."

"It is,—yes awful' 'steerious, 'cause it's by the 'chanted forest where my Fairy Auntie lives with her Esau."

"Good!" he nodded, "I'd like to meet a fairy."

So, hand-in-hand, away they went, by shady lane, over stiles, across lush, sunny meadow where lazy cows blinked at them, puffing fragrance as they chewed sleepily and flicked their tails drowsily.

"You're not afraid of cows, eh, Sweetheart?"

"No. I like them lots 'cause they smell so nice and cow-y, and they're always eating 'cept when they're being milked and sometimes even then. Our Tom let me try to milk Daisybell once, she's the oldest and has had lots of children, Tom says. Yesterday at supper I tried to chew like a cow, side-

ways you know, only my Granny said I might be struck
like it an' grow horns, an' I shouldn't like that. And why
are you so changed, Uncle Sam?"

"Eh? Changed? D'you mean——"

"I liked you more in your nice sailor's clothes, your shiny
hat and bright buttons!"

"Oh?" he questioned, glancing down at the neat stockings
and knee-breeches that now moulded his brawny limbs. "Did
you, my Jane? Why?"

"'Cause now your legs look so 'normous and bumpy."

"Aha!" said he, chuckling. "But then just look at my
lovely shoes, Sweetheart, so trim and shiny,—with real silver
buckles, too! So watch my buckles flash and forget my
legs."

"But how can I when they're so long an' big?"

"However," said he, smiling down at her, "I hope my
face is still nice—in places, here and there, eh, my sweetness?"

"Yes," she nodded, "'specially when you smile. And
over there's the Deep Dark, look!"

Now glancing whither she directed Sam glimpsed beyond
tangled thickets and lofty trees, a ruin of broken roof and
crumbling walls.

"Ah!" he murmured, halting suddenly. "You mean the
old mill pool, Jane?"

"Yes, but you mustn't go a-nigh it 'cause my Granny says
'tis a bad place waiting to drownd folks like it nearly drownded
me once long ago when I was only a child."

"Lord!" exclaimed Sam, clasping his arm about her, instinctively. "How was that, my Jane?"

"'Cause I went with some other children to peep at it
and they pushed me in. So the Deep Dark took me and tried
to drownd me dead only my Fairy Aunt came down to me
and took me out and dried me and telled me tales and kissed
me and took me safe home, that's how I found her. And
to-day I'll let you kiss her, if you like. Should you?"

"Yes," he laughed," I should like to kiss a fairy aunt——"

"Look!" said she again, pointing to a little shady coppice
they were approaching. "There's our 'Chanted Forest and in
it there's a great, big tree with 'normous waggly branches
what was struck by lightning so it's a magic tree. And my
Fairy Auntie says if you stand there in its shade and wish—

it'll all come true, if you're very good an' say your prayers an' wish hard enough, so I did, and that's how I got my Batilda."

"By just wishing under the old tree, Sweetheart?"

"Yes. I wished out loud and said my prayers every night and was a good, p'lite, obedient child every day—'cept now and then. So on my birthday my Batilda came to me by James Purvis, the Carrier, in a great, big box tied with blue ribbon. So this time, Uncle Sam, I'm going to wish for a nice big cradle for Batilda with curtains, what rocks, 'cause in two days I've got another birthday an' so has my Fairy Auntie, our birthdays are always together, and I'll have growed myself to seven!"

They were close upon the coppice when from its green shadow leapt a great, shaggy dog, such powerful, fierce-looking animal that Sam instinctively took firmer clutch on the heavy stick he carried and was about to snatch Jane up to his shoulder; but with a cry of "Esau! Esau!" she sped forward and dog met child in a glad and riotous greeting. And despite ferocious look, a dog of dignity this who now quelling his joyful exuberance, sat down to proffer one great paw, though with much flicking of tongue and thumping of stumpy tail; having thus welcomed the child he advanced stiff-legged and cautious, to take stock of the man, and they surveyed each other like the strangers they were until a voice, sweet though imperious cried:

"Friends, Esau,—shake hands!" Instantly the dog obeyed, and Sam, grasping his shaggy paw, glanced up to see Jane being clasped and kissed by Andromeda,—but this Andromeda glorified by a new tenderness very lovely to behold, or so thought Sam as he stepped forward, hat in hand, the great dog at his heels.

"Oh, Auntie Mee," cried Jane, "in two days I'll have growed myself to seven and then it'll be your birthday too, so I've brought you two lovely presents,—and one's only just me—here I am,—and the other's my great, big, nice Uncle Sam, and there he is, so if you want to kiss him like I do, I shan't mind a bit——"

Sweet as trill of bird or ripple of brook Andromeda laughed, for the first time in Sam's hearing, and showed the more beautiful for the rich colour that swept from rounded chin to night-black hair, or so thought Sam as her golden eyes met his in swift up-glance ere their long lashes veiled their light.

"Oh, but . . . Jane dear," she laughed, "such great, big uncles are only meant for little girls like you to kiss."

"Yes, I know," said Jane, smoothing Batilda's somewhat rumpled petticoats, "only he said how he'd like to kiss a fairy aunt an' she's you, so—why don't you?"

"Not to-day, Jane dear."

"Very well, Auntie Mee, only if he ever kisses you you won't please smack his face like our Nancy did to our Tom in the dairy, will you?"

"Indeed, I—might!" laughed Andromeda, with another swift up-glance at silent Sam who now, laughing also, said:

"So you are Jane's mysterious lady, her wonderful 'Fairy Aunt'! I might have guessed it."

"So now," said Jane, setting Batilda beneath Sam's ready arm, "please let's all take hands and go into the 'Chanted Forest' and I'll wish to our dear, old, magicy tree."

So, thus linked together, they entered the coppice, the great dog pacing solemnly behind, until they came where stood a gnarled, old oak tree, its massive trunk storm-riven and warped by Father Time yet still hale and hearty, judging by the myriad leaves that decked its knotted wide-flung boughs.

Here Jane stayed them and stole forward on tip-toe; and now, standing beneath this aged tree, Jane did a quaint and Jane-like thing, for clasping her small arms about its huge bole, she kissed its rugged bark and laying her soft cheek against it, spoke to it in her clear, young voice:

"Please, dear old Tree, I have come to wish you many happy returns of my berfday in two days and please I do so want a nice big cradle for my Batilda, with curtains, that rocks. So 'cause I know you won't let me be dis'pointed, I'll thank you in my prayers every night till I've growed myself to eight. So now thank you and good-bye you dear, old Tree."

"A child's faith is very beautiful and touching," murmured Andromeda.

"Very!" answered Sam. "She'll get her cradle, of course?"

"Yes, by Purvis, the Carrier, on her birthday."

"I'm wondering what I can give her, Miss Andromeda?"

"Well, I know she hasn't a doll's house."

E

"Ay, b'Jingo, the very thing! Where could I get one?"

"Hush, here she comes! But I happen to be driving to Lewes to-morrow."

"Splendid!" exclaimed Sam. "Then will you, that is, could you,—would you allow me to go with you?"

"If you don't mind our shabby, old cart, Mr. Felton."

"Where, and when?" he enquired, almost eagerly.

"At the end of Willowmead Lane, about half-past ten."

"There!" cried Jane, returning to clasp their hands again. "Did you hear our dear old Tree whisper me with all its leafs, like it was saying: Yes, Jane dear, Yes-s-s? So now, Auntie, let's go an' make a fire an' boil your big, black kettle an' brew tea,—though my Granny says I ought only drink milk—so let's."

"But, Sweetheart, it isn't time for tea yet, or is it, Miss Andromeda?"

"It will be, when the kettle boils. Though," said she, as they began collecting dry sticks, "I suppose, being a sailor you prefer ale and rum and such like, Mr. Felton?"

"Ay, but," he answered, "since coming to Willowmead, I'm learning to appreciate tea though it seems uncommonly expensive at twelve shillings the pound. Yet to be sure this is Sussex . . . a free-trade country and everyone's a smuggler more or less, I suppose. By the way, do you know the Willowmead folk, Kate, Aunt Deborah, Grannyanne?"

"I've met them, but I know Mrs. Leet best—through little Jane."

"When you saved her from drowning?" he enquired. "And in that . . . that hateful pool."

"Yes. And it is a horrible place. I always avoid it. But that day I was looking for Joshua who had wandered away, and got there quite by accident and—just in time, thank God!"

"Ay, thank God!" repeated Sam, fervently. "She is such a sweet little soul, ay, and I'm proud to tell you she adopted me the instant we met, or very nearly."

"Yes," said Andromeda, gravely, "that was a great compliment because Jane does not take to many people, for instance —poor Uncle Arthur, she can't bear him."

"How is Mr. Verinder?"

"Very well, thank you. He is away at present. Staying in London with friends."

"London?" repeated Sam. "Oh? Ah! And for how long?"

"He said a week, but it may be longer."

"And you," growled Sam, "in this desolation—alone!"

"Oh no, I have my Esau dog. And I—like solitude."

"But have you no friends in London to stay with?"

"No," she answered, stooping to pick up more firewood, "no, not now. Besides, I prefer the country."

"So do I!" nodded Sam.

"And I'm such a very unsociable person."

"Same here!" nodded Sam.

"And I cannot make friends easily."

"Neither can I!" quoth Sam. "And that's what surprises me,—for here we are, d'ye see . . . making friends in spite of ourselves."

"Oh?" she questioned, sitting back on her heels the better to survey him. "Are we?"

"Ay, to be sure," he answered, with his transfiguring grin, "or we shouldn't be here gathering sticks together,—it stands to reason."

"Oh!" said she again, pondering this; then her ruddy lips curving to the smile that was all too rare, she enquired, "Can gathering firewood inspire friendship?"

"Hardly, but it can help, like a favouring breeze. Ay, and friendship, d'ye see, is one of the truest blessings of this life! So, Miss Andromeda, if you can so honour me you will bless me also."

"But," she demurred, her golden eyes holding his steady grey, "can a man and woman be and remain—only friends?"

"Ay, most certainly,—speaking for myself, they can. For d'ye see, Miss Andromeda, I'm a cove,—a fellow who's run foul of and—well—seen so much of—t'other thing and the troublesome foolery of it, that nowadays I take mighty good care to give that sort o' thing a wide berth, keep it well to loo'ard and steer clear,—if you know what I mean."

"Yes, I think I do," she murmured, "if by that sort of thing, you mean 'love'."

"Ay," he answered, rather grimly, "or that which goes by the name in home ports and foreign all round this world. So, d'ye see, Miss Andromeda, I'm a man you can trust as a friend and no more, ever and always. So pray, what's your answer?" But at this moment (of course) came Jane her arms full of kindling wood with Esau pacing beside her, bearing in his powerful jaws a diminutive twig.

And now Andromeda led them to a merry chattering brook that guided them by devious leafy ways to a grassy clearing where stood the luxurious caravan, the dingy tent and Joshua chewing busily as usual.

"So then," quoth Sam, glancing around, "you have changed camp!"

"Yes, we often do. Uncle Arthur can never bide in one place very long, though we seldom go far from our dear Sussex and usually keep on Wrybourne land."

"Oh?" murmured Sam. "Ah? Why?"

"Because there's so much of it, I suppose, and besides, Uncle knows the agent, a Mr. Joliffe."

"Ah!" nodded Sam. "And does he likewise know Lord Julian Scrope?" Instead of replying Andromeda knelt and began arranging sticks for the fire until Sam interposed, saying:

"No, please let me."

"Thank you! Then I'll go fill the kettle and——"

"No, I'll do that too."

"Very well. Jane and I will get the tea things and——"

"Not yet," said Sam, kneeling to build the fire. "Do pray sit down and be idle for once!"

Mutely she obeyed, crouching nearby with her work-roughened hands folded in her lap, watching Sam very pensively.

"Yes," she murmured, at last, "you know how to lay a fire."

"I ought to!" he nodded. "For when not aboardship I've lived in some pretty wildish places, d'ye see."

"Tell me of them."

"Ay, so I will. But first let me say how glad I am you're camping so much nearer Willowmead, and gladder still you have that great, hairy ferocity,—a regular fighting-dog by his looks."

"Yes, he is," she sighed. "Esau has saved me from . . . hatefulness more than once. Last time a two-legged beast stabbed him——"

"Eh—a man?" demanded Sam, scowling.

"Of course! A horrible man who caught me alone . . . he had a dog too . . . . and he . . . . but I called Esau . . . and when he had killed the dog, he would have killed the man if I had not called and dragged him off."

"Hurrah for Esau!" quoth Sam.

"It was not until I had allowed the man to run away that I found he'd stabbed my poor Esau so badly that I had to take him to Mr. Robbins in Lewes to be doctored."

"Ah," nodded Sam, "that's why I didn't see your Esau until to-day. Well, I'm heartily glad he's such a savage creature."

"Yet he can be gentle too! Look at him now!"

Glancing whither she directed Sam beheld the dog crouched and with Batilda between his big paws while Jane was twisting wild flowers in his shaggy coat.

"Ay," nodded Sam, "a grand fellow despite his looks, Miss Andromeda."

"A ragamuffin," she nodded, "with the manners of a courtly gentleman. I bought him years ago from the gipsies for two shillings. He was all eyes and hair and paws then, so very hairy that of course I named him Esau. Then he grew and grew until, well—there he is! Just what, or how many breeds is he, d'you suppose?"

"Evidently all that's biggest and best," answered Sam, taking out his tinder-box, "mastiff, retriever, sheepdog and bull most likely—though I don't know much about dogs." Here Sam set fire to the kindling that blazed with merry crackle. "So now," said he, returning to his previous question, "does your Uncle know Lord Julian Scrope, are they friends?"

"No," she answered, vehemently. "Oh—no! Quite the reverse! And I must ask you never—ah, never to mention that name in Uncle Arthur's hearing, it affects him so terribly."

"Ah?" murmured Sam, "then of course I won't. But why should it?"

"Because years ago, before I was born, I believe they had a dreadful quarrel . . . I remember vaguely to have heard they fought a duel."

"A woman, I suppose?" Sam enquired, gently.

"I . . . don't know."

"Could she have been the Lady Barbara Stowe?"

Andromeda started to her knees with hands outflung against him in strange, wild gesture.

"Hush!" she whispered, "Oh, hush! This is another name must never be spoken! This is the dread, the terror that haunts me day and night! Ah, what must I . . . what can I do?"

Now taking these outstretched, trembling hands in his strong, warm clasp, Sam drew her nearer and strove to comfort her, saying with look and tone very humbly gentle:

"Andromeda, tell me your fear, let me share your trouble as a friend should. You poor, lonely child, honour me with your confidence and trust. . . . Is it . . . your uncle?"

"Yes," she whispered and, with the word, all strength seemed to fail her and she leaned to him, pillowing her troubled head upon his breast and, with her face thus hidden, continued in whispered, feverish haste:

"Sometimes he frightens me because I don't understand him. . . . Not long ago I found him rolling on the ground in a sort of fit, crying on God for vengeance and, oh—clasped to him he had . . . the pistol and he . . . was kissing it! When at last I coaxed it from him and asked what he meant, he told me it was a means to God's purpose—to rid the world of evil and that he only waited for proof and then God would show him how and where and when. So that night after he was asleep I crept away and threw the pistol into that . . . dreadful mill pool. But since then he has bought others and hides them from me now. . . . And this terrifies me."

"Ay," murmured Sam, "you think, because of their old quarrel he means to kill Lord Julian?"

"I . . . don't know! Don't ask me! But I'm so dreadfully afraid that sometimes at night when the wind rustles the leaves I have to steal out of bed to go and make sure he is sleeping,—as he always has been—so far, thank God! Yet some night when I'm asleep, he may go . . . creeping . . . away in the darkness to some . . . awful purpose. Yes, some night he may elude my care . . . and no one to help me!"

"Oh yes," said Sam, "I shall."

She had whispered all this in the strong comfort of his arms, her cheek pillowed upon his breast, but now she lifted her head to look up at him wide-eyed:

"You?" she whispered, "but how?"

Looking down at this lovely face, in especial these sensitive, quivering lips, Sam was about to reply when they started and turned to find Jane beside them who, nodding small bright head enquired casually:

"Are you kissing him, Auntie Mee, like I said you could?"

"No—oh no!" answered Andromeda, rather breathlessly. "No, dear, of course not."

"Well, you looked just as if you——"

"Tea!" cried Andromeda, leaping afoot. "Tea, Jane! Come and help me while your—your Uncle Sam fills the kettle and sets it to boil, come!" So off they sped together, leaving Sam very grave and thoughtful.

However, with a good deal of merry bustle and chatter, especially on Jane's part, a dainty cloth was spread upon the grass, then while Jane set out the crockery, Andromeda began cutting thin bread and butter:

"Though," said she, ruefully, "I have no cake to offer you."

"Aha, but," quoth Sam, stoking the fire, "you have, or had, some most delicious wild-strawberry jam, Miss Andromeda."

So tea was brewed and they began a meal the more joyous because of Jane's merry, inconsequent chatter until Esau, who of course made one of the happy party, growled suddenly with show of sharp white fangs while the hair on neck and crest seemed to rise and bristle; and now it was that Sam pulled his hat lower above his betraying scar.

"Someone is coming!" said Andromeda, glancing swiftly up and round about, with expression so very like terror that Sam glanced about also and with look threatening as the dog's growl.

"It must be a stranger," said Andromeda, huskily, "or . . . someone he doesn't like. Esau, come here!" Instantly the great dog obeyed and she grasped his brass-studded collar as somewhere amid the surrounding thickets was a leafy rustle . . . growing louder, nearer until—out from the undergrowth stepped a slim, elegant person who, beholding Sam, halted suddenly, then glancing from him to round-eyed little Jane, smiled and baring sleek, black head, bowed with an odd though graceful writhing movement.

"Miss Andromeda," said he in tenor voice altogether too sweet (or so thought Sam), "I fear you may deem this . . . my advent . . . an intrusion." Nevertheless and even as he uttered the words, he strode forward with a serene assurance at odds with his soft-spoken words. "I was not aware

. . . I could not know you would be—entertaining company, or——" Here Esau growled again and was silenced by his mistress who, glancing from her elegant visitor to Sam in his yeoman-like homespun, made them known to each other, saying:

"Mr. Jennings, this is . . . my friend, Mr. Felton."

"Friend?" questioned Mr. Jennings, softly but with shapely lips grim as Sam's own. "Friend? Indeed! Mr. Felton should feel extremely honoured."

"I do!" retorted Sam, "and I am!" Then he reached for another piece of bread and butter while Mr. Jennings fidgeted nervously with a portfolio he carried beneath his arm, yet when he spoke, his voice though soft as ever, sounded vaguely aggressive, or so thought Sam.

"Dear Miss Andromeda, am I graciously permitted to join you? May I sit down?"

"Of course," she answered, though almost before she spoke, down sat he between Andromeda and Jane who immediately shrank nearer to Sam.

"Will you have tea?" enquired Andromeda, making to rise.

"Ah, no!" he answered, staying her with gracious gesture. "Thank you, no, pray do not trouble yourself. I am here only to show your Uncle Verinder another . . . and latest . . . composition of mine and to crave his valued opinion——"

"But, Mr. Jennings, I thought you knew he was away——"

"Indeed no, dear Miss Andromeda, I was not aware . . ." he answered, gazing upon her almost possessively while his white hands trembled, fumbling nervously as he opened the portfolio. "But since Mr. Verinder is absent, perhaps you will be so good, so very kind as to afford me your judgment upon my . . . my poor efforts . . . though you will find them nothing very great, I fear." Saying this, he gave Andromeda certain sheets of manuscript music beautifully written and, while she studied them, sat watching her bold-eyed, yet all the while his long pale hands were clasping and wringing each other as in a very agony of nervousness. And indeed a gentleman of violent contrasts was Mr. Jennings and apparently at odds with himself; for beneath a dreamer's brow his eyes, large and softly luminous, showed deeply sad and wistful, while beneath jut of delicately aquiline nose, a mouth, shapely though thin-lipped above long, pointed chin, had in its close, down-trending curve something harsh, sneering and utterly relentless.

An old-young man was Mr. Jennings, for though his face had the ivory pallor of age, it was unmarked by any line or wrinkle, yet his sleek, thick hair was touched with silver.

All this Sam noted as he sat munching bread and butter while Andromeda studying this music, uttered such expressions as:

"But, Mr. Jennings, this passage in the minor is simply heavenly! . . . Oh, and this sudden change of key and tempo . . . so unexpected! Almost terrifying! . . . Ah, but these arpeggios leading up and up to the finale. . . . These grand chords! . . . Mr. Jennings, this is the best you have ever done or that I have seen, and truly beautiful! I'm sure Uncle Arthur will tell you the same."

"Oh . . . Miss Andromeda!" he exclaimed breathlessly, leaning swiftly towards her, his pallid face radiant, his lithe, shapely body performing that graceful writhing movement which Sam thought so peculiarly revolting. "Dear Miss Andromeda, do you . . . ah, do you really . . . really think so?" he stammered, his great, sad eyes even more beautiful now because of the sudden tears that gemmed and softened them until,—turning to meet Sam's lowering gaze, these same tearful eyes took on a fierce glitter while the sweet, soft voice no longer stammering, deepened instead to harsh menace, or so it appeared to watchful Sam as Mr. Jennings addressed him:

"Ah, do not mock me, sir! Do not contemn me for these tears which spring from purest joy and gratitude that any work of mine can evoke such kindly praise and—understanding. For this little moment I am happy—almost. So, Mr. Felton . . . do not . . . mock me!"

"Not I, sir!" answered Sam, gruffly. Here Esau thought fit to utter another growl that ended in sharp-fanged snarl as Mr. Jennings leaned slowly towards him, saying mournfully:

"Alas,—even your nice, ugly dog hates me, dear Miss Andromeda! I wonder why, for I never gave him cause. Indeed I should greatly like to win his friendship, for even the love of a dog would be a joy in such loveless life as mine——"

"Ah—no!" she cried. "Don't touch him!" But she warned

vainly, for Mr. Jennings reaching suddenly across her, laid his hand upon Esau's shaggy head, a slender hand that stroked, patted then clutched bristling hair as the great creature, cowering beneath this unwelcome caress, snarled fiercely and attempted to snap.

"Down, Esau, down!" cried Andromeda, striving to hold the powerful animal.

"Let me!" said Sam, rising to his knees.

"Ah no!" sighed Mr. Jennings, tightening the grip of his long, white fingers. "Pray do not trouble or be alarmed, he will not bite me,—he shall not! Dear me, no—I will not allow him. So please let him rave and struggle till he weary, I have him quite securely."

"Ay," growled Sam, "but he'll have you unless you cast loose and sheer off,—easy now!" So saying he took such grasp of Esau's collar that the dog aware of the power and mastery of this big hand, ceased his fierce struggles, and bowing shaggy head, whimpered and lay still.

"Ah sir," said Mr. Jennings in gentle reproach, "pray be more gentle, do not hurt the poor creature on my account, I beg you, I implore——"

"No need!" quoth Sam.

"Instead, sir," sighed Mr. Jennings, rising, "I will take my departure."

"Ay, I think you'd better!" said Sam, ungraciously.

Mr. Jennings instantly sat down again and meeting little Jane's wondering, round-eyed gaze, smiled.

"Little girl," said he, in tender, pleading tone. "Oh, Sweet Innocence, could you . . . will you . . . bless me with a kiss?"

"No! Oh no . . . thank you!" she whispered, shrinking from his outstretched hand with such very evident aversion that he cowered also, hiding his bowed face in clutching fingers,—then, glancing up and around, with sudden, wild gesture:

"Oh—am I accursed?" he whispered through clenched teeth. "First the dog, now the child! Am I so loathsome? So utterly repulsive? Is there some hideous mark, some foul stain upon me that all creatures shun me? . . . Lonely as a child, solitary as a youth, desolate as a man . . . am I fore-doomed, predestined to be for ever loveless, friendless— an outcast? . . . Well, I have in music an outlet for my grief, a comfort for my sorrows. . . . And you, Miss Andromeda, you at least can find a gentle word to greet me,—and for this your sweet mercy I am and shall ever be most truly and very humbly grateful!" Cramming his manuscript back into the portfolio, he leapt afoot, then stood hesitant, looking here and there like one dazed and lost.

"Dear Miss Andromeda," said he, at last, "kind and gentle mistress, I—bid you good-bye—for the present! Mr. Felton, sir—your servant." Having said which, he writhed at them, turned and hastened away at such rapid pace that soon all sound of him had died away. Then, loosing Esau's collar, Andromeda enquired:

"Jane dear, why wouldn't you kiss that gentleman?"

"'Cause he made me all shivery cold."

"Same here, Sweetheart!" quoth Sam. "He's a very shivery sort of customer."

"And I think," said Andromeda, "that he is a very sad gentleman and greatly to be pitied."

"But I," Sam retorted, "I'm pretty sure he is a hysterical fellow and could be deadly dangerous. So, consequently, I hope he doesn't often trouble and spoil your solitude,—with his 'dear Miss Andromeda's', confound him!"

"Oh, but he does, Mr. Felton—I mean he visits us quite frequently."

"Does he, b'Jingo? And why, pray?"

"For one reason because he is such a very clever musician. Uncle Arthur esteems his compositions most highly."

"Ha!" growled Sam. "That's only one reason! What are the others?"

"Perhaps because he is indeed a lonely man."

"However, he is no fit company for you, that's mighty certain."

"Oh? Indeed, Mr. Felton!" she exclaimed, knitting her dark brows at him. "And who are you to pass judgment?"

"Marm, I'm a fellow, d'ye see, who's roughed it ashore and afloat, ay, and run athwart enough evil to know it on sight. Ay, b'George,—and I'm warning you as yon fine gentleman who can weep for and pity himself so readily, would have small mercy on anyone else. So, I'm warning—no, I'm begging you to give Mr. Jennings a wide berth,—I mean steer clear of him,—that is—discourage the fellow—no friendship —if you get my meaning?"

"Oh yes, I can guess what you mean, Mr. Felton, and now I mean you to understand that you must leave me to choose my own friends. And I take it very ill in you to so vilify this poor gentleman and—in his absence!"

"Marm, but for your presence he should have heard it to his too-smooth face. Next time I——"

"Sir, there shall be no 'next time'!"

"Oh?" growled Sam, pondering this. "Ah! Just how must I take that, pray? I mean to say what d'you mean—exactly?"

"That if you intend to insult this unhappy gentleman and in my presence——"

"Not likely, marm."

"But I think it so very likely that I must ask you to . . . please keep away from here."

"Very—good, Miss Andromeda! Ay, ay, marm, so be it. Though I should like to know why you must call the fellow 'poor gentleman', so very tenderly?"

"Because I believe he is very sad, very lonely, and I pity him deeply."

"Ha!" exclaimed Sam. "And pity is akin to love, they say!"

"Mr. Felton, you are presuming!"

"Ay, I am. However, no one can ever call me 'poor gentleman', thank God!"

"No," she retorted, with flash of eye, "that would be quite impossible!"

"Too true, marm," said he, rather grimly, "I'm only a seafaring fellow and no fine gentleman, but I'm pretty sound and wide-awake, and I tell you again——"

"Indeed, I beg you won't."

"Right-ho!" he growled and at his grimmest. "Thanks for the tea. I'll slip my moorings and bear away."

"Thanks for nothing! And you'd better!" said Andromeda, at her stateliest. So, for a moment they eyed each other; then as Sam made to rise, Jane spoke:

"Ooh, Auntie Mee, you're frownding at my nice Uncle Sam an' he's frownding at you an' you're bofe cross 'n' angry at each other, so won't you kiss 'n' be friends again —just to please me?"

"Sweetheart," answered Sam, his grim features instantly transfigured by that winning smile of his, "dear little Jane,

I should—love to and—not only to please you, my Heart's delight."

"Well then, Uncle Sam, whyever don't you?"

"Because, my Jane, I've never kissed a fairy aunt and feel too shy,—so I'm waiting, ay, and hoping she will do her best to please you by showing me how."

"Oh! Then, Auntie Mee, I suppose you'd better kiss him first,—he isn't hard to kiss 'cause his face is nice an' bare. I don't like kissing hairy faces, do you?"

"No, dear, I—— Oh, I don't know—I've never tried——" Andromeda's ruddy lips quivered, she smiled, she laughed; then rising to her knees and reaching out her arms, said: "Anyhow I had much rather kiss you,—so come!" So, having propped Batilda against a tussock of grass, Jane came to kiss and be kissed,—but in this same moment she reached out to Sam who now rose also to his knees; and thus standing between them with her small arms about both, she compelled them to each other, drawing them slowly ever nearer, until—Andromeda closed her eyes. . . .

"There!" demanded this small so fateful person. "Wasn't that nice an' easy?"

"Yes," answered Sam, a little unsteadily, marvellously shaken by a now unforgettable memory of the shy, soft caress of lips that had met and quivered beneath his own. "Yes, Jane . . . my darling!"

"So now you're bofe friends again, aren't you, Auntie Mee?" But, with sound that was neither sob nor laugh yet something of each, perhaps, Andromeda kissed her again, saying:

"Now come and help me to wash up the tea-things,— both of you."

When this was done, and all too soon, thought Sam, a distant church-clock, chiming the hour of six, warned him of the amazing flight of time, he rose to be gone, saying awkwardly:

"Miss Andromeda, if we . . . or I . . . should chance to bear up for the 'Chanted Forest' now and then . . . and spy you in the offing . . . may I hope to . . . find a welcome?"

"Of course!" she answered, lightly. "And especially from Esau, he has accepted you . . . quite surprisingly."

"Dogs," quoth Sam, "are highly intelligent creatures and your Esau being as wise as he's big knows honesty when he

sees it and whom he may trust—ay, and his mistress too!
At sea," he continued, his voice hushed now and solemn as
his look, "we have a saying—'there's a sweet, little cherub
who sits up aloft to look after the life of poor Jack' and . . .
Miss Andromeda, I'm . . . I'm wishing this same cherub,
ay, and all the holy angels may look after you and . . .
have you in their keeping . . . ever and always."

"Oh!" she murmured, her eyes widening in surprise, as
she looked up into his grave face, "that sounded . . . almost
. . . like a prayer."

"It was!" he nodded. "And is!"

"Then," said she, giving her hand to his ready clasp, "I
think . . . I know now that Esau was right. So I shall trust
you as he does and accept you as my friend—most gladly, yes
more gladly than I can ever tell."

"And like Esau, I shall never fail you," he answered, looking down at her slim, toil-roughened hand as if he meditated
kissing it.

"I know it," she answered, softly. "Yes, I'm sure of it.
But"—and here her lovely sensitive mouth quivered with her
rare smile, "shall you be obedient as he?"

"Almost!" answered Sam, smiling also. "But now, before
I go,—mine isn't much of a name, I know, d'ye see, but will
you,—I mean I should like to hear you say it."

"Sam!" she murmured, obediently.

"Ay," he nodded, "it can sound better than I thought.
Good-bye, until to-morrow morning—at the end of the lane."

"At half-past ten!" she added.

"Pray, how long should it take us to fetch up with Lewes?"

"Over an hour, I'm afraid."

"Good!" he nodded. Then, still looking down at her hand
as if he would have kissed it, he loosed it instead that she
might bid Jane farewell. Then with this small personage
perched jubilant upon his shoulder, homewards they went,
through the 'Chanted Forest' where birds near and far were
already beginning their evensong, past the Deep Dark gloomy
and sullen, waiting with a dreadful patience for that which
was yet to be, and so at last to Willowmead as evening shadows
lengthened.

CHAPTER XXII

"MIRACLES," quoth Mrs. Leet throned this same evening in the ingle, knitting in hand, "miracles still happen and wonders will never cease!"

"Very true, Anne!" nodded Aunt Deborah, glancing up from her tatting. "For indeed it is a monstrous and mighty miracle that any clutching, clawing grimly-grasping, scoundrelly Scrope should ever part with an inch of his ill-begotten heritage."

"Ah, but," said Mrs. Leet, "every now and then a good Scrope happens somehow or other, and The Admiral was one, and a very good one too!"

"What Admiral, Anne? Who, what and when?"

"Lord Japhet Scrope, Admiral of the Blue, wounded in the three days' battle with the Dutch off Beachy Head."

"Goodness gracious, Anne! That happened so many many years ago that your Admiral must be very completely dead and dusty by now."

"Yes, Deborah, of course he is, good, brave gentleman. But The Family lives on and maybe the good Admiral or his spirit has come back to live again in our new, young Earl."

"Holy heavens, Anne, what an idea,—so grim and ghostly, so spookey and spectral!"

"But," said Captain Ned, glancing up from The Document whose abstruse legalities still engaged him, "a very interesting idea, Aunt Deb. The transmigration of souls has been argued long before we hammered the Dutch off Beachy Head. However, this new earl must be a pretty good sort of fellow, according to Mr. Joliffe——" Here Aunt Deb, Kate and Mrs. Leet demanded in chorus:

"What did he tell you?"

"Well first," answered the Captain, smiling at their so evident curiosity, "that his lordship is a young man——"

"Is he tall and handsome?" demanded Aunt Deb.

CAPT. NED: Ay, he's pretty tall—a burly fellow, though his looks are nothing in particular.

KATE: Is he dark or fair?

CAPT. NED: Neither, Kate. Mr. Joliffe's word was "darkish".

MRS. LEET (*Knitting-pins, suddenly idle*): Was he ever a seaman, Ned. Did Mr. Joliffe tell you that?

CAPT. NED: No, Grannyanne, he merely said the earl had been a great traveller, has lived mostly abroad, is at present greatly busied with family affairs and that his first name, oddly enough, is Japhet.

MRS. LEET: Ha! That was the Admiral's name! Yes, this was the good Admiral's name! Did Joliffe tell you anything more of our new Lord Japhet, his air, speech, manner?

CAPT. NED: Not a word, Granny.

"Well!" exclaimed Mrs. Leet, glancing where Sam, in corner of the long, cushioned settle, was puffing thoughtfully at his second-best pipe. "Well, what say you to all that, Grandson Sam? Has Admiral Japhet, the good earl, come back again as this new Lord Japhet, think ye?"

"Maybe," answered Sam, meeting her keen scrutiny with his flashing smile, "but if he shows anything like your old Admiral, the poor fellow must look a regular-beetle-browed ruffian."

"And yet," said Captain Ned, folding up The Document very carefully, "he has let us have dear, old Willowmead and for such surprisingly moderate price that he must be better than his looks, handsome or no."

"And a dear!" sighed Kate, glancing up and around with eyes gladly bright. "Yes, he is—he must be a good Scrope, as Granny says, a generous, kindly gentleman! I only wish I could thank him. I shall if ever we meet and—if I dare."

"You will, m'dear!" quoth Mrs. Leet and with the utmost finality. "Tell me, Ned, did Lawyer Joliffe say when the Earl would be coming to The Great House, Wrybourne Feveril?"

"No, Granny."

"Or—where he is at present? You enquired, of course?"

"I did, but he evaded the question."

"Which does not surprise me. And may I know what you paid for Willowmead?"

"Exactly one thousand pounds, Anne."

"Ha! Reasonable indeed!"

"Yes. I was prepared to offer double, ay and more!"

"However," quoth Mrs. Leet, "this doesn't surprise me either."

"Why not, Granny, for it astonished me."

"Because, Ned, my Admiral was reputed to be generous as he was brave, and Admiral Lord Japhet was an extremely valiant gentleman. Ah well, well, 'tis time I was homing to my cottage with its dratted leaky roof."

"Not yet," said the Captain, "for before you go we are all of us going to drink a toast to Lord Japhet, Earl of Wrybourne—and in something worthy."

"Yes, Ned dear," said Kate, rising, "the special port wine you sent me out of Spain, so long ago and we then so unhappy. . . ."

Thus presently standing all and with glasses abrim, these dear folk, so rare yet truly English (thought Sam) drank "health, happiness and long life to their new, young Earl of Wrybourne."

Thereafter, Mrs. Leet having been tied into her vast bonnet by Kate's gentle hands and received her club-like staff from Ned, took Sam's ready arm and with him sallied forth into a fragrant night radiant with stars.

"Hum!" quoth she, after they had gone a little way. "Ha! That was very excellent port wine, Sam!"

"It was!" he chuckled. "I mind the time we took it out of a French prize, for d'ye see, Granny, 'twas meant for Old Boney himself."

"I can well believe it! Though such noble wine should not be guzzled by such Beast of blood and suffering as Buonaparte!"

"Too true, Grannyanne!"

"Sam, we have left wonderful happiness there in Willowmead."

"And well they deserve it!" said he, fervently. "Ay, they do so and indeed, Granny!"

"And how," she demanded, peering up at him in the dim starshine, "how are you feeling to-night, Sam?"

"Hale and hearty, thankee Granny——"

"So you should!" she nodded. "Ay, so you should, Sam, for never in this world was toast drunk with deeper, truer sincerity—Health, Happiness and long life to—my lord Japhet, the Earl."

"Oh-ho!" murmured Sam, peering down at her.

"Ah-ha!" quoth Mrs. Leet; after which they walked some while in silence.

"How glorious," said she, at last, "how bright and beautiful the stars are to-night!"

"Yes, Grannyanne. I've seen them so many a night at sea. I think they show better from the deck of a lonely ship."

"Maybe, Sam, maybe. But I'm hoping they are going to shine brighter upon Wrybourne Feveril and bring more true comfort and happiness to its many folk than ever they did through all the long, past years. How think you, grandson Sam?"

"That you are right," he answered.

"Ay, I know it!" said she, nodding up at him, "and having the power, what gladsome privilege to make this poor, old world a little better . . . a happier place. That brute-man Buonaparte has power, Sam, and just see how he is misusing it—the countless dead and maimed, the breaking hearts and bitter tears, a devil's work, Sam. Ah, but how godlike to use such power for the joy, the comfort and preservation of the sorrowful, the weak and helpless—instead of ruinous desolation, a flowery garden, in place of tearful anguish, song and laughter. . . . Well, here's my cottage, so good-night, tall grandson,—though I'm not sure I should continue to name you so——"

"Grannyanne," said he, taking her hands, club-like staff as well, "when you honoured and adopted me it was for good and all, d'ye see—besides I shall need your wise counsel later on,—so as the years draw on they must only . . . draw us with 'em, closer; ay, closer, d'ye see, Granny."

"Ha!" she exclaimed, almost fiercely. "Now for that I shall even dare to kiss you—stoop, tall grandson, stoop! There and—there again! Oh, what a world it is! I feel as happy to-night—yes, even as your Captain and his Kate. Now good-night, grandson mine, home with you and as you go—look up at the stars and think of all there is to do."

Thus presently home went Sam a very thoughtful Sam indeed.

Now as he walked the moon arose, making a pale glory all about him.

CHAPTER XXIII

TELLS HOW MURDER STRUCK AMISS

SAM was reaching to open the gate at Willowmead when he stood instantly arrested, heavy stick clenched in ready hand, for, in shadow of the tall hedge a denser shadow moved, —then from this imminent leafage a voice whispered, hoarsely:

"Hold 'ard, Mr. F., the word is—'Jarsper'!"

"Dammit!" exclaimed Sam pettishly, though greatly relieved. "Is that you, Daniel?"

"Ar's me, sir! And I were to say as Jarsper needs ye very special and immediate."

"What's he want? And at this time o' night?"

"You, sir."

"Yes, yes,—but why?"

"Jarsper'll tell and likewise show ye."

"Where is he?"

"Not s'very fur, sir,—and I've got the gig handy."

"I'm asking you whereaway is Jasper?"

"Up along by Dickerdyke Spinney, sir."

"Never heard o' the place! Is it a mile away?"

"Ay and more, sir."

"Two miles?"

"Nearer six, sir, but I've got the——"

"Oh, come on!" And away strode Sam at great pace though Dan'l kept beside him with no apparent effort.

"Here's a dev'lish time to be abroad!" growled Sam.

"Ay, sir. And yonder's the gig."

Into this vehicle they mounted forthwith and away they drove by leafy by-ways fretted by pale moonbeams, through a bowery countryside ghostly and all unreal in this pallid radiance

"Can't you tell me what Jasper wants with me at such an hour?"

"Ay, sir, I could but, orders being so, 'twouldn't do no-how."

"Shrig is always so confoundedly mysterious and over-cautious!"

"Mebbe so, sir. But then—mebbe not. And sir, I notice as you ain't rigged in your sailorly duds,—coat, sir, 'at, sir, nor yet your fine neckerchief."

"No."

"Ar! You give 'em away, sir, p'raps?"

"Not I."

"Then mebbe they was took, p'raps, nabbed, filched or stole?"

"Ay. And my favourite pipe along with 'em."

"Bad luck, sir! Hows'ever, seamanly duds ain't particklar healthy in these yere parts! So mebbe 'twas all for the best, sir."

"Eh? Daniel, just what d'you mean?"

"Jarsper'll explain, sir."

"Ha—damme!" exclaimed Sam as a distant church clock struck eleven. "How much further?"

"Top o' the 'ill yonder, sir, then down along by the spinney."

"And a cursed odd hour to be meeting in dam' spinneys, or anywhere else!"

"Ay, so 'tis, sir. But the carcumstances is precious odd, sir,—and growing odder!"

They topped the long hill at last and turning down a narrow by-way, rounded a sharp bend and thus beheld Mr. Shrig seated on grassy bank and puffing his short, clay pipe.

"Eighteen minutes and a bit!" said he, rising as the gig drew up. "You've been pretty slippy, Dan'l! Greetings, sir and pal! I've had Dan'l fetch you along so as I could show and prove t'ye as your pal J.S. don't paint no roses, gild lilies nor yet cry 'fire' without doo cause."

Sam frowned and shook his head, saying:

"Jasper, you're too dam' mysterious as usual! Be plain, for I haven't the vaguest notion what you're——" Sam's voice died away and he stood mute and strangely disquieted; for Mr. Shrig's head was bare and, perhaps because of the ghostly light for the moon now stood right above them, Mr. Shrig's face placid no longer, showed strangely pale and haggard as slowly he turned and moved aside.

"Pal," said he, pointing with his stick, "take a peep at this!"

Sam looked—gasped, recoiled suddenly and caught his breath, yet staring down in horrified amazement at a frightful object that sprawled half in shadow, a ghastly, blood-soaked something had once been a powerful, burly man but whose face was now only a flattened, dreadful smear; but beside this shattered head lay the glazed hat; about the gory throat was the neckerchief, its gaudy design of anchors blotted out here and there; buttoned across the broad and motionless chest was the jaunty coat,—that too smart, fatally betraying jacket with its rows of gleaming buttons. . . .

"God—Almighty!" whispered Sam, at last. "It might be—me!"

"Ar!" nodded Mr. Shrig. "There you lay, pal, or so I thought, and small vonder, seeing as this yere misfort'nate cove is rigged as I see you last and his face shot off into the bargain! Ay,—there y'are!"

"Yes," said Sam, hoarsely, "even now . . . he looks the very image of me."

"Ar!" sighed Mr. Shrig. "So werry much so that b'goles,—it give me quite a turn! Even arter I rolled him over, him laying face down'ards,—even then, pal, seeing his chivvy is all blowed off, I could ha' took my oath as he was you,—till I noticed as his right daddle lacked a finger, as you can see. Yet still I couldn't be quite sartin sure, because fingers can be shot off easier than faces."

"Jasper, I've seen many, too many dead men in my time, but . . . nothing worse than this! A fowling-piece and fired at close quarters, eh, Jasper?"

"Yes, pal, his murderer stood just behind yon bush, his tracks is werry plain."

"Poor fellow!" murmured Sam. "Poor, unlucky cove,—for if our suspicions are right, he died of—my hat and coat."

"Nary a doubt o' that, pal. Said hat and coat marked you for death so soon as Tobias J. tipped the office to—US knows OO."

"Well?" enquired Sam, turning from this horror, "what now?"

"Now, sir and pal, this yere poor relic must—wanish! The Law shall take charge of it and—all unbeknown to a living soul except The Law and us. Ar, and unbeknown it shall remain till I lays my awenging daddle on its murderer!"

"Ay, and what must I do?"

"Nary thing, sir and Sam, except con-tinny to lay low."

"But, Jasper——"

"Sir, take another peep at our misfort'nate relic and be dooly varned! Creeping Murder has crawled and struck wrong but thinks it has struck right! Werry good! So let it think, ar—and so must it think till 'tis fast in my trap, stuck tight to my twig or wriggling wainly on my hook! So now, sir, while I sit yere along o' this werry de-funct party oo might ha' been you but for ass-tounding luck, Dan'l shall drive ye back to Villersmead and pleasant dreams—I hope! Good night, pal, and thank your stars for a poor thief as saved your precious life."

"Ay, Jasper, so I do indeed! Good night—no, first,—how did you chance to find the poor fellow?"

"Not b'chance, pal, 'twere obserwation, sir! I've other eyes besides mine and Dan'l's vatching over ye now. So ever since yon poor cove nabbed your clobber he's been trailed——"

"How? You saw him steal my——"

"Not me, Sam 'pal, 'twere other ogles as see the fact, other feet as follered in hopes as in your garments he'd lead us to US knows OO,—vich he might ha' done if he hadn't dodged too clever and so got hisself shot thereby—and unseen, more's the pity! Good night, sir and Sam pal, and remember, more than ever now, the vord is Caution, vith a werry large C."

CHAPTER XXIV

OF TWO IN A FOUR-WHEELED CART

IN this busy old world, besides the woeful discordancy of man's evil to man, there are, thank God, many lovely sounds to charm the ear, warm the heart and gladden the soul; and yet (thought Sam) never a one of them all, and especially upon this particular summer morning, so gladly welcome as the steady, very deliberate clip-clop of hoofs with the creak and rattle of a certain weather-beaten, four-wheeled cart. Though Sam, the dunderhead, had no idea why this should be so—as yet! Not even when Joshua was reined to a stop and Andromeda was smiling down on him; nor when he was seated beside her and so near that their knees and shoulders touched whenever this small, rickety vehicle jolted over some rut or stone, no—not even then!

"Of course," said Andromeda, poking this sleek, very deliberate Joshua with the whip to no apparent effect, "the question is, Mr. Felton, just how much money you wish to spend."

"Money?" he repeated, glancing at her profile—delicate line of nose, full, ruddy lips and rounded chin.

"Yes, for little Jane's birthday present."

"Ay, to be sure. Well, anything you think right."

"You can buy quite a good doll's house for about—ten shillings."

"Ay, but I want the best, d'ye see, something worthy of our Jane."

"Then naturally that will cost more."

"Yes," said Sam, eyeing a wind-blown curl apeep below the brim of her small, close bonnet, "I thought—about five or six pounds."

"Goodness!" she exclaimed, turning to look at him and thus becoming aware of his intent gaze, looked away again. And now except for the creak and rattle of the cart, they travelled in silence awhile, yet a very pleasant companionable silence until, as by mutual consent, glancing at each other again, she smiled, as did Sam; then with her lovely mouth thus up-curving:

"Five pounds would be ridiculous!" she said.

"Oh? Why, pray?"

"Because it is a great deal too much!"

"It can't be," he answered, "for, d'ye see, I owe our small, sweet Jane so very much more. Now will you please ask me how and why?"

"No!" said Andromeda, and though she smiled again, the rich colour deepened in her cheek. Here ensued another brief silence; then, quoth Sam, wistfully:

"You haven't said it once, yet!"

"I know I haven't."

"I mean my name."

"Of course!" she nodded. "Nor have you uttered mine,—though 'Andromeda' is such a very awkward name."

"Yet it suits you,—that is—what I mean is,—it's beautiful, though it would be easier said—without the 'miss'," he suggested, almost shyly.

"Yes," she agreed, "at least it would be that much shorter."

"Then will you—would you mind—may I——" Sam floundered and she let him, until, words failing, he was dumb—while the cart rattled and creaked as if in derision; then above its clatter,—sudden, unexpected yet ineffably sweet rose her laughter, ending all too soon, as she answered:

"Yes, Sam, you may. And I'll call you 'Sam'—though to be sure it seems quite too shockingly familiar, considering we scarcely know each other."

"Oh, but we do!" quoth he.

"Having met each other exactly three times!" she retorted.

"Ay, too true!" he admitted. "But then, d'ye see, ours is to be a friendship that shall never hope or ask for anything more, Andromeda."

"Never?" she demanded, turning to regard him with her level, calmly-appraising glance.

"No, never!" he repeated.

"But you are a sailor, are you not?"

"Ay, I am—or was. And how then?"

"Don't sailors—have wives in every port?"

"Ay, and that's my trouble! I never have and never could take women lightly enough, d'ye see. That's why I very nearly ran foul of wedlock twice and weathered it each time by a miracle."

"Oh?" enquired Andromeda, quite unaware that Joshua's

leisured trot had become a lazy amble. "Tell me of it, if you—can."

"Ay, willingly," he answered. "Yes, you'd best know the sort of fool I am. The first time was in Old Mexico, a Spanish donna——"

"Was she young and beautiful?"

"Both!" he nodded. "Ay, she was indeed! A devout Catholic and seemed too good, ay—too pure and holy for such rough fellow as myself,—I was only a fore-mast jack, then. But . . . I discovered she was . . . well . . . so unspeakably the reverse that I came pretty nigh death. For, like the young fool I was I'd taken it all—too seriously! So I shipped aboard a regular floating hell, hoping to die. But 'twas others did the dying and I ended that voyage as master's mate. The second time, ay, and the last, happened when I was prisoner o' war in France . . . she was a lady too and kindly gentle as she was beautiful and I, like the too-serious, dam' fool I am, broke my fool heart again—or nearly so."

"Why . . . Sam?" Two words only, but in their soft utterance was that which lifted Sam's bowed head, banished his painful frown, softening his grim features so wonderfully that in this moment, as he turned to look at her, he seemed younger than years of hardship had made him, and—yes, almost handsome, or so it seemed to this woman whose calm, deep eyes were so quick to see and determine. Also when now he spoke her name it was in voice gentled and deepened with gratitude.

"Andromeda . . . then you know? You understand how such fool as I . . . can suffer?"

"Yes," she answered, softly, "yes . . . and I know that a fool never did or ever could feel such grief."

"Andromeda," said he again, and both of them totally unaware that Joshua, this artful creature, had stopped to graze, "you are and have been a constant surprise to me ever since we met."

"Such a little while ago!" she reminded him, with her grave smile. "But tell me of the French lady, was she—like the Spanish?"

"Well, no, for d'ye see, contrariwise, she was a wife already and the Spanish lass should have been."

"I see. And so you were a prisoner in France?"

"Yes. But enough of me, pray what of you?"

Here Andromeda becoming aware that the cart was motionless, poked Joshua to his leisured trot and enquired:

"What would you know of me?"

"Everything!" answered Sam, promptly. "Or—as much as you'll honour me by telling. I'd greatly like to know why you always look so sad, yes—even when you smile?"

"Do I?" she questioned. "I didn't know it . . . the looking-glass in my tent is very small and I don't use it often. I'm growing too careless of myself, I'm afraid."

"Yes!" said forthright Sam. "You are."

"Oh—indeed?" she exclaimed, flashing her golden eyes at him.

"Yes," he repeated, "and more's the pity because you are shaped so . . . so very beautifully."

"How do you know?" she demanded, glancing from him down at the garments whose shabbiness was the more manifest because of the splendours they half revealed; so much so that she spread their close, betraying folds with whip-hand and gracefully dexterous kick of slim foot, then flushing consciously, looked at his defiantly, saying casually, "This happens to be my marketing dress and quite good enough for me to——"

"No!" said he, almost harshly. "It's nothing like good enough for you, Andromeda, any more than that tent! B'George, I hate to think of you in that flimsy thing—at night."

"But I like it!" she retorted. "Day or night . . . perhaps because I was born in a tent."

"Oh?" murmured Sam.

"Yes!" said she, turning to face him. "My mother Rosalind Verinder committed the social crime of marrying an inferior, or so her family deemed it,—she ran away with an actor, though they called him a strolling player and vagrant! And so he was, I suppose, though he had his own travelling company and was a great actor,—the Robert Sheldon Players were famous everywhere—except London. However, my poor mother was outcast by her family, the Verinders were too proud of their ancient lineage ever to acknowledge her again."

"Was your brave mother happy?"

"Supremely and my poor father was devoted to her."

"Then, outcast or no, she did right well."

"Yes, she was very happy, though not for long, she died giving me life—I killed her, and my father too, almost. For when she died all the best of him died too. He lost all ambition . . . became a hopeless drunkard,—though always kind and gentle to everyone, especially to me—— Oh, the poor, poor dear! So from famous actor and master of all, he sank to last and the willing drudge of all—oh, the pity of it."

"Ah, and what—what of you?"

"Oh, I lived somehow until I was old enough to—take care of him . . . he became my great, big helpless child . . . until he died. And then I should have been lost! But then . . . ah, then, by God's mercy, my Uncle Arthur found me, my wonderful, rich uncle—ah, he was very different then, so vital, so grandly masterful—he swept me up and away from all that sordid misery—to the wonder and luxury of his great house. He loved me, had me educated, yet taught me far more by his own inspiring genius. He took me to all the great centres of art in Europe, opened to me the glorious world of music. He was, oh, so much more to me than a father that when ruin came, loss of money and the woman he adored,—when he was stricken, as you see him now, and all friends except very few, deserted him,—can you, do you wonder that I devoted myself to him, to shield and care for him in his helplessness, as I always must and shall,—do you wonder that I love and shall serve him so long as he needs me?"

"No," answered Sam, though rather gloomily.

"Well then, why are you frowning?"

"Because," he answered, heavily, "you are indeed Andromeda! For according to what Ned tells me, he's a classical scholar, d'ye see, the first Andromeda was exposed as a—a willing sacrifice for others."

"Well," sighed Andromeda, "if I am or—must be a sacrifice, I also shall be willing . . . even though it break my heart at last."

Here for some while the cart rattled its four wheels and creaked its worn timbering while Joshua from lazy amble betook him to lazier walk and all unheeded for Sam was thinking unhappily of Andromeda and she stealing sideways glances at his grimly woeful visage and guessing the reason therefore, roused him at last with the question:

"Were you at Trafalgar and have you been in many battles?"

Hereupon Sam (as only English sailormen usually do, unless inspired by Bacchus) told the dashing exploits and valiant deeds of shipmates with scant mention of himself until she "brought him up with a round turn", demanding:

"Yes, but how did you get that ugly wound—there above your left eyebrow, Sam?"

Over this betraying scar he instantly jerked his hat-brim, saying as he did so:

"It was either a Froggie's pike, cutlass or musket-butt, I could never be sure which, the time we boarded the——"

Horse-hoofs on the narrow road behind them and approaching at such furious gallop that Sam turned, in angry alarm while Andromeda reined aside and only just in time as a horseman dashed by in cloud of dust, a wild figure who glanced back at them from a face contorted and streaked very oddly.

And when this choking cloud had subsided, Sam enquired:

"Did you notice who that was?"

"Oh, yes,—the hateful Honourable Scrope."

"Ay, and looked as if he had been weeping,—shedding tears and plenty of 'em."

"Yes, Sam. But can such man ever shed tears? If so, I hope they sting."

CHAPTER XXV

OF ANDROMEDA, SAM, AND FRIENDSHIP

THE doll's-house had been purchased, though indeed this was a veritable palace in miniature and as sumptuously furnished even to pictures on the walls; a toy of such dainty splendour that Andromeda (despite its costliness) clasped her hands and exclaimed for sheer feminine joy of it.

This magnificence having been duly packed and stowed in the cart, Sam decided they must both wine and dine,—unheeding Andromeda's protestations that she was not hungry, was too untidy . . . dusty . . . in her very oldest bonnet. . . . However, Sam's sailorly eye having singled out the White Hart Inn—thither he led her; and once within these hospitable portals, no high-bred lady in all Christendom more sweetly dignified, more stately and gracious than Andromeda despite her aged bonnet.

Thus with obsequious waiters to attend, they enjoyed such meal that Sam, because of its growing intimacy, was to remember with a wistful yearning,—such meal that Andromeda even forgot her aged bonnet, or very nearly.

This magical repast ending, too soon of course as all such happiness must, forth they went into the busy street that Andromeda might do her marketing. Now while she was thus busied, Sam chancing upon a jeweller's shop entered forthwith and accosted the presiding genius who beamed on him through a ferocity of curling whisker:

"I want something in diamonds—not too overpowering."

"Sir," quoth the jeweller, exhibiting a circlet of flashing gems, "behold the very article!"

"No!" said Sam. "Nothing like it."

"Ah!" sighed the jeweller, grasping the whiskers with restraining hand. "You desire something less expensive,——"

"No!" answered Sam. "Something less showy."

"Aha!" exclaimed the jeweller, releasing the whiskers. "Then here, sir, behold this brooch or pendant, a perfect work of art, or should we say 'heart'—ha, ha—being indeed a

149

heart involved or enwrought with a cross for Truth and an anchor for Hope."

"Yes, this'll do!" nodded Sam, thrusting hand into pocket. So, the brooch being paid for, was neatly boxed and away rolled Sam with his seaman's lurch, and was pondering just how and when he should bestow this gift when Andromeda rejoined him. He was still meditating this vexed question when the cart was rattling and creaking under them, and so profoundly that she questioned him at last:

"Why are you so thoughtful,—or is it only drowsiness? I'm sleepy too. . . . For I seldom or never take wine . . ." Here she yawned behind slim fingers and quite bewitchingly, or so thought Sam—as he answered:

"Well then, why not have a nap?"

"I should love to . . . but how can I?"

"By closing your eyes, in the wood yonder, or any other shady place. I'd take care nothing and no one disturbed you, though you know that, I hope?"

"Yes," she answered, meeting his look with her serenely direct gaze, "and I haven't been sleeping very well, lately." Now here, there rushed upon him the dreadful memory of that ghastly, bloodstained thing he had looked down upon last night . . .

"Andromeda," said he, impulsively, "I hate to think of you so utterly alone in your camp . . . that wilderness!"

"Oh, but," sighed she, looking up at him slumberously, "I'm a very light sleeper—when I have not had wine, of course! Besides I have my Esau dog. I left him on guard in my tent . . . and there he will be . . . waiting to greet me, bless him!"

"Ay," growled Sam, "thank God for those sharp fangs of his!"

"Yes, though I'm never afraid—except for Uncle Arthur. And to-day . . . just for the present, even that dread is . . . soothed away . . . I never felt so . . . deliciously sleepy! So, won't you please take the reins?"

"I'd much rather take you into the shade where you can lie and sleep properly . . . know complete rest if only for a little while."

"I should love to!" she murmured. "Oh, I ought not to have drunk . . . so much wine."

"You should have drunk more, Andromeda. You are

mentally exhausted. I'll warrant you slept little, last night."

"Not very well," she admitted.

"Then you shall sleep here and now."

"Oh, but I couldn't . . . it would be too ridiculous!"

"But very sensible, Andromeda. You're dead beat with anxiety and constant worry. So now—lean against the seat-back and my shoulder! And if I set my arm about you it will be only because I'm compelled to save you from lurching overboard—into the road, d'ye see! There,—are you quite comfortable? You don't look it, but—are you?"

"Yes," she murmured, drowsily.

"Then," said he, setting long arm about her, "close your eyes and sleep." The which she did, and so profoundly that once or twice she snored, though very gently to be sure. . . .

Now looking down at this sleeping face too strong and resolute for prettiness, too haggardly pale for beauty, Sam felt the heart within him surge and swell, his eyes grow dim, his arm tighten about her,—yet still the dunderhead fellow didn't guess.

Thus at a plodding walk they traversed these leafy by-ways and the vociferous cart now so hushed and silent that Sam could hear Andromeda's soft, slow breathing that told of deep, untroubled, soul-refreshing slumber.

How often he looked down at this head now pillowed on his breast, at this face with its black, low-arching brows, these wide-set, long-lashed eyes, this gently-aquiline nose and well-rounded chin that, together, held more than suggestion of indomitable will and courage, though softened by the sensitive, full-lipped, ruddy mouth all sweet curves and so lusciously provoking that he averted his eyes and stared at Joshua's ears instead, though it is doubtful if he noticed them. Yet so long and fixedly he gazed that he was unaware the sleeper had waked until she spoke, and almost gaily:

"Goodness, how he scowls! Am I such a burden?" Sam started and Andromeda sat up to smooth her petticoats, glance around and enquire:

"How ever long have I slept?"

"Scarcely half-an-hour."

"My gracious, and we are not half-way back! Joshua must have crawled."

"He did, lest he should wake his mistress."

"And don't tell me she—snored."

"Only now and then, and very sweetly!"

"Can any snore be sweet?"

"That depends upon the snorer."

"However, I feel wonderfully better for my sleep. But now, since there is no possibility of my falling, or—'lurching overboard'—was it? I think you can venture to release me."

"Ay, to be sure!" said he, withdrawing his arm.

"I suppose," she murmured, straightening her bonnet, "considering how long you have been embracing my slumbering form, I ought now to be all blushing, maidenly coyness, don't you think?"

"Lord, no!" he answered. "Why should you?"

"The question is," she demanded, looking up at him with her gravely wistful gaze, "why shouldn't I and why don't I?"

"Because," answered Sam, believing he spoke merest truth, "the arm around you was simply the arm of a friend."

"Ah yes!" she murmured. "To be sure, yes. I'm glad you—did not forget."

"Of course not!" quoth Sam, with a vehemence that surprised himself. "Certainly not! As though I ever should— or could!"

"Is it so unthinkably impossible—Sam?"

"Quite!" he answered, with the same excess of fervour. "Oh—quite! This is why I ventured to buy you a small gift, a keepsake, a memento of the occasion, d'ye see——" So saying he produced, opened and presented the jewel-box, in as many moments.

Motionless and silent Andromeda gazed down upon it, then closed her eyes as if the flash and sparkle of the gems had dazzled her, while up from round, white throat to raven hair rose a painful flush; then with sudden, almost fierce gesture she thrust this gift back into his unwilling hold, saying as she did so:

"This would be too absurdly out of place on me . . . my general shabbiness would be——"

"No!" exclaimed Sam harshly.

"Yes!" she retorted, positively. "Your jewels would be ill-suited to me as Shakespeare's 'pearl in an Ethiope's ear'."

"Don't you like the thing?" growled Sam.

"Of course I do! Yes! Any woman would love it. . . . Only this woman cannot accept it."

"Then, damme, I'll throw it away——"

"No, don't do that. And, Sam, do—not—swear! Instead, let me look at it again." So, once more she sat gazing down at these sparkling gems that were no brighter than her eyes, nor so lovely as the smile that slowly curved her sensitive lips —or so thought Sam, who now ventured to explain his gift:

"The anchor, d'ye see, stands for steadfast hope and the cross for faith—truth everlasting——"

"Yes," she murmured, "but what does this heart mean?"

"Friendship!" he replied, instantly. "Unfailing loyalty, reverence and friendship. And it is in their name that I beg you'll—honour me by accepting their token."

"Then," said Andromeda, closing the box and folding it between her two hands, "in their name I will and do accept it . . . gladly and more . . . gratefully than I can tell——" Here she turned to smile up at him though her eyes brimmed with tears bright as any jewels.

"But, Andromeda, why are you crying?"

"Because at last I do, I must believe such reverent friendship is real and true. And so," said she, giving him her two clasped hands, "now with your token I take you for my friend . . . I that was so terribly, bitterly alone yet never allowed myself to realize it . . . because I have always known I must be lonely. So I shall wear your precious gift . . . round my neck . . . hidden . . . upon my heart."

Now looking down upon these hands that nestled so confidingly in his, Sam stooped and kissed them—hard, and yet so reverently that, though her lips quivered to a smile, her voice matched her tearful eyes as she enquired:

"Was that for merest friendship—Sam?"

"Yes," he answered. "Yes—indeed!"

"But mine are not kissable hands,—so rough and two broken nails!"

"Ay," said he, very gently, "these are hands glorified and made holy by unselfish devotion and service. My beloved mother had such hands—though I never thought to kiss them."

"Tell me of her, Sam."

And so, while Joshua ambled at his laziest pace, even pausing

F

when so minded to crop succulent mouthfuls of grass, Sam
with all his heart, told of his most sacred memory while with
all her heart Andromeda listened and questioned.

And never had any cart, on four wheels or two, borne a
man more glad to be alive, through countryside so altogether
lovely; though Sam, the addle-pate, still had no idea of how
or why this should be so.

CHAPTER XXVI

14, Clifford's Inn,
June 21, 1807.

MY DEAR SAM:

I begin this hurried letter with the word BEWARE writ large, since Shrig's latest despatch informs me that you and your whereabouts are now known to that Walking Evil who must contrive your destruction or perish himself. For I have spun such web and to such effect that soon he will be in close durance whence shall be no deliverance or escape. But, alas,—he is also aware of this and in fury of desperation and to avoid his own utter and final ruin will (as I fear and Shrig confidently hopes and expects) make some determined effort against your life by any and every means. Wherefore, my dear Sam, in God's name and for your own sake, do not be fool-hardy, run no avoidable risk, be constantly alert day and night and above all be guided in everything by Jasper Shrig who has lately called certain others to his aid. And this alone doubles my anxiety for you. Five weeks and two days hence this Deadly Menace, this Two-legged Evil will be removed, shut away for good and all and you in safety may enjoy your Inheritance. But in this space of time what will and how much may happen? I can but trust in the continued mercy of a Divine and all just Providence, in your own prudence and the often proved sagacity of Shrig who, in my experience, has so frequently outmatched devilish cunning by a guileful astuteness and methods as unexpected and original as himself. And here I end this most unbusiness-like but entirely friendly epistle as I began, viz: with that same ominous word—Beware!

This from your sincere friend and well-wisher,

EB. JOLIFFE.

Outstretched at ease in the shady orchard, Sam read this letter very carefully, then having pondered it awhile, went indoors to his cosy bedchamber, the gable room where stood his brass-bound, seaman's chest and battered ditty-box whence he rummaged in turn a formidable sheath-knife and belt, together with a brace of small, beautifully made pocket-pistols which he duly loaded and primed.

Thus armed, downstairs he went and taking hat and stick, stepped out into the sunny yard just as Nancy fitted a yoke upon her buxom shoulders whereby to carry two large pails of creamy milk.

"Nancy, belay!" said he. "What I mean is—pray allow me."

"La, sir," she exclaimed, returning his smiling look, "I be so used for to carry a yoke——"

"However," said Sam, yoking himself instead to these luscious burdens, "your pretty shoulders and white neck will show prettier without it."

"Nay, sir," said she, dimpling. "Oh, Mr. Felton, ee du say such things—I be all of a blush."

"Good!" he nodded. "It well becomes you, for you're even handsomer when you blush. Ay, a right seamanly eye has Tom——"

"Lud, sir, what's Tom got to do wi' my blushes?"

"Everything, Nancy, or so I thought, but now—well, I'm nowise sure——"

"Not—sure? Oh, Mr. Felton, whatever do ee mean?"

"Nay, faith, Nancy—Tom must do his own explaining, if he will or if you can wheedle the truth out of him, coax him to tell you who she is and—when ·it's to be. However, if she does or has said 'yes' I shall be first to wish him joy and so will you, I'm sure. Though she's a lucky, ay, a right fortunate girl to have won such a smart, handsome fellow as Tom—and he one of Lord Nelson's 'hearts o' the oak'——"

"What 'she', sir? Oh please, please tell me who . . . who and what like she be."

"Not I, Nancy, 'twouldn't do! Only Tom can tell you—if he will. Not that he's likely to say a word till it's all over and done."

Nancy stopped to clasp her large though shapely hands upon her splendid bosom as if to still its tempestuous surge.

"Oh, sir . . . Mr. Felton," she said, breathlessly, "du ee mean . . . oh, can it be . . . is it that . . . Betty Noakes, or Mistus Cec'ly Croft over tu Deepways Farm? Yet no, 'twouldn't be she, her be breaking her poor heart for that Mr.

Ralph—and him a Scrope! No, 'twill be that Betty . . . and if 'tis . . . Oh, Mr. Felton sir, be she the one?"

Instead of replying, Sam hastened his steps and setting down pails and yoke in the dairy, glanced at Nancy's flushed and troubled face saying, gently:

"Nancy, I must not tell you of the fortunate lass Tom means to make his wife, it wouldn't be fair. But you're clever as well as lovely, use your wits and find out from Tom himself: for no sailorman could resist such handsome lass—and especially such eyes as yours when they are gentled and lovelier for their tears as they are at this moment." Which said, away strode Sam hastily to avoid further questioning and to find Tom and presently espied him busied with a pitchfork among the fragrant ricks.

"Tom," said he, "Tom, you chuckleheaded lubber, you've been so far out in your reckoning that I've just left your lovely Nancy ready to weep all over you because she thinks you mean to wed another——"

"Eh? Another, sir? What—me?" gasped Tom. "What could ha' put such dam' fullishness into her pretty head?"

"I did, Tom! And to right good effect. So now, here's your course, d'ye see,—keep away and well to wind'ard, plying off and on, till of her own accord she bears up and ranges alongside or runs you aboard."

"Ay, sir, ay, ay!" said Tom, eagerly, his blue eyes very bright. "Ah—but," he sighed, glooming again in sudden doubt, "suppose she don't."

"Still keep the weather of her, and she will, Tom, she will."

"Ay, and if so—how then, sir?"

"Leave her to loose the first broadside. Be dumb as a dead eye till she question you. I'll lay my oath she will, like the honest-hearted, high-spirited, sweet lass she is."

"Ay, she's all that, sir! And how then?"

"Tell her the truth, of course, and then, old Victory-man, use those arms o' yours as a sailorman should, and 'twill be victory again, I'll warrant—or damme!"

"Sir," quoth Tom, in awed tone, "Mr. Felton, sir,—if I bring it off, if only I can, sir——"

" 'If' is no word for a Navy man, Tom, as well you know and have proved afore now! The word is 'when'! . . . And when you have, good luck and happiness t' both o' ye, say I, and a right prosperous wind."

Then away went Sam with his long, rolling stride, off and away in the one and only direction and wondering, like the addle-pate he was, just why the green world around him seemed more lovely than usual, the sky bluer and why the birds were singing and piping in blither chorus. . . . Ah but,—as he passed that place of gloomy trees and tangled thickets which little Jane called "The Deep Dark", he was checked suddenly, smitten by such ghastly dread as for the moment left him sick and faint,—the sound of a woman's desperate weeping . . . a breathless, wailing cry:

"Oh God . . . make me . . . brave enough——"

Then Sam leapt to action swift though silent until coming in sight of that sullen, dismal pool, he stopped again, breathing his relief in a deep, shuddering sigh.

She lay face down upon the very margin of the pool, so near indeed that her long, yellow hair was already afloat,—heedful of which, he spoke her very gently:

"It would be very cold, dear lass. And besides I hate swimming in my clothes."

She started violently and turned showing thus a face of surprising beauty though now all marred, blotched and swollen with her grief.

"Who . . . who be . . . you?" she sobbed.

"A friend—I hope. And my name is Sam, d'ye see and I——"

"Oh—go away . . . leave me alone . . . I . . . want to be . . . dead!" she gasped.

"Why so you will, someday, but not here or in that dam' pool. No man is worth such death,—no—not one! And more especially," said Sam, hazarding a guess, "such fool and villain as Ralph Scrope."

"He's neither!" she cried, sitting up to say it the fiercer.

"He's both!" said Sam, sitting down to say it the more provokingly. "Ay, he's both, and a liar besides! A worthless scoundrel—it stands to reason."

"No, he's not . . . he's not!" she panted, glaring on Sam through the tears that filled her very beautiful though grief-reddened eyes.

"Then why is he breaking your heart? Why are you here in this vile, desolate place? The fellow's a heartless rogue——"

"No!" she wailed. "His poor heart be breaking likewise, for he do love me true."

"Oh?" murmured Sam, pondering this. "Ah? Then why d'you wish for death?"

"Because he be such great and noble gentleman and I be— only me."

"Ay!" nodded Sam. "And so beautiful—when your lovely eyes and pretty nose aren't so red,—that I'm right certain you are much too good and lovely for such as he. Why d'ye love the fellow?"

"Because I do! I always have and always shall."

"Even though he deserts you and breaks your heart along with all his promises?"

"Yes, but—'tis only because he must leave me . . . to save his family from ruination!"

"Ah?" murmured Sam. "Tell me—how?"

"By marrying a very rich lady . . . and I'm only a farmer's daughter to . . . milk and churn, and bake and brew . . . though I've tried to speak and act like a lady should . . . for to be his . . . lady wife. But I . . . haven't any money. . . . So that's why cruel Fate compels my poor Ralph to break my loving heart . . ."

"Lord!" exclaimed Sam, shaking his head in helpless manner. "Whoever heard the like o' this?"

"We've loved each other," she continued as if now her sorrow found some relief in speech, "ever since we were boy and girl . . . and with every year my love grew . . . and so 'tis I know I'll have to go on loving him till I die."

"Such love," murmured Sam, "is perfectly unreasonable, very pitiful, but b'George,—altogether wonderful."

"And so," she continued, heeding only her own grief, "this is why I came here to end it all . . . because it is all so hopeless! But when I saw the pool . . . so still and dreadful dark . . . I was afraid and . . . couldn't."

"Good!" nodded Sam.

"Though maybe," she whispered, gazing down into these same dark waters and shivering, "maybe . . . someday I shall be . . . braver."

"No!" said Sam. "Oh, no! If you can love such fellow so wonderfully, you must have the fellow. We'll see what can be done about it——"

"Ah—what, what do you mean by 'have him'?"

"Marrying him, of course."

"Ah, but how . . . how can I?" she wailed, beginning to sob again.

"In the usual way," answered Sam, "parson, ring and so on. Now swab your tears,—dry those pretty eyes—or shall I?"

"Nay but . . . who be—who are you?"

"Your friend, Sam. So take my handkerchief, clean this morning, and dry your eyes, Cecily. You are Cecily Croft, aren't you?"

"Yes," she answered, taking the handkerchief, but gazing at Sam in growing wonder, "yet how du ee—do you know my name?"

"Put it down to friendship, Cecily. For Friendship, d'ye see, especially mine, can and shall work wonders, if you'll do your part."

"Oh, but what—what must I do?"

"Be patient, have faith in yourself and the future, never say die and soon or late you shall be your beloved Ralph's lady wife." Sam uttered these words in tone of such convincing sincerity and with look of such serene assurance, such absolute certainty that Cecily started to her knees, looking at him above hands clasped as if in prayer.

"Oh," she whispered, "if only this could come true!"

"It shall!" he nodded. But now, once again, tears blinded her.

"Ah, no—no!" she wailed, bowing golden head and cowering in hopeless misery. " 'Tis past my hope . . . and you . . . you be only . . . making mock o' me."

"Not I, lass! No, damme! Do I seem the sort of animal to mock any woman's grief? Sit up—take a good look at this figurehead,—this face o' mine! Do I look such vile brute?"

Obediently she raised her lovely head, shook it miserably and sobbed:

"No . . . no, you don't. But how . . . oh, how ever can I . . . how dare I hope for . . . or believe such joy when I do know 'tis so impossible? Oh, how can I?"

"Because," he answered, with his flashing smile, "in this old world there's nothing impossible to our Navy, and I'm a sailorman, d'ye see! So all shall come right for you soon or late,—it stands to reason."

"Oh, but—how?" she questioned, with a new eagerness and (hopeful sign) beginning to pay attention to her beautiful, corn-coloured hair, "I don't understand you."

"Of course you don't," he answered, with another cheery grin, "you don't have to. Your part will be to—work instead of weep, hope instead of despair, never say die or even think of it, say your prayers and trust to the Lord and the Navy and Friendship. So, what d'ye say?"

" 'Deed I don't know what to say or think," she sighed,—but beginning to braid her lustrous hair, "you talk so strange and—wild! I seem like I were in some dream."

"Ay, and in dreams all things are possible! So dream on, lass, till Friendship makes your dream a reality and you wake to find 'tis true."

"Oh, but," sighed she, "my Ralph be gentleman o' The Quality, like I tell you, and must wed money, and I be only——"

"Your own beautiful self," nodded Sam, "a loveliness far too good for your Ralph,—ay, a woman any man would be right proud to wed, money or no! There'll be plenty will envy your Ralph when he marries you."

"Marries . . . me?" she repeated breathlessly.

"Ay, to be sure!" quoth Sam and with the utmost conviction. "And when you are his wife I'm pretty certain you'll be his salvation also, if anyone can save the fellow,—I believe you'll raise him, lift him up to be worthy, almost, of your sweet lovely self." Her busy hands fell idle, her long-lashed eyes gazed upwards as if, for the moment, they looked upon a rapture ineffable.

"If I only could!" she whispered. "Oh, God, most merciful, if only I could. . . ." Then she drew a long, shuddering breath, crowned herself with the shining coronet of her hair and rose.

"I think," said she, looking on Sam now as if noticing him for the first time, "you must be Captain Harlow's friend back along with him from the wars and staying at Willowmead. And so now, sir, I be—I am—trying to thank you for doing your best to comfort me in—in my black hour. For though you talked a lot of fullishness, I know 'twas well meant."

"It was, Cecily, it is! And my name's Sam. And now you are going straight home, I hope."

"No. My home went when father died. So I'm going back to Uncle Roger's farm to help to milk his cows, and churn and brew and bake, same like as usual."

"However," answered Sam, as they went on side by side,

"even such hard work is better than lying dead—back there in that hellish pool?"

"I wonder?" she murmured.

Thus, presently they came up from that place of gloom, out into the pure, blessed sunlight. And here Sam halted to enquire:

"I suppose you don't believe in fairies any more, Cecily?"

"No," she sighed, "not since I were a child—and happy."

"But do you believe in prayer?"

"Yes . . . I suppose so . . . of course," she faltered, "though I've prayed and I've prayed but all to no purpose."

"Only because you haven't prayed quite long enough. So keep at it and someday sure as a gun, I shall salute you like this, hat in hand saying: 'Your humble servant, madam. Good day and God bless you, my Lady Scrope!'"

And so, having bowed with a flourish, Sam turned and strode away, leaving Cecily gazing after him wide-eyed but with the dawn of a smile upon her lips.

Sam also was smiling as he strode these sunny meads (always in the one and only direction) his grey eyes alight with such purpose that presently he began whistling softly an old sea-chanty as he meditated how best and soonest to effect this same purpose. On he went and in such profound abstraction that he had passed little Jane's 'Chanted Forest quite un-noticed when he halted again, arrested by a sound of all sounds most unexpected in such place—the high, sweet notes of a fiddle with the sweeping chords of a harp; but this, as he quickly realized, a fiddle played as he had never heard before, —an instrument that sang in joyous triumph, that laughed awhile then was hushed to wailing supplication, a murmurous, sobbing melody of heartbreak and despair, rising anew but swelling now to fiercer, wilder strain until the very air seemed to throb with diabolic scream of hate, of vengeance—changing, all at once, to a trill of ecstasy that sank and was lost in the deep, sweet chords of the harp.

"Glorious. . . . Oh . . . wonderful!" sighed Andromeda.

"Mag-nificent!" cried Mr. Verinder.

"Good morning!" said Sam.

CHAPTER XXVII

TELLS, AMONG OTHER MATTERS, OF A STEAK AND KIDNEY PUDDING

INTO Sam's ready hand the dog Esau thrust his shaggy head, though his mistress, standing tall and stately, uttered no word of greeting; wherefore Sam looked grim as he demanded:

"Why did they, your Uncle and that Jennings fellow sheer off at sight o' me, Andromeda?"

"Well," she answered, resentfully, "perhaps because you made it so very evident that you cannot and do not appreciate great music."

"But I do,—especially when played so very well."

"Then you showed your appreciation very strangely!"

"However," growled Sam, "I can enjoy the fiddle without adoring the fiddler or looking at him with eyes of such confounded worship."

"Pray—what are you—suggesting?"

"I mean that a fellow is no better because he scrapes a fiddle pretty well."

" 'Pretty well'!" she repeated, scornfully and turned away with a hopeless gesture. "If you had the faintest conception of music you would know that Mr. Jennings is not only a wonderful composer but a most brilliant . . . an exceptionally great violinist,—a master——"

"Well, I prefer your dog!" quoth Sam, fondling Esau's shaggy head. "He at least is glad to see me and was so kind to give me welcome."

"Being—only a dog!" she retorted.

"Was that worthy of you, Andromeda, or just to your dog?"

"No!" she admitted. "For I do believe my Esau has more taste for glorious music than Mr. Felton,—at least he did not howl!"

"Nor I, as I remember."

"No, you merely gloomed and scowled,—black as a thundercloud! You also growled."

"Maybe I did—while you gazed on that Jennings fellow as if you longed to devour him—fiddle and all!"

"A hatefully repulsive suggestion!"

"Ay—like the cove himself!"

"That is a hideously vulgar word."

"And suits him."

"Mr. Felton, I will bid you 'Good morning'——"

"And time too!" said Sam, removing his hat with a flourish. "Good morning t'you, marm, your humble servant! And now, Andromeda, come down from aloft,—be your own sweet self, let's enjoy each other's friendship and talk as friends should."

"I do—not feel at all friendly this morning."

"Nor look it!" he agreed. "However, I'll put up with all that just because you're Andromeda and may presently bless me with a smile or kinder looks, as a friend—Lord!" he exclaimed, for they had come within sight of her tent and he halted to view it with the utmost disapproval:

"Lord love me!" Sam repeated.

"It is to be hoped so!" she retorted. "And He may, of course, being all merciful! But why call on the Deity—and so suddenly?"

"That tent-thing of yours! It's a menace! A sudden squall, or mere cap-full o' wind and it would carry away."

"Carry what away?"

"Itself—and you along with it."

"It never has yet, so why should it?"

"First of all—the stays are rotten."

"If you mean the guy-ropes, they are much stronger than they appear."

"And those bits o' stick instead o' proper pegs! They'd never hold——"

"But they do hold, and very well—as you see!"

"Only because there's no wind to strain 'em. Should it blow hard and the confounded thing came down on you with a run''twould half stifle you before you could crawl free. So why not have proper pegs?"

"Because they were all lost ages ago."

"Why then," said Sam, drawing his broad-bladed seaman's knife and testing its keen edge, "though I can't scrape catgut I can shape you some proper pegs."

"Pray do not trouble yourself, Mr. Felton."

"Andromeda, don't be silly,—so dam' statuesque and aloof."

"Mr. Felton, I refuse to be sworn at!"

"Then don't waste your dignity on me, dear lass."

"I also object strongly to your—your maritime familiarity."

Sam chuckled; gave a sailorly hitch to his belt fore and aft, executed the first steps of a hornpipe, struck an attitude and exclaimed in tone extremely hoarse and nautical:

"Marm, you may keel-haul me if you ain't taken me all aback! I'm shivering in the wind's eye, falling off and on and drifting to loo'ard! Raked fore and aft I am by that theer 'maritime familiarity' broadside o' yourn!"

"Don't be so ridiculous," said she, frowning still but with the ghost of a dimple beside her ruddy lip.

"Andromeda," he rejoined, suddenly grave, "I'd do or give a great deal to bring laughter to that lovely mouth of yours and see happiness in your eyes."

"Oh? Why?" she demanded. "Why ever trouble about me? Why are you here now?"

"All in the way of friendship!" he replied.

"I see! Of course!" she nodded. "Though you think I have—a 'lovely mouth'!"

"I do! I do indeed. I were blind else. And you know it, too, of course."

"I know it serves me to eat with. And this reminds me!"

"Of what?"

"Steak and kidney pudding! I promised Uncle Arthur and it is a favourite dish of his."

"And no wonder!" quoth Sam. "Where is he, by the way, and that—that Jennings blo—fellow?"

"Talking music together somewhere, you may be sure. And now I think you had better go, I'm going to be busy."

"Good!" exclaimed Sam, cheerily. "So am I, d'ye see. While you're making your duff and so on, I'll get busy with your tent pegs."

"That great knife of yours looks horridly sharp."

"Ay, it is. But a saw would be useful, if you have one, though I suppose that's too much to expect."

"Of course I have a saw," said she, indignantly, "quite a large one! You will find it with my other tools in the box over there."

And true enough, amid a jumble of rusty pliers, pincers, shaftless hammers and jagged chisels, Sam extracted that which had once been a saw; he shook his head at it, sighed over it and enquired, gently:

"Do you use this for cutting through bolts and nails, Andromeda?"

"Of course not!" she replied, tying herself into a large apron, "I never do except when they get in the way. I sometimes have to saw up boxes for kindling, in wet weather, and they are such naily things."

"You dear soul!" he murmured and so tenderly that she turned to frown at him, saying—though not very angrily:

"I believe you are—daring to—pity me."

"No, I'm picturing you on a damp, chilly morning, turning out to hack away with this poor, blunt old saw, to light a fire with your only dry kindling—for my lord's breakfast."

"And my own! So, I'll not be pitied,—do you hear?"

"Ay, ay, Cap'n!" said he, saluting her with the rusty saw as if it had been a cutlass; then away he went in quest of wood suitable for his pegs and presently returned with a stout sapling and in time to prevent her dragging a table from the tent.

"Where will you have it?" he enquired, picking it up.

"There, in shade of the big tree. Though I can manage quite well alone."

"I know you can—and do!" said he, rather grimly. "But just at present you are not alone, and while I'm about you shall neither haul, heave nor hoist, d'ye see. Is that understood?"

"Ay, ay, Captain!" she mocked, saluting him with the rolling-pin.

"Very good!" said Sam, and began cutting his sapling into precise lengths with the almost toothless saw while Andromeda, rolling up her sleeves, commenced to make and knead her dough.

The saw whose teeth were so very blunt and gappy, required and received dexterous manipulation, yet long before it had been coaxed to successful performance, Sam was perfectly certain he had never seen arms so deliciously round and smooth, their dazzling whiteness the more apparent because of sun-browned wrists and hands,—nor elbows so bewitchingly dimpled. . . .

All this, Sam contrived to notice while Andromeda, working her dough with both slim fists, was as truly aware of him, his lithe strength, the balanced ease of his every movement, his grim features which yet could soften to such unexpected gentleness that, with his wide-set, grey eyes and shapely mouth, made him quite handsome—or almost.

Thus though both were apparently intent upon their work, each was supremely aware of the other.

The saw having been persuaded to do its duty, Sam now took his knife and seated with his back against the tree and legs crossed sailor-fashion, began to shape and trim the first peg with quick, sure hand. And now as they wrought, they talked—thus:

SHE: That knife looks horribly sharp!

HE: Yes, a knife should be.

SHE: I've heard sailors are handy men.

HE: They have to be.

SHE: However, you'll cut yourself if you don't watch your work instead of staring at me—with such odious slyness.

HE (*With flashing grin*): Not slyness, Andromeda.

SHE: Yes, a detestable furtiveness.

HE: No, 'askance' is the word. I merely venture to glance up at you now and then sideways or a-jee.

SHE: Just because my arms are bare!

HE: No. Just because they are yours.

SHE: Whatever is the difference?

HE: That they belong to you and no other woman, of course. So I thank the Lord for their beauty.

SHE: You are extremely personal.

HE: Certainly I am, and also perfectly sincere, and you too, I hope. So let's go on being personal—tell me now of myself—or the sort of fellow you think I am.

SHE: I won't be so cruel.

HE: Ah well, I asked for that,—and got it because I admired your arms and was honest enough to say so, eh, Andromeda? What more d'ye think?

SHE: That you are supremely—impertinent.

HE: Yet very meek and humble,—and yourself so proud and fierce—and in such naughty temper! Your cheeks flushed and eyes so bright! B'George, anger suits you, for your mouth could never be anything but its lovely self——

SHE: Are you trying to offend me?

HE: You know I'm not.

SHE: Then cease your odious personalities! (*Here she turns her back on him with movement that is almost a flounce.*)

HE: Very well, Miss Andromeda. And may I humbly suggest a sprinkle of salt?

SHE (*Glancing down at him over her shoulder*): Salt? Whatever do you mean now?

HE: (*Becoming gruff jack tar*): In your duff, lady. 'Twill sweeten it ye'll find.

SHE: What do you know of such things?

HE: Plenty, missis. I were ship's cook years ago.

SHE: Ah—indeed!

HE: Ay. And don't look s' scornful, lady, for I were a mighty good 'un, d'ye see. Bake or boil, stoo or fry, there was few to ekal Sammy! And as for puddens, you should ha' tasted my spotted dog.

SHE (*Shuddering with extreme violence*): Repulsive! I feel unwell at the mere suggestion.

HE: Then besides, marm, I could do more wi' a good, fat lump o' pickled pork than most——

SHE: Horrible! If I must endure your company do—not talk of such utterly revolting things—or like a vulgar sailor.

HE: But these revolting things are what poor sailormen must eat or starve,—and I am a vulgar sailor.

SHE: Well, if you must talk—speak as you usually do.

HE: Why, so I will—if instead of showing me your back, which I'll own is very shapely and perfect as feminine back should be, yet I——

SHE (*Turning in sudden appeal*): Oh, Sam, why are you trying to anger and annoy me?

HE (*Speaking in tone suddenly gentle as his look*): My dear, for this little while you haven't thought of your anxieties,—I've made you even forget that Uncle of yours, haven't I?

SHE (*Softly*): Yes, you have.

HE: Because, Andromeda, I'd do much, very much—anything to make you a little happier. You believe this, don't you?

SHE (*More softly*): Yes.

HE: I hope we are going to be—closer, better friends than ever, because very soon I shall be . . . pretty lonely, ay, I shall so! For in a week's time my friend Ned, Captain Harlow will marry his Kate.

SHE (*Sighing*): I hope they will be very happy.

HE (*Rather bitterly*): Oh, they will! So happy they won't
want me cruising in their waters. That's the worst o'
marriage, it so often casts off Friendship and sends it adrift.
So don't you go marrying anyone, Andromeda.

SHE (*Beginning to line a basin with dough*): I never shall—
never.

HE (*Fervently*): Good! Neither shall I.

SHE: Why not?

HE: Because having made two fool attempts I shall never
make another—not I. Besides, should this threat of invasion continue I shall ship myself off to fight the mounseers.

SHE: So should I,—were I a man.

Here she began cutting up the steak, but made such a
business of it that Sam rose and taking the knife from her
(very gently to be sure) shook his head at it, saying:

"As I thought—blunt as my finger! Use my knife while I
find a stone and put an edge on this."

So Andromeda took the keen, glittering blade and found
such ease in its usage that Sam promptly gave it to her, showing how she must wear it in its sheath belted around her
slender waist.

The pudding was duly tied up and set to do its best in the
black pot above the fire; then while Sam went on with his
peg-making, Andromeda, throned upon a stool nearby, prepared the vegetables. . . . And now they worked and talked
in an ever-growing intimacy and understanding.

"Have you met Kate Ford?" he enquired.

"No, but I have seen her frequently at Lewes Market. She
is a splendidly handsome creature."

"Ay, she's all that. Ned's a mighty lucky fellow—and
deserves to be."

"Have you many friends, Sam?"

"I had, but most of 'em got killed, one way or another
ashore or afloat. So to-day my only real friend is Ned, Lord
love him."

"No lady friends, Sam?"

"Only one—with golden eyes that ought to laugh yet never
do."

"Perhaps they can't," she sighed, "or don't know how."

"Then I'll try to learn 'em. For, d'ye see, no laugh is
real unless it somehow gets into the eyes."

"I fear I am a very depressing person, Sam."

"No, for there's a dimple in your cheek sometimes, and that mouth of yours was made for laughter and——" Sam closed his lips on the word, whereupon she, of course, instantly demanded:

"What, Sam?"

"Smiles," he answered. Here she glanced up from the potato she was peeling, and with smile so unexpected, so altogether lovely and dazzling that Sam very nearly cut himself.

"You were going to say 'kisses', weren't you?"

"Yes," he admitted.

"And very silly, very foolish of you, Sam,—if you want my friendship."

"Oh?" he murmured. "Ah? Why?"

"Because my kisses would destroy friendship—utterly and forever."

"How?" he enquired. "Why? Just what do you mean?"

"Think and find out!" said she, and went on peeling the potato. And when Sam had chipped and pondered awhile, he changed the subject by enquiring:

"Do you happen to know Cecily Croft?"

"Quite well, why?"

"What sort of person is she?"

"A fool, of course, but a very beautiful one. She is sweet and good and gentle, but a fool because she is wasting herself on that abomination called Ralph Scrope."

"Ay, she told me some such——"

"Oh! Indeed!" exclaimed Andromeda, and dropped a potato. "Do you know her so well?"

"I met her for the first time this morning on my way here."

"I see!" murmured Andromeda, reaching down for the errant vegetable. "Well, don't you think she is a—supremely beautiful girl?"

"Ay, I do indeed."

"With—the most glorious hair?"

"Yes, like ripe corn."

"And you admire that colour, of course?"

"Yes, though I prefer black."

"You feel compelled to say that, I suppose?"

"I do, for d'ye see truth compels."

"Are you so extremely truthful—always?"

"I hope so,—except when truth is like to hurt."

"Yes, and how then?"

"Why then I pipe down, stow my jaw-tackle and hold my tongue."

"Are you going to hold it now?"

"No,—why should I?"

"Then tell me how Cecily came to be so confiding to you—a stranger?"

"First, do you like her, Andromeda, are you her friend?"

"Yes, she saved my life."

"Did she, by George?"

"No, by her strong arms—and they are as 'round and white' as mine, please understand."

"Tell me about it."

"It was that day I brought our little Jane up from death in that awful pool. I am a strong swimmer but the horrid weeds caught and held me down . . . there in the frightful dark . . . grasped and clutched me like slimy hands and arms. . . . It was Cecily who lifted me half dead from that ghastly water at last."

"Hurrah for Cecily! And it was by that same accursed pool I met her this morning, crying her eyes out and so near death that her long hair was awash."

"That horrible place!" gasped Andromeda. "Oh, my poor, poor Cecily! There is something very—terrible about that pool!"

"So I think," Sam agreed. "'Tis an evil place. should be blotted out, and shall be—someday, and pretty soon, maybe——"

"Yes, Sam. Too many have died there in the past. . . . And now—poor, distraught Cecily! Do you think she too——?"

"Only the Lord knows that."

"Ah," whispered Andromeda, shivering, "love can be very frightful . . . such an agony . . . to drive one so sweetly simple, so purely good as Cecily to even think of death so dreadful and for such brute beast as Ralph Scrope! Love can be the bitterest curse!"

"Too true!" nodded Sam. "And yet the holiest blessing and comfort also, my dear,—for such happy ones as Ned and Kate. As for Cecily—her love is so deep, so true and marvellous that I can only wonder and feel—well—humble and almost envious of such a love."

"Oh! Why?"

"By the glorious unreason and beautiful folly of it. For in spite of everything she adores the dam' fellow still! Told me he was only breaking her heart because 'twas his duty to save his family from ruin and that she'd love him till she died, ay—and that he was breaking his own heart, too."

"Impossible!" exclaimed Andromeda, scornfully. "Such abhorrent wretch has no heart to break!"

"I wonder?" queried Sam.

"Good gracious,—why?"

"That time we saw the fellow gallop past us in the lane his dusty face was all streaked with tears,—and I'm hoping they were for Cecily."

"Why ever should you?"

"Because d'ye see, I promised she shall wed the fellow,—ay, and within the year!" Here, Andromeda gazed at Sam in such speechless amazement that he enquired:

"What's so wonderful?"

"Not wonderful!" she retorted, indignantly. "Only wickedly foolish and cruel. You told her that—that absurd nonsense merely to soothe and comfort her, I suppose?"

"Of course! And it acted like a charm."

"An evil charm that can only work greater misery and evil later on, as you must know."

"But I don't. Why should it?"

"Because your easy promise is quite beyond your power to fulfil! You know it is all quite, quite impossible. So why deceive the poor soul with false hopes?"

"Not false but sincerely true, my dear——"

"I am not your dear. And it was a cruelly impossible promise! So why make it?"

"Well, let's say because I am a seaman."

"What on earth has that to do with it?"

"Everything! For d'ye see my—Andromeda, seamen are always doing the impossible and always will——"

"Oh, Sam, what preposterous nonsense! Seamen are only human, the poor men often drown and their great ships are wrecked because it is impossible to save them——"

"No! Because they are summoned aloft by the Lord High Admiral of us all."

"Sam, you are evading the question."

"However," said he, shaping the last peg, "I believe nothing is impossible until we make it so. And I'm so sure Cecily shall wed her confounded Ralph that I'm ready to lay you a wager on it. Let's say—a new collar for Esau here, bless his shaggy hide,—to one of your oldest shoes." At this she glanced up in a surprise made utterly delightful by the swift, conscious flush that could soften the too-austere beauty of her too such shy and gentle loveliness,—or so thought Sam, as she exclaimed, though very tenderly:

"How absurd! What ever could you do with such a thing —supposing you won?"

"Treasure it!" he answered, adding promptly: "As a token of friendship—and patient service. So, what do you say?"

"No, of course not! First, because my shoes are never too old until they fall to pieces and then I burn them or throw them away. And secondly, because when not going to town, I usually wear things like these, as I'm sure you have noticed, but—look again!" And she thrust out a slender foot and ankle tied into such thick-soled, clumsy boot that Sam frowned, demanding:

"Why wear such things?"

"To keep out the early morning dew. I usually change them later, but to-day I forgot because of Mr. Jennings' magnificent playing. Why do you so dislike the poor man?"

"Well," enquired Sam, "why does Esau? He and I are of the same mind. Eh, old lad?" said he, patting the great animal who lay couched beside him. "Well, your pegs are finished, Andromeda."

"And I'm very grateful, Sam."

"Then come and help me to fix 'em."

"I'm afraid the hammer is broken."

"Only needs a new shaft. I'll make one."

"The axe is over there."

"Ay, and blunter than your knife. I'll sharpen it presently."

"You have made these pegs quite—beautifully."

"Because they are for you. To-morrow I'll rig new stays——" At this moment a distant church clock struck the hour.

"Twelve!" gasped Andromeda. "Twelve o'clock—already!"

"Am-azing!" exclaimed Sam, driving the last peg.

"And those vegetables ought to be on!"

"Well, let's put them on!" quoth Sam; which done, he set

to work sharpening the axe with a stone from the brook that made a soft rippling nearby like elfin laughter, while Andromeda, seated upon the stool again, now busied herself with needle and thimble. And after she had stitched and he had ground awhile in silent though eloquent communion, Sam enquired:

"Are you never idle?"

"Yes, often. Why?"

"I can hardly believe it."

"Oh, but I am. Sometimes I sit doing nothing for hours."

"Then do it now—for half-an-hour. Give those hard-worked hands a rest."

"When I have mended these stockings."

"Such silken splendours!" said Sam.

"Yes, they are lovely."

"Your uncle's, of course."

"Yes, he can't bear anything coarse or common."

"Though others must."

"If by 'others' you mean me, pray understand that I also wear silk—sometimes, though I prefer worsted or wool to work in."

"Does he ever work,—ever try to help you?"

"He does his best."

"Does he ever turn those soft, white hands of his to anything besides his confounded harp and paint-brush?"

"Oh yes—sometimes. But why should he when I am only too glad to do anything—all I can for him?"

"Precisely! You are his too-willing slave and he accepts all your ceaseless labour as his due because he is a wilful do-nothing, a selfish, domineering autocrat,—a tyrant who is killing you in his service, stealing your youth, spoiling your life and will leave you desolate at last . . ."

"Have you done?" she enquired gently when Sam paused for breath.

"No, I could go on and——"

"Then please don't, it would be of no avail, I must and shall live for and serve him so long as he needs me no matter what the end may be."

"Ha!" growled Sam, looking up at her beneath close-knit brows. "So you will sacrifice yourself because he saved you—his own sister's child—from poverty, which was no more than act of common decency to his own flesh and blood! So why make a kind of saint of him, why glorify him for being human and doing no more than his duty? Ay, and to one of his own family! Any man worth the name would have done as much."

Andromeda's busy needle was suddenly stilled, and for a moment she sat as if lost in unhappy reflection: when at last she spoke, it was unwillingly and with an effort:

"Then I must tell you . . . how Uncle Arthur not only saved my young mind from . . . ruinous evil but my childish body also. . . . I can never describe all the sordid shame and misery I endured after my poor father's death. . . . But I was nearly fourteen and had become the wretched drudge of a cruel mistress and . . . a man so unspeakably vile that . . . at last . . . one day . . . he——" The words died on her quivering lip, her eyes widening to such remembered horror that Sam instinctively cowered, waiting in sickening apprehension of what he must hear:

"Andromeda——?" he said, at last; and in this one word, harshly whispered, such agony of dread that instinctively she reached out her hand to comfort him, saying and more tenderly than he had ever heard:

"Dear Sam! No! God sent my salvation—it was then Uncle Arthur found me at last! And when he had nearly killed the man, he bore me away to his loving care—a great, glad life at last. He saved me from living death and gave me instead all the best and noblest of life. . . . So to-day, in his weakness, I remember him for the wonderful man he was and shall love him, watch over and serve him—to the end. So now, Sam, you understand, don't you?"

"Yes," he answered, mournfully. "Yes, I understand."

"Well now—don't look such a woeful Sam,—come and help me to dish up our dinner."

"Ours?" he enquired.

"If you will honour our simple board, Mr. Felton, sir."

"Ay, but—what of Mr. Verinder? I'm pretty sure he don't like me, d'ye see——"

"He will welcome you, of course, like the gracious gentleman he is." At this moment Esau cocked his ears and wagged stumpy tail, for, as if conjured up by mention of his name, Mr. Verinder appeared, advancing with his short, tripping stride.

"Ah, Mr. Felton," said he, bowing hat in hand, "do I see you yet?"

"Ay, sir," answered Sam, returning this salute rather awkwardly, "though I was about to bear up and stand away,—go, d'ye see, sir."

"That is well, Mr. Felton, that is very well, for I am not well, indeed no! Meda, my love, I think I will lie down a while."

"But, Uncle, the steak-pudding! See, it is all ready——"

"There are kidneys also, I trust?"

"Of course, with onions and seasoned as you like it——"

"Then you may bear us a small portion to the caravan, child,—though we doubt if we can touch a morsel,—but we will attempt it—for your sake, Meda love. Pray do not tarry. . . . Good morning, Mr. Felton, or—should I say—Good-bye?" Uttering which, Mr. Verinder turned and tripped away to his caravan.

"Now I wonder," sighed Andromeda, "what can have upset him,—he looked dreadfully pale."

"However," said Sam, rather grimly, "it is just as well you didn't forget the kidneys! Well,—now, Andromeda, 'a dieu' as the mounseers say, but—I shall see you to-morrow."

"To-morrow," she repeated, glancing towards the caravan with look almost apprehensive, and Sam frowned to see the trouble was back in her eyes again. "No—not to-morrow," she sighed.

"Ah?" exclaimed Sam, also glancing towards the caravan. "Well, if not to-morrow—when?"

"I . . . I'm not sure," she answered in voice troubled as her look, "I'll send you word by Cecily Croft."

"Then please," said Sam, baring head in farewell, "please let it be soon and I hope . . . no, tell me you'll be glad to see me—a little."

"Yes," she answered, giving him her hand, "yes, I shall be—very glad."

CHAPTER XXVIII

IN WHICH IS MENTION OF A MOTHER AND SON

VERY thoughtful was Sam as he trudged homewards, indeed so profoundly abstracted that he went astray and became lost in a maze of field-paths, cart-tracks and narrow lanes; but guiding himself with sailorly instinct, came out at last upon an unfamiliar road shut in by trees and tall hedges. Therefore he paused to take his bearings and thus espied the thatched roof of a cottage, a small, wicket gate and a motionless woman who leaned across it, peering intently away from him along this shady road. So thither went Sam, his feet soundless upon the grass bordering this road, while the woman continued to gaze away with the same fixed and motionless intensity. Now as he approached thus silently, he became aware of two things,—that this slender, graceful woman was no rustic cottage-body, and that there was something almost dreadful in her strained attitude and utter stillness . . . a fearful, an agonized expectancy.

He was close enough for speech, when, as if warned by some sense other than hearing, she started violently, turned and shrank away, showing a face, haggard though still beautiful, framed in grey hair and lit by dark eyes wide in such swift terror that Sam halted amazed beyond words, and before he could find utterance, she spoke in dreadful, gasping voice:

"He is . . . not . . . here! I tell you . . . he is not . . . here! Why is he being . . . spied upon? Why do you . . . follow him?"

"Madam," Sam replied, gently as he might, "I've no idea what you mean. But don't, pray don't be so alarmed."

"But, he told me," she whispered, "of . . . eyes that watched . . . through the leaves, footsteps that . . . creep——"

"My poor soul," quoth Sam, strangely moved by the agony in her voice and look, "Lord love you now, here is nothing to dread ye. I'm but a stranger who has lost his way, d'ye see, off my course and beg to ask if you can direct me to Willowmead Farm."

"Oh—oh, then, I—I crave your pardon," she said, in the same nervous, breathless manner. "I . . . I am not well . . . my nerves . . . pray forgive me. Yes, this road will take you there . . . to Willowmead, though a quicker way is by the field path . . . the lane opposite . . . across the stile to your left."

"Thank you, lady," quoth Sam, hat in hand, "I'm mighty sorry I so frightened you . . . and if you are in any trouble, say the word and I'll be glad to do my best——"

"No—no!" she answered hurriedly. "Thank you—no! And your way is—down the lane you see opposite and over the stile to your left."

So thither went Sam, and more thoughtful than ever. He had crossed the stile and gone but a short distance when again he stood arrested, this time by the sound of hasty, strangely uneven footsteps upon the road, feet that strode apace and broke frequently into a stumbling run. Now peering through the tall screening hedge beside him, he saw this hurrying pedestrian was Mr. Jennings; the lady had seen also, for throwing open the wicket gate, she sped to clasp and welcome him, but—sinking to his knees he buried his face in her gown, half stifling his wailing, desolate cry:

"Oh, Mother . . . beloved . . . I'm lost again in the dreadful dark! Oh, Mother, now . . . you are threatened . . . homeless . . . destitute——"

"Eustace," she answered, stooping to lift and comfort him, "my darling, never mind! He can never hurt me any more, never again! Come you indoors, my dear one, music shall make us forget awhile . . . I have schemed an accompaniment to your Rondo, come let us try it over, my own darling —come!" So saying, tender mother led grievous son away into the little cottage.

Thus, gazing wistfully after them, Sam must needs remember that sweetly gentle woman who, despite poverty and hardship having mothered him so wonderfully, had died worn out and, of course, too soon! And thinking of all he might now have done for her, the cottage chimney, thatched roof and little wicket gate grew suddenly all blurred upon his sight. . . .

Thus, when a hand touched him and, starting, he beheld Mr. Shrig, Sam forthwith cursed and damned his eyes the more fervently because of the tears that were half-blinding his own.

"And nobody," said Mr. Shrig, placidly, "has ever cursed me more fluent and hearty! But talking o' mothers, pal Sam, these yere eyes o' mine as you've damned so eloquent, never see my own ma to remember, yet if I could pick me a mother —yonder she goes along o' Number Two."

"Ay," nodded Sam, as they went on together, "a lovely person, Jasper, though very sad and—strangely fearful."

"'Sorrer' is often another name for 'mother', pal . . . and there's more o' same a-coming yonder! And talking o' sorrer and grief nat'rally brings us to steak and kidney pudden."

"Eh?" exclaimed Sam, halting in surprise. "Why what the devil——"

"No, pudden, pal, coupled vith the name o' Mr. A. Werinder as has lately took sich a werry strong awersion agin you b'reason o' Number Two and all because of a certain young female party vith a crack-jaw name as I'll call Miss A, same as kips or dosses in a tent——"

"Avast, Jasper! Haul your wind and speak plain! Just what are you trying to tell me?"

"That you are raising more windictiveness agin yourself, ar,—you're driving Number Two frantic and ditter Mr. Werinder and my anxiety is rose according."

"How so, Jasper?"

"Along o' you making love to Miss A, aforesaid——"

"Making love? Who? Me?" gasped Sam, in fury of indignation that swept him above all mere rules of grammar.

"Ar,—you, pal."

"What dam' nonsense! Who says so?"

"Seeing's believing."

"Believing what?"

"Sir and Sam, if a young cove—'specially a sailorman, looks at a young fe-male party as if he could eat or as you might say, de-wour her, it argufies love on his part. And if aforementioned young fe-male looks at him as if she yearned to run into his arms and be de-woured or give him the chance thereof, it argufies love on her part. Vich I therefore repeats seeing's believing."

"Now damme!" exclaimed Sam. "This means you've been prying on us,—a spy, eh?"

"No, sir, 'tis others is the spies. I'm your own partickler hark-angel in top-boots to see, according to Holy Writ, as

you don't dash your stamper agin a rock neether run yourself into any kind o' danger. And there y'are!"

"Hell!" exclaimed Sam, striding on again. "Are you
always on my heels?"

"Not always,—no, that ain't hardly to be expected, but I
do my best, as in dooty bound."

"This is perfectly damnable!"

"It is!" said Mr. Shrig with fervour. "Damnable's the
vord, pal, for dog bite me if you ain't more leery-skittish
than any vill-o'-the-visp, risking your precious carkiss here
and theer, if not afoot, then in a cart along o' that young
fe-male party aforesaid——"

"Lord love me!" groaned Sam, with hopeless gesture.
"This is sheer, dev'lish persecution! Ay, b'gad, the whole
countryside must be full o' your spies, for Mr. Joliffe writes
you have called others to help you."

"Ar!" sighed Mr. Shrig. "But I called in wain! For
because o' this hot weather, Crime in London and Wiciousness in general has growed that rampagious that The Law
has all its limbs occupied com-plete. So to-day here's only
self, Dan'l and my Gimblet to prewent you being measured
untimely for a vooden overcoat. Now if you ax me about
said Gimblet——"

"I don't!" quoth Sam, lengthening his stride.

"Then," said Mr. Shrig, following suit, "I'd better tell
ye all about the same, for your own sake hereafter. Are
y' listening?"

"Ay, ay, since I must."

"Then, pal, my Gimblet is a London street arab, a little
orphan vaif as I've took under my ving to eddicate up to
The Law and sich sharp young shaver that I've named him
Gimblet and for oo's be-hoof I now take partickler care vith
my h-aitches! A werry bright lad rising fifteen or thereabouts for nobody can't be sure to a year or so, and you'd
better look him over so as you'll know him again." Here,
Mr. Shrig whistled a trill of soft, melodious notes and
out from the leafage close by a small shape emerged with
hardly a rustle; a trimly clad boy with the quick, bright
eyes and sharp, impish features of the true cockney urchin.
Halting before them he touched cap with up-flung finger,
saying:

" 'Ere I ham, Gaffer."

"Ar," nodded Mr. Shrig, "but you've got your aitch in the wrong place, Gimblet. And don't call me 'Gaffer'."

"Very good, Gov."

"Tell us, lad, oo is this here gen'leman?"

"Felton, Gov'nor, likewise Sam-u-el, First Orficer o' the *Fortun'* privateer."

"Right, lad. But oo else is he, and speak soft." And the boy answered, whispering:

"Jaff-et, Lord Scrope, h-earl o' Wrybourne."

"Right again, Gimblet, only you've got a aitch now as shouldn't be."

"Ax par'din, Gov, but them aitches is allus a-ketchin' of me onexpected like."

"Ar!" nodded Mr. Shrig. "They do! For, Gimblet, this here letter Aitch is a reg'lar double-faced leery-lurcher. He's a dodger and a ducker, he's as slippery as a werry moist eel! He's a changeable customer, sometimes hissing like snakes and sarpents and sometimes silent as ghosts and phaintums, so take doo heed, my lad! Now, anything to report?"

"No, Gov—'cept when I tracks 'em to the cottage I hears Number Two cryin' and sobbin' like billy-o and so was she, but I left 'em fiddlin' and playin' the h-arp."

"Werry good! Now cut along to your dinner and tell Dan'l to have summat kept hot for me."

"Right-o, Gov'ner. An' if Mr. Felton wasn't a h-earl, and in our charge, I'd cock a fair snook at 'im I would, for frownin' at me like as he is now." Sam chuckled suddenly, laughed and took out a half-crown, saying:

"Let's see." Instantly Gimblet set thumb to snub-nose, spread his fingers, wagged them and shot out his tongue with hideous grimace—all in as many moments.

"Pretty good!" Sam nodded and tossed the coin which Gimblet caught dexterously, spat upon for luck, spun aloft and finally pocketed; which done, the boy took off his cap to say, with odd little bow:

"Thankee, sir, best respex, sir!" And away he sped.

"Yes," said Sam, looking after him with a smile, "a smart little fellow, Jasper."

"Ar,—and though full of impidence, fuller still o' grati- tood. And you'll know him again, I hope, because like as not you're a-going to see him pretty often—so soon as Number Vun makes a move as he's bound to do before long."

"The sooner the better, and when he does—how then?"

"Pal, ekker alone replies! But—so soon as Number Vun finds out as you ain't so nice and dead as he now hopes and believes, then—Murder'll be up and arter you again, ar—morning, noon and night. If you should wenter abroad in lonesome places, every bush and tree'll be a wital menace! Death'll creep in your werry shadder! So, Sam and sir,— take heed!"

"Ay, ay, Jasper. But now, talking of steak and kidney pudding——"

"Eh?" exclaimed Mr. Shrig, halting in surprise. "Did you say steak and——"

"Kidney pudding—yes!"

"Ar!" quoth Mr. Shrig with quick side-glance. "Coupled, I suppose, vith the name o' Miss A."

"Yes, Jasper. I'd have you tell me again exactly how she looked."

"Prime!" answered Mr. Shrig, his keen eyes twinkling. "A ree-markable handsome young fe-male. She looked prime, pal, and werry kissable."

"Did she, b'George?"

"No, by you, sir and Sam."

"Jasper, if you are friend o' mine—talk sense."

"So be it. Then hark you and heed! In hopeful expectation as Numbers Vun and Two must shortly make a move, I'm keeping a werry sharp ogle on same. Consequently this morning I ob-serve Number Two peeping and prying on Miss A and you."

"Then curse the fellow!"

"He is so, pal! For if ever I see a cove in torment— 'twas him! Every look you give her is vips and scorpions for him,—ar, but—'twas a dagger in his buzzum every time she looked at you!"

"Oh?" murmured Sam. "Ah? Just how did she look at me, then?"

"Love, pal! All her throbber or as you might say, heart in them big, soft eyes o' hers,—lovely sad eyes she's got— like a cow."

"Eh?" gasped Sam. "Damme,—a what, Jasper?"

"Cow, Sam and sir. Some cows can look at ye so werry plaintive, vith ogles sad enough to make some folks veep for sympathy. So there's this lovesome Miss offering herself to you in every look and you all unregardful, chopping sticks vith that sharp knife o' yourn, then looking at her as if you could eat her! Vich therefore your friend J.S. now makes bold to ad-wise you. . . . Are you listening?"

"Of course I am!" Sam answered, rather pettishly. "So carry on, man,—what is your advice?"

"That you coax or veedle her into that there pony-cart and drive off vith her as fast and far as ye can go, ar— the further the better! Result—con-tentment for both o' you, con-flummeration for Vun and Two, relief for me and the pot set a-biling generally."

"How," demanded Sam, halting again, "are you suggesting I—elope with her?"

"That i-dentical."

"But . . . good Lord,—to do such thing I'd have to be desperately in love."

"Well—ain't you?"

"No, certainly not."

"Sure o' that?"

"Yes . . . yes, of course I am."

"Then," said Mr. Shrig, easing large, silver watch from his fob, "it being now thirty-two and a half minutes past twelve, all I can say is—Good-arternoon!"

"The same to you, Jasper, and I'll thank you not to make your care of me so all-pervading, dammit,—and overpowering."

"Werry good, sir and Sam,—and so soon as you've got yourself com-pletely flummaxed you'll allus find me, if you ain't a cadaver, under the name of Caleb Brown at the Ring o' Bells t'other side Wrybourne Willage. So pray, remember —Caleb Brown allus at your service." Then with airy flourish of his stick, Mr. Shrig trudged off.

This same evening after supper, Sam indited the following letter:

Willowmead, June 26.

SIR AND MY DEAR BEN,

Thanks for yours of the 21st with its warm-hearted and friendly warning. But I have to inform you that the Walking Evil you mention now supposes me dead, thanks to a poor wretch who stole my clothes and thus got himself shot and killed in my stead. Thus our Two Legged Evil imagines me a corpse and Shrig, fostering this belief, now

waits the next move. Meanwhile I am the victim of Jasper
Shrig's unrelenting care, he watches over me so remorselessly that he is continually running athwart my hawse
and falling aboard of me and always when least wanted
or expected. However, I write now to beg you as friend
(and command you as my esteemed man of business) to
meet me not later than Thursday next two days hence at
the 'White Hart' Lewes on matter that can best be trans-
acted face to face and man to man. Also I shall be right
glad to see you, Ben. Therefore, Mr. Joliffe, fail not

Your obliged and sincere friend,

SAM.

CHAPTER XXIX

TELLS OF THE DAY BEFORE

WILLOWMEAD was in a feminine turmoil for to-morrow was—the Wedding Day.

Light feet tripped and sped to and fro, upstairs and down, gay voices called, laughed and chattered; Kate in the parlour with Grannyanne and Aunt Deb attendant and critical, was trying on her wedding-gown; Captain Ned, having got himself in everybody's way, finally wandered forth in a sort of daze, to look at his new pig-sties, while Sam in the orchard was hard at work constructing a rustic seat in the shade of his favourite apple-tree. Thus, presently guided by the purposeful ring of hammer, thither wandered the Captain to watch and pace restlessly to and fro nearby as if upon the quarterdeck of his ship and with never a word until Wrybourne Church clock struck the hour, whereat Captain Ned halted to say and very wistfully:

"Twelve of the clock, old messmate!"

"Ay!" replied Sam, busied now with saw.

"And to-morrow, Sam, to-morrow at this hour, we shall be just about completing it."

"What, Ned?"

"The service, messmate,—the—wedding. And this is a very solemn thought."

"It is so, Ned.

"At this hour to-morrow, old fellow, I shall be a Benedick!"

"Eh?" enquired Sam, glancing up. "A what, Ned?"

"A bride's-man, shipmate."

"Oh! Ah!" said Sam, driving another nail. "Well, long life and happiness to you, old lad, ay—to both of you."

"Thanks, Sam!" quoth the Captain and turned again to his quarter-deck walk and Sam to his hammering. But soon, back came the Captain to say:

"I shall be mighty glad when 'tis all over, messmate, the ceremony, I mean."

"And so shall I!" answered Sam, fervently. "For, d'ye see, Ned, I'm nowise sure I shan't miss stays or be taken

185

aback—botch the whole business and 'stead of your 'best man', prove the opposite——"

"Not you, Sam! Your sole duty will be to stand by and leave it to the parson and me. To-morrow! B'gad I can hardly believe it even now . . . that Kate and I . . . at last . . . so soon! Seems too wonderful for belief . . . such marvellous happiness!"

"Ay, you're mighty lucky fellow, Ned, yet you deserve it all—or damme if ye don't."

"Thanks again, Sam. When are you going to follow my example, old fellow?"

"How, Ned?"

"Marry of course and settle down."

"Now God love ye, Ned, who'd want me for her brides-man or—Benedick, was it?"

"Ay, and how about that handsome Miss Andromeda?"

"Well," demanded Sam, changing saw for hammer, "what of her?"

"Messmate, that's what I'm asking you."

"Ay, Ned, and why should you mention her?"

"Because,—well, you've been in her company so often lately that we were hoping, Kate and I, that perhaps you and she might make a match of it and settle down some-where near us, neighbours, Sam! Could anything be better?"

"Nothing in this world, Ned, only I'm pretty sure it can't ever be, d'ye see."

"Why the devil not?"

"Well, since you ask, because I'm nothing near so well educated as yourself, Ned, I'm too rough and ready, little better than an ordinary fo'c'sle jack . . . and I'm not up to my ears in love like you. As for Miss Andromeda—the chief reason for my visits is that little, precious niece o' mine—Jane."

"Gammon!" laughed the Captain. "Is little Jane the reason you have been so moody of late?—not she! Has little Jane put you off your feed? Not she! Did little Jane drag you unwillingly in a certain direction so often lately? Cer-tainly not! No, Sam, my poor, old juggins, you're in love, and you've taken it badly as I foretold. Andromeda haunts you. Her beautiful, sad face is in your thoughts morning, noon and night! Isn't this true? Come, speak up, ship-mate, tell the truth and shame the Devil."

"Well," Sam began, then paused as his roving glance espied a hat emerging slowly from behind a tree at no great distance, a familiar hat followed by the wrinkled visage of old Mr. Toop who, catching Sam's eye, winked his own and beckoned with stealthy though portentous finger.

"Sam, what now?" demanded Captain Ned. "What the devil are you staring at?"

"Yonder, Ned—our aged Mr. Toop."

"Ay, so I see. Well, Gaffer, what can I do for you?"

"Nowt, Cap'n!" answered the old fellow, hobbling forward. "Nowt wi' you, maister, my business be wi' Mus' Felton an' strickly private, strickly!"

"However," said Sam, "you can speak out now, Gaffer. For Ned, d'ye see, Mr. Toop, has been good enough to choose me your wedding present——"

"Ay, that Oi 'ave!" chuckled the aged man. "Ar and 'ad the toime o' me loife, I 'ave! To fairs and markets I 'ave druv and nigh two wiks it's took me choosin' an' checkin' —and allus the best,—if not, then: 'Tek 'em away' say Oi, for Oi be buyin' f'r a gen'leman as wants only the proimest o' the proime! Money's no objec', Oi sez. Ar and b'the pyx Oi've got 'em tu,—the best as eyes ever see."

"Good!" nodded Sam. "Where are they?"

"Comin' 'long lane yonder. And theer ain't another 'erd to ekal 'em in arl the South Country nor nowheers else! Coats so silky, s'smooth and glossy as the down on a babby's 'ead! Udders on 'em like so many gally-oons!"

"How many?" Sam enquired.

So many as we can 'commodate, maister,—twenty and four, and every one on 'em—in milk!"

"Lord!" exclaimed the Captain, hushed of voice but eyes aglow, "Lord love you, old shipmate, I—— Damme, I've no words to thank you——"

"Don't ee try, Cap'n!" piped Mr. Toop. "Norra word till you've seed 'em. Come now and lemme show ee!" Thus jubilant of air though rather tottery of gaitered legs, old Mr. Toop hurried them into the spacious farm-yard that seemed full of tossing horns, sleek bodies and swishing tails, —a truly magnificent herd whose lowing had drawn hither an amazed and admiring audience.

"Ours, Kate, ours!" cried the Captain. "Sam's wedding present!"

"My merciful Maker!" exclaimed Aunt Deb.

"La, what booties they be!" cried Nancy.

"Ha,—a very lordly gift!" quoth Grannyanne.

"Oh!" sighed Kate, viewing these splendid animals with eyes of knowing and rapturous appraisal. "Oh, Sam . . . my dear . . . you must have spent a fortune! Ned, how can we ever thank him?"

"We can't!" replied the Captain, shaking his comely head. "It goes beyond mere words, yet we can try——"

"No need!" quoth Sam, almost gruffly. "None at all, Kate and Ned, because d'ye see—you've given me such home and you're learning me to love the good land so much more than I thought possible that 'tis I am the grateful one. And if the herd is so good, 'tis old Mr. Toop here you have to thank—he chose 'em, d'ye see——"

"Ay—'tis me!" chirruped the aged man. "'Tis me as done arl the choosin' and chafferin', 'tis me as picked they—every one! And, oh me, dear souls, a pretty penny they costed,—ah, a mort o' money, never see s'much in arl me days, if I wur to tell ee 'ow much——"

"No, no," laughed Sam, "mum for that, Gaffer, not another word and . . . why, Lord love me, there's my little sweetheart!" So saying, he sped away where Jane was singing her song of "Barbree Alling", in her sweet, high voice.

CHAPTER XXX

TELLS HOW LORD JULIAN LAUGHED AND SAM FOUND HAPPINESS

"OH, Uncle Sam, I have come to tell you 'bout my dollys-house what my dear, old Magic Tree sent with the cradle what I asked him for and I love it. So now please I want you to take me so I can thank him—so will you?"

"Ay, to be sure I will, sweetheart. So you love your dollys-house, do you?"

"Oh, Uncle Sam, I just 'dore it and so does my Batilda, too. So now let's go, shall us? 'Cause when I've said my thanks, we can call for a visit to my Auntie Meda an' I can tell her about my lovely dollys-house too!" So away they went along the winding lane and seldom speaking because Jane was giving all her thought to her wonderful dollys-house while Sam pondered the whether or no of the Captain's words:

"My poor, old juggins, you're in love with her and you've taken it badly."

"By—George!" he exclaimed at last, removing his hat to run fingers through his crisp-curling hair. "By Jove and Jingo—I am!"

"What are you?" enquired Jane, turning to look up at him.

"In love, sweetheart! Isn't that wonderful?"

"Oh no, 'cause everybody's always in love with somebody, like Tom an' Nancy this morning, 'cause I heard him say 'Oh, Nancy, I love you more'n I can say'—so then he kissed her an' she kissed him lots an' lots—an' another time I heard my Uncle Ned say, 'Oh Kate, I 'dore you', then he kissed her. An' I like you best without your hat 'cause your hair's so nice an' twisty. . . ."

And now it was that round a bend in the lane, his horse's hoofs unheard upon the turf, came Lord Julian Scrope, riding for once, at a walk; also he sat bent in the saddle, arrogant head bowed as if in utter weariness or profound thought. Slowly he advanced until suddenly espying Sam's burly figure and scarred brow, he jerked swiftly upright, checking

his horse so violently that the animal, snorting to pain of
fiercely-drawn bit, reared, subsided and stood shivering while
his master neither spoke nor moved. Rigid and dumb Lord
Julian stared haggardly from a face whose deathly pallor was
the more ghastly because of the awful fixity of his wide-
lidded, smouldering gaze. . . .

So indescribably dreadful was his look that little Jane
clasped Sam's nearest leg; even the horse appeared to sense
something terribly amiss, for he fretted and champed, backed
and sidled until at last came his rider's hand to pat and
soothe him, in which moment Lord Julian spoke and with
all his usual arrogance of look and tone:

"Tell me, fellow,—have I not seen you before?"

"Ay, my lord, you have," answered Sam, taking firmer
grip on his heavy stick. "If you'll trouble to think hard
enough, you may remember 'twas at Willowmead. We
became somewhat familiar there; in fact quite—closely connected."

"A-h-h!" sighed his lordship. "At—Willowmead!"

"Yes, my lord. Though I was in sailor rig then, but,
d'ye see, somebody shot my seafaring clothes and in 'em the
poor thief that stole 'em, which though hard on him, was
lucky for me and confoundedly disappointing for—others.
How think you, my right noble lord? Let's hear your opinion
on't, come now."

But instead of speaking, Lord Julian did that which Sam
was never to forget,—his pallid lips quivered, parted to slow,
terrible smile that grew and widened upon sharp, white teeth,
then—back went his stately head and he began to laugh . . .
and laughed loud and louder . . . until his nervous horse
whinnied shrilly in unison, and breaking into a canter, was
spurred viciously to such furious gallop as soon took them out
of sight; yet even then the echo of that frightful, mockery
of laughter rang upon the startled air,—or so it seemed to
Sam.

"Ooh!" cried Jane, clinging to him close as ever. "Didn't
he laugh—drefful?"

"He did, sweetheart."

"And why d'you suppose?"

"Perhaps, my dear one, because he fancied he saw a
ghost."

"But do folkses laugh at ghostesses?"

"Ay—some do, it seems, now and then, sweetheart. However, let's forget all about it and talk of your fairy aunt, instead."

"Yes, let's. An' I think we ought to kiss and comfort her a bit, Uncle Sam dear, 'cause sometimes her eyes look so weepy, don't they?"

"They do, my Jane and so we will."

But at the end of this winding lane they beheld Cecily Croft hastening towards them, and Sam was struck anew by the beauty of her. Swiftly she came and flushed with haste, said breathlessly:

"Oh, Mr. Felton, sir . . . I come from—someone in trouble, someone who wants you, please." Now saying this, she glanced furtively at Jane and shook her head.

"Thankee, Cecily," answered Sam, then stooping to Jane, he kissed her, saying:

"Sweetheart, we must put off our visit because I'm wanted, d'ye see. So now go home with Cecily and you shall take me a walk soon as I come back."

Then up and away strode he, heedless of lurking perils and forgetful of all things on earth except this "someone" who wanted him.

"And," said he, between shut teeth, as he lengthened his swinging stride, "by God she shall have me!"

Very soon and with not even a glance towards the "Deep Dark",—that place of brooding evil, he reached Jane's 'Chanted Forest, then halted, suddenly breathless with great leap of his heart, for, Andromeda was coming towards him; thus it was beneath the broad, kindly shadow of little Jane's "Magic Tree" that they met.

"Oh, Sam!" she sighed, and gave him both her hands.

"Andromeda!" he said, and took her in his arms, drawing her near, folding her close upon his heart. "My own . . . beloved . . ." he whispered, brokenly, and kissed her hair, her sad eyes, her ruddy lips that, quivering beneath his, kissed him back. . . . And in this moment Sam knew at last the Joy Ineffable,—for now he felt her clinging arms about him, her whole lovely body yielding to his in mute surrender. Then leaning back that she might look up into his eyes, she questioned:

"Ah, Sam, is this your—mere friendship?"

"No!" he answered and quite fiercely. "No, this is love

at last, thank God! Ay, such as I have never known or
imagined. You are mine and I am yours forever! So,
Andromeda . . . oh, my dear, when shall—how soon can
we get married?" Now instead of replying, she clung to him
again and, sobbing, began to kiss his rough coat until he
lifted these caressing lips to his own, murmuring:

"But, Andromeda, why must you weep?"

"For our love," she whispered, "because it is so vain . . .
so hopeless."

"No!" said he, at his grimmest. "Oh no! We belong
to each other, we always have and always shall——"

"Dear love," she sighed, in tone sadder than any tears,
"such happiness is not for us . . . it can be only a passing
dream because reality is so vile, so hatefully cruel and wicked
. . . and may become so horrible that now . . . at last . . .
I am terribly afraid."

"Afraid?" he repeated, kissing her bowed head. "All the
more reason for you to marry me soon, my beloved, ay—
soon as possible."

"Loose me, Sam dear,—let me show you a horror of the
past and a—growing terror of the present——"

"Is it your uncle again?"

"Yes, but—oh Sam, let me show you why——"

Instead, he swung her up in his arms and carrying her
beneath this aged tree of "magic", sat down with his back
against its mighty bole, her loveliness still close in his embrace,
and for a never-to-be-forgotten while, she nestled to him,
clinging instinctively to his strength; and thus with his lips
upon her fragrant, midnight hair, he said, rather breathlessly:

"I know now . . . that I've always . . . loved you,
Andromeda . . . yes even before I saw you . . . it was
you I was looking for . . . you, the other part of myself,
d'ye see! So I shall always love you . . . because I must,
it . . . it stands to reason. So when . . . how soon shall we
be married?"

"Oh, my dear, my dear," she sighed, "how can I answer
when you know I shall never forsake poor Uncle Arthur,
you know this."

"Ay, I do. And so, if you must be his devoted slave,
I'll be yours and . . . help my sweet wife to take care of him
by taking dam' good care of her. Yes, my Andromeda,

besides your husband, I'll be your lover, your 'hewer of wood and drawer of water', yours to serve——" Here, with soft, inarticulate cry, she drew him to the grateful passion of her kiss; and thus sweetly dumb they, for a while, knew a rapture far too deep for any words. And now being conscious only of each other, how should they be aware of the furtive eyes that watched their happiness with such deep anguish, the pale lips close-set to such relentless purpose? Until:

"Oh—listen!" gasped Andromeda, roused to swift anxiety by a distant though ferocious barking, "something is wrong! I left Esau tied up because he's been so strangely fierce and nervous lately . . . but he never barks so without reason! Oh, hark to him! Yes, something is very wrong! Oh, how glad I am to have you beside me, for I am nervous too! Come with me, Sam dear."

"To the world's end!" said he, drawing her hand within his arm. Side by side they hurried through this shady coppice until they came where stood tent and caravan—with Esau straining at the stout cord that held him, at sight of them he ceased his raving clamour, wagging stumpy tail, but kept his fierce eyes glaring in the one direction.

"There must be someone hidden in the wood!" said Andromeda, glancing around apprehensively as she stooped to pet and soothe the great dog.

"Lord!" muttered Sam, and invoked a silent malediction on Jasper Shrig's all-pervading watchfulness.

"Whoever it was has gone now," said Andromeda as Esau, having flicked red tongue at her caressing hand, composed himself in stately attitude yet with shaggy ears cocked and bright eyes alert.

"Dearest lass," said Sam, kissing the hand he had retained, "why are you trembling? What is it so 'frights you?" And drawing his long, and very ready, arm about her shapeliness, she answered:

"Sit with me under our big tree yonder, your tree, Sam dear, where you made my tent-pegs, and I'll tell and show you why at last I am so greatly afraid." So thither they went and there seated, he drew her close and feeling how she nestled to him, kissed her, saying very tenderly:

"You've a very beautiful body, Andromeda, and for this I love you. Ah but, d'ye see, in all this loveliness you have

such sweet, ay, such strong and valiant soul that for this
I . . . oh, I worship you so truly, so reverently that I'm
shamed by my own unworthiness. For, d'ye see, I'm such
rough sort o' fellow with none of the airs and graces I
would have for your dear sake. So now I'd like to know
. . . well—just how you think of me. And if you can say
'Sam, I love you' 'twould hearten me, for you haven't
yet——"

"Oh, but I have—repeatedly!"

"Not in so many words. So if you can, pray do."

"Well then," said she, obediently, "Sam, my darling, I
admire you for your strength and grimly dogged manliness,
but—— Oh, I love you for these dear, grey, truthful eyes
that have shown me so much of your great, clean, gentle
heart. And mine is a love shall comfort you in adversity,
suffer with you in pain or grief, glory in your triumphs and
welcome hardship and, with you, death itself, rather than
life without you. This is how I love you now, but if we
are to be so blest—to share life together, the years shall
only make me more your own to serve you, cherish and
comfort you to—the end,—and beyond. So now, Sam, are
you content? Why—— Oh, now you are crying!"

"Ay, I am!" he confessed, blinking. "For . . . oh, damme—
how can I ever be worthy such wonder of——"

But here, she proceeded to silence him; when at last she
permitted him speech:

"Andromeda," sighed he, "though you're such angel o'
light, ay—so holy I'd scarce dare touch you, yet thank God
you're a woman also—for my lips to kiss, these arms o' mine
to clasp, this rough body o' mine to——" Here she silenced
him again; which done, she resettled herself beside him and
holding his nearest hand in both her own, spoke now in tone
so dreadfully altered that Sam enquired anxiously:

"Eh,—why, dear heart, what now?"

And, drawing a deep, shuddering breath, Andromeda told
him:

"Last night Esau woke me and sitting up in the dark, I
heard a strangely awful mewing sound. Sick with fear, I
lit the storm-lantern and with this in one hand and my other
on Esau's collar, I went out to see what it was. Esau led
me in among the thickets until I saw something on the ground
. . . a dreadful shape that moved and twisted. . . . Then

I heard that awful sound again, but . . . it was not a poor animal mewing—ah no, it was Uncle Arthur weeping more terribly than I ever heard. I ran and lifted him, his poor face all stained with earth and wet with tears . . . and then I saw that in his hand he grasped a crumpled paper. And with his terrible weeping he was whispering these words, over and over again like a prayer,—'Oh, God of Justice, give me strength, give me vengeance'. For a long time he lay there writhing and twisting as if in torment and I could do nothing with him. So I prayed too, for God to help me, and my prayer was answered, for at last my poor Uncle suffered me to bring him into his caravan. The fire was not quite out, so I warmed some milk and made him drink it, then stroked his poor troubled head until he was soothed and fell asleep. Then very gently I drew the crumpled paper from his fingers. . . . This letter, Sam, this cause of my dear Uncle's anguished madness and my growing terror! Read with me this frightful, heart-breaking message—though I know it almost by heart." From her bosom, Andromeda drew a folded paper, smoothed it out and together they read these words:

Julian, your heartless abandonment of me at such time as this, must be God's punishment on me for my sin and wicked treachery to poor Arthur. Without you I am desolate, and since you are so merciless I must seek through death the abiding mercy of God—or solace of forgetfulness. Yet, oh Julian, I am so greatly afraid of what I must do, yet even so and with my last breath I pray God forgive you, for your wretched, dying Barbara loves you still. So now for the last time, Good-bye and farewell.

"The Lady Barbara Stowe!" murmured Sam, "Poor soul . . . God pity and bless her!"

"Lord . . . Julian . . . Scrope!" hissed Andromeda, between shut teeth. "He drove her, through anguish of love, to her death. He drove my Uncle Arthur, through anguish of grief, to ruin and madness! Oh!" she cried, leaping afoot. "Such inhuman monster is too vile to live— I, yes, I—could kill him!" And flashing that keen knife from the sheath at her girdle, she struck such passionate blow that Sam, rising swiftly, cried:

"No—for God's sake, not you! Here's no work for a woman's hand, 'specially this dear, gentle hand o' yours!" Seizing this hand he kissed it until she let the knife fall and turning, hid her face against his breast, saying breathlessly:

"Oh Sam . . . had he been here . . . I should have . . . killed him! Ah . . . horrible! Hold me close, close . . . take care of me for I'm afraid of . . . the·future and . . . myself. Marry me if you will . . . when you will! Take me and keep me . . . safe in your strength——"

"Ay," growled Sam, "this will I, by God!"

"Alleluia!" exclaimed a voice so near that Sam turned, scowling, as out from the leafage tripped Mr. Verinder.

"Glory!" said he, baring his white head reverently. "Glory to God, alleluia and amen! And frown not, young man, for you are become my blessing."

"Uncle Arthur. Oh, my dear, what——"

"Beloved child, God has called me to his most holy work, His inspired instrument I and in His mercy will presently free me of this futile body and lift me, perfected by death, to His light and perfection of achievement at last. My only grief in dying was that I must leave thee, my beloved niece, solitary, forlorn and unprotected. Ah, but God has now raised up this Felton, sent us this young, strong man to espouse you and free me of all care, banish my last grief and strengthen me to God's holy purpose and thereafter— bless me with death——"

"What purpose, sir?" Sam enquired gently. "And if you are His instrument, how will God make use o' you, pray?"

"Dear Felton," said the little gentleman, patting his hand affectionately. "Ah, my dear, dear youth, here is subject too sacred, and far, far too holy to discuss, even with you. Instead, go you, I beg, I plead, rouse fire and fill kettle . . . Meda, my love, the day wanes, I suggest tea,—let it prepare. And yes,—thereafter, my loved ones both, I will play for you a solo on my great harp, a song of Life's supremest blessing—death. So now let tea brew for I thirst, likewise hunger."

With Sam's deft aid the meal was soon prepared—and who so witty, so glad and unaffectedly joyous as Mr. Verinder. Thereafter, down sat he to this imposing instrument and from quivering strings wooed, plucked and compelled such splendour of sound as held them rapt, enthralled by the wonder of his artistry until evening shadows began to creep.

The wonder of this music was still haunting him when at last, with Andromeda's parting kiss sweet upon his lips, Sam left her in the shadows and turned unwillingly homewards.

CHAPTER XXXI

TELLS HOW SAM SAVED HIS LIFE AND TOLD A FORTUNE

THE sun had gone down in glory, but the sky was still radiant with a soft light that blessed the quiet world about him with a gentle, wistful loveliness much like the beauty of his own so beloved Andromeda. . . . He would see her again to-morrow . . . ay, to-morrow he would know again the rapture of her touch, her kiss, the softly-yielding, vital feel of her in his arms . . . to-morrow. . . . Thus homewards fared Sam, musing happily of her and all the joys to be—until, from dreaming lover he was suddenly transformed to grim, fierce-eyed man strung for instant deadly action,—and this merely because a partridge had whirred unexpectedly from the woodland to his right—where now every tree seemed a threat, each bush a menace, especially a certain dense thicket. Sam halted, took out his pipe and setting it between his teeth, thrust hand into pocket and fumbled as if for his tinder-box, but all the while his keen gaze was upon this particular thicket; he heard it rustle faintly, saw leaves stir gently and whipping out pistol, fired and tumbled headlong as from these leaves leapt roaring red flame and death that hissed close above him. And now rose a shrill scream with tempestuous flutter of petticoats and Cecily Croft was kneeling beside him, had lifted him in soft, strong arms, then, seeing his white-toothed grin, loosed him, saying breathlessly:

"God ha' mercy—I thought—you was killed!"

"So did I, Cecily."

"Be you anywise—are you at all hurt, sir?"

"No, thank God!"

"It looked like you was being shot at deliberate, Mr. Felton!"

"Ay, so it did. Confound these poachers! 'Twas from that bush—yonder!" said he and while Cecily glanced thither, Sam stole the pistol back into pocket.

"Hush!" she warned. "They're still there—listen!"

"Yes!" said Sam and leapt afoot; for now indeed the

wood seemed full of stir and movement, a distant leafy tumult
swelling to vague clamour suddenly hushed to a rustle that
presently died away. So came silence sweetly broken all
at once by the plaintive fluting of a blackbird.

"Well," said Sam, still watching this ominous wood where
shadows gloomed darker, "they've gone now, whoever they
were, and we may as well do the same. I'll convoy you—
see you safe home, if I may."

"Thank you, Mr. Felton, but you don't have to. Uncle's
farm do lie down yonder, scarce five minutes if I run. But
before I go, sir, I'd like to know why you told me all that
fullishness about. . . .Oh, about my poor Ralph wedding
me when he can't and never will, and about me being called
. . . Lady Scrope! Such fullish nonsense, Mr. Felton—and
why?"

"Cecily, did you ever have your fortune told?"

"Well,—once I crossed a gipsy's palm with sixpence."

"Well, what did she prophesy?"

"She said I'd . . . marry my love and have . . . oh
. . . sixteen children."

"Lord!" exclaimed Sam, with his transfiguring smile. "She
gave you full money's worth, Cecily. Now I'll tell your
fortune, give me your hand,—either will do."

For a moment she hesitated, saying:

"Mine isn't a fine lady's hand all soft and white—'tis a
hand to work itself rough and hard——"

"So much the better!" quoth Sam, fervently, "for it is
such hands are our blessing—ay, and only such hands can
make and keep a home, Cecily." So she gave him her hand
warm with young life and strongly capable; then gazing down
into its open palm, Sam uttered this prophecy:

"Here I see gold, much wealth. You are going to be a
very rich woman. But here I see a prison also and in this
prison—your Ralph——"

"No!" she wailed, trying quite vainly to free her hand.
"Ah, no!"

"Oh yes!" quoth Sam. "But to this vile prison and in
splendid coach, drives a grand and beautiful lady named
Cecily Croft——"

"Me?" she gasped.

"At her command the prison gates open, by the power of
her money the poor prisoner is freed, and when he kneels

to thank her she cries his name and he recognizes his loving
faithful Cecily. And in that moment—I hope—he knows his
own unworthiness and growing humble, becomes a better
man."

Now when Sam released her hand she stood a while as
though entranced—until a shrewish voice at no great distance,
cried:

"Cec'ly! Oh, Cec'ly, where be ee gone—and all they
cows to milk! Come your ways now!" So, waking from
her dream Cecily glanced at its inspirer through sparkle of
tears, nodded dumbly and hurried away to her never-ending
labour.

Sam was still gazing after her when once again he heard a
rustling behind him and starting round, saw how the ever-
deepening shadows had transformed the woodland to a
glooming mystery wherein something stirred. Every bush
and tree became a menace, a stealthy threat to his life—a
life now so very precious because of Andromeda; wherefore,
thrusting hand into pocket Sam drew his second pistol,
cocked it and stood waiting. The leafy rustling grew louder,
nearer until out from the shadows stepped a figure bloody
of face, dishevelled of person and bare of head, who, beholding Sam, let fall a battered hat and leaning heavily upon his
stick, exclaimed in shaken accents:

"Blow . . . my . . . dicky!"

"Jasper!" cried Sam, hurrying to him.

"Dog . . . bite me!" sighed Mr. Shrig distressfully. "Ar,
you can burn my de-woted neck if I didn't expect to find
you a bleeding . . . stiffening . . . ca-daver—instead o'
threatening me with that pop."

"Sink me!" exclaimed Sam, uncocking and re-pocketing
his weapon. "What happened, Jasper, old fellow? You've
been grassed and your head cut——"

"Scratted, sir, only scratted, but—oh, pal, I have been
diddled and ditched by—your vould-be ass-assin! I hears
the shot, I speeds thereto, I has my daddles on the murderer
—almost, but——"

"Then you saw him, Jasper?"

"Ar, but——"

"Who was he?"

"A countryman, a yo-kel, ar—werry much so, hat, neckercher, smockfrock and gaiters—all complete."

"Oh, ah, you mean a poacher?"

"No, a murderer—as proved too much for J. Shrig. So my sperrits is low, sir, and I'm shook mind and body! J.S. is so hu-miliated, ar—I'm that humble I can hardly bear my own company!"

"No, no," laughed Sam, setting arm about the speaker's drooping shoulders. "Cheer up, old fellow, we're not beat yet, far from it. So let's sit down, smoke a pipe and talk it over, come."

"Sir," said Mr. Shrig, mournfully, "ven I named you 'pal' being flashed for 'brother', I named you right! For if Failure—vith a werry big eff—chills the beating throbber and o-bases the soul, Friendship can varm it and give a leg-up. So, now, tobacker it is!" Down they sat forthwith, and when their pipes were alight and drawing, Mr. Shrig sighed:

"Pal Sam, no man can't trooly enj'y sitting down till he's been shook up and flattened out by the butt of a gun."

"That was the way of it, eh, Jasper. I fancy I heard something of the business, but never guessed it could be you."

"And . . . I had him!" said Mr. Shrig with sigh like a groan. "But he broke free and fetched me such clout vith his gun as must ha' done for me and been my final and to-tal qui-eetus but for this here noble dicer o' mine!" And taking up his hat, Mr. Shrig gazed wistfully at a great dent in its crown.

"Looks ruined, Jasper."

"No, pal, all as it needs is a hammer."

"Eh, hammer?"

"Ar, 'tis lined wi' iron, y'see, my inwention again. Windictiveness in the form o' brick-bats, bludgeons and a occasional chimbley-pot, though a gun-butt is coming it a bit strong! Consequently here upon my tibby is a lump like a negg! Ar, but for my dicer I'd be at this i-dentical moment, laying flat as a flounder and dead as mutton."

"And the fellow was dressed like a countryman, eh, Jasper?"

"Ar,—even to his boots,—hobnails."

"Did you see his face?"

"No, his chivvy vas hid by his neckercher and hat, and 'twas pretty darkish among the trees, but—I see the end

of his conk and caught a glimp' of his eyes and—I shall
know 'em again!"

"Then we're still in the dark, Jasper, still not sure of his
identity?"

"Ar! And us had better get on afore it grows any darker
and somebody tries another shot and makes surer this time."

So up they rose and on they went, both somewhat gloomy
and silent, until before them lay Willowmead, its latticed
casements beaming homely welcome. At the wide yard
gate they halted and, sighing gustily, Mr. Shrig held out
his hand, then let it fall, saying mournfully:

"Sir, I've growed that humble as I can't expect you to
take the hand of a failure, but——"

"Now damme," exclaimed Sam, seizing this hand to grasp
it firmly, "don't be such a juggins, Jasper! I've never
felt such kindness for you as I do to-night, because d'ye see
I'm going to be married."

"To Miss A?"

"Ay, none other."

"Then sir, Sam and pal, though grievous and werry des-
ponding, I humbly vish ye j'y, first a gal and then a b'y."
Having said which, Mr. Shrig sighed, shook his head and
trudged heavily away.

CHAPTER XXXII

HIS LORDSHIP COMMANDS

MR. JOLIFFE'S trim wig was somewhat askew, his lean face showed slightly pink, his eyes sparkled as he sat opposite Sam at this choicely-laden table; he ate with gusto, drank with the respectful deliberation due to such noble vintage, he talked and laughed,—yet all the while was sternly repressing some powerful emotion, or so thought Sam. Thus when at last they leaned back in their chairs, comfortably replete, Sam enquired:

"Well, Ben, what's on your mind?"

Mr. Joliffe smiled, viewed the wine in his glass with look very like an ogle and sighed happily:

"This has been a meal worthy the occasion, a great—hem—truly memorable and very singular occasion, for this is indeed a day of days. So now, and before I explain more, I think since you informed me how your fire-eating Captain Harlow is so happily tamed by matrimony and even now upon his honeymoon, we should recharge our glasses and pledge——"

"Ay, with all my heart!" cried Sam, reaching for the wine. "Thanks, Ben! Come now and no heel-taps—health, joy and long life to them—bless 'em!"

Now when this toast had been properly honoured, Mr. Joliffe set down his empty glass, took out his snuff-box, glanced at it absently, fobbed it again and leaning forward, said in hushed though jubilant tone:

"And now, Sam, now—'tis my pleasure to inform you that I have—hem—spun webs to such effect that your blackguardly young cousin the Honourable Ralph is—under lock and key, safely and securely prisoned with no hope or possibility of enlargement or escape!"

"Good!" nodded Sam.

"Ah, but—better yet, his villainous sire, my lord Julian will be as closely jailed three days hence! Yes, Sam, positively in three short days you will take your lofty station in Society as your true self, Japhet, Earl of Wrybourne!"

"Oh?" murmured Sam, rather gloomily. "Ah! And what then?"

"This of course is for you to decide, though, upon my soul, the prospect appears to distress you!"

"It does, Ben, it does, damme! For, d'ye see, I'm merest sailorman and shall make such a fool of an earl! Ay, sink me,—I shall be a sheer hulk·. . . all adrift . . . or forever on my beam-ends."

"No, Sam, dear me no! To provide against such awkward contingency, I shall engage the offices of a certain gentleman of ancient very noble lineage to be your Maecenas, your mentor, guide and perambulating *vade-mecum* who shall instruct you as to your dress, address and general deportment."

"Which," groaned Sam, "sounds very perfectly damnable!"

"Yet—most necessary!" said Mr. Joliffe, hiding a smile, what time Sam scowled at his wine-glass.

Out came Mr. Joliffe's gold snuff-box again, but this time he extracted a pinch, saying as he did so:

"Cheer up, my dear fellow. Things might be worse— even though you are young, an earl and stu-pendously rich! Yes, indeed, there are worse troubles. And now regarding the business you wrote about, pray how can I serve you?"

"Well—first, Ben, at a rough estimate—about how much am I worth?"

"Ah!" sighed Mr. Joliffe, closing his snuff-box and laying it carefully upon the table. "Such vast possessions constantly increasing since money begets money, are difficult to compute exactly, but I can confidently assert that your total fortune already amounts to considerably more than a million sterling!"

"Hell!" exclaimed Sam, "I was afraid it would be pretty much but this is worse than I expected——"

"Eh?" gasped the lawyer with clutch at his toppling spectacles. " 'Worse', d'ye say?"

"Ay. So much worse, Ben, that I can't bear it."

"Can't . . . bear——" Mr. Joliffe's voice failed him.

"No, Ben, I can't and won't! So I must get rid of some of it, let's say half a million, and soon as possible."

"Half a mill——" Mr. Joliffe seemed to choke.

"So you'll please draw up a deed of gift to this amount in the name of——"

"Sam . . . my dear fellow . . . you are joking——"

"Ben, I was never more serious."

"But . . . a gift . . . five hundred thousand pounds . . . such vast sum . . . a gift——"

"A million would be more, of course, Ben, so on second thoughts——"

"Sam . . . Sam . . . what are you saying?" gasped Mr. Joliffe, peering at him anxiously through and over his spectacles. "You are not yourself,—the wine perhaps——?"

"I'm sober as a barn owl, Ben."

"Then—a touch of the sun,—or that wound in your head! However, my dear Sam, do nothing in a hurry, I beg—I plead! Defer this matter for a day or so, give yourself time to think . . . I protest you confound me, indeed you alarm me, Sam!"

"Ben," he sighed, a little wearily, "I'm neither drunk nor sun-struck nor crazed with my wound, and being perfectly sound o' mind and body, I now desire you to draw up the necessary legal what-nots, deeds, indentures, conveyances and so on, for the bestowing of half my heritage to——"

"Good, great Je-hovah!" gasped Mr. Joliffe, dabbing at moist brow with a table napkin. "Oh, Sam, think—for God's sake think what you would do! Be advised and give up this incredible, this preposterous folly."

"Mr. Joliffe," quoth Sam, becoming quite grim, "here and now my lordship Japhet, Earl of Wrybourne commands you as his lawyer to prepare the proper legal instrument whereby my Lord of Wrybourne can give, bestow and transfer half this fortune to Mistress Cecily Croft—at once."

"A million!" repeated Mr. Joliffe in ghostly whisper, writhing as if in bodily anguish. "This . . . oh, this is unheard of . . . unbelievable! It's utterly preposterous!"

"Ay, damme, preposterous it is, Ben, that one man should own so much, and that man myself. For, d'ye see, I never wanted all this cursed money. In fact, had these Scropes not been scoundrels they should have had this dam' Wrybourne heritage, ay—every penny. As it is, I'm mighty glad to rid myself of even this small part of it."

"Small part!" repeated Mr. Joliffe in voice like a moan. "Small! Good Lord deliver us! Ha, Sam, d'ye know how much, have you any conception of the vast sum you are throwing away so lightly, so recklessly, so——"

"Not throwing away, Ben, I'm giving it to a very worthy young——"

"Woman, of course!" snapped Mr. Joliffe. "A poor creature who will be victimized, hunted, pursued, hounded and beset by rogues and rascals of every sort, fortune hunters all."

"Ay, but, d'ye see, Ben, she's of such sort herself that she desires and will accept only one of these rogues and rascals, one only, Ben, because he is truly of all rogues—the one, ay—her own particular, long-chosen rascal. So get the business done soon as you can, according to my lordship's herewith express order and command, Mr. Joliffe."

"Then," said the lawyer, miserably, "you positively mean it? . I am actually ordered by your lordship to proceed in this—this matter?"

"Mr. Joliffe, you are. And immediately."

"In-credible!"

"Yet true, be assured, sir."

"Ah-ha!" sighed Mr. Joliffe, relaxing and with the twinkle back in his eyes. "Do I comprehend? Am I to infer that this so extremely fortunate young lady is . . . your future countess?"

"No, Mr. Joliffe. This lady is quite determined to marry a scoundrel."

"Then," groaned Mr. Joliffe, with gesture of hopeless resignation, "I—give up!"

"And no wonder!" said Sam, with flashing grin. "So, Ben, let's finish the bottle——"

But even as he spoke, came a hollow knocking on the door, and Tragedy entered in the dusty person and woebegone whiskers of "the man Dan'l".

CHAPTER XXXIII

TELLS OF "THE HOUR OF VENGEANCE"

"WELL," enquired Mr. Joliffe, "well, Daniel, my good fellow, what news this time?"

"Sir, all as I can say is, gen'lemen both, the word is 'Jarsper'. You're wanted immediate and very special,—gig's a-waiting."

"But this," said Mr. Joliffe, sitting up, "this is very sudden and most unusual. Has anything happened?"

"Mr. Joliffe, sir, things is always so a-doing. And, sir, 'tis nigh on three o'clock and gig's a-waiting. So's Jarsper! Therefore, and by your leaves, I'll desire you to obleege by stepping down to the gig and, sirs, the livelier the better."

"But where are you taking us?" enquired Sam.

"To Jarsper, sir."

"Damme, I know that! Where is Jasper?"

"Half-a-mile or so t'other side o' Wrybourne village, sir."

"But where, you oyster, where exactly?"

"That old mill, sir."

"Ah!" exclaimed Sam, and said no more until they were throned aloft on this high-wheeled vehicle and driving rapidly out of the town; then:

"That accursed place!" said he abruptly. "Ay, it would be there!"

"What would be where?" enquired Mr. Joliffe, clutching his hat as they took a corner at speed.

"D'you know that old mill, Ben, a desolate ruin by a murderous pool?"

"Of course I do. It pertains to the Manor estate. Lord Julian's property."

"Well, it has always seemed to me there's a curse hanging over it. If ever a place should be haunted—that's the place!"

"Haunted? Pooh, Sam, tut-tut! You surely don't credit such tarradiddleish foolery? Yet to be sure I've heard superstition still sails the seas and you are a seaman though, being also educated——"

"Half-educated, Ben! However, if bitter grief, blank despair and merciless evil can haunt a place they're lying there, ay, and with springs on their cables ready to let go,—ghosts o' vengeance waiting their hour!"

"Dear me, Sam, you're very fanciful!"

"Ay, I am, for I hate the place! And you must have heard evil has been there more than once."

"Oh yes, I'm aware people have been drowned there—two only, I believe. But, my dear Sam, if the act of self-destruction can eternally curse a place with ghosts, then what multitudes of apparitions must forever haunt London Bridge, for instance."

"But, d'ye see, Ben, what I mean is that there are particular places where the evil once wrought, still lives—waiting and forever on the look-out."

"Good gracious! What for?"

"Lord knows,—vengeance, maybe."

"Vengeance on whom?"

"Well,—let's say the first cause of all the suffering and despair."

"Nonsense, Sam!"

"May-be-so, Ben. But there are places on this old Earth where strange things do happen——"

"Con-found it!" exclaimed Mr. Joliffe, clutching at his flighty hat again. "Daniel, I forbid such perturbing speed! Drive less recklessly!"

"Ax pardon, but not recklessly, Mr. Joliffe, sir—no!"

"Then abate this most discommoding pace."

"Can't be, sir."

"Why not?"

"Jarsper's orders, sir! 'Dan'l', says he to me, 'you should do it under the hour', says he."

"Pree-poss-terous!" cried Mr. Joliffe jerkily as they jolted in and out of a rut. "Scandalous. . . . Insane——"

"Very good, Mr. Joliffe, sir!"

"Oh, confound you, Daniel!"

"Yessir!"

"Bah!" exclaimed the lawyer in indignant bafflement. "Sam, I shall be boxing his ears if we don't talk and forget the crass fellow and his driving. So tell me,—you must have seen some queer things in your travels."

"Plenty, Ben, especially in the wilder parts along the

Main, Inca, Aztec and Maya Indians. I lived with 'em
once and right folk I found them. Then among the savages
o' the islands I've known a magic whereby a man may kill
by word or just pointing with a bone or some such—'You',
he'll say, 'must die in three days', and damme, Ben, die
he does and in the three days! How it's done, I don't know,
but done it certainly is."

"Ah," nodded Mr. Joliffe, "I opine by the power of
suggestion, hypnotism or the like deviltries, of course."

"Ay, may be. Then there are cures just as wonderful . . ."

Thus Mr. Joliffe questioned, Sam held forth and Dan'l
drove until they were speeding through Wrybourne village
just as the church clock struck four.

"Astounding!" quoth Mr. Joliffe, resettling his ever-restive
hat, "we are here already and—alive! How much further,
Daniel?"

"About six minutes, sir."

Turning from the high-road down a narrow lane Dan'l
whistled, reined up and out from some leafy nook shot the
boy Gimlet who, taking the lathered horse by the bit, cried:

"Right-ho, Dan! Shall I drive him up an' down a bit to
cool 'im off?"

"Ar!" replied Dan'l, socketing whip and reins. "And
you've dropped an aitch!"

"Oh, blow that, Dan'l! 'Op down and lemme git h-up!"

"Now," sighed Dan'l, descending to earth with lithe agility,
"now you've got 'em in the wrong places! This way, gents
both, foller me."

Off from the lane amid thickets he led them by a mazy
track, past that sullen, gloomy pool, and so at last through
a yawning doorway into a musty twilight shut in by moulder-
ing, age-old walls, up crumbling steps to a place bright with
sunbeams flooding in at a jagged hole that once had been
a small window, a pleasant light which showed them Mr.
Shrig, pipe in mouth, seated upon a broken box beside a
long, muffled form couched upon a bed of rotting hay and
wind-drifted leaves.

"Afternoon, sirs!" said Mr. Shrig, rising and tapping out
pipe upon broad palm very tenderly. "I have made bold to
send for you to inform you as how this here case has turned
itself upside down and inside out! Vich sirs, J. Shrig here
and now is bound to con-fess as Fortun'—not content vith

diddling and ditching same, has now fetched your humble a leveller as has fair doubled me up, sirs, and knocked me and this here case sky high! And if you ax me how so, I now begs you, sirs both, to—take a look at this."

As he spoke, Mr. Shrig stooped, twitched away the dingy covering—to show that at sight of which Mr. Joliffe recoiled with a strangled cry, while Sam leaned nearer to gaze down with expression of speechless disbelief changing to certainty and sickening dread:

For there, gazing up at him with awful fixity, faint-smiling, couched with gracious ease, white hands folded reverently upon motionless breast, lay Lord Julian Scrope.

"Not . . . not dead, Shrig?" whispered Mr. Joliffe.

"Ar! . . . As mutton, sir."

"In-credible! For . . . oh, my God . . . he looks alive . . . and younger . . . handsomer even than I ever remember him and actually . . . saintly! His hands . . . folded in prayer——"

"Vell—no, sir. I shouldn't hardly call it prayer, Mr. Joliffe."

"But why not? What d'ye mean?"

"This, sir!" answered Mr. Shrig and stooping, drew and held apart those so reverently folded hands to show what they had been clasping. And now Sam also recoiled, lifting his hands instinctively as against some blinding horror . . . the haft of that knife had once been his own, its keen blade now deep-driven . . . Andromeda's knife. . . . While he yet stared, sick with an ever-growing dread, Mr. Shrig covered this awful thing with the stained old horse blanket that did duty for a shroud.

"Sam," whispered Mr. Joliffe, taking his nerveless arm, "now I'm remembering your words, yes and almost believing —this is the ghostly hour of vengeance."

CHAPTER XXXIV

TELLS OF A PARTING

THEY were out again all three in the sunny air, Mr. Joliffe pale, shaken though full of pertinent enquiry. Sam as livid, but frowning and speechless; yet it was upon him that Mr. Shrig kept his keen gaze as he answered the lawyer's questions.

"When did this happen?"

"From information received, sir, I'd put it about dinnertime, 'twixt ha-past twelve and two o'clock."

"Have you any clues, Shrig, any suspects?"

"Ar, cloos a-plenty, sir, and suspects three or four. Because, as corpses go, his lordship's a pretty informative stiff and has told me two or three helpful fax."

"You mean, I suppose, by his general appearance?"

"I do, Mr. Joliffe. In the first place he tells me as how he has come to this here bee-utifully lonesome spot to meet a friend—an ooman, p'raps, some willage beauty or, p'raps again, a young ladylike fe-male!" Here, the keen eyes watching Sam's motionless, silent figure, saw the powerful hands clench suddenly.

"But, Shrig, why should you suspect any woman?"

"Sir, his lordship being a Scrope was therefore nat'rally add-dickted to The Sex. Also this here solitood! Also the motive ain't robbery. Then you'll ha' noticed as he died smiling werry loverlike! Verefore and therefore my first suspect is of the femmy-nine gender."

"Ye-es, the inference is reasonable, Shrig. Well—hum— to whom do your suspicions point? Have you any particular woman in mind?"

A moment of tense silence, of agonizing expectancy and Sam's eyes closing as against some unbearable vision.

"Well, Shrig, I asked you——"

"Ar, Mr. Joliffe, you did. And, sir, I now answers you full and free—ekker alone responds—as yet."

"Ah, then you are not certain the—hem—culprit is a woman?"

"No, sir, not by no manner o' means—so fur!"

"And indeed," mused Mr. Joliffe, "on second thoughts this would hardly seem a woman's crime. The fatal weapon, I noticed, was powerfully driven, completely buried, suggesting strength with perfect accuracy, which argues coolness and determination."

"Werry true, sir. But some females can be cool as icicles and most ex-tremely determinated. How say you, Mr. Felton, sir?"

"Eh?" exclaimed Sam, starting. "Oh, I'll sheet home, bear away and leave you to it." And off he went at leisurely pace until beyond their sight and hearing,—then he began to run as if Despair itself were on his heels, nor checked until he was in the leafy shade of Jane's "'Chanted Forest". Here he paused to fetch his breath and seeing the great old "magic tree" before him, went and leaned dejectedly against its rugged bole while he strove desperately to order the wild and fearful commotion of his mind.

For some while he stood thus until hearing a cry he glanced up and saw Andromeda speeding towards him.

"Sam. . . . Oh, Sam!" she panted and sinking into his ready arms, clung to him shuddering so violently that fearful doubt grew to a great horror surging over him like a wave. Then she was looking up at him wide-eyed:

"My dear," she whispered, fearfully. "What is it? What have you come . . . to tell me?"

And whispering also, he answered:

"Lord Julian is dead."

"Yes," she sighed, hiding her face against him. "What must I do now?"

"Then . . . Andromeda, you . . . knew?"

"Yes . . . I knew . . . hours ago."

"But how . . . how could you?"

"Because . . . Uncle Arthur told me."

"When, Andromeda, when?"

"What can it matter now . . . why are you so strangely, so dreadfully altered?"

"Oh, my dear," he whispered, gesturing towards the empty sheath at her girdle, "where is the knife?"

"Why, Sam—ah, why do you ask?"

"Because it was that knife . . . mine . . . your knife that killed him!" Now at this, she cried out as if he had struck

her and crouching against the tree, covered her face. Then
Sam's arms were about her protectingly.

"My own dear," said he, drawing her close, "nothing matters
except our love——" Swiftly she looked up at him, and seeing all the agony in his too honest eyes, nodded her head,
saying in oddly expressionless voice:

"Why, of course—only yesterday you saw the knife in my
hand,—you saw me strike that murderous blow,—you heard
me say I could kill him! And now he lies dead! Oh, my
poor dear—and you love me still."

"Of course, and for ever."

"Even though you think, you suspect——"

"Hush, for God's sake!" he whispered harshly. "Yesterday I saw you drop that cursed knife—tell me—did you pick
it up again?"

"Why do you ask, Sam dear?"

"Because I've been hoping, yes and praying—as I am
now—that you forgot it—left it lying here by this tree, and
that someone else found it."

"And suppose," said she, looking deep into his eyes, "suppose I tell you that I found it—and used it?"

"Then to-night, no—this very hour, I'll carry you away
to the coast . . . a harbour I know . . . there I'll buy or steal
a boat o' some kind . . . stand away down channel and pray
God we may win to France or be picked up by French or
Spanish cruisers so we get clear of England and English
ships."

"And what," she whispered, "oh, what of poor Uncle
Arthur? Would you take him with us?"

"Ay, even that—for your sake."

Andromeda sighed deeply and hiding her face against him
murmured:

"Oh, my brave, faithful, beloved man! Then so you must
—for I did lose the knife and Uncle found it."

"Thank the Lord!" Sam breathed. "You saw him find
it?"

"No. But last night I kept watch. I heard Wrybourne
Church clock strike eleven and a little while after . . . he
stole from the caravan . . . the moon was up and I saw the
flash of that hateful knife and—Oh, my dear—he raised it
heavenwards and kissed it as if it had been some holy thing.
Then I called to him and ran, but he fled from me into the

wood and I lost him. . . . So I sent Esau after him, but the dog loves him, and after all he is only a dog. Uncle Arthur was away all night but returned to-day all broken with fatigue and . . . Oh, from words I heard him muttering—I knew Lord Julian was dead and . . . Lady Barbara avenged. So then I prayed God to send you to me—and here I am, safe in your dear arms and at peace for a little while."

"And here," said Sam, folding her closer, "here you shall be safe while I have life and strength——"

"Meda! My love, my joy and only consolation . . ." Wailing these words, Mr. Verinder tottered into view, a woeful figure, his finery of garments rumpled and stained, his un-shaven face convulsed by sharpest agony. "Oh Meda," he gasped, "I am lost—lost, broken and abandoned of my God . . . disappointed, heartbroken, hopeless and abject. And now since God has denied me the vengeance I hoped, prayed and lived for, you cannot, must not, shall not desert and render me utterly desolate——"

"Sir," began Sam, but she checked him with a gesture, saying:

"But, Uncle Arthur, your enemy is dead, so how has God denied you? Lord Julian is dead——"

"Yes, yes, I know this, I saw him, child. Yes, I beheld him lying—in his glory, beautified by death! Yes, he—this vile wretch, this foul, black-hearted villain lay there with his youth renewed, hands folded upon his dead breast, showing like a sleeping saint—his face so evil in life, now in death, most fair, its wickedness all smoothed away by deadly steel deep driven and, oh malediction,—by other hand than mine! He at peace and glorious in death—I alive and woeful—So does God mock me——"

"But, Uncle, you had the knife."

"The knife, yes—ah, the sweet, sharp knife, I had it but— Oh God, Oh God—I lost it in the wood, dropped it in the hateful, blinding dark. I sought it, upon my knees I sought it, praying—yet vain, all vain alike my seeking and my prayers, for I found it not. But in the dawn I came upon a stone, a sharp-edged, jagged flint-stone, though I yearned for the sharp, bright knife . . ."

"Yes, Uncle, and what did you do then?"

"Fell asleep, child, and dreamed gloriously until the birds waked me with their singing. So I lay and harkened to this that is the very music of God—until I heard a laugh that changed to the bleating of a sheep and after this a rush and rustle of wind. . . . Then I found myself close to that ruined mill I have twice essayed to paint and there I found him dead and mocking me with his glory. So, because it seems God has turned from me I fled to thee, my one remaining comfort and only joy, confiding in the hope, nay, the assurance that you will never abandon me, never—never forsake me——"

"Neither will I, sir," said Sam and rather grimly. "You shall find me ever ready to serve you when Andromeda is my wife. Here will we live and together we——"

"No—and no!" cried Mr. Verinder, wildly. "You are but common clay with no music in your soul. Your presence is a blight I cannot, must not endure. Your very shadow chills the genius within me and for which alone I endure life! Wed him, Meda, if you will, yield that sweet and lovely body to his brutish love, but——"

"Avast!" growled Sam. "Hold hard, Mr. Verinder! How can my love be 'brutish' now when last time we met I was your 'dear Felton' and 'a man raised up by God'! Ay, and you gave us your blessing into the bargain——"

"Yes, yes I did!" said Mr. Verinder, peevishly. "Of course I did. But since then, God has changed towards me and therefore all else is changed,—quite, quite altered and—especially my unhappy self!"

"Ay," nodded Sam, "you're a confoundingly changeable customer, sir, but then, d'ye see, I'm not, and especially as regards Andromeda. So the sooner you change back again the better. However, instead of one slave you're going to have two, ay—just as soon as wedlock can make me so——"

"How—how?" panted Mr. Verinder, clenching plump, white fists. "Do I understand you will force your attentions upon my beloved niece, this sweet child of my adoption? Will you actually defy me?"

"No, sir, ignore you."

"Oh, insolence! Had I a whip I should strike you——" Here Andromeda took him in her arms, but even while she strove to soothe him he flourished dimpled fists, crying: "Ah, were you a gentleman I'd call you out and shoot you——"

"Uncle Arthur, hush now! Oh, my dear, calm yourself—there, there! Come and rest while I brew tea—come!"

"Tea? Ah, yes, yes. I'm all foredone, I languish! Tea that blessed panacea,—yes, go prepare it, beloved child, and hurry, hurry! Felton and I shall follow. Dear Felton, forgive me, I was hasty. I am not myself,—so pray, dear Felton, say I am forgiven."

"Ay, sir, heartily."

"So, you hear the dear, good fellow, Meda? Go you now, my ever precious, go—go!" Slowly she turned and unwillingly obeyed.

Now scarcely was she out of sight than Mr. Verinder uttered a pitiful, wailing cry and leapt headlong at Sam who thus surprised had some difficulty in fending off this attack, so that Andromeda, speeding back to this outcry, arrived just in time to see her Uncle fall heavily.

"Ah—trickery!" exclaimed Sam. "Damme, I scarce touched him;" but writhing upon the grass, Mr. Verinder gasped:

"Meda . . . Oh Meda, now . . . you see . . . how he hates and misuses me——"

"No!" retorted Sam, bitterly. "You aren't worth my hate, I scorn you for the deceitful, miserable half-wit you are."

"No, no!" wailed Mr. Verinder, covering his face. "I am not mad—not that—Ah God—not mad!"

"Better so," growled Sam, driven beyond endurance, "better mad than selfish liar and trickster."

"Andromeda," gasped her uncle, crawling to her feet and writhing there, "oh, my brave darling, comfort me, cherish me, save me! You are my very life——"

"Be silent—you!" cried Sam harshly. "Now, Andromeda, be warned. . . . Oh, my dear, you are wasting your life and mine for a selfish, cowardly trickster who plays upon your fears and makes your devotion fetters to enslave you to his service, damn him——"

"Beloved child," sighed Mr. Verinder, rising feebly to his knees, "without you I cannot and will not live. Wed this man if you will, this cruel man so harsh, so brutal—wed him and in that hour I die. Yes, here kneeling before the Great God of our Salvation, I swear I will end my hated life and give back my poor soul to my Creator! So choose between us, my dearest one, choose."

"Ay," muttered Sam, bitterly, seeing her look and reading it aright, "choose and be done."

Now glancing from yearning, stalwart man down to the piteous suppliant at her feet, she hesitated, yet when at last she found speech she answered as he had dreaded and expected, saying firm-lipped though with lifeless voice:

"Sam dearest, I have chosen . . . as I must . . . because I am . . . Andromeda."

"You mean," he demanded, brokenly, "sacrifice? That you . . . I . . . this is the end?" And in the same dull, passionless tone, she answered:

"Yes . . . my beloved."

Sam's powerful fists quivered, his grim lips parted in a snarl, but—reading the supplication in her golden eyes, he choked back bitterness of despair with fury of reproach and bowed his head, saying after a moment and very humbly:

"As you will . . . but I shall always love you."

"And I," she murmured and always in the same dreary monotone, "I shall be . . . always . . . only yours." But saying this, she drew from her bosom the gold chain and jewelled pendant, his gift, and held it out to him on her open palm, whispering:

"Oh, my darling, I have never worn it because I wanted your dear hands to set it about me, so do it now, but kiss it first that it may comfort me the more when I shall touch and kiss it—in my loneliness. Kiss it, dear, then fasten it about my throat." Dumbly he obeyed though his big hands were very unsteady as he locked the chain about this round white neck. And when this was done at last:

"Kiss me!" she murmured. So their lips met in a sweet agony of farewell.

"Now," she sighed. "Oh now, my ever dearest, go . . . in mercy to us both—ah, beloved—go!"

Then, uttering no word, Sam turned and with not one backward glance, trudged away to—emptiness.

H

CHAPTER XXXV

TELLS HOW AND WHY SAM WAS "TOO LATE"

AND now treading this well-remembered path, Sam checked and stumbled more than once, for, though his scowling eyes were tearless, grief was blinding him to all save the memory of Andromeda's last despairing look in such pitiful contrast to the firm-set, too-resolute lips that for duty's sake had bidden him away; thus now, because of her indomitable will, Sam despaired also.

The countryside about him, radiant with sun, was beautiful as ever, birds near and far piped and chirruped joyfully as ever but Sam blundered and stumbled through a bleak desolation towards a blank dreariness where for him was no future. Only with him went the memory of Andromeda's beloved, stricken face that seemed to blot out the very universe.

In this state of bitter despair and hopeless dejection Sam had reached a certain familiar stile when he espied a woman crouched beneath the hedge nearby and was about to pass on, but something in her look and attitude arrested him and he knew her for the lady of the lonely cottage in the by-road and he paused.

"Your pardon, marm," said he, hat in hand, "but is anything wrong?"

"I—I'm afraid so, sir," she answered, with shyly rueful smile. "Crossing the stile very awkwardly, I have turned my ankle so painfully that I can neither stand nor go, and my cottage is too far to hop, though I have done my best."

"Then of course I'll carry you—if you'll allow."

"Oh, but I—I could not—you could not. I mean it is some distance."

"However, we'd manage it by easy stages."

"You are greatly kind, sir . . . and this is such a lonely place . . . and I cannot remain here all night."

"No, marm, it stands to reason you can't."

"But to—to so burden you, sir, a stranger."

"Not quite, marm, I spoke to you some days ago."

"Yes, of course you did. I remember now you are the gentleman who wished to be directed."

"Not gentleman, just a sailorman and my name is Felton, Sam Felton—you may have heard mention of it—perhaps?" Now as he propounded this question, Sam watched the almost too-sensitive features of this lady, the luminous eyes, delicate nostrils and mouth with its sweetly-gentle curves, and read in this face such unaffected surprise, such artless sincerity that he knew she spoke truly when she answered:

"No, Mr. Felton, how could I and why should I?"

"Well," said he, keen gaze still intent, "I thought maybe my name had been mentioned by your son."

"My son?" she repeated, her pale face suddenly glorified by the mother-light beaming in her long-lashed eyes. "Then you know my Eustace? I am glad, for he needs a friend, poor boy—he like his mother is very solitary and much too sensitive. So I should like you for his friend—if it may be."

"Why, marm, d'ye see, I . . . we have met only once or twice and then I . . . we . . . well, didn't seem to have much in common."

"I . . . I am not surprised, sir," sighed she and with such mournfulness of look and tone that Sam flinched. "He is much too high-strung and of a quite painful shyness,—but then so am I, so perhaps I'm to blame. As it is, he lives only for his music—and me, and yes, poor hopeless boy, one other! And he is my hope, his tender love has been my one joy and solace, for Mr. Felton in this one particular I am humbly like the Man of Sorrows, because I too am 'acquainted with grief', —though thank our kind God, I have my dear son."

"And he," murmured Sam, "should be thankful for such mother, mine's dead, d'ye see."

"Poor boy!" she whispered, touching his sleeve very gently. "I see you loved her deeply. So now this mother would comfort you if she could—please know me better if you will. I am Ruth Jennings and——"

"Now God love you!" exclaimed Sam impulsively, " 'Ruth' was my mother's name and therefore the loveliest in all this world—except one"—and speaking, he bowed his head to kiss this slender, comforting hand.

"Dear boy!" she sighed. "I dare to think your so loved mother looking down on us from God's light, is blessing me now in her son's kiss. So more, oh, more than ever I hope that someday perhaps you may bless my son with your friendship. And now—if you will help me I shall be so very grateful."

Laying by his stick, Sam raised her in his powerful arms, saying as he did so:

"Now pray rest easy. Try to think we are very old friends."

"That will not be difficult," said she, smiling, "though you are quite a boy really, but then all men creatures are great big children. . . . And I do hope you don't find me too heavy."

"On the contrary you are much too light," he answered, striding along with her easily. "But I'm wondering why you were so—startled when first I spoke you in the lane?"

"That was because my poor Eustace has been so terribly nervous lately. He imagined he was being followed—especially in the woods—a pale man and an impish boy who grinned and peeped—which sounds absurdly fanciful, and yet for the moment I thought you must be one of them."

"But why should anyone watch your son?"

"I don't know, I cannot imagine. I hope and believe it is all his fancy,—though for some time now he has seemed changed."

"Oh? Ah?" said Sam, keeping his gaze on the path before them. "Since when?"

"More than a year. He came flying to me one evening crying out that he was lost in the dark,—as he used to do sometimes when a little boy. But I comforted him at last by playing part of a sonata he was composing—such lovely music! Yet there are times even now when he seems—dreadfully troubled . . . and it hurts me to know he has a secret from his mother. To be sure he is deeply in love, but this is no secret."

"Oh?" murmured Sam. "Who with?"

"A very beautiful young lady though rather odd, I think, because she lives like a gipsy in the woods with an even odder relative. . . . Perhaps, after all, she may be the true reason for his grief—you see, he has loved her so long and quite without hope, he tells me. It is when he visits these people, they are very musical, that he thinks he is being watched and followed. Only the other day my darling came to me in quite frantic state—indeed I do not know what I should have done but for that good, kind Mr. Brown——"

"Eh, m'lady—who?"

"Oh, a Mr. Caleb Brown, such a dear, quaint, kindly person. Do you happen to know him?"

"Oh yes. Pray how did he manage—I mean how did you meet him?"

"Months ago! I was trying to dig my garden, but the ground was so hard and I am not at all clever with a spade. Mr. Brown happened to see me and proffered his help and he was so very kindly, so quaint and gentle that I could not refuse. Since then he has helped me quite often."

"Does he know your son?"

"Oh, yes. Mr. Brown loves to sit and hear him play his violin while I accompany on the harp or pianoforte—though he often says,—I mean Mr. Brown, of course,—that he has an untutored ear, though he calls it an 'untootered year'. Now do pray put me down and take a rest——" But at this moment was a cry and Cecily Croft hurried to meet them, enquiring anxiously:

"Oh, Mr. Felton, is she hurt? Dear Mrs. Jennings, whatever is it?"

"Dear child, nothing more than a sprained ankle."

"'Tis bad enough, mam,—so terrible swollen! Can I help?"

"If you will hurry on to the cottage and put on the kettle for tea——"

"Yes, I'll run. I was on my way there with your butter and a loaf I made special for you. . . . And I'll have things ready to tend that poor ankle!" And away sped Cecily, fleet and graceful as a stag and despite the basket she carried.

"So beautiful!" sighed Mrs. Jennings, looking after her. "So sweetly good! I do hope she at least will have a happy life."

"D'you think she won't, m'lady?"

"Well, her uncle and aunt are not very kind to her and I'm afraid the dear innocent has given her love unwisely."

"Ay, you mean young Ralph Scrope. D'you know him, m'lady?"

"Yes," she answered, averting his look. "I did once, but now I—do not."

"Would you say he might be altered for the better?"

"No, never—with such a father."

"D'you think such a father would be much better—dead?"

"Yes!" she whispered.

"So do I!" nodded Sam. "And others ha' thought the same. And, m'lady, now we'll carry on, if you're ready?"

"Yes," she answered, smiling up at him now. "Yes, my gentle Hercules. But please why do you call me your lady?"

"Because, next to 'Mother' and 'home' and 'woman', it's the best word I know."

Then Sam bore her on again nor stayed until somewhat breathless and spent, he reached the cottage gate at last and there halted and scowled—to see Mr. Shrig in the trim garden standing very still and apparently lost in profound contemplation of a flower-pot.

"Oh, Mr. Brown, how nice to see you!"

Starting violently, Mr. Shrig turned, stared—then hastened to open the gate, hat in hand.

"Dear Mr. Brown, how pale you are! And there really is nothing serious, merely a twisted ankle. Pray come indoors and when Cecily has helped me bathe it, we will all have a nice, cosy tea."

Unspeaking, Sam bore her into the cottage, laid her gently upon a couch, smiled away her thanks and stepped out into the garden where he beheld Mr. Shrig staring fixedly at an onion, one of a row.

"Jasper," he demanded, "how the devil can you do it?"

"Eh?" murmured Mr. Shrig, his gaze still intent.

"How can you trick yourself into such home as this— worm your way between such mother and her son? Damme, it's not decent!"

"Ar!" sighed Mr. Shrig. "And, pal, talking o' vorms I'll ax you to remember as I'm Caleb Brown yereabouts."

"Yours is a cursed deceitful profession!"

"Ar, that it are, so right you are, Sammy pal. And I'd like you to in-form me at vich partickler p'int in the landskip you found Mrs. J?"

"The stile beyond the second spinney."

"Vas she a-coming or a-going?"

"I don't know, and shouldn't tell you if I did."

"Ho!" exclaimed Mr. Shrig. "So? Im-pede The Law now, is it? For J. Shrig being a Limb o' the Law is thereby, as in dooty bound, com-pelled——"

At this moment Mrs. Jennings called to them through the open lattice.

"Do please come in and sit down, Cecily has nearly finished with me and so cleverly, bless her! Then we—Oh, Mr. Brown, I hear the kettle boiling over—in the kitchen, will you please see to it?"

"A pleasure, marm!"

Thus presently seated all four in this small parlour, a strangely pleasant meal they had, thanks to the charm and unaffected grace of their gentle hostess. Thereafter, assisted by Mr. Shrig's sturdy arm, she crossed to the piano, saying very diffidently:

"Now . . . if you do not mind, I—I should like to show you why I am so proud of my dear son . . . I will play for you—music he composed for and has dedicated to his mother, may I?"

"Do please!" answered Sam.

"Honoured, marm!" murmured Mr. Shrig.

"You know I always love to hear you play it, marm," said Cecily.

Then reaching her slender hands to the keyboard, this mother filled the air with a son's love wrought into splendid sound, a sweetly plaintive melody often lost in surging counter-themes, yet as often recurring,—a melody that was to haunt Sam hereafter.

"Oh . . . lovely!" sighed Cecily, when the last echo had died away.

"That," said Sam, "that is noble music."

"Yes," she answered, smiling, "Eustace has genius . . . someday . . . perhaps it will bless the world. I have great hopes of my dear son."

And presently, with her gently spoken thanks and farewell in his ears, Sam followed Mr. Shrig out of this small, lonely cottage and for some while neither uttered a word. When at last Sam spoke it was with a diffidence very strange in him.

"Jasper, you're a law officer and will think me a sentimental fool when I tell you I feel as if we had been on—holy ground . . . for d'ye see, that gracious, gentle lady makes her little cottage a holy place . . . sacred . . . just because of her own goodness."

"Agreed, pal—ar, werry much so!"

"And now, Jasper, now damme I'm wishing, for her sake, I'd been . . . a little kinder, less hostile to her son. However, I'll make up for it next time we meet, ay, I'll be more friendly."

"You can't, pal."

"Eh? And why the devil not?"

"Because you're too late."

"How can that be?"

"Pal," said Mr. Shrig, easing out his large, silver watch and consulting it, "you have missed him by eggs-ackly two hours and fifty-three minutes——"

Grasping his arm, Sam halted him and thus face to face, demanded in harsh whisper:

"Jasper, are you trying to tell me it was—her son killed Lord Julian and is now safe away? If so, good luck to him say I! Come, let's hear,—speak man, speak will ye."

"Pal," sighed Mr. Shrig, "never in all my puff have I been so near piping my eye as this here afternoon, and the cause thereof—his mother's vords,—you'll mind 'em: 'Someday', says she, 'he'll bless the vorld! I've great hopes o' my dear son', says she—and all the time this son she's so proud of—is laying stiff and cold and werry damp—poor lady!" Sam fell back a step and when he spoke it was in dreadful, broken whisper:

"Jasper . . . oh, Jasper . . . you never mean . . . ha—what do you mean?"

"Death, pal! Her son has took the only road, the best, ar—and the cleanest road up and out of it all. Fellerdesee! That conwenient pool! By my con-nivance! For his mother's sake!"

"Christ-Jesus," gasped Sam. "Christ pity her . . . the poor, sweet, gentle soul . . . God comfort her!"

"Same here and amen!" muttered Mr. Shrig. "I come to break the noos to her, but s'soon as I see her in your arms s'helpless, I couldn't say a word, my chaffer refused its office, ar—burn my neck if it didn't! And now——" here, fumbling in breast, he drew thence his bulbous pocketbook wherefrom he extracted a folded paper, saying: "Seeing as how there's mention o' your lordship herein, your lordship had better look it over." Unfolding this paper he passed it to Sam, who read these words hastily though firmly written in pencil:

I scribble these lines in gratitude to that kind friend who for my mother's sake permits me the better way. I killed Lord Julian because he was my father. I discovered this but lately with the fact that he had deceived my beloved mother with a false marriage and would have harmed her yet again. I have also to inform you that together with the lately deceased Lord Julian I was concerned in the death of his brother and my uncle, the late Earl thirteen months since. Now in my turn I go where I must but in the comforting hope of joyous reunion with the one solitary soul whose faith and love never failed me, she who has made my sorry existence bearable, this pure angel on earth —my beloved mother. May I venture to hope the new Earl Japhet, known as S. Felton will care for her in this pitiful life until she in due time shall join me in the greater and happier. In which hope I subscribe myself, for the first and last time

EUSTACE (by natural right) LORD SCROPE.

"And," said Mr Shrig, taking and refolding this letter, "there y'are!"

"But, oh damme!" exclaimed Sam, greatly troubled. "This frightful news will pretty near kill her! It must be broken to her very gently by someone she knows well . . . a friend. . . . Ay,—Jasper, this must be your duty for she calls you 'friend'——"

"No, pal! That's the reason as I can't. It must be you— ar, you've had her in your arms,—so you it is!"

"Never in this world!"

"Werry good, then I must make it that there handsome young fe-male Ces'ly, Mistress Croft. Let's turn back and meet same."

"No, Jasper, I've had enough for one day, ay—too much, damme! For, d'ye see, had I only been a little kinder to the poor fellow . . . been his friend . . . this might never have happened."

"And yet again, it might, Sam pal. For I can lay sich information agin Number Vun deceased as'll make you vonder as he didn't get hisself de-ceased long afore to-day, and makes

his bloody finish werry nat'ral and proper—though being
Murder and hence The Capital Act, the Law must take its
course, Justice be windicated and myself the means of——
Ah, by Goles,—there's Missis Ces'ly crossing the medder
yonder,—now's our chance!"

"Ay, so I'll leave you to it, Jasper and bear away for
home."

CHAPTER XXXVI

THE old farmhouse lay very hushed and silent for Captain Ned and his bride were still away. Aunt Deborah was visiting Grannyanne and Sam finding it thus deserted, went forth into the orchard and the better to occupy his troubled mind, set himself to construct a rustic table to match the seat that now stood invitingly beneath his favourite tree.

But in a little while, as if lured by the rasp of saw and ring of busy hammer, came Nancy light of foot, bright of eye and flushed of cheek who having saluted him with shy curtsey, said between ruddy, smiling lips:

"La, sir, you was all wrong about—my Tom! 'Twas me as he intended for arl the time."

"Good!" sighed Sam. "And you said 'yes', I hope?"

" 'Deed, sir—I had to, for Tom were that sudden—so fierce and masterful that ef I hadn't give him 'yes', I du b'leeve—Oh my—he'd ha' stifled me, he would!"

"All quite proper and ship-shape, Nancy. I hope he'll stifle you as properly and pretty often when you are his . . . wife." Here Sam, hesitating at the word, sighed again.

"La, sir, what things ee du say! But, oh, Mr. Felton, why du ee sigh so heavy and show so grievous?"

"Do I, Nancy?"

"Ay, that ee du. Your eyes be that woeful sad! Shall I bring ee a jug o' our home-brew? There be nought like strong ale for to comfort a man's sorrows."

"Thanks, Nancy. You're wise as you're lovely. Lord, what a wife you'll make! Tom's a mighty lucky fellow!"

"Lud,—Mr. Felton!" she exclaimed, with smiling, conscious blush, and away she sped.

Sam was miserably contrasting Tom's happy lot with his own misery when Tom himself came striding to salute in smart, quarter-deck manner, saying:

"Sir, by your leave I'm here to report operation com-pletely successful and now begs to express gratitood for same, very much so, sir."

"Good!" quoth Sam again, with another deep sigh and scowling blackly at his hammer. "Though damme if I know why some fellows have all the luck!"

"Ay, sir, true enough. And I'm one o' the luckiest and all b'reason o' you, sir. For, according to your orders, I stood away to wind'ard, plying off and on, kept her in my lee until of her own accord, sir, she bore up, run me aboard and brought me to close action."

"Ay," nodded Sam, dejectedly, "and how then?"

"Why then, sir, she demands the who of it, so I grapples her and lets her have the truth of it."

"With a—a kiss, I suppose, Tom?"

"No, sir—with a whole broadside of 'em—till she was breathless and finally struck her colours with a 'yes'. So the banns'll be read for us at once, and all thanks to you, Mr. Felton, sir."

"I'm—glad!" said Sam, though with sigh like a groan.

"Thankee, sir, though, axing pardon, you don't hardly look it, sir."

"However, I am glad, Tom, and wish you and your Nancy every happiness."

"Thankee again, sir, and heartily. And talking o' happiness—why, Lord love us,—here be mine coming now—on her two pretty feet——!" And, indeed, back came Nancy bearing the ale, but now with no eyes or thought except for her comely Tom, as he for her. And beholding their radiant joy, Sam could not bear to look, so commenced banging away with his hammer until this happy pair left him to his labours, whereupon he must needs watch them go and bitterly envious, poor fellow.

But there was the good ale, so he gulped at it fiercely, and there were the tools, so he wrought with them furiously until a voice arrested him and glancing up, he beheld Cecily looking at him through glitter of tears.

"Mr. Felton, 'tis so awful! That poor lady . . . her dear son! However can I tell her? Mr. Brown do say 'tis I must break the news . . . this dreadful accident to her only son! And 'tis I must tell her——"

"Yes, it must be you, Cecily. You are so sweetly gentle it will come better from you than any other."

"But . . . her only son as she so loves . . . and him so
clever . . . and now dead . . . and in that same dreadful
pool! How ever can I bear to tell her?"

"Just because your tender sympathy can make the blow
less harsh and cruel, Cecily. Your gentle arms may be her
comfort, your gracious strength may help her to bear this
new sorrow."

"Mr. Felton," said she, dashing away her tears to view
him the better, "you're a strange man and talk so that you
make me feel better and stronger than I really am or ever
thought I could be."

"Only because you are naturally good and so may be able
to comfort this poor stricken lady—if you will only try."

"Yes, yes, of course I'll try, though 'twill nigh break my
heart!"

"Indeed, Cecily, you are so very much too good for any
Scrope, especially young Ralph—do you really love him?"

"Yes, yes I do—only God knows how much . . . and this
be my own grief he is now to London, for to woo and wed
that rich lady——"

"No, my dear, oh no! Your rogue Ralph shall never marry
this lady, never! So don't grieve——"

"Oh, but—Mr. Felton, how—how can you be so certain-
sure? Oh, please, what do ee mean? For dear God's sake—
what?"

"Just what I say, Cecily, and by your dear God I swear
it! Now go comfort that sorrowing mother like the good,
beautiful angel you are."

Slowly she turned and went her way, taking much of the
sunlight with her, or so Sam was thinking when back she
sped to say:

"Oh, my gracious, I was forgetting! Miss Andromeda met
me and gave me this note for you, here 'tis. And," she added
shyly as Sam took this precious thing, "I do hope as you . . .
and she will be happy, very happy . . . together."

"Thanks!" muttered Sam, hoarsely, gazing down at this
very small missive. "Thank you, Cecily—dear!" When
she had gone, he unfolded this paper and read these pencilled
words:

Oh my dear, I cannot sleep to-night without writing you
one last word. And this word, beloved, is Hope. Without

this I think my heart would die within me. If you can wait, if only you can be patient—someday I shall come back to you. This must be a short note because I cannot bear to write more, yet these few words and this small piece of paper bear to you all the best of me with the yearning, deathless love of your

ANDROMEDA.

Seated upon his rustic bench Sam read this message over and over again and was still thus intent when he was roused by a familiar voice and glancing up, exclaimed, peevishly:

"Damme, Jasper, you're dev'lish silent and sudden!"

"Ax your pardon, m'lord——"

"Belay all that, the very word sickens me! What d'ye want with me, Jasper?"

"Sir, this here case having con-clooded itself so fur as I'm con-carned, seeing as how Numbers Vun and Two at this i-dentical moment is being carted to the mort-u-ary at Lewes in a vaggon borryed for the o-ccasion, I've dropped in for a parting vord and puff at my steamer along o' you—if agreeable?"

"Yes, of course, old fellow. If I seemed a bit short with you I ask pardon, but you startled me as usual, and besides this frightful business has upset me."

"Ditto here, pal."

"Isn't Mr. Joliffe with you?"

"No, sir, he's off to ketch the night mail. For, says he, 'tell the Earl (meaning you o' course) as how this terrimendious happening calls me (that's him) back to London for some days at least, but that I (him again) shall visit his lordship (that's you again) in Wrybourne soon as possible and shall write in the meantime'."

"Oh well, sit down, Jasper, light your pipe and tell me how you found the—the killer."

"I didn't, pal, 'twas him found me! Ar, and I'll tell jest how, s'soon as I've got my puffer a-going."

This being accomplished, Mr. Shrig puffed, sat down and talked, nor did Sam utter a word until the narration was ended.

"Dan'l and me has got his lordship's carkiss into the aforementioned vaggin and are having a delayed bite at the Wrybourne Arms and in strolls Mr. Jennings carrying his fiddle in its case. 'Mr. Brown', says he, wery affable, 'may I beg

the favour of a vord vith you alone?' So arter Dan'l has left
us, 'Sir', says Mr. J., ''tis only lately as I've found our supposed friend Mr. Brown is also a Bow Street Orficer'. 'Correct, sir', I says, 'but that don't alter friendship o' same,
'specially for your lady mother'. 'I'm glad o' that', says he,
'because I'm here to inform you as I killed Lord Scrope
because he vas my father and also to rid the vorld, but
especially my mother of a cruel, black-souled villain.' 'Vich,
sir,' says I, 'don't sap-prise me, seeing as I've suspicioned
you might kill same ever since I diskevered how he come to
be your father'. 'Oh!' says he, 'then you know some part of
his vileness. I myself discovered this fact only recently or I
should certainly have destroyed him before now'. 'Sir', says
I, 'your motive vas werry powerful thereto, but Murder is
The Capital Act and myself being a limb o' The Law must
per-form according'. 'Oh, certainly', he says and werry agree-
ably. 'You must do your duty and I must pay the penalty,
that's the reason I'm here. So pray tell me, Mr. Brown,—
arter they've hanged me—must my wretched body be jibbeted,
hung in chains and—hereabouts'? 'Sir', I says, ''tis usually
so done on or near the site o' The Deed'. 'Yes', says he, nowise troubled, 'so I understand. But, Mr. Brown, if you are
truly my mother's friend, I beg you will arrange for my jibbet
to stand as far from Wrybourne as possible—for (and here
he gives a little cough) her sake—my mother'. 'Sir', I replies,
'for the sake o' that same (and here I gives a cough) dear,
gentle lady, I begs to suggest a method by vich you can pay
the aforementioned penalty vithout eether hanging nor yet
jibbeting,—you might con-trive a accident with a firearm or
tumble into a pool'. 'Oh, Mr. Brown', says he, looking
remarkable grateful, 'you are indeed a true, kind friend'—
and here for the only time his big eyes is tearful, 'sich friend',
says he, 'that vere-ever I must go, be it heaven or hell, I shall
treasure your memory for my dear mother's sake. And now
p'raps I'd better put my admission in writing, Mr. Brown?'
'Ar, it would be best', says I, so I lends him my pencil, gives
him a page out o' my pocketbook, and he writes cool and
calm as if to his tailor. Then, never troubling to read it over,
he gives it to me, saying: 'Mr. Brown, I have ventured to
address Mr. Felton the noo earl on my mother's behalf. I
may be wrong, but he seems a somevat hard sort o' person,
if therefore you'll be good enough to second my appeal, a

humble but desperately anxious plea, you'd add to my deep gratitood'. 'Sir', says I, 'all as you ax I'll do for your own sake and your lady mother's'. Then up he gets, puts on his dicer and takes up his fiddle, saying: 'If you don't object I'll take my wiolin along o' me because 'twas a present from my mother. And now, Mr. Brown, good-bye and farewell and', says he, hesitating, 'I should esteem it greatly and find it a comfort if you'd, for one moment, take the hand of a ass-assin'."

"Jasper, I hope you did?"

"Ay, I did so, pal. Then he looks at his vatch and says he, 'Pray give me half-an-hour'. And off he goes. . . . Pal, I give him a full hour, then calling Dan'l, off I goes to that there Mill pool. And the first thing I sees is—the fiddle-case a-floating like a little barge, and as I'm trying to fish this ashore, Dan'l says: 'Here he is, Jarsper, here among the reeds',—and, pal, there he is—floating too—and face uppards. And so—there y'are!"

"Jasper, he was a man!"

"Werry true, and a aristocrat besides."

"Ha—damme!" exclaimed Sam, leaping afoot. "I shall regret him all my life!"

"Howsomever," said Mr. Shrig, rising also, "seeing as how his life has been neether a bed o' roses not yet all beer and skittles, I hope as your lordship'll do summat in regard to his dewoted and now grieving lady mother."

"Good God, man, of course! She shall have every comfort, every care. I'll do all—— Oh, hell—what can I or anyone do for such grief as hers?"

"Ekker," murmured Mr. Shrig, shaking his head, "ekker alone responds!" Then having tapped out his fragmentary clay pipe very tenderly as usual upon his palm, he rose, saying rather mournfully:

"Pal Sam, sir, this here has been a werry onsatisfactory case—'specially for your humble,—but you still draw the wital air instead o' being meat for worms, and that's summat arter all,—you're all a-blowing and a-blooming vith the best o' life afore you and happiness—I hope. So now in bidding ye Good-bye, Sam and sir, being also your pal, I now begs leave to offer you a bit of adwice."

"Well," enquired Sam, as they clasped hands, "out with it, Jasper."

"Talking o' steak and kidney pudden, same being wholesome and succulent,—I suggest that there pony-cart or any other conweyance in the hope that someday mebbe I shall make my bow to your lovely young count-ess. And so, my lord, good-bye!"

For some while after Jasper Shrig had departed, Sam remained gazing thoughtfully at Andromeda's note, until slowly his grief and yearning gave place to indignation, and this again to a coldly purposeful anger; inspired by which, he rose, donned his coat, rammed on his hat and went striding furiously, to achieve this purpose.

CHAPTER XXXVII

ANDROMEDA was busied preparing supper while **Mr.** Verinder seated comfortably nearby played dreamy music to her on his flute,—when up leapt Esau with joyous clamour; thus rudely interrupted they looked up to behold Sam scowling at them. Andromeda gazed speechless and utterly still. **Mr.** Verinder, on the contrary, flourished his silenced flute as it had been weapon of offence, demanding truculently:

"What, sir, will you trouble us again? Must you plague us yet?" Then finding himself quite disregarded, he laid down his flute and rose, saying desperately:

"Mr. Felton, if you come to plead your selfish love, you may begone. If you are here to assail my ewe lamb her precious innocence, I shall defend her with my very life."

"Avast, Chatterbox," growled Sam. "Belay your silly prattle. Stow your gab. I'm not come pleading, but to make an end o' this foolery one way or t'other. Andromeda, I've read your note. I know it by heart. You bid me wait, you ask me to be patient—why? Must I waste months, ay, maybe years till my lord here changes his mind again? Not I, no damme! And will you allow this sly, drivelling lubber to trick you into ordering our two lives now and in the future? If so, then I'll not be a party to such curst, sickly, sentimental nonsense."

"Is this an ultimatum?" she enquired, gently.

"Ay, call it that. However, I'll not drag out my days in empty yearning, hoping and waiting until your sly hypocrite here graciously permits you to become my wife. I tell you he shall not rule my destiny or victimize me as he does you——"

"Liar!" cried Mr. Verinder.

"Andromeda, I tell you this thing you call 'uncle' is a clinging misery, a vampire sucking your very life away! So it's now or never,—will you die his worn-out slave or live as my beloved——"

"Oh, abom—abominable!" panted Mr. Verinder. "Ruffian and liar depart or I shall certainly assail you! Go, I say!"

"You——!" snarled Sam, at his worst and grimmest, "you cursed little pest, you shall, damned tyrant. You——" Sam choked back the fo'c'sle epithet and ended the more lamely, "Come on and I'll trounce ye across my knee." Instantly Mr. Verinder rose, clenched dimpled fists and leapt —to be as instantly collared and whirled face downwards across Sam's brawny thigh and so viciously that Andromeda interposed.

"Ah," she cried, grasping Sam's upraised, vengeful hand in both her own, "you would never strike him——" And scowling down on his writhing victim, Sam answered, fiercely:

"Loose me and see!"

"No!" she answered as fiercely, "you shall not."

"Watch now!" Despite all her efforts, Sam freed his hand, raised it.

"Don't!" she pleaded. "For my sake! I beg you——"

Even as she spoke, Sam's big hand fell with resounding slap—then his hat went flying and stung by this blow, he loosed his struggling prisoner and turned to see Andromeda poised to strike again.

"Hold!" cried Mr. Verinder. "Stop now and listen to me." Seating himself cross-legged upon the grass like a plump though indignant imp, he reproached them like the odd, serenely dignified, little gentleman he was:

"Mr. Felton, behold how you can debase a gracious gentlewoman to the odious level of a screeching fishwife,—your detested face bears the stigmata of her fingers and I am glad. Ah, but—my niece comported herself like vulgar harridan and this shames and grieves me! And you, Andromeda, now see what coarse, horrid brute is this Felton, a common, loutish sailor who, as your husband, would drag you down to his own sordid depths and might even beat and outrage your tender loveliness with——"

"Yes," nodded Sam, "I probably should if she deserved it, as she does now for being so easily bamboozled by the like o' you. Ay, she ought to be slapped. However, I'll go instead, like the dam' fool I am——"

"And a monster!" added Mr. Verinder. "A coarse tar, a savage and barbarian!"

"As you will, sir," quoth Sam, mournfully, stooping to pick up his hat and putting it on dejectedly, "yes, I am coarse, I suppose, according to your lights, and maybe a bit brutal

. . . I shouldn't have slapped your poor, little tyrant, Andromeda. But I'm just a roughish sailorman, as I told ye, with no manners, no airs or graces and never a spot o' polish. No proper spouse for a fine lady—though she don't wear silk stockings, poor soul, and clumps about in heavy boots, working her pretty hands rough and horny for a selfish do-nothing——"

"Do not heed him, Meda love! Do not listen!"

"But she must, sir. She's going to hear me say that had she followed Love and wed this brutal sailor she might ha' gentled him and maybe learned him the trick o' prettier manners. As it is, he remains his brutish self, but will love her truly as any fine gentleman. So now, here's my final good-bye, Andromeda, unless you bid me otherwise."

But as she neither moved nor spoke, Sam turned, sighed and trudged away. But he had not gone far when his heart leapt to the flutter of her petticoats and he saw her speeding after him.

"Andromeda——?" he questioned, striding towards her, but she stayed him with a gesture saying, rather breathlessly:

"Did I hurt that . . . dear, scowling face?"

"It would be all the better for a touch of that lovely mouth," he suggested.

"No, stay where you are or I shall fly." Sam frowned but obeyed. "Once," she continued, "when you were less fierce, —indeed almost gentle, you wished for one of my worn-out shoes—here is one!" And she tossed it towards him, adding: "And nearly always I do wear silk stockings, as someday . . . perhaps . . . I will show you——"

"Oh, Andromeda," he pleaded, "will you marry me and damn your tyrant——"

"Never!" she cried and fled from him, swift and graceful as a dryad.

"Ay, ay—never it is!" he shouted after her; then spying her shoe within reach, kicked the poor little thing into a bramble bush—and scratched his passionate hands getting it out again; which done he cursed it, kissed it, crammed it into his pocket and strode away like the furious, disappointed sailorman he was.

CHAPTER XXXVIII

IN WHICH SAM IS MY LORD PROCLAIMED

"A WEEK!" said Aunt Deb, plying busy needle as she sat upon the rustic seat while a gloomy Sam laboured at his half-completed table, "a whole week since this truly terribly tragic affair! The entire County agog and all astir, Sam,—and still no sign or word of our new lord. One would have thought that as head of The Family he would certainly have attended the funeral—and such a funeral! But, oh dear no,—there was no least sign of him! Now mark me, my dear, in his persistent and so absolute absence, I sense a strangeness, Sam, a mystery of moment!"

"What did you think of the funeral, Aunt Deb?"

"Intensely impressive, my dear! Such crowds,—horsed and afoot! So many carriages of The Quality—and all so truly decorous."

"Ah!" snorted Sam. "And all to see the last of a Scrope, which of course means a scoundrel——"

"Hush, Sam! My dear—forbear! One should not speak ill of the dead."

"Why not, Aunt? For, d'ye see, it's the way folk talk of us when we're gone, the memory we leave is our true epitaph, the monument to be honoured or spit upon——"

"Very true!" quoth Mrs. Leet, thudding across the grass towards them with her ponderous stick. "Though I wouldn't waste my good spittle on such Scrope as Lord Julian. As for Eustace Jennings, poor boy, I'm glad they buried him away from Wrybourne."

"I suppose you knew him well, Grannyanne?"

"All his life or nearly, Sam," answered Mrs. Leet, seating herself beside Aunt Deborah and loosing the strings of her vast bonnet.

"His was a sad life, eh, Granny?"

"Yes, poor boy. And no wonder!"

"You mean because Lord Julian was his father——"

"Oh—never!" exclaimed Aunt Deb, busy needle suddenly arrested. "Sam, whatever are you saying?"

"Truth, Deborah!" nodded Mrs. Leet. "I learned this years ago on a night when Lord Julian and the Earl quarrelled; they were drunk, of course, at least the Earl was, and taxed Julian with it—a vile, wicked tale of how he had deceived Ruth Jennings, poor lady,—actually rigged one of his friends as a clergyman! This the Earl was shouting as I went in to 'em crying them hush for decency's sake. And so they did but took their swords to each other,—then I, like a fool, snatched a tablecloth and caught their blades—ha, better I'd let 'em kill each other! But I was young then."

"Yet, Granny, how came Eustace to live with such a man?"

"Because he never knew the shameful secret of his birth. When his poor mother discovered Julian's vileness she fled, but he never rested till he found her, for he loved her——"

"Oh, but, Anne, he couldn't have."

"But he did—as much as such man could. That's why he stole her baby away—to keep her near him. He used the boy kindly, had him well educated as the son of a friend and thus won the boy's gratitude—a shy, too-sensitive boy as I mind him,—won him body and soul, then used him to compel his helpless mother! Ha, the monster should ha' been slaughtered long ago! Pah—let's talk o' something cleaner."

"Yes, Anne, though—my Gracious, what a wicked family! 'Tis dreadful to think there's yet another Scrope somewhere about who may be just as bad."

"And if not, Deb, if this new Scrope should be of the better sort, think of all the evil for him to undo, all the wrongs to be righted—and my dratted cottage roof yet to mend!"

"We must hope that he will be good, Anne, though he is not beginning at all well."

"Oh, why not, Deborah?"

"He ought to have been at the funeral, his absence was marked, folk are scandalized and talking."

"Well, our Scropes are, or were, a scandal,—so let folk talk. Our new Lord Japhet will have the more to live down, that's all."

"If he ever can, Anne!"

"I think he will, Deb."

"Then he will have to be a brave, strong-souled young man, Anne."

"I believe he is, Deborah."

"Oh, why should you?"

"Because, as I said before, it's about time a good Scrope happened."

"Well, Anne, seeing is believing."

"How say you, Grandson Sam?"

"I'm hoping your kind faith will be justified, Granny-anne. But where's my little sweetheart, what's become of our Jane?"

"Away to Deepways Farm with Cecily Croft. A right grand girl that! Yes, without her I do believe poor Mrs. Jennings would ha' died, for she was beyond my power to comfort."

"So you were with her, Granny, I'm mighty glad o' that."

"Sam, of course I was. But as I say, 'twas Cecily she clung to in her desolation, Cecily it was who soothed her! I never saw such grief and hope I never shall again! Yes, a fine, a splendid girl is Cecily."

"True, Anne, though far, far too dangerously, bewitchingly beautiful! And a fool of course to waste herself on that Ralph Scrope! Which reminds me—I didn't see him at the funeral either—and his own father's funeral too! Terribly odd, hatefully unfilial, dreadfully disrespectful and surpass-ingly strange, eh, Anne?"

"Of course, but then he's a Scrope. So no more o' him! Instead tell me when must we expect Ned and his Kate?"

"About six o'clock."

"And what have we for dinner, or is it supper?"

"Both or either, Anne. And we have fried soles, boiled beef, a green goose, peas, beans, a gooseberry pie and currant tart."

"Then, m'dear, I hope they won't be late for I'm hungry already."

"Grannyanne, how often do you visit Mrs. Jennings?"

"Every day, Sam."

"Then I should like to go with you to-morrow if I may?"

"Of course. She speaks very kindly of you—how you car-ried her. Yes, and she seems to have taken a great fancy to that queer person Mr. Brown, she was asking after him——"

"Hark!" cried Aunt Deb, laying by her sewing. "Surely I hear wheels in the lane——" As she spoke came a seaman-like roar mellowed by distance:

"House ho! Ahoy, Sam! Messmate—ahoy!"

And instantly, his gloom forgotten a while, Sam bellowed in cheery response. Then with Grannyanne on one arm and Aunt Deb on the other away they hastened to welcome Captain Ned and his lady. And a right joyous reunion it was; the old farmhouse rang again with laughter and happy voices which, after some while, were somewhat muted by reason of the boiled beef, goose, etc.

And afterwards, seated about the wide hearth, with its cosy ingles, where winter and summer a fire blazed or smouldered, they talked or were comfortably silent like the real friends they were.

And it was upon this scene of happy peaceful domesticity that Nancy opened the door to announce:

"Mr. Joliffe, if you please."

Forthwith in he came bowing and smiling as they rose to greet him.

"God bless you all, how snug you look! I am the more ashamed to disturb you, but by your leaves, I must crave a few words with his lordship here."

"Eh, sir?" questioned the Captain. "His lordship did you say?"

"Ay, to be sure I did," said Mr. Joliffe. "How then," he chuckled, seeing Captain Ned's blank look, "are you not aware—Sam, haven't you told them—aha—evidently not! Then, my dear friends, in this scowling Sam of ours, I have the honour to present my lord Japhet, Earl of Wrybourne . . ."

CHAPTER XXXIX

TELLS HOW SAM MADE A DECISION

THESE words, so merrily spoken, smote Sam like an icy blast, a blighting wind that swept the spirit of warm, sweet intimacy from this homely fireside where now these faces so dearly familiar became all suddenly cold and strange; Kate, wide-eyed, shrank from him nearer her husband who regarded him beneath brows knit in perplexity or anger. Aunt Deborah stared open-mouthed, only Mrs. Leet, watching all, knitted serenely in a breathless silence, an unnatural stillness growing ever more unbearable, a hush broken only by the click of her knitting-pins, even this homely sound ended at last—and then she enquired:

"Well, why are we all so speechless?"

"Because," Sam answered, bitterly, "I'm cursed with the name of Scrope! Ay, and the curse is come on me already, shutting me away from you all, shattering this that was my home, making me an outcast——" With the word he started afoot and strode out and away to the orchard where shadows were deepening.

And here presently Grannyanne found him crouched disconsolate on the rustic settle.

"Sam," she murmured, touching his bowed head, "dear boy, make room for your granny."

"Oh, Grannyanne," he sighed, setting his arms about her, "thank God you're here and—didn't use my accursed title."

"Not yet," said she, seated herself beside him, "but Sam, my dear, 'tis for you to make this title honourable again, respected and I hope—loved. . . . But, my word, a fine to-do you've made yonder, there's Kate weeping, Ned swearing, under his breath, Joliffe trying to explain and apologize for springing such surprise and Deb still goggling in amaze, and here's me come for my grandson's arm."

"Which is always at your service, God bless you! But you're not bearing up for your cottage yet because, d'ye see, I need the comfort of you—so you won't leave me yet awhile?"

"No, my hearty, oh no," she replied, as her sailor father

might have done, "we'll beat to quarters and square away for the parlour——"

"Not yet, Granny, I can't face 'em so soon——"

"Ay, but you must, if only to put 'em all at their ease, for if you're taken all aback, Sam, they're on their beam-ends! So it's tack about and bear away, my hearty. And for goodness' sake don't look such a hang-dog, guilty wretch, for though you are a Scrope 'tis no fault of yours."

"Grannyanne, when were you sure I was of this cursed family?"

"The night we looked at the stars, Sam, though I suspected it when you stood beneath the Admiral's portrait. Come now, my Admiral Two, tack about and smartly."

"God love you, Granny, what a joy and comfort you are!" So back they went . . . to be met and welcomed by Kate's glad cry:

"Oh Sam, dear, dear Sam—oh, my lord, I'm trying to thank you as I said I would, though even now I hardly dare and don't know how——"

"Why then," said he, rather hoarsely, "kiss me instead and make our Captain jealous!" And kiss him she did, right heartily, and after her Aunt Deb; then Captain Ned grasped his hand, saying:

"Sink me, old messmate, this calls for a bottle!"

Thus that invisible, so English barrier of Caste melted away, the awesome spectre named Rank fled before the genial Spirit of Home, and my lord Japhet, Earl of Wrybourne became also Sam and one of this joyous family circle. Though Aunt Deb murmured at fitful intervals:

"Amazing! Astounding! Our Sam! My Saint George! Astonishing!"

So once again they drank the toast: "Health, happiness and long life to Japhet the Earl."

"Well now," said Sam, rather awkwardly, fumbling his wine glass, "I'm going to pledge you all . . . God love and keep you all and may you be the . . . the same dear folk when I come back, for, d'ye see, I'm off to fight the mounseers again, but this time—in my own ship."

"Oh—no!" gasped Kate.

"Ah—don't!" cried Aunt Deb.

"Pre-posterous!" exclaimed Mr. Joliffe. "Sam . . . my lord, you must not——"

"Folks," said Mrs. Leet, rising majestically, "I dare to think he won't. And now I'll get me beneath my dratted leaky roof. Grandson, your arm!" And so, when she had been tied into her bonnet and armed with her formidable staff, forth she went with Sam into a fragrant night.

"But, Granny," said he, opening the gate, "surely it's every man's duty to defend his home 'gainst invasion?"

"Of course, Sam. But thank God, there are thousands of brave men to do that, but only one man to do what you must. So your duty is to fit yourself for your new responsibilities and they are great. 'Tis London for you, Sam, to take your place as peer o' the realm and help to govern our troubled old England. Any man that is a man can fight with his hands—you must fight an everlasting battle with your mind, your wits, the influence of your character and the enormous power of your wealth."

"But, Grannyanne, I'm a sailor with little education, and besides a hard life has made me such a rough, mannerless sort o' fellow——"

"But the good Lord made your body strong, your heart clean and true and fearless. Fortune has made you an earl, 'tis for you to make yourself a gentleman. Ha, Sam, you are going to be right busy here in England with fights a-plenty, battles with yourself and circumstance without seeking 'em at sea! Then besides, and lastly——"

"Well, Granny?"

"There's Jane's Fairy Aunt."

"Yes," he sighed, "there will always be Andromeda. Do you know her, Granny?"

"No, not properly, but I mean to, if you love her, do you?"

"Ay, beyond the telling!"

"However, did you tell her?"

"Yes," he answered again and with another sigh.

"Ha! And she denied you?"

"Well, she has and she hasn't——"

"Under the hedge, Sam—here in the moonlight, sit down and tell me all about it."

There seated beside her, Sam told of his love briefly yet with such deep sincerity and unconscious eloquence that when he had finished, Grannyanne instantly rapped him with her ponderous stick though not very hard, saying:

"Sam, y'great silly numps, you lubberly jack, you handled the affair quite wrongly!"

"Oh, did I, Granny? Pray how?"

"You slapped the little gentleman abaft, didn't you?"

"Ay, I did and now regret it."

"And so you should, you great gowk, for making such fool mistake."

"Eh? Mistake, but—how d'you mean?"

"I mean you slapped the wrong one. You should have ignored the uncle and slapped the niece! Such delicate, fine lady would take it kindly—done properly and by the right man, of course. However, this can always be amended next time you meet her. . . . Ha, and yonder comes Ben Joliffe seeking you. Here we are, Ben, under the hedge!"

"Well," enquired Mr. Joliffe, anxiously, "have you talked our hot-head into reason, Anne? Have you convinced him of his duty?"

"I think so, I hope so—ask him!"

"Then, Sam, will you waste yourself at sea—or to London and follow your high destiny?"

"You must give me time to decide," answered Sam, aiding Grannyanne to her feet.

"Of course," sighed Mr. Joliffe wearily, "but how long will that take you?"

"Until we reach Granny's cottage," answered Sam, whereat she gave his arm a squeeze, saying as she did so:

"And must I remind your lordship that the cottage your lordship permits me to inhabit at a price, has a leaky roof—drat it!"

"Ay, but then, Mrs. Leet, d'ye see, marm, I'm hoping you will take command again at my lordship's house called Wrybourne Feveril."

"Sam—you never mean it?"

"Ay, but I do."

"No, no, I'm too old for such responsibility."

"Then I'm too young ever to live in such a confounded old rabbit-warren without you, Granny."

"And here," said Mr. Joliffe, "here we are at the cottage. So which and what is it to be, Sam?"

"Why London, of course, Ben. Who can resist Grannyanne? Not I! She's but to fire a shot athwart my forefoot and I strike my colours. God bless her! So kiss me Good-bye, Grannyanne and wish your loving grandson good luck, b'Jingo he'll need it!"

So kiss him she did and left a tear on his cheek, saying thereafter:

"Oh, drat you, Sam, you've made me cry! But with these tears I'm praying our Almighty Father will give you strength to be a true noble-man, the best and greatest of all the Scropes to bring love and honour to the name at last. Good-bye, Grandson and God bless you!"

"And there," said Sam, when the cottage door had shut her from his sight, "there is a truly grand soul, Ben!"

"I have known it these many years, Sam! Anne Leet was always profoundly wise and utterly fearless. She only could manage or dared outface your—hem—lordly sire in his drunken furies. While she ruled the Great House there was at least some show of decency."

"Ay, truly 'tis privilege to know such as she!" So saying, Sam turned and slipping hand within Mr. Joliffe's arm enquired, rather gloomily:

"When d'you propose we start for London, Ben?"

"At your convenience, m'dear fellow, but—the sooner the better."

"Then," quoth Sam, sighing deeper than ever, "let it be to-morrow."

TO THE READER:

who having followed Sam thus far, the Author dares
to regard as his friend.

Here this narrative might conclude, since here end the
bodily dangers of this Heritage Perilous. Yet because in this
life are perils more insidious though no less deadly, your
Author, and friend (I hope) ventures to describe briefly as
possible those dangers that still awaited Sam amid the teeming
riot of London's then cobbled streets and in the perfumed
bowers of great Vanity Fair that has been, is, and ever will
be the lure to buoyant, exuberant youth for eventual good
or ill.

Here then begins Book Number Two called:

The Aristocrat.

BOOK NUMBER TWO

THE ARISTOCRAT

CHAPTER I

OF SIR JOHN ORME AND VANITY FAIR

THE clock of St. Clement Danes was striking the hour of three as Mr. Joliffe turning from the roar and clatter of the busy Strand, led Sam beneath a shadowy arch into the comparative quiet of Clifford's Inn where, beyond cobbled walks, grass grew and trees made pleasant shade for buildings which, though grimed and dingy, were yet gracious and digni-fied by age and long tradition.

Entering a certain gloomy portal they ascended a gloomier stair, up and up until they arrived at the dingiest of doors which opening promptly to Mr. Joliffe's knock, disclosed a sombre person who, bowing speechlessly, conducted them to a bare little room with no carpet, one picture, two small, hard chairs and a shock-headed man in faded dressing-gown and slippers performing on a squeaking quill pen.

"M'lord," said Mr. Joliffe ceremoniously, "I have the honour to present Sir John Orme, Sir John, the Earl of Wrybourne."

"Servant!" snapped Sir John, his pen still squeaking. "You are a little before your time, Joliffe. Pray sit down until I have slaved my allotted span. Be seated."

"Thankee," answered Sam, a little grimly, "I'd liefer stand."

"And rightly so," said Sir John, still writing busily, "those four-legged discomforts are meant to discourage idle sitters and fatuous chatterers, for this, sir, is my room of penance. Five minutes longer and I shall give you my attention."

So while Mr. Joliffe perched uncomfortably on inadequate chair, Sam glanced from this harsh-spoken, shabby man, round about this ostentatiously barren little room until arrested by the one picture, the portrait of a young, delicately-beautiful woman; he was yet regarding this when Sir John's harsh voice exclaimed:

"My wife, sir! She died twelve years ago. I killed her. She came to me like sweet flower of Spring, and I killed her. She was for me the one dearest thing in life and I murdered her as surely as if these hands had strangled her."

"Though," Mr. Joliffe interpolated, "she was always extremely delicate."

"My lord," continued Sir John, more harshly, "I was one of those human curses known euphemistically as a dashing sportsman, a gambler on the heroic scale and comported myself so heroically that in one night of heroic folly I lost all—yes even the bed she lay upon! Three months later, in room small and wretchedly bare as this, she died in the arms of the remorseful wretch who had killed her. Then, having lost all that made life endurable, I should have tossed that away also, but for my good friend Joliffe . . . later he found me work as a law-writer, thus I eke out an existence and better than I deserve thanks to my man Jeremiah. So I have made life a penance, part of which is thus to trample pride underfoot and make confession so painful to you, sir, a man so much younger than myself. Well, my lord, what have you to say?"

Now looking down at the speaker, Sam beheld a face framed in shag of long, grey hair, pale, high-nosed, square of chin and lit by eyes so much the reverse of his abrupt, harsh manner that, finding no words, Sam held out his hand instead, to have it grasped with such unexpected heartiness that he said, impulsively:

"Sir, I hope we are going to be friends."

"Joliffe," said Sir John, rising, "he'll do! Now leave we this room of penance for one where we may talk in more comfort. This law-writing is weary business, I've been quill-driving since dawn. Come away!" And presently seated in cosy chamber: "My lord," said he, "our friend Joliffe has of course informed me of you and your change of fortune and I am curious to know what you intend to do with yourself and how I can help you?"

"Sir," answered Sam, "a few weeks ago I was a seaman and a rough sort of fellow, to-day greatly against my will, I'm an earl and what's worse, a Scrope! I belong to a family of blue-blooded scoundrels who have been a curse to themselves and others—back through the ages. And now it seems I must assume my lordly position and responsibilities and my trouble is how to do it worthily being only myself and cursed beforehand with such villainous name?"

Sir John, sitting up in his chair, was now regarding Sam with new and keenest interest; Mr. Joliffe watching both, was hiding a smile in his hand as Sam continued:

"What's more, sir, besides my accursed name, you must know I'm no fine gentleman, I've no graces o' manner and little education. Yet I've a mind to lift this damned name of Scrope out o' the mud and do something to better the condition of my tenantry and the country at large, use the power o' my money,—Joliffe says I've lots of it,—for good 'stead of evil and—well, d'ye see—be an earl to the best o' my ability."

"So," repeated Sir John, leaning forward to say it, "you would be an earl—to the best of your ability—and how, pray?"

"By service, sir. Giving as well as taking. By mixing with my folk, giving 'em a lead in their work and pastime. For, d'ye see, I know and ha' proved this aboard ship, —that I can get the best out of a fighting crew by leadership rather than command. 'Boarders away—go to it, lads'! is one way—'Follow me, my hearties'! is another and better. I know, for as I say, I've proved it. But, sir, to be a proper earl, it seems I must bear up for the Fashionable World, learn the manœuvres of Polite Society, eh, Joliffe?"

"Undoubtedly, my lord!"

"So, d'ye see, Sir John, my need is for someone to pilot me among these shoals, learn me the ropes and how to box the social compass, to learn me gentlemanly ways with the how and what of it all. Well, Sir John, our friend Joliffe speaks of you so highly that here am I to beg you'll so oblige me—if you will I shall be very truly grateful. So, what's the word, sir?"

"My first word," answered Sir John, sinking back in his chair again, "is astonishment! And my second—gratitude! Yes, Joliffe old friend, I am profoundly grateful for chance of such joyous adventure, which I accept gladly! For, 'pon my soul, Ben, our young lord is like a fresh, clean breeze and one that may become a gale to scatter age-old cobwebs, even shake Vanity Fair and of course eventually prove his own social ruin."

I

"Oh?" murmured Sam, pondering this. "Ah! Pray how, sir?"

"By contravening those unwritten laws, breaking every rule whereby Vanity Fair troubles to govern itself."

"And what," enquired Sam, "what is Vanity Fair?"

"Aha!" exclaimed Sir John, with something very like a chuckle. "There spake our innocent man of the sea! Vanity Fair, my lord, is a—sentient nebulosity that judges all and every thing by externals, believes only what best pleases itself, refuses to see or hear anything disagreeable to itself, troubles itself only for itself, exists but to pleasure itself, and may be summed up therefore in the one word— Itself. By such criterion you must see how entirely wrong are your values. In Vanity Fair the name of Scrope stands high, your family being old and of long tradition is therefore honoured. Your Uncle, the late Lord Julian will be politely lamented as a mordant wit and famous sportsman. Consequently you as a Scrope of Wrybourne will be hailed and made free of Vanity Fair not for yourself or because of your prodigious wealth, but for your blue blood and long ancestry, in fine because you are an aristocrat."

"Lord!" exclaimed Sam, with hopeless gesture, "Lord love me! Now I'm greatly minded to turn farmer along o' Ned or fit out a ship against the mounseers."

"And in either," sighed Sir John, "you would find more true happiness and content."

"But," said Mr. Joliffe warningly, "your duty points another way!"

"Ay, ay!" groaned Sam. "But now I'm fairly out o' my reckoning."

"And no wonder!" chuckled Mr. Joliffe. "This is why we sought aid of Sir John."

"Which I am happy to afford."

"Then, sir," quoth Sam, "since we are to be associated, will you favour me by dropping my title, cutting it adrift and calling me Sam?"

"Gladly, on condition that you reciprocate."

"Thankee. Then how do we begin, John and how?"

"I suppose," suggested Mr. Joliffe, "the first and most urgent need is—a tailor?"

"No, Ben, not a tailor—the tailor, my own! I believe he still condescends to fashion creations and create fashions for the favoured few. We will call on him to-day, so soon as I am ready."

"Excellent!" exclaimed Mr. Joliffe. "For in the hope you might prove agreeable, my dear Sir John, all is prepared for your reception at my lord's town house."

"Though," added Sam, dismally, " 'tis more like an hotel —with a crew o' servants, butlers, footmen and what not— enough to man a ship o' the line, besides a host o' women."

"And one other," said Sir John, smiling, "my man Jeremiah who is a host in himself. Which reminds me!" And rising, he pulled the bell-rope whereupon the door opened and the sedate Jeremiah entered bearing a tray laden hospitably with bottles and glasses. Towards these Sir John gestured, saying:

"Give me half-an-hour."

"Well, Sam," quoth Mr. Joliffe, as the door closed, "yonder goes your guide, philosopher and, I hope, friend, than whom I could have chosen none more able as events shall prove. For Sir John was once a famous and brilliant denizen of Vanity Fair—to-day a man of even greater parts . . . made wise by bitter experience. I hope you approve my choice?"

"Why, so far as I can tell at present, Ben, I echo his words and heartily—'he'll do'. No wine, thankee! And I've been thinking, Ben."

"Oh, indeed?" enquired Mr. Joliffe, filling his own glass.

"Yes, a matter of business—Joliffe!"

"Ah, what now, my lord?" he enquired, apprehensively. "No more stupendous bequests, I hope?"

"Yes and no. I'm wondering what I can do to make life a little easier, if possible, for that very unfortunate and gentle lady, Mrs. Jennings."

Mr. Joliffe sighing heavily, set down his wine untasted: "Money, my lord?"

"Of course!" Mr. Joliffe moaned faintly as Sam continued: "The question is—how much and how best I can get her to accept it without hurting her pride, d'ye see? I've been trying to scheme how we might let it appear to be a legacy from Lord Julian's estate . . . and yet, considering he's proclaimed bankrupt and his son at present in a debtor's prison——"

"Whence he can never win free!" added Mr. Joliffe, sipping his wine with relish. "A prisoner for life——"

"Precisely, Joliffe . . . I thought about five hundred a year and the cottage she occupies or any other she may choose——"

"But, my lord, my dear fellow, Oh, Sam, consider—Mrs. Jennings has but her own simple needs—she is alone, and for a single woman five hundred per annum is quite exorbitant——"

"Then, Mr. Joliffe, considering her loneliness, let's make it six hundred and a house or cottage. Is this understood?"

"Yes—yes!" gasped the lawyer. "But, my lord, permit me to remark——"

"That you think we should do better, another hundred or so——"

"No, no! Great good Jehovah—no!"

"Very well, my dear Ben. Now as to the method, the how and when of it. I think the only person who can help us is your old friend and that wise Grannyanne o' mine. So, to-morrow, Joliffe, you will proceed to Wrybourne and consult with her."

"To-morrow, my lord? But, my dear fellow, I——"

"To-morrow, Mr. Joliffe, sir! For, d'ye see, I want the matter completed at once. Then besides, regarding Mistress Cecily Croft——"

"Yes, oh yes!" moaned the lawyer. "Very soon this innocent young creature will be harassed by this fabulous wealth which——"

"And, Mr. Joliffe, I must impress upon you again how she must have no idea—not the least suspicion as to the who or why of it! Is this also understood?"

"It is, my lord, I do assure you."

"Then, Ben, my dear old fellow——" At this moment the door opened and glancing thither, Sam was dumb, for upon the threshold stood a tall, stately person, such truly imposing figure that Sam rose instinctively to his feet.

Sir John's wild shag of grey hair had been combed back into a queue, his patched and faded dressing-gown had given place to garments whose sombre elegance lent him an added dignity while his lean face lit by wide, bright eyes, showed power in its every feature and line,—gentled all at once by a smile that seemed oddly wistful as he said, and in voice altered as was his appearance:

"Gentlemen, I am at your service."

"Ah, Sir John," said Mr. Joliffe, rising in his turn, "my dear Sir John, I am happy to welcome you back to life . . . the world of action——"

"And," sighed Sir John, "the tragical follies of Vanity Fair."

CHAPTER II

A MONTH has elapsed and my lord the Earl of Wrybourne stands scowling at the resplendent young gentleman who scowls back at him,—a tall, shapely young exquisite whose garments seem moulded upon his powerful body, more especially his skin-tight pantaloons, that reveal his nether man from hip to ankle with an almost disquieting frankness.

It is at these brawny, too-evident limbs of his that my lord is gazing with such very Sam-like scowl while his two valets hover anxiously in the background, when the door opens to admit Sir John, whereupon my lord turns from his reflection in the long, cheval-glass, saying gloomily:

"John, I'm well enough aloft, but alow—damme, I feel and look like a skinned rabbit!" At this, my lord's two valets exchange glances and even venture to appear horrified, while Sir John, lifting gold-rimmed quizzing-glass adangle on broad ribbon, inspects my lord from curly pate to gleaming pumps, walks slowly round about my lord, inspecting him from every angle and finally remarks:

"I find nothing about you to disparage,—indeed you are quite point-devise! And knee-breeches, my dear Japhet, are becoming démodé, and this new, hideous fashion of cossack trowsers is not permissible for such occasion as this! Also at such function to be a trifle late is modish, to be devilish late is deuced bad form and—we are a trifle late!"

Thus presently side by side these two fine gentlemen descend wide, curving stair to spacious, pillared hall where four ornate footmen moving as one, open ponderous door, bow them down marble steps and into luxurious carriage that bears them away through, but not of, these busy London streets.

And now as they bowl along, my lord still very conscious of those legs of his, says unhappily:

"Damme, I'm shaking fore and aft! I'm nervous, John!"

"Well, thank heaven you don't show it! And after all you've only to look the part, which you do,—say little, bow often and remember our many lessons in speech and deportment."

"Ay, you've been very patient with me, John, all these weeks, and taught me a great deal."

"You are an apt pupil, my dear Japhet, and quick to learn, though to be sure Nature made you a gentleman. I have but added a little polish I venture to believe."

"And I'm grateful, John, and only hope I may do justice to your instruction. Though, 'pon my soul, I'd rather be fighting a close action in gale o' wind than front all these fine folk. Have you any last orders?"

"Merely to reiterate—first—do not stride with your sea-man's roll and lurch. Second—bear yourself always like the aristocrat you are. Third—when you converse modulate your voice and use few gestures. Fourth—if you are angered or troubled, smile. Pray remember that you must, under all circumstances, preserve an immutable calm, an unshake-able, nay a pertinacious serenity! Rein in and govern your emotions——"

"Ay, but suppose some fellow affronts me?"

"Be gracious and return his insult with a bow. And this reminds me, being a fighting seaman you are used to fire-arms?"

"Of course, John, though I'm happier with a boarding-axe or cutlass . . ."

Talking thus, they arrive in due season at another great house, vast of gates, portico and courtyard where other stately carriages trundle in, deposit their precious cargoes and rumble away, making room for others. For here to-day Her Grace the Duchess of Camberhurst is to introduce my lord the Earl of Wrybourne to the World of Fashion which is eager to take him to its polite bosom since he is "One of the Wicked Scropes, my dear"! also, "One of the wealthiest young bachelors in England, my love"!

Wherefore, as these many carriages rumble and roll, be-plumed and turbaned mamas give final keen scrutiny to their daughters, with such instructions as: "Remember to bear yourself swimmingly, child! When you make your reverence, miss, your curtsey must be graciously slow with becoming droop of lashes and—forget not to surge your bosom a little pantingly, my dear and do—not point your elbows!"

Up carpeted steps, between rows of powdered flunkeys, sweep stately dames, gallant gentlemen and visions of youth-ful loveliness; dainty petticoats flutter, plumes nod, jewels sparkle, bright eyes beam,—and all to meet to greet and give welcome to this Child of Fortune, this blue-blooded aristocrat my lord the Earl of Wrybourne-Feveril. . . . But he, completely overwhelmed and giving way to sudden panic, eludes Sir John amid this crowded magnificence, steals away like hunted wretch, finds a door that opens upon the free air and is off and away. He is speeding along a path between tall yew hedges when he collides with one who, reeling from the impact, splutters a strangled curse, a tall gentleman this, chiefly remarkable for teeth that are large and cruel-looking and eyes that are small but exceedingly fierce.

"Curse you, sir!" gasps this gentleman, large teeth bared and small eyes narrowed. "What the devil, sir—hey, sir——"

"Damn your eyes!" retorts my lord, harshly as any sailor-man possibly could. "If y'must run me aboard, speak me more mannerly or be dumb, blast ye!"

"Eh—eh?" cries the gentleman, opening his eyes wide as possible. "Who the—what the devil——"

"Avast!" snarls my lord, becoming Sam at his grimmest, "I'm in no mood to parlez-vous with the likes o' you, so sheer off—and lively!" At this, the gentleman seems to breathe with difficulty, he chokes, gives a ferocious tug at his high cravat, then snapping large teeth hisses:

"S-s-sir, you are addressing . . . and provoking Sir Robert Chalmers,—the Chalmers——"

"Deah me!" says Sam the mariner becoming my lord the Earl. "Then I take joy to inform Sir Robert Chalmers that I do not like the sound of him any better than the sight of him and beg him to oblige me by removing himself——"

"Oh, I see," nods Sir Robert, "you are a stranger to town—ignorance excuses you, also I am pressed for time! But—should you annoy me again—if you are then no wiser, be warned now." So saying, Sir Robert strides rapidly away. My lord is still gazing after him when he hears a slow step nearby, glances thither and beholds a slender, youthful though extremely languid gentleman who bowing feebly, says, as if speech were an effort almost beyond his strength:

"Sir, not th' faintest notion who y'are, but f' sake o' pure humanity, beg t'offer word o' warning 'f I may."

"Oh?" enquires the Earl. "Ah? Pray do."

"F'ler Chalmers, dooced notorious, dead shot, killed

several. Don't do t'quarrel with,—dey'vlish dangerous f'ler. Hope m'advice don't 'ffend ya."

"I'm grateful, sir. Whom have I to thank?"

"Standish, sir. Henry—no one in particular—'d afternoon!" And with another feeble bow, young Mr. Standish ambles away rather like a tottery old gentleman.

And now, hearing a merry babblement of voices chiefly feminine, away speeds my lord in the opposite direction and turning a corner in full career, comes upon a lady so suddenly that before he knows it, she is in his arms.

"Gracious mercy of Heaven!" she exclaims. "What a bear! My feet yards above the earth! Put me down this moment, sir." All stammering apology my lord obeys and sees her for a very small person of indeterminate age, an extremely dignified, small lady whose curls are suspiciously black, cheeks as suspiciously pink, though her eyes are remarkably bright and quick with perennial youth; now looking down into these beautiful and quite wonderful eyes, my lord (this hunted wretch) feels instinctively that here is a friend so for a brief space they regard each other eye to eye, then before he can speak, she demands:

"Well, sir, where on earth were you going in such furious hurry?"

"Anywhere, marm—madam, so long as I keep well to wind'ard of the Duchess——"

"Oho! So you're running away from the Duchess, are you?"

"Ay, I am indeed——"

"Then give me your hand and let's run!"

"Lady," says my lord, taking the very small hand she proffers. "God love you—those eyes o' yours spoke me true, for the moment they looked at me I——"

"Run!" says she, imperiously! So away they flee, hand-in-hand, until this very small lady gasps: "Wait . . . oh, I'm breathless . . . wait—no, you must carry me if you——" Powerful arms swung her lightly aloft and thus cradled, she directs him until in remote corner they reach an arbour shaded by trees and bowered in roses. Here he sets her down and she having adjusted her somewhat ruffled frills and furbelows, seats herself upon cushioned settle and beckons him beside her, saying:

"Now continue! What were you remarking about my eyes?"

"That they are mighty sharp, marm—madam, very wise yet kind, like the eyes of a friend."

"Ho! Is this all? Don't you think they are very beautiful eyes?"

"Yes, marm——"

"Then why not say so?"

"Because a friend's eyes are always beautiful——"

"Fiddle-faddle and nonsense! I know friends with eyes like pigs' eyes, and holes in blankets, and Friendship cannot alter the fact, so don't you try."

"No, madam, for just at present your eyes are a bit too sharp for friendship——"

"In-deed! Well now, tell me why you are running away from the Duchess."

"Not from her so much, madam, as the fact that she's to introduce me to her lady friends,—hundreds of 'em! I'm to bow and scrape and be paraded before them all which you'll agree is enough to shake any man."

"But I do not agree. Oh no, not for a moment! Most men would adore such occasion and why not you?"

"Because I'm clean out o' my reckoning and no soundings! All these fine folk! This isn't my world. I'm a stranger here and what's more I don't belong and never shall."

"Then why are you here?"

"All John's fault, marm, Sir John Orme, he's a friend o' the Duchess and well, here I am, and heartily wishing myself anywhere else."

"So,—you are the Earl of Wrybourne!"

"Ay, I am," his lordship admits and with look so abject and sigh so very like a groan that the lady's mobile lips twitch, her bright eyes twinkle though her voice is perfectly solemn as she enquires:

"Why so miserable, pray?"

"Oh, marm," exclaims the Earl, forgetting everything except that he is Sam, "I loathe the very idea of it, because of the hateful name I bear and all that goes with it! Then besides I'm a sailor and pretty rough though Sir John, bless his heart, has been schooling me in ways of speech and gentle manners, ay, he's done his best with me but I'm only the more certain my proper place is aboard ship instead of a palace the like o' this. As a sailorman I was well enough, but as an earl and aristocrat I'm all adrift and like to founder.

So here am I on my beam-ends, as I knew I should be, feeling mere clumsy fool and terrified of all these fine ladies. This is why I'm so glad, so thankful to have found one like you!"

"Why?" she demands, studying his troubled face with keenly appraising scrutiny. "Because of my so beautiful eyes?"

"Yes!" he answers gravely. "And all the rest of you. So, marm, although I'm Japhet and an earl by law and must so be to everyone else in London, I'd like you to know me for what I truly am——"

"I believe I do!" she nods.

"Then if you'll bless me with your friendship will you call me 'Sam'?"

"I will, on condition that when you are made known to the company as you must be, you will play your part as boldly as you did on your ship in battle—— Oh, I've heard a few facts about you from Sir John. And now, if we are to be friends, tell me why you so hate the rank and wealth you have inherited?"

"I despise my name because the Scropes have generally been such scoundrels, and I hate all the money because it makes me grieve all the more for my dead mother."

"I should like to hear of her, if I may—Sam."

So once again he told that tale of hardship, grinding poverty and a woman's selfless devotion, told it simply, briefly though with such deep and tender sincerity that when his last words had been uttered, there ensued a silence—broken at last by sound of hasty footsteps and a dignified, somewhat flurried personage stands to bow profoundly and say breathlessly, though with the utmost deference:

"Madame, your guests are all assembled and await your Grace's pleasure."

"Very well, Smedley, you may inform them that we, Lord Wrybourne and myself, shall join them shortly."

"I thank your Grace!" with which the personage bows himself away.

"Marm . . . madam——" stammers Sam, rising in no little dismay. "So you—you are—the Duchess."

"My lord," she answers, rising also and sinking before him in graceful curtsey, "I have the honour to present myself to your lordship! Now Sam—bow! A trifle lower—y-e-e-s. Ha! Sir John's efforts have not been wasted, as I shall tell him. Come now. Your arm!"

CHAPTER III

TELLS HOW VANITY FAIR RECEIVED MY LORD

SO, beneath the aegis of this small but very potent lady, my lord makes his obeisance to the World of Fashion; he bows to noble dames stately and otherwise, who smile, chatter, or merely stare; he touches hands with gentlemen who talk of the weather, the war, Old Bony, our Nelson, England's glory and loss, they shake grave heads, snuff and pass on; Beauty parades itself with demure coyness or shyly provocative glances—until a voice somewhat muted, drawls:

"Takin' liberty t' warn y'again,—Gorgon 'pproaches! Advise y'dodge,—this way!" Turning, my lord beholds the languid form of Mr. Standish who, beckoning feebly, moves with unexpected celerity, guiding my lord who follows instinctively until in remote corner of broad terrace, he sinks upon a cushioned ottoman, saying:

"She was after y', m'lud, the Juggernaut, full cry, champin' the bit, all maternal determination!"

"Who was?" enquires my lord, glancing about uneasily.

"The Marwood mama, th' dem dowager, awf'lest of 'em all, wi' th' loveliest daughter in Creation,—can't think how she managed it!—t'mother such daughter! One o' Nature's mysteries and—demme, she's flushed us,—I'm an off 'un!" And off goes Mr. Standish, vanishing in the moment that a full-throated imperious voice exclaims:

"Japhet—oh, Japhet! My dear, dear Wrybourne! Oh, my heart!" Glancing round in no little apprehension, my lord beholds a tall be-plumed dame of commanding presence, whose awful stateliness overwhelms him, whose determined graciousness saps his will-power, whose appalling familiarity smites him dumb. Sinking magnificently upon the ottoman she beckons him beside her with a dreadful coquetry.

"Wrybourne, my dearest boy," says she between carmined lips that smile beneath arrogant nose and eyes that languish soulfully, "my poor heart so beats, so leaps and flutters—as of yore! For, ah me,—you are the breathing image of your splendid gallant father, your handsome sire, the Japhet of my adoring youth!"

"Indeed, marm?" his lordship mutters.

"And indeed!" she sighs. "Ah, what a man,—so charmingly compelling! So deliciously audacious! Years ago . . . he and I. . . . Ah me, how fleeteth cruel Time! The rose of yesterday—alas, so soon to fade!" Here my lady pausing to sigh and gaze upon him as in fond recollection, his lordship shifts uneasily yet contrives to murmur:

"Really, marm?"

"Yes," she sighs, "the dear past is real again, my dear boy, lives again in you—so does your noble father." Here my lord seems about to protest but sighs instead and the Dowager Lady. Marwood continues: "Oh memory, memory! And you are Japhet, too, with his chestnut, curling locks! The years roll back and I am young again! Then there was Julian, poor, gallant Julian! Alas, what an end for such gay Lothario! So tragical! So dramatic and yet how like dear, wild Julian! How handsome, how witty, how splendid was he! I mourn him as loved friend! Ah, but now you shall tell me of yourself, Japhet, you are or were a sailor?"

"Yes, m'lady."

"Well, I adore all sailors from our lamented Nelson our national hero, down to the humblest tar. Were you with our Nelson, one of his glorious 'band of brothers'?"

"No, marm."

"A pity! He was so truly heroic though small, not so tall as your shoulder! I danced a gavotte with him once in Italy it was. And he so debonnaire, so graceful despite his empty sleeve pinned across his breast ablaze with stars and orders, though it flapped so comically each time he bowed! You were at Trafalgar, of course."

"Yes, marm, though had no part in the action, we were carrying despatches."

"No matter, you were there and—ha, yonder is my dove at last, my olive branch, my one beloved pledge—my only child! So wilful, Japhet, I spoil her but so do the gentlemen, such homage,—a reigning toast already!" Here, in rich contralto the Dowager calls: "Oh, my love! Rowena, my precious one, be pleased to approach!"

My lord glances up, draws a deep breath and sits motionless, gazing at the most radiantly beautiful vision of loveliness he has ever seen: slowly, gracefully she advances all dainty seduction from slender, sandalled foot to the crowning glory of her gleaming yellow hair.

"My own," says her mother, tenderly, "you behold here beside me the dear son of a dearer old friend of my girlhood —Rowena, my love, I make known another Japhet, Earl of Wrybourne-Feveril!"

Dumbly my lord rises, speechlessly he bows before this shape of splendid young womanhood. . . .

Her watchful lady-mother seeing him thus spellbound smiles happily while the arching nostrils of her haughty nose palpitate slightly as she rises, saying:

"I must have a word with the dear Duchess. Meanwhile, Japhet, I charge you with the care of my beloved child. Ah, youth—youth!" sighs she, striking an attitude of rather awesome ecstasy as she gazes upon them, "ah, youth—the rosy, rosy hours, alas how soon they fleet, how fast they speed away! Bring me my precious Rowena within the hour, Japhet."

My lord bows and still dumb, glances again at the radiant creature beside him, smitten anew by the exquisite daintiness and delicate grace of her, as she stands gazing down at her own slim, sandalled foot, yet so perfectly aware of his admiring scrutiny that, still motionless and without even glancing towards him, she enquires:

"Well, my lord, what do you think of me? I'm for sale, you know."

"Sale?" he repeats, and in such tone of shocked amazement that she troubles to look up at him and with eyes shrewd as they are beautiful.

"Why, of course," she replies, delicate brows lifting, "surely you know? This is the marriage market, the highest bidder takes me—perhaps! And this is my first season,—so what offers, my lord?"

"Lady Rowena," says he, trying not to scowl, "I think we'll change the subject."

"Oh no, my lord," and now in her soft voice is a note of bitterness, "business is business!"

"Ay, but I'm no business man, I'm only a sailor."

"Why—of course," says she, more naturally, "this explains why you are so different."

"Oh?" he murmurs, pondering this. "Pray how?"

"In every way."

"You mean I'm awkward . . . clumsy, ay, so I am."

"Wrong!" And now her voice is kind as her look. "You are just natural. Yes, I think—no I'm sure that you are the most unaffected person I have ever met. And now, my lord, what is your estimation of—me?"

"I—well—it goes beyond my poor words."

"Which is mere evasion!" she nods. "Then since you won't venture to pronounce judgment on me, what do you think of—Her?—with a very capital aitch!" and the beautiful head inclines itself in a certain direction. "I may tell you that some call her the Carronade because she's so very devastating at close quarters, some—the Buccaneer, others —the Juggernaut and lots of other things! So what say you of her, my lord?"

"Which 'her'? Who, pray?"

"Darling mama, of course!" And lo—the bitterness is marring this sweet voice again.

"Why since you ask me," says my lord, a little stiffly, "I think of her as your ladyship's mother."

"Goodness gracious—a snub! You reproach me for being unfilial! You'll dare to censure me——"

"Oh no! Only I respect all mothers because of my own, for, d'ye see, I loved her——"

"Because she did not put you up for sale to the highest bidder! Twice I have been nearly sold, once to a man old enough to be my grandfather, and once to an awful creature who should have been buried! But I escaped thanks to Henry and my own wit—oh, pray let us walk! No, not that way," says she, as they descend the terrace steps, "I cannot bear company just yet . . . to-day I hate them all!"

"All?" enquires my lord.

"Yes—yes!" she exclaims, fiercely. "I detest all this fulsome make-believe, our superior affectations, for we are all so cat and doggy, really,—oh, most politely inhuman,—bows and curtseys, teeth and claws!"

"Lord!" murmurs the Earl, glancing askance at this beautiful Ferocity. "Lord love us!"

"I wonder if He can?" says she bitterly. "Such pompous Insincerities as we are, such charming shams. And I'm as bad as any—a niminy-piminy claw-cat! To-day I meet my three closest friends, we embrace, we kiss, we call each other 'my love', 'my darling', 'my dearest', though our real names are Jealousy, Malice and Envy. Yes, I'm a cat with very sharp claws, or I should have been gobbled up before now! And being such a very catty cat, I'm wondering what sort of dog you are,—my lord?"

For the first time to-day he laughs and so joyously that beautiful Ferocity shows less fierce as he answers:

"I'm a dog with no pretty tricks, that seldom barks, never bites—except with just cause, wags his tail to friendly whistle and his name, to his friends, is—Sam."

"Sam?" she repeated, as if trying the sound of it, her mouth lovely and smiling again.

"A somewhat plebeian name, I suppose," he suggests, "but then, so is Tom, Dick and—Harry!"

"Ah?" she murmurs, the smile vanishing. "You know him?"

"If he is Mr. Standish I met him about half-an-hour ago."

"Here?" she exclaims, in sudden anxiety. "Oh and I warned him! I told him not to come . . ."

"May I ask you if he is—the one?"

"Yes," she replies, after momentary hesitation, "yes, it is Harry. It would be the poorest of them all! You see his reckless father gambled everything away before he died leaving his son almost destitute. Yes, it's Harry—and always will be. . . . Though I don't know why I am talking to you so—so very unreservedly."

"Perhaps because you believe I'm the kind of dog that seldom barks and never bites—a friend."

Now at this, she turns to look at him very wistfully.

"Oh," she murmurs, "you can never guess how friendless we are, how utterly helpless, poor Harry and I. Some people have good angels to watch over them—ours must have flown very far away!"

"However," says my lord, rather diffidently, "a dog can be useful now and then."

Lady Rowena is looking at him now through a sparkle of tears as she enquires:

"Does this mean that you—you of all people would help us, my lord?"

"Ay, it does. And this dog's name is Sam."

With her eyes still tearful she laughs, saying rather brokenly:

"Oh, Sam, you are going to be . . . a terrible disappointment to . . . darling mama! For at this very moment she fondly imagines you . . . a sighing victim of her daughter's . . . all-powerful charms! And instead . . . here you are . . . offering me a chance of freedom at last : . . of happiness with my Harry! You are very, very wonderful, but nobody can possibly help us,—not even you."

"Of course not," he answers, "until you begin helping yourselves."

"How, tell me—how ever can we?"

"Are you afraid of poverty?"

"Not with Harry."

"Then why not elope, marry and dare the future?"

"So I would," sighs she, clasping her hands. "Ah, God knows I would have done, but I . . . dare not!"

"Oh?" murmurs my lord, "may I know why?"

"Take me into the arbour yonder, and I'll tell you."

So in that same fragrant bower where the Duchess had listened to his story, Beauty now tells hers, though with more fire and passion:

"There is a hateful brute and loathly beast named Robert Chalmers, we were children together and he was my boyish sweetheart though he was a beast of a boy, selfish and masterful, said I belonged to him and says so to-day— he persecutes me, haunts me——"

"Yet he must love you very greatly."

"Yes, though his love would frighten and shame me were I a timid miss, but I am not easily terrified, thank heaven!"

"What says your mother of him?"

"Oh, darling mama favours him, of course, because failing a better, he is a very good match, highly connected and plenty of money! And besides, she is terribly afraid I shall throw my precious self away on Harry."

"Then she knows of him?"

"Of course! Darling mama has eyes everywhere and knows everything. She must have warned Robert for he came to me and in his dreadful, smiling way suggested I had better discourage Harry or he would. Of course I did not, and of course he did—with a bullet."

"Was Mr. Standish wounded?"

"Desperately! Robert forced the meeting and then—while my poor Harry lay between life and death, the beast told me he had spared his life just this once but that if there had to be a 'next time'—these were the brute's very words,—'he would be less merciful'!"

"Oh?" murmurs my lord, thoughtfully. "Ah! And is this gentleman so deadly?"

"Indeed yes—yes he is. Oh, Robert is terrible! They say he can 'hit his man wherever he chooses' and that 'he never misses'! He has fought very often, here and in France—— Oh, and he always wins! This is why the beast is so honoured and respected wherever he goes!"

"No," murmurs my lord, "only here—in Vanity Fair. . . ." It is now that Lady Rowena shrinks instinctively, whispering a startled "Hush!" For, as if conjured thither by their words, this very redoubtable gentleman is seen approaching, an angry-seeming gentleman in such hurry that he would have passed without espying them had not my lord coughed loudly, whereat Sir Robert halts, stares, and comes striding like the perfectly assured, extremely formidable person he knows himself to be.

"Aha," says he, with show of large, white teeth, "a game of hide and seek, m' sweet soul? Well, I've found you as I always do and always shall, because I am your destiny—and you know it! I am also your devoted slave joyous as ever to serve you, but—a slave who must not be denied——"

"Oh, be done!" sighs she, wearily. "For mercy's sake—leave me in peace."

"Rowena," he retorts, his smile widening, brows knitting above small, glittering eyes, "sweet fool, you cannot escape your destiny. Come, I will escort you to madam your mother."

"No, Robert! Darling mama placed me, her so precious asset—in charge of Lord Wrybourne whom you see here."

"E'gad!" he exclaims, glancing at my lord, in affected surprise, "now you mention him, I do. Servant, m'lord. Now, Rowena, go with me—or must I show you how there is no escaping your destiny? Come, I say!" And he reaches out a hand so possessively that she recoils with a fierce, gasping: "Don't!"

And now it is that my lord thinks proper to intervene; he rises languidly, makes a leg, sailor-fashion, corrects this into a ceremonious bow with elaboration of gesture and advances slowly, saying in carefully modulated, sweetly dulcet tones:

"My dear, my very dear sir, three times—no less, you have proclaimed yourself to be—Destiny! To this remarkable, not to say astounding claim, I must beg leave to take exception, though with all the humility possible, and for the following reasons——"

Now as he speaks, my lord continues his insidious advance until the crested gold buttons of his coat (this work of art) are in contact with the person of Sir Robert who instinctively steps back—and yet back, for my lord, while talking, continues his slow and gentle advance; in which ridiculous posture, breast to breast, these two fine gentlemen move on together, Sir Robert backward, my lord forward, saying as he smiles into the baronet's narrowed eyes: "For, d'ye see, my dear sir, that any mere human, ay, even you, should dare claim to be Destiny, makes me bold to imagine that I may become—Nemesis."

By this time they are screened from the arbour by a tall yew hedge—and here my lord suffers a dire "sea-change", for the smilingly-gracious, gentle-spoken Aristocrat is transmuted into the grim, harsh-voiced, fighting sailorman whose large hand, swift-moving, grasps the baronet's startled face, covers it, shakes it, hurls it away—and Sir Robert, thus outrageously surprised, falls backward and lies for the moment shocked beyond speech or movement, staring up at his aggressor who scowling down on him with eyes quite as merciless as his own, says in fierce, snarling voice:

"'Destiny', d'ye call yourself? Why, y'poor, damned, lubberly hulk, what's to stay me running ye under, treading ye into the earth? Get up, Mister Destiny and Nemesis shall knock ye flat again! Stand up!"

Still dazed and shaken, Sir Robert struggles up to an elbow, glances around, is relieved to see that no one has apparently witnessed his discomfiture, and looking up at his assailant, draws a deep breath and despite his lowly posture, contrives to speak with a certain dignity and the utmost venom:

"My lord, though you speak and act like blackguardly ruffian, I promise you shall die like a gentleman."

"Sir Robert," my lord replies, becoming again the urbane fine gentleman, "of this I am perfectly aware."

"Naturally, my lord! But what you cannot and shall not know until I so please, is the precise hour when I shall accord you this honourable death, which shall be sudden and preferably in the open air—at dawn or sunset. But, pray mark this,—at my pleasure and in my own time! I shall allow your lordship a brief span of living, a few days, weeks, or even months, as best pleases me and suits my convenience. So while I permit you to live, let me urge your lordship to make the most of it, enjoy it to the full—with this certainty that soon or late, whenever the whim takes me, I shall call you to account and shoot you like a dog."

"Oddly enough, sir, Lady Rowena and I were talking of dogs a while since, before an odd creature calling itself 'Destiny' intruded, and I was saying something to the effect of how some dogs are all bark and no bite and others all bite and never a bark,—now you, sir, not only bark quite demnably, but you also yap."

"Bark or yap, my lord, I shall permit you to live awhile that you may ruminate as to the exact hour of your dying and become aware of this fact that 'in the midst of life we are in death'. Think on this, my lord, eat and drink with it, sleep and wake with it, expect me to summon you at any moment to die—and be damned!"

"Sir," says my lord, shaking his head as in gentle though shocked reproof, "I find you so very truly detestable, such pernicious pest and ugly blot that when you summon me and we meet, then, sir, instead of simply maiming you for life as I intended, I shall be greatly minded to end you for good and all, ay, and for the good of all. We shall see when the time comes. However, sir, do not let us have any more of your 'destiny' nonsense. And now, finding your air, face and person so repulsive I'll be rid of 'em. But until I am gone, pray make no attempt to rise or I must pleasure myself by flattening you out again, therefore pray lie still. So, until our next happy meeting, ay, and after, the devil keep you, sir."

Then with airy flourish, my lord strides lightly away.

CHAPTER IV

RETURNING to the arbour he is met by a pale, great-eyed Rowena who, clasping her hands, exclaims tearfully:

"Oh, what have you done? Merciful heaven—how will it end? Oh, my lord, my lord!"

"The name is Sam!" he reminds her.

"That beast means to kill you—and he will! There was death in the way he looked at you."

"Ah, then you saw?"

"Of course! I heard your voice so I stole and peeped. . . . And, oh God, forgive me—this is my fault! I led you into this! Your blood will be upon me——"

"Oh no! No indeed! Sir 'Destiny' and I ran into each other before I had the joy of meeting you. Ay, we ran foul of each other in every sense."

"Ah my lord—Sam, is this true?"

"Abs-lootly!" drawled a familiar voice and into the arbour stepped Mr. Standish, saying: "Hope I don't intrude. But, m'dear . . . simply must tell you! Amazin' business! Wrybourne's method is quite dooced original and arrestin'—he merely takes his man by the face and—throws him away!"

"I know, Harry, I know!" gasps Rowena, "I saw—he did actually throw Robert away! Oh, and this means bloodshed, —death! But, oh, did you see how Robert fell? Legs in the air—feet above his head! Oh, Harry—Sam——" Here, not knowing whether to laugh or cry, Rowena does both, to the consternation of her hearers.

"Hold hard, m'dearest!" Mr. Standish implores. "Curb now—curb! Sit tight, m'love! Oh dem, she's goin' t'swoon or somethin'! Take her other hand, Wrybourne—now open it—now slap it like I do,—smartly, m'dear f'low, smartly!" So, while Rowena sobs, laughs and chokes, these two dismayed gentlemen slap her pink palms until they glow pinker and their lovely owner gasps:

"Stop—stop, you great sillies . . . I'm only laughing . . . now!"

"Eh? Only laughing? Sure o' that, m'dear?"

"Yes, though it's perfectly horrid of me when—it may mean —death! Oh, my lord——"

"Yes, b'James! I was f'gettin' too! Chalmers'll be after your blood, Wrybourne—thirstin' for 't,—tongue lollin', m'dear f'low. And, oh demme, he'll have it too, for he's calamitous wi' the barkers or sharps! And he'll keep y' in suspense—it's a trick he uses t' shake his 'ponent's nerve!"

"However," says my lord, glancing from one anxious young face to the other and touched by their very evident sincerity, "pray sit down, Mr. Standish, and let us converse of something more pleasant, ourselves, for instance, for I'm happy to say your lovely and gracious Rowena has honoured me with her friendship."

"Yes, indeed, Hal!" she breaks in, giving a hand to each. "Here we sit joined in friendship because, Harry, instead of the sighing, ogling wooer I dreaded and darling mama hoped he would be, I have proved Lord Wrybourne so truly a friend that he is 'Sam'—yes, and almost before I knew it, I was telling him—confiding to him all about—us!"

"Ha! Did y' tell him how and why you eternally blight me with a continual, dem, everlasting 'no'?"

"Yes," she replies mendaciously, "I said it was because I fear poverty."

"Naturally, m'dear, so do I! Yet with you I'd dare even that. . . . I'm keepin' the old farmhouse—last bit o' the mater's dowry, in hopes! Not much of a place, but with you in it, well—you could make it—home, y'know."

"Could I, Hal?" she murmurs, leaning towards him.

"Yes," he answers, leaning towards her. "That's why I haven't sold the old place, hopin' you might—some day! I shall always hope, y'know."

"Shall you, Hal?" she whispers; no bitterness now in beauteous face or tender voice, also Mr. Standish has quite forgotten his languor and shows for the vitally-eager, manly young fellow he truly is—or so thinks my lord, watching them critically, and they so completely oblivious of him and everything except each other that they start almost guiltily as he says in his hearty seaman's voice:

"Ay, hope's the word, never say die! And if we're to be friends—I'll take a stroll, as a friend should. But before I leave you together a while, here's an offer for your consideration, Mr. Standish—I need a private secretary who will also be a friend, will you accept?"

"Eh? A secretary? Me? But, m'dear, old lord, I hardly know how t' write——"

"Harry!" exclaims his lady, indignantly. "Do not be so ridiculous! He writes extremely well, Sam,—indeed quite legibly—sometimes!"

"No, m'angel," sighs Mr. Standish, "can't let him be deluded b' friendship! Fact is, old f'low, as a scribe I'm a poor fish——"

"Harry, you shall not disparage yourself so outrageously! He writes beautiful letters, Sam—to me!"

"And no wonder!" smiles the earl. "Then, Mr. Standish, I've quite a number of horses in town, but I ride like a sailor and shall need some lessons."

"Aha!" exclaims Mr. Standish. "That's certainly more in my line——"

"Harry can ride anything, Sam."

"Then I hope he will oblige me by accepting."

"He will! He shall! He does—say so, Harry, at once!"

"And, by the way, I offer six hundred a year to begin with —if you think this adequate!"

"Adequate!" sighs Rowena, clasping her hands.

"No, Wrybourne, no!" says Mr. Standish, forgetting to drawl, "it's too much! I should never be worth it——"

"You will, Harry! You must be——"

"But, m'dearest gal, I never earned a penny in my confounded life!"

"Then begin now, for—my sake, Hal."

"Eh? Your sake? It's a go! Then what about yoke o' matrimony—nothing to stay you—double harness—what's to stop you?"

"Nothing!" says my lord, rising. "So I'll leave you to talk it over." Scarcely has he stepped from the arbour than he espies Sir John Orme approaching and hurries to meet him.

Now though Sir John's fine face shows serene as ever, his voice is low and troubled as he says:

"Ah, Sam, you have shocked me profoundly! For I was a distressed witness of your quite ruffianly assault upon Sir

Robert Chalmers! Instead of quarrelling with dignity and finesse as gentleman should, you comported yourself like a veritable—coal-heaver!"

"No, John—like the sailorman I am. The fellow deserved knocking down, instead I merely pushed him over." Sir John's mobile lips twitch, but his black brows knit themselves above hawk nose as he continues:

"I warned you repeatedly how when a gentleman sees fit to quarrel, he should do so with grace, and eschew all violence of tone or gesture. Also I am much concerned for—— Oh, my dear boy, you are not aboard ship now where such affairs are settled by honest fists and forgotten, but in Vanity Fair, this world of make-believe which is yet so terribly real and nothing more so than the abstraction called 'Honour' which, though possessing here a far less noble meaning than that given in the dictionary, is yet so precious that noble gentlemen must fight and die for it or be outcast. Thus Sir Robert will certainly call you out and do his utmost to kill you."

"Ay, so he assured me, John."

"Consequently I am gravely anxious on your account—for he is esteemed a dangerous fellow, a much experienced duellist, or so the Duchess informs me."

"Eh? The Duchess, John? But how——"

"Unfortunately Her Grace was with me and also witnessed your very lamentable exhibition of—how *not* to do it."

"Oh Lord!" exclaims the Earl, greatly dismayed. "Lord love me!"

"It is to be hoped so," sighs Sir John, "all things considered!"

"Was she as shocked as yourself, John?"

"I cannot say. But she desires to see you alone before you depart."

"Does she, b'George! Then I'll slip my moorings now—— Oh, damme, there's 'darling mama', Lady Marwood, John, bearing down on us! Hold her in play while I go speak word o' warning!"

Back to the arbour speeds my lord at sight of whom up starts Mr. Standish, saying:

"So ho—the Juggernaut approaches, I see b'your look.— I'll vanish!"

"I shall expect you to-morrow!" says my lord, as they shake hands.

"Without fail, Wrybourne, and many thanks! But th' dear soul still says 'no'! Can't think why—no reason now! Goo'-bye!"

"My lady," begins the Earl so soon as they are alone.

"No, Sam, please use my name."

"Rowena, why is it still 'no'?"

"Because I still dare not say 'yes'—and if I explained to Harry he would fight again and be killed."

"Oh!" murmurs my lord. "Ah? Then you must think I shall also be killed?"

"Oh, pray do not talk of it—don't! It is too frightful! You—we—might have all been such dear friends and yet it must end so horribly whenever Robert desires."

"So you are quite sure he will end me?"

"He is so terrible! But I shall—pray for you, Sam, yes with all my heart, day and night——" So saying she gives him both her hands so impulsively and with such eloquent look that my lord, as impulsively, stoops and kisses them, then starts as a throaty voice cries:

"Oh, fie upon us, Sir John, we intrude! We shall fright away shy Eros, terrify sweet Cupid the rosy roguish archer, let us fly! Dear Japhet, my sweet child, enjoy the brief, glad hour,—we will waft ourselves hence——"

"Then, darling mama, we will waft along with you!"

Thus presently, back went they all four to mingle with the throng (and more or less envious mamas) wherefore my Lady Marwood's stately head is so proudly borne, her plumes nodding so triumphantly that Rumour is bred and Envy indeed follows in her train.

CHAPTER V

IN WHICH MY LORD BECOMES MERELY SAM

MY lord finds the little Duchess in small, cosy chamber, performing with a very large, silver teapot.

"Well, Sir Ferocity," says she, nodding, "you may sit down and take tea with me; you probably detest it but you shall drink it as a penance—though to be sure I'm grateful to you for affording me a thrill by out-bruting Sir Brutality Chalmers so outrageously."

"Oh?" murmurs my lord. "I was afraid your Grace would be shocked."

"Indeed I was—delightfully! You showed like battle, murder and sudden death all rolled into one, though considering you are a sailor your language fell much below expectation, neither oath nor curse—and only one chastely demure 'damn'! However, your actions were completely satisfactory, Sir Brutality fell beneath your arm with a pleasing violence that must have shaken his nasty person from top to toe, inside and out. Ah, but—though you stood above his writhing form like Ajax defying innumerable thunderbolts, he will probably slay you for it soon or late,—and all for that Marwood minx."

"Minx, madam? Can you possibly mean——"

"Rowena,—certainly I do! Is it any use warning you that she is heartless as she is beautiful and mercenary as her odious mother—is it?"

"No, madam, not a bit, because——"

"Ha! So she has her pretty claws in you already, has she?"

Now here my lord abandoning his fine airs, becomes merely Sam, and retorts bluntly:

"No, marm! And you do her gross injustice."

"Oh, do I—indeed!"

"Yes, marm, that you do! Your judgment of her is entirely wrong, ay, you're completely out o' your reckoning."

"Well!" exclaimed this little, great lady, setting down her cup, the better to stare and give effect to her amazed resentment. "Great goodness! Upon my immortal soul I never heard such—such audacious impertinence!"

"No, only truth, marm. For indeed you are very cruelly wrong. Lady Rowena has honoured me with her friendship and I——"

"Fiddle-de-dee and a flap-jack! Tush, boo and bah! No mere man could be merely a friend to such beautiful witch as she!"

"Probably not, marm, unless a man happened to . . . well . . . love another 'she' just as beautiful."

"Eh? Aha—another? Then you are already in love?"

"Heart and soul, marm!"

"Deeear me! What passion is here! How sighfully romantic——"

"No," said Sam, beginning to scowl, "pray don't try to make light mockery o' this love of mine, because it is the best part of me. Ay, 'tis clean and sweet as the open sea, 'tis better suited to fragrant countryside, the leafy solitude of woods at twilight sweet wi' the song of lonely bird, rather than this mockery called Vanity Fair. So, my lady, pray don't try to make joke of it because this, to me, is a—very holy thing."

The Duchess lifts her tea-cup as if about to drink, sets it down again and says in voice marvellously altered:

"No, Sam, I will not mock your love. God forbid! For such great passion ennobles man and woman, makes this world the sweeter—and alas, is all too rare! Indeed there are very few so blessed—to find such love."

"Ay," nodded Sam, "I've knocked around the world and I'm sure o' that—and so it is all the more precious to me, d'ye see?"

"Does she return your love?"

"So she tells me."

"Then why is she not your countess?"

"Because she places duty first."

"May I know her name?"

And after brief hesitation, he answers:

"Andromeda."

Her Grace, in the act of taking up the teapot, pauses, blinks those beautiful though very sharp eyes of hers, but all she says is:

"Let me refill your cup, Sam."

"Thank you!" he answers.

"So you actually do like tea?"

"Ay, marm, though I didn't know it until she learned me."

"Your Andromeda, of course. A quaint name,—will you tell me about her?"

Quick to heed the speaker's new gentleness of look and tone, Sam responds and with such simple eloquence that the Duchess utters no word (a remarkable fact) until he ends with sigh and the question: "So that's how things are, and what can I do? What d'you think of it all?"

"Girl's a fool, of course! And you trounced the uncle across your knee, did you?"

"Ay, and grieve to confess it."

"So you should, for he has always been most tragically unfortunate, poor Arthur!"

"Eh? Oh—you know him, madam?"

"All his unhappy life, he is a kinsman of mine. Ah—so greatly gifted he would have achieved greatness but for his cruel reverses. The woman he adored jilted him and he nearly died of grief. Your Uncle Julian shot him in a duel, a head wound and he was never the same after. Then his fortune was lost in some bank crash or other. To-day he is little better than a child, his great gifts all wasted and he now a peevish recluse, would be entirely desolate but for his niece's perfectly self-less, untiring devotion!"

"Yet, marm, you called her a fool."

"So I did, so I do, and so she is——"

"And so it is I love her—though, d'ye see, I'm all too rough and unworthy such an angel——"

"Stuff and nonsense! No man ever can love an angel, her wings would be so incommodious and forbidding, not to mention her halo,—if angels wear the things. However, it's high time Andromeda remembers she is merely a woman all flesh and blood with a dash of the divine, like the rest of us and acts accordingly. You say she loves you—then we must see that she behaves as a fine, healthy woman should."

"Ay, if she only would!" he sighs. "But what of her uncle, for, d'ye see, he vows he'll end himself if she leaves him or marries me."

"Fiddlesticks! And yet—he might, poor soul—unless I take him in hand as I have before now. Yes, I'd manage him——"

"Oh, marm!" Sam exclaims with an almost breathless eagerness. "If you only could and would!"

"Of course I could and would,—and will,—on a condition!"

"Anything," cries Sam. "I'll agree to anything——" here, warned by her look, he sat up, became the earl, and added: "except one thing, madam."

"Ah!" quoth she, nodding. "You've guessed aright, my condition is that you give up your meeting with that death-dealing monster Sir Robert Chalmers. And of course you're going to say 'no'."

"True, madam, 'no' it is and must be."

"You know he carries certain death in that right hand of his?"

"I have heard so, your Grace. But the weapons I shall choose will set us upon a pretty fair equality."

"Sam, if I beg and entreat you not to fight—for my sake, how then?"

"No, my lady."

"If I implore you for Andromeda's sake?"

"It must still be no, madam."

"Even though I offer to set Andromeda in those nice, strong arms of yours,—to hold and to have till——"

"Oh, madam, in mercy don't torment me!"

"Very well, then—if instead of the warm, sweet loveliness of your Andromeda with the blessed joy and hope of children, you will choose death and a clammy grave, so be it, my poor Sam. Good-bye, my lord, I shall send a very large and lovely wreath for your coffin."

"Your Grace, madam—— Oh, marm, will you allow me to call and see you again? May I, please?"

"Why, of course, Sam. I shall always be glad to see you at any time—so long as you are alive. When do you fight this abominable duel?"

"I've no idea."

"Well, to-day is Friday,—I shall expect you next Thursday, without fail—if you happen to be alive. However, you shall hear from me. Now good-bye, and I think I like the sailor of you, Sam, better than the earl, Japhet—so far. However, time shall prove this—unless Death should supervene, which God forbid, my poor, my foolish, my dear Sam."

"Lord love you," says he, gratefully, "what friends we are going to be!"

"Perhaps," she sighs, "only perhaps!"

"Pray marm," he enquires, gazing down at the small vital hand that clasps his big one so heartily, "just what might you mean by 'perhaps'?"

"Well, instead, let us make it 'if', Sam—if you are not killed too dreadfully soon."

"Ay," he murmurs, "Old Man Death is never very far from some of us, I guess. . . . Now suppose, marm, I had accepted your condition and the . . . joy of Andromeda instead of doing what I must and shall,—how then?"

"Why then, Sam, my dear, I should have commended your prudence highly—but from a very great distance and never, never have compelled you to drink tea with me again of course!"

"Oh, marm—my lady," he exclaims, his grim features all at once transfigured by his flashing smile, "what a blessing and comfort you are!" Then stooping, he kisses her small, rather bony fingers with such fervour that when he is gone, she glances down at these same fingers very wistfully.

CHAPTER VI

MY lord is a success, Vanity Fair throws wide its portals and all within may be his—at a price. Favoured by Fashion's small arbiter her Grace of Camberhurst, Fashion does the like; and thus, backed by his ancient name, his prodigious wealth and forthright personality, he becomes a, or rather, the celebrity more especially with The Sex. His occasional lapses into "merely Sam", his blunt turns of speech and vigour of gesture are declared "so essentially male" and he is pronounced "an absolute original" and "charming oddity". So in drawing-room and assembly he becomes "the rage" and "persona grata" in the clubs.

Then besides, having more money than he can ever spend, he spends it so lavishly, wins and loses with such placid disregard, that he becomes almost too popular among the younger element, dashing bucks and superb dandies,—gilded youth but sportsmen all,—by whom his somewhat awkward gestures are copied together with the tie of his cravats, cut of his hair, tilt of his hat and seaman's rolling stride which Sir John has endeavoured so vainly to correct and eradicate. So my lord achieves Popularity, this panoply of glittering tinsel, and wears it with a careless ease, to the more or less articulate jubilation of Mr. Standish, now his devoted and trusty henchman, and the dignified surprise of Sir John, which sentiment he expresses on a certain morning at the breakfast table, thus:

SIR JOHN: I find your popularity, Sam, quite surprising.

SAM (*Busied with the luscious fare before him*): So do I.

MR. STANDISH: 'S amazin'! Sam's positively the glass o' fashion and mould o' form! Acme of elegance and so forth, —put Brummel's nose out o' joint, y'know. They're advertisin' a new line o' waistcoats à la Wrybourne—fact 'pon honour! And then the ladies, bless 'em—such sighful languishin's, b'Gad——

SIR JOHN: What astonishes me, Sam, is that all this does not seem to embarrass you in the least.

SAM: Well, no, John, for, d'ye see, I don't bother about it.

MR. STANDISH: 'Xackly, John! Sam's cold-blooded as confounded fish!

SIR JOHN: Indeed? Then pray inform me, Sam, why I am so frequently hearing your name associated with that of Lady Rowena Marwood?

SAM (*Puffing at the hot coffee in his cup, to Sir John's very evident and startled disapproval*): For a very good purpose. Harry—explain. (He drinks.)

MR. STANDISH: Well, S'John, it's all f' my sake and the behoof o' The Juggernaut, Darling Mama——

SAM: He means Lady Marwood, John.

MR. STANDISH: 'Xactly, sir, t' draw the wool over her dooced uncommonly keen peepers. Sam woos Rowena f' me, proposes romantic midnight elopement, Darling Mama agrees with joy. At 'pointed hour, Sam's fastest carriage 'pears, out gets Sam, gives signal, to him steals Rowena—watched, be sure, by gloating Mama,—and away they go—pull up here—out pops Sam, in pop I and away we dash, Rowena and I, to Matrimony and rapture while Darling Mama sleeps blissfully content. That's it, John, in nutshell. What d'ye think of it, sir?

SIR JOHN (*Shaking stately head in grave reproof*): I forbear comment! Except to declare that—— He pauses at sudden rap on the door which opens to discover Robins the stately butler, portentous of mien, who bears a silver tray whereon repose two cards, the which he presents with solemn bow, saying:

"My lord, the gentlemen desire instant speech with your lordship on matter of extreme moment!"

"So?" says my lord, glancing at these cards "Then you may inform Major Topham of the Guards, and Viscount Twily that I will see them here and now."

"But, my dear boy," demurs Sir John, a little anxiously, "in your dressing-gown?"

"Precisely so, John."

"This will be Chalmers' formal challenge, Sam."

"Ay, so I think. Harry, d'you know these gentlemen?"

"So dooced well, my dear old f'low, that I—don't! Especially Twily, bit of a blackleg, y'know.—Here they are!"

Again a tap—the door opens and two exquisite beings appear, the Viscount slim, pallid and slightly vulpine, the Major tall, red-faced, bewhiskered and inclined to swagger and corpulence. Bows are exchanged, my lord wafts his visitors to chairs, suggests refreshment which is refused, takes up his coffee-cup and enquires:

"Well, sirs?"

The Major clears his throat, Viscount Twily smiles thin-lipped, and they speak alternately:

"M'lord," booms the Major, making the most of his whiskers, "we have the honour to represent our friend Sir Robert Chalmers who has appointed us his seconds——"

"To demand," smiles the Viscount, "a meeting with your lordship, satisfaction, my lord, and I may add—to the uttermost and last extremity!"

My lord, sipping his coffee, looks at the speaker, sets down his cup and says, musingly:

"Sir, until now I have never had the extremity of joy to see or hear you, yet you sound remarkably bloody, why? Or is this your natural charm of manner? But no matter,—instead pray tell me just when does your principal propose to kill me, where and how?"

"Yours, my lord," answers Major Topham, "yours is the choice of weapons, pray be good enough to name 'em."

"And," says the Viscount, with muted eagerness, "our principal, Sir Robert, will perform upon your lordship at Barn Elms, ten days hence. The hour he sets you is eight o'clock precisely, morning of course   You will choose pistols, I presume?"

"Well—no," answers my lord, slowly, as if pondering the question, "no, sir—not—pistols."

"Ha!" exclaims the Major, nodding brightly. "Then small swords, of course."

"N-no," murmurs my lord, still hesitant, "no, Major, nor small swords."

"Oh? Eh—not? Then E'gad—sabres!"

"No," answers my lord, as if making up his mind at last, "certainly not sabres."

"Why then," says the Viscount, acidly, "suppose my lord your lordship troubles to inform us?"

The Earl takes up his coffee-cup, finds it empty and shakes his head at it, saying:

"I am deliberating, gentlemen, whether to make it boarding-axes or cutlasses."

K

Major Topham falls back in his chair, redder of face than ever, he emits a strangled gasp and then:

"B-b-boarding-axes!" he repeats, explosively, while Viscount Twily, pallidly vicious, rises to his feet.

"Cutlasses?" he hisses. "If this is a jest, I resent it! B'God, sir, this is no matter for jest or lightsome trifling,—no! This affair is to be without respite—to the death! So I warn you——"

"Sir," my lord breaks in, setting down his coffee-cup very tenderly but speaking in the voice of Sam, "be damned t'you and your warning! My choice is cutlasses, ordinary ship's cutlasses, d'ye see, thirty-two inch blades,—these or nothing."

"Oh, but—but," splutters the Major, groping for his whisker rather dazedly, "these—oh, I beg, I plead,—my lord, pray consider,—these are no weapons for a gentleman!"

"However, they are mine," nods my lord, "you may take 'em or leave them. If Sir Robert feels himself too much of a gentleman to use them, let him send me an apology for thus disturbing me at my breakfast and we'll say no more about it. But, gentlemen both, pray understand—cutlasses it shall be—or an apology I must have."

"Ap-pology!" whispers the Viscount, between lips tighter now than ever. "Ha, my lord, I take joy to inform you that Sir Robert Chalmers never apologizes,—never."

"Very good!" nods my lord. "Then in ten days' time, he and I will chop at each other with cutlasses. And now, gentlemen, since we have settled the matter so happily, unless you will join us, be good enough to permit that we finish breakfast."

Scarcely have these indignant gentlemen stalked out and away, than Mr. Standish is convulsed with uncontrollable mirth, he gasps, he groans and finally wheezes:

"Sam . . . oh, Sam . . . m'dear . . . old lord . . . oho—cutlasses! Their dem faces! Cutlasses—what a prime move. . . . Oh, Sam!" Even Sir John's gravity relaxes and he smiles though with shake of stately head, saying:

"With the exception of your one regrettable show of temper, Sam, you bore yourself well. Your choice of weapons is original and should make your chances more even—I hope!"

"Though, demme old f'low, they were right, y'know, a cutlass is no weapoh for a gentleman—never heard o' such thing!"

"However, I've used one pretty often, Harry, and am fairly handy with one."

"D'y'think you'll—get him, old f'low?"

"Well, d'ye see, it's his pistol-hand I'm after. By the way, John, I'm hoping you'll act for me—my seconds, you and Harry—make all the arrangements—will you, please?"

"Assuredly!" answered Sir John, sighing.

"Honoured, my dear, old lord!"

Breakfast done, my lord ascends to his sumptuous bed-chamber where with the aid of his valets he is prepared and attired for the street, when a bowing footman appears to inform him that "a Mr. Joliffe desires speech with him". So my lord in his splendour presently greets the lawyer with a very Sam-like heartiness.

But Mr. Joliffe is in state of such indignant perturbation that no sooner is the door closed than he exclaims:

"Sam—oh, Sam, he's free! My months of planning and contriving are proved to-tally vain! Villainy triumphs! Your cousin the Honourable—no, confound him—Lord Ralph Scrope—is free!"

"Good!" nods my lord.

"Eh—good? Good, d'ye say? But I'm telling you he is free, and moreover—a rich man!"

"Soho!" says my lord, becoming Sam. "She's married him already has she, bless her loveliness!"

"Eh? Married? She?" gasps Mr. Joliffe. "Then you know? You've heard?"

"Nothing, Ben, I only guess. For, d'ye see, I schemed for this——"

"You—you schemed——?" Here, words failing him, Mr. Joliffe snorted instead.

"Sit down, Ben, old fellow, compose yourself and tell me all about it! Come, let's hear." And very indignantly Mr. Joliffe obeys, saying:

"No sooner has this young Croft person become possessed of her immense legacy and recovered from the shock, of it, than with her friend Mrs. Jennings, she hastens to London, outfits herself like a princess, drives in state to the Marshalsea and having beforehand paid your cousin's liabilities to the last farthing, frees the prisoner, marries him by special licence and is now back at the Manor House which is being renovated from cellarage to attics,—and all this your own doing by the bestowal of such vast sum to an inconsequent, irresponsible, hare-brained miss——"

"No, Ben, a very lovely, strong-souled woman who has acted precisely as I wished and hoped she might."

"Wished?" repeated the lawyer, staring, "do you mean me to infer——"

"Ben, this was the best way I could think of,—I mean— how to share some portion of this dam' heritage with the family. And Cecily Croft, God love her,—was the means. So all's well, for if anyone can ever make a good man out of a Scrope, it is she. And therefore," says my lord, rising and crossing to the sideboard where stood promising array of bottles, decanters and glasses, "let us drink to her, this dear, faithful soul, may her beauty be her husband's inspiration and he prove her abiding happiness." When they have honoured this toast, my lord enquires:

"Ben, does she guess—about this money, has she any suspicions?"

"My dear Sam, of course! Being an astute young person, she suspected it was your doing, at once,—and was oddly unwilling to receive——"

"Ay, I guessed she would be! And how then?"

"I was necessitated to argue and finally—almost to compel her acceptance. And a fine time I had of it, for then she began to weep, which profoundly upset me, then she laughed, and then did both together, which perfectly dismayed me, then she told some wild, quite fantastic story of how you had told her fortune. So that when at last the business was settled and she gone,—well, I am a more confirmed bachelor than ever! And now, Sam, I'll quit your lordship's noble mansion for my dingy office—though, as a friend, permit me to remark your desperate gambling is a by-word—Sir John is greatly perturbed, and I venture to——"

"However, Ben, I don't always lose, d'ye see. So never worry—instead tell me of Cecily—you said she actually brought Mrs. Jennings here to London with her, which surprises me, considering——"

"Ah, to be sure, Sam, there was something of a miracle, or so says Anne Leet. She vows that, but for this girl, Mrs. Jennings would certainly be in her grave. . . . Eh? Twelve o'clock!" he exclaims, as a clock chimes the hour. "And I've an appointment! Good-bye, my lord, for the present, Sam."

Mr. Joliffe having departed, my lord takes the air with Mr. Standish who opines it will be a busy day. Reaching Whites, they lounge, wine and exchange news with other "busy" gentlemen; they saunter as far as Wattiers to yawn over the gazette; thence they amble to Boodle's for a glass or so of a certain famous sherry; they dine at Brooke's where my lord elects to gamble, which he does for preposterously high stakes and with varying success until supper-time. Thereafter, wearying of the cards and Mr. Standish having departed long since, my lord calls for hat and cane, when he is accosted by Major Topham who says, engagingly:

"Will your lordship be so very obleeging as to follow me?" My lord does so and comes face to face with Sir Robert Chalmers who bows and smiles, at least he shows his large teeth, as he enquires and quite pleasantly:

"Ah, my lord, pray what is this fantastic nonsense my friends report to me concerning your choice of weapons for our little affair?" And my lord, bowing in turn, answers as pleasantly:

"If your friends befool you, sir, I suggest you chide 'em——"

"Sir, they talk of—of—cutlasses!" says Sir Robert, spitting out the word as if it were something extremely nasty.

"Then they speak truly, Sir Robert, cutlasses are my choice."

"Damnation, sir—these are no weapons for gentlemen! They are irregular, they are utterly preposterous, and outrageous!"

"However, Sir Robert, permit me to assure you that one gentleman may hack another gentleman very well indeed with such tools. Yes, sir, properly used cutlasses are excellent for chopping, you'll find—though should you prefer boarding-axes or even pikes——"

"Oh, the devil! Here will be a very ridiculous exhibition. The vulgar travesty of what is and should be a very solemn, gentlemanly business! Suppose I refuse to accept such plebeian, such cursedly boorish weapons?"

"In that event, Sir Robert, I shall take joy to publish you in all the clubs as a cowardly braggart."

Sir Robert's small eyes open their widest to glare, his big teeth snap, his hands clench to quivering fists; noting all of which, my lord smiles provokingly and nods:

"Pray do,—but this time I shall not merely—push you down!"

Sir Robert's fury being now far beyond words, he says nothing, he merely looks all he cannot utter, then turns and strides away, gesturing like a madman.

CHAPTER VII

WHICH, HAVING LITTLE TO TELL, IS ADMIRABLY BRIEF

THE rarified atmosphere of Vanity Fair is vibrant with rumours of the impending duel; whereby my lord's now assured popularity is decidedly increased. The Sex is bewitchingly horrified; bright eyes now languish more soulfully or contrive to dim their radiance with anticipatory tears more or less genuine; there are even signs that angels, extremely feminine of gender, would fain comfort his few remaining hours.

In club and coffee-house he is greeted more warmly, his hand clutched in heartier grip, voices hail him more jovially, —and thus, wherever he goes, my lord becomes aware that he is regarded as a dying man whose hours are numbered to the precise minute, a victim fore-doomed to certain death.

Wagers of course are freely laid upon his chances of survival, which are esteemed so poor that certain gallant sportsmen are bold enough to offer heavy odds that he "will be snuffed out at the first exchanges".

Yet my lord goes his way apparently serene as ever, his smile as ready and laugh as hearty as usual,—no Sam-like frown is ever seen to furrow his well-marked, low-set brows— until a certain afternoon. . . . He lies drowsing in shady corner at Brooke's, remote from the throng, when his sleepy ears are assailed by a high-pitched voice, arrogant, assured, uttering these words:

"Wrybourne's a goner, of course,—good as dead already!"

"Agreed, Denby," says a second voice, "but no need to proclaim the fact, dem bad form, I call it!"

"Bad form or not, Hewitt, that's my belief and I'm backing it at ten to one! Who'll take me? What, none o' you? Then b'God, I'll make it fifteen, d'ye hear? Fifteen to one I'm offering against the earl lasting five minutes! What, still no one?"

"Ya-as," drawls a new voice, "I take y', Denby."

"Eh? Oh, it's you, Standish. Well, what'll you lay me—fives?"

"No, tens."

"Oho, you're dev'lish bold! Will you venture to make it twenties?"

"No, 's make it hundreds——"

"Eh—what—what?"

"Layin' y' a hundred at twenty t'one, Denby. Are y'on?" Here ensues an excited babblement:

"Well, how about it, Denby?"

"Aha, Denby, won't you take him?"

"Are you backing down now, Denby?"

"Certainly—not!" shrills Mr. Denby. "I'll book him at the figure—or any other man. But as for you, Standish, come again—make it two hundred."

"No, Denby, let's say five—a monkey. Though per'f'kly willing t' make it a thousand, y'know——"

This bold challenge causes an uproar,—and it is now that my lord's dark brows knit in a Sam-like scowl.

"That's got you, Denby!"

"Aha, that's a leveller!"

"One right in the wind, eh, Denby?"

"What's the word, Denby?"

"If," says Mr. Standish, "if y' want any more shall be dooced glad t'oblige, y'know."

"No, demme, I'm satisfied . . ."

My lord being now extremely wide awake, consults his watch, rises without noise and as silently steals away, for this is the afternoon he is to visit Her Grace of Camberhurst.

CHAPTER VIII

TELLS HOW MY LORD MET TEMPTATION

THUS the clocks are proclaiming the hour of four when my lord entering the ducal portals, is relieved of hat, cane and gloves and ushered into that same small, cosy chamber where, as once before, he is to drink tea with the Duchess; just at present he finds it is vacant wherefore he crosses to the window and stands there gazing out, so lost in thought that he is unaware the door behind him has opened, so does not move until a soft voice says:

"My lord!" Then, starting violently, he swings round and stands motionless and dumb.

For instead of the little Duchess he beholds a lady graciously tall, whose raven hair parted on white brow, falls in glossy ringlets to frame the proud, high beauty of her face; her silken robe, high-bosomed, clings her loveliness, revealing such shape as the first Andromeda showed the happy Perseus who beholding thus beauty's perfection, had no eyes (of course) for the grimly, snake-locked Medusas, sea-monsters or anything else.

So here before my lord is beauty far more wonderful than Sam had ever dreamed, a glowing, dainty thing of loveliness looking at him with the golden eyes of gipsy drudge, woodland dryad and—the one woman.

"An-dromeda!" he breathes at least and makes a step towards her, then halts, awed by the sheer wonder of her.

"Sam!" she murmurs, reaching out both hands to him. . . . Then he has her in his arms and, trying to speak, is dumb now for very joy. So he kisses her instead,—lustrous, silky hair, these fragrant, midnight tresses, long-lashed eyes and vivid mouth that with an equal passion, meet and return his caress.

Now leaning back within the fervour of his embrace, she looks up at him, saying tremulously:

"Oh, my beloved . . . you are . . . marvellously . . . wonderfully changed!"

"Only outwardly," he answers, "for I'm still truly—only

Sam, a common sort o' fellow, but . . . all yours if you'll only take him . . . and here am I crushing your dainty finery in such brutal hug——"

"Well—crush it!" she whispers, clinging to him. "For . . . oh Sam, if you are mine, I am all yours, as I always have been and must be. Life is an empty dreariness . . . and I am lost without you—ah yes," she murmurs, seeing where he looks, "your keep-sake, the cross and heart and anchor I wear it always upon my heart and it shall never leave me so long as you are my Sam!" and she lays slim finger on the small gold chain that gleams about her round white throat; so he kisses finger, chain and throat, whispering:

"Oh, Andromeda . . . beloved, are you here to give yourself to me at last—my wife?"

"Yes, beloved man, I am here for your taking—soon, oh, soon! You can marry me by special licence and take me away anywhere you will,—away from this hateful London."

"But, your uncle?"

"He is here with my godmother and will remain——"

"Godmother?"

"The Duchess, yes,—so if you want me as I need you, it must be soon, my dearest, very soon." Now as she utters these words his arms relax, wherefore she hides her face against his breast and clings him the tighter.

"Andromeda," he demands, kissing her hair again, "then you have heard, you know I am to fight?"

Without lifting head she nods "yes".

"And you have come," he demands, "to cheer and strengthen me for it with your love?"

Now at this, she shakes her head, saying:

"No, I have come to shield you with my love,—to stand between you and death!" Here she looks up at him wide-eyed, "I am here to command you,—beg and entreat you not to throw away your life, our happiness, and my love—wasting them all to such foolish, wicked purpose and so needlessly! Oh, Sam, my own dear, you shall not, must not."

"Now Lord love me!" he groans, "you should know me better than to ask of me such thing as this——"

"But I do ask it, I must—I must——"

"Don't!" he gasps. "Ah—don't!" His arms fall from her and she, as if bereft of strength, sinks to her knees before him.

"Oh, my beloved," she sighs, looking up at him above clasped hands, "here at your feet I do now implore you not to peril your life and our future—all the wonder that may be for us . . . because, if you are killed I think I shall die too . . . it is for you to choose. Think, dearest, think, I might . . . be so blessed to . . . give . . . an heir to your name. . . . Oh, Sam, how can there be any choice—what, what is it you would die for?"

"Now God help me!" he groans, lifting clenched hands to his temples. "Why, why a God's name must you be so sure I shall be killed—why?"

"Because the Duchess is so dreadfully certain—and tells me that everyone—yes everyone believes the same. So now again, for the last time, I beg—entreat you to live for me and —our future—instead of dying for this—this code of honour which has nothing to do with honour that is real and true. Be brave enough to refuse this duel and if you are branded craven, wear the stigma like a glory, for my sake."

"Ay, so I would, for I care nothing for the opinion of these grand folk,—and I fight for no dam'-fool code of honour, d'ye see, but to make it impossible for a fine gentleman to kill or maim any other fine gentleman ever again, more especially a certain one. So, Andromeda, don't tempt me with your beauty—to run away and shield myself in your arms. Could you love me if I did? If so, then such love would shame us both. Ay, by God, I would rather die loving you as I do now with honour, than, taking all you offer, live to despise the beauty that made me despise myself. So now, Andromeda, 'stead o' weeping, be furious and glare those golden eyes at me,—reproach and berate me and I will be my lordliest,— like this: Madame, my hand—suffer that I aid you to rise——"
But this she does unaided and avoiding his touch.

"Yes," says she, viewing him through tears that do not fall, "yes, I have indeed shamed myself bitterly . . . for your sake, and this I shall not forgive. Deeply and truly as I loved my rough seaman, my simple, clean-hearted Sam, just so truly do I hate and despise this selfish wretch called lord and Earl of Wrybourne. . . . To Sam I would have given myself utterly, sharing his poverty joyfully,—to my lord of Wrybourne I say —go, fight your vile duels, shed your foolish blood, waste your precious life so vainly if you will, but expect no tear from me! A man who will die for such useless folly is not worth any woman's grief! Yes, my lord, when you go to fight this duel, I shall abominate your lordship because—you take my beloved Sam with you."

"Madam," says my lord, with elaborate bow, "through the lips of my so detested lordship, your ever-loving Sam speaks you his sincere gratitude and undying hope of you. And now, dearest madam, my lordship humbly begs leave to say that though you now show in your splendour, beauteous as Venus glorified by the golden eyes of Andromeda of the sorry cotton hose and clumsy boots, you talk like very peevish, excessively petulant miss! And so, madam, pray give me leave to bid you a very fair good afternoon!" Then my lord turns and leaves her . . .

And now indeed her tears fall at last, hot and painful, tears of yearning for this her chosen man and he so wishful to die and be done with her.

So Andromeda sinks to her knees sobbing a prayer, and then to her face and thus outstretched abandoned to her grief, weeps more bitterly than she has ever done in all her not too-happy life.

CHAPTER IX

TELLS OF BARE FLESH AND COLD STEEL

IT is a fine autumnal morning when in pleasant rural surroundings remote from chance of interruption, two gentlemen accompanied by their friends, reasoning creatures all, meet—with the avowed and sole intention of maiming or killing one another as expeditiously and, of course, politely as possibly.

Hats flourish and backs bend in gracious salutation, grave voices murmur, solemn eyes take heed to the angle of a new-risen sun this giver of life, to the evenness of ground and smoothness of turf destined to be enriched anon by something other than rain.

Sir John is here, placid and stately as usual, with Mr. Standish a trifle paler than wont, yet bearing himself with a confident air that is almost jaunty. Major Topham is here, very stiff as to back and whiskers; Viscount Twily is here, smiling and sardonic; here also the two surgeons standing together in muttered confab.

And here of course are the two protagonists,—my lord apparently lost in thoughtful contemplation of a skylark carolling joyously above them and thus perfectly oblivious of Sir Robert Chalmers' persistent, lowering stare, until Mr. Standish draws his attention thereto, saying low-voiced:

"Remark our Sir Bob, his demd fighting-face, his fee-fi-fo-fummy expression! That's 'nother trick of his,—t'stare his man out o' countenance t'shake his nerve."

Made thus aware of his antagonist's lowering scrutiny, my lord nods airily, draws out his handkerchief and enquires:

"Eh, a smut, Sir Robert? On my nose,—my chin? Be good enough to tell me which or where."

Sir Robert mutters fierce incoherencies and turns his back whereat Mr. Standish nods derisively and murmurs:

"First blood t'you, my dear, old lord!"

But now the Major approaches to say:

"M'lord, as this is to be the cold steel, it is proper and

usual, also my principal demands you fight bare-chested. Is this agreed?"

"Certainly," answers my lord and begins to cast off surtout and close-fitting coat in which business he is assisted by Mr. Standish.

Thus presently bare of arm and breast the two adversaries front each other . . . Viscount Twily now advances to present their weapons,—my lord bows to Sir Robert who takes the nearest, swings the broad, curved blade with practised hand, cursing its weight and clumsiness, while my lord stands with point to ground, waiting.

"My lord," says the Viscount, backing away, "pray remember, Sir Robert demands this shall be without stay or respite— to the death!"

"Gentlemen," booms the Major, "are you ready?"

"Yes!" hisses Sir Robert between those big teeth, of his that seem crueller than ever,—my lord merely nods.

"Then, engage—go!" The keen blades flicker in swift action to meet with ringing clash, and for a moment they remain thus crossed, then—with fierce "Ha!" and stamp of foot Sir Robert, swiftly disengaging, thrusts straight at his antagonist's throat, his deadly point glitters dreadfully near, is beaten aside—and he leaps back from the counter-stroke.

Mr. Standish, gasping relief, takes off his hat, looks at it and puts it on again; Sir John, keen eyes intent upon this murderous steel, fumbles unsuccessfully for his snuff-box and frowns, while this combat rages with ever-growing fury.

Sir Robert, well-used to the more delicate small-sword, relies chiefly upon the point, but my lord, expectant of this, watches this swift-leaping point, meets and parries its every darting thrust, and waits for the full-armed lunge that will give him the opening for the stroke which shall end this murderous business . . .

And now while the spectators scarcely breathe, is close, desperate flurry of cut and thrust, point and edge, the broad blades clashing in fierce attack and violent parry, whirling in glittering arcs or flashing in lightning thrust . . .

Mr. Standish has doffed his hat again and clasps it to his bosom; Sir John has found his snuff-box but forgotten to open it. For as this relentless combat progresses it becomes ever more terribly apparent that Sir Robert indeed means to kill. . . . Time and again his vicious thrusts are turned only just in time,—quick of hand he is also swift of foot, avoiding counter-blow and thrust as much by agility of body as skill of blade, while my lord, keen-eyed and watchful, stands his ground—waiting.

"Oh—demme!" murmurs Mr. Standish, donning his hat only to take it off again. "This can't. last, y'know! Can't possibly! 'Tisn't human—never saw such dooced endurance . . . ha, look at Chalmers, there's animus . . . hate and bloody murder! There—and there again——"

"Hush!" says Sir John, fingers clenching his forgotten snuff-box. "The end will be . . . sudden and . . . soon——"

"Oh God, John. . . . Oh God . . . look at Sam, he's failing . . . ah—blood!"

"I see, Harry! Yes, Chalmers means death."

Ceaseless ring and clash of ever-whirling steel, stamp and shuffle of feet. . . . Thus, hand-to-hand, foot-to-foot, and eye-to-eye, they strike, parry, and thrust at each other's lives, circle and sway,—Sir Robert sweat-streaked, fiercely relentless as ever,—my lord grim and steadfast. Both now are breathing hard, both seem tiring at last—and upon my lord's sweat-glistening sword-arm is trickle of blood . . .

Mr. Standish stifles a groan, crushes his hat shapeless, lets it fall and holds his breath in horrified dismay. For my lord's blade seems to waver, he shifts his ground awkwardly—then reels back with Sir Robert's weapon driven through his arm, —but this arm is his left and, recovering balance, he laughs grimly, his own blade whirls, flashes down in the stroke for which he has watched—and Sir Robert, losing his weapon, stumbles backward and is caught in the Major's embrace while my lord stands looking down at the dangling steel transfixing him.

Then Sir John drops the crushed fragments of his snuff-box and with Mr. Standish hastens to support him, while the surgeon proceeds to withdraw the clumsy blade from my lord's ugly wound, at which Mr. Standish winces as if this arm had been his own, exclaiming:

"Oh dooce and the devil . . . my dear old f'low . . . how the devil are you?"

"Better than I look," answers my lord rather breathlessly and between pallid lips. "But, Harry—his pistol hand,— tell me——"

"M'dear old lord, no need t'tell you—look yonder!"

Now glancing whither he is directed, my lord beholds, lying upon smeared grass, that which will never more grasp murderous duelling weapon.

"Lord!" murmurs Sam, between lips even paler now. "Ned . . . tells me I always strike . . . harder than necessary——"

CHAPTER X

THE duel and its unexpected ending sets the crowning glory on my lord's popularity, and he is now famous. He is also a scowling, gloomy misery. Cards and flowers pour in upon him, visitors of both sexes, old and young, call to do homage, but are received with gracious urbanity by Sir John who, pleading my lord's wound, fills his place with a charm that tempers disappointment at my lord's non-appearance;—so they enquire the more tenderly after his health, commiserate his hurt, glorify his success and depart, feeling themselves more his friends than ever. . . . While my lord, having shut himself away with his wound, his pipe, a few books and his broken hopes, becomes ever the more dejected.

Thus daily he languishes,—for this fighting seaman whose precept has been "no surrender and never say die", now does both. Weakened by his bodily hurt, he despairs at last and sinks to such deeps of woeful, hopeless despondency from which Mr. Standish strives to rouse him and so vainly that both he and Sir John becoming daily more anxious, summon the most eminent doctors—surgeons and physicians (to my lord's disgust)—even nurses are threatened (to my lord's indignant horror) for no one, not even his devoted Harry, suspects that it is not so much bodily wound troubling him as a bewitching affliction called—Andromeda . . . until:

Upon a certain morning, my lord having cursed his two valets out and away, Mr. Standish finds him doing his one-armed best to clothe himself.

"Goo' Lord!" exclaims that gentleman, aghast, "m'dear old tulip, no, no, naughty-naughty! Y' ought ta be in bed, y'know!"

"Not me!" snarls my lord, becoming Sam at his worst. "No, damme, I've had enough o' this cosseting and cursed inaction,—I'm off!"

"Eh, off? Off where? What for——"

"No matter! Bear a hand wi' this dam' shirt."

Mr. Standish, alarmed by something wild in my lord's looks and tone, becomes extremely articulate and quite determined as Sam himself, as he says:

"No, dear fellow! Your place at present, is bed,—and it's not the least good your cursing me, for back to bed you're going—and at once!"

"Well, damn your eyes!" growls Sam, actually clenching his one good fist. "D'ye think you or any other man could stay me or keep me from her?"

"Ah!" exclaims Mr. Standish, recoiling as if indeed from a physical blow. "Then . . . yes, that's it—you're in love with——"

"Ay, what else! Come, bear a, hand with my shirt."

"I ought," says Mr. Standish, swallowing with difficulty, "ought to have guessed. Yes . . . of course . . . it was only to be expected! You have not——" here another difficult swallow, "told her yet, naturally?"

"What of?"

"Your . . . love——"

"Ay, that I have."

"Oh? A trifle hasty, weren't you?"

"Well," says Sam, pondering, "yes, come to think of it, I was."

"And does she," again Mr. Standish gulps, "does she . . . return your sentiments?"

"If you mean my love, Harry, yes—yes, I believe she does, and this is my one comfort."

"And I wish," sighs Mr. Standish, "you were cured of your wound because then I should express to you—my sentiments."

"Oh?" murmurs Sam, pondering this. "Ah? Harry, what d'ye mean?"

"That were you a sound man, Wrybourne, I should express myself rather forcibly—as it is I merely suggest it would have been fairer to me and more honourable in you to have warned me first."

"Warned you? Damme—what about?"

"Your love for Rowena."

"Oho!" exclaims Sam. "My poor, old Harry-fool!" And for the first time since his scene with Andromeda he laughs, while Mr. Standish, pale and stern, watches him. "B'George!" he exclaims, his merriment subsiding. "That's done me a power o' good! So now for your good, Harry, I tell you my love instead of gold is black as midnight, her eyes a golden glory, herself the only woman for me in all this world. Sit down, my hearty, and let me tell you. . . ."

And thus, with many other particulars, Mr. Standish, this faithful, trusty friend, learns the wherefore of my lord's disease that has perplexed everyone.

"So d'ye see, Harry," he ends mournfully, "she's braced about, borne away and left me in the dam' doldrums, no—worse, a dismasted hulk, helpless, waterlogged and rolling gunn'le under for the final, everlasting plunge!"

"Nothin' o' the sort, m'dear, old f'low—no! All that's needed is judgment and manage. First, did your lady toss your engagement ring back at you—with scorn and so forth?"

"No, but——"

"Good——"

"Only because she never had one to toss."

"Ha! And she's stayin' wi' th' Duchess?"

"She was."

"And the Duchess is her godmother you tell me? Well, she thinks no end o' you, th' Duchess, fact! Called three times t' enquire—pity you refused t'see her."

"Yes, Harry, I was a curst fool! But I felt such a poor, miserable, sick dog—I couldn't bear anyone near me."

"No wonder! You'd lost gallons o' gore—artery or something 'cording to the surgeon. And e'Gad, 'Sam, I thought Chalmers had skewered more than your arm—frightful minute for me, old f'low! How the dooce did it happen?"

"Chalmers was so clever, Harry, I had to give him an opening to get in the blow I wanted,—ay, he certainly could fight!"

"But never again, m'dear, old lord, unless he's ambidextrous, for the hand that shot me—and others, is now rotti——"

"And now," says Sam, rather gruffly, "I'll thank you to help me into my clothes, Harry."

"Cer-tainly not, old f'low—you're not fit,—lot weaker than you think, loss o' blood and so forth, y'know."

"But damme, I must see the Duchess."

"So you shall, by proxy. I'll see her for you, give her any message and, better still, a letter to your Andromeda, a few heart-felt words—if you can manage to write——"

"Of course! Bring me the pen and ink, Harry."

Thus, with writing materials before him, Sam (and despite the weakness that surprised and angered him) contrives to scrawl, very shakily, these words:

> EVER BELOVED, I am not dead, but it is for you to bless me with the very joy of life, if only you will. So if you will, pray come to me. However I am now and always—only your SAM.

Folding this missive he superscribed it

TO THE ONE.

Then Mr. Standish seals it carefully, thrusts it tenderly into the bosom of his coat and turns to go, saying gaily:

"Have patience, old f'low, don't work y'self into another dooced fever——"

"Into her hand only, Harry!"

"None other, old lord—I'm an off 'un!" And off he speeds accordingly. Scarcely has he gone than my lord buoyed up by hope, summons his valets and makes an elaborate toilette, tries vainly to get himself inducted into his newest, tightest coat, is folded into loose dressing-robe instead and sits down to await the outcome of his written appeal. Hoping against hope, yearning for sound and sight of her . . . to see the door open and Andromeda standing with arms reached out to him. . . . He ponders just what his first words shall be, how he will greet her—he even selects the chair that shall be so blessed as to support and embrace her loveliness. . . .

Thus he frets and fumes, alternating between radiant hope and black despair until the door indeed opens at last to admit—only Mr. Standish, his gaiety somewhat dashed, but saying, cheerfully as possible:

"No luck, old f'low!" And he gives back the letter and Sam, seeing the seal unbroken, crams it fiercely into his pocket, demanding:

"Was she out?"

"Well," answers Mr. Standish as if considering this question, "no—not exactly."

"Ah—then she saw you?"

"Oh yes. Yes, certainly—she saw me."

"And you gave her my—my dam' letter?"

"Well—not precisely."

"Harry, what the devil d'you mean?"

"I handed it to her, old fellow, at least I—held it out to her, but she . . . didn't——"

"Ha! She refused even to touch it, eh, Harry?"

"Yes, Sam."

"Did she—say anything?"

"Yes, something that I didn't and don't understand—dooced perplexing, y'know, Sam, can't make head or tail——"

"Well, out with it, man—her very words."

"When I proffered your letter she merely smiled at it, shook her head at it and said, 'No, sir, you have brought Lord Wrybourne's billet-doux to the wrong person'."

"Eh, wrong person? Did you ask what she meant?"

"I did, but she merely smiled and left me."

"So, Harry, that ends it!"

"No, old fellow, this begins it! We now attack her with flowers. Nothing like flowers, old boy, t' touch the feminine heart, blooms and blossoms—properly applied, y'know. So I'll away and begin our flowery campaign,—violets t' begin with or lilies o' the valley, suggestin' a sweetly tender humility! So cheer up, old f'low. I'll set about it at once." And off he speeds again, but very soon reappears, to say in awed tone and with looks of consternation: "Sam, oh, Sam —the Juggernaut's below with Sir John, demanding speech with you. So, dear, old lord,—will you, for my sake,—the elopement business,—will you?"

Sam scowls but unwillingly and perforce agrees,—whereupon his faithful Harry murmurs gratefully and hastens away on his self-imposed mission.

Thus presently my lord rises as Lady Marwood is ushered in by Sir John who, after a few perfunctory remarks, bows himself out again.

Lady Marwood surveys this hoped-for son-in-law, her eyes large with yearning, and strikes an attitude:

"Ah—he is pale!" sighs she, as to an invisible audience. "Pale yet so romantically pallid! Ah, Japhet, thou art our hero, our conqueror triumphant! Thou art indeed the——"

"Oh, madame, pray be seated," says my lord bowing, and reaches for a chair wherefore my lady emits a tender scream:

"No! Ah—no! Thine arm—thy wound that badge of glory,—trouble it not. See, unaided—I sit! Come you beside me, dear, heroical boy. Ah, what maternal bosom but would swell with pride for such son? What gentle, sweet-shy feminine heart could resist you? Surely not mine nor the heart of my beloved Rowena——"

"My lady, you overwhelm me!"

"Dear Japhet, if I do, 'tis with a mother's devotion,—for doth not my sweet child adore you—her hero? Thus when I surprised the secret of your proposed elopement I kept the secret locked within my bosom, even from my own child—for the sweet romance of it all—to fly together—upon speedy wheels—at midnight's hour—— Oh, very ecstasy! Ah, but, I have to warn you, there is a—hitch! And all owing to the Duchess! For her Grace has sent us such pressing, such very urgent invitation, indeed she is so persistent that I cannot possibly refuse. So that, dear boy, on the night appointed for your elopement Rowena and I shall be domiciled with the Duchess."

"I see!" murmurs my lord. "We must alter our arrangements somewhat."

"Precisely! Ah, dear Japhet, could you but enlist her Grace's aid—you are already high in her esteem—with her to assist you, all would be well."

"Yes," nods my lord, "it would be mere plain sailing then. I'll try it."

"Then—you will succeed! Yes, you will bear from me my olive branch, my one beloved child—you and she to rapture! Ah, but my lonesome pillow will be moist with a mother's tears—tears of woe for my loneliness, but of joy for her and your happiness!"

My lady Marwood's large, soulful eyes are indeed moist with tears, real or so well simulated that my lord feels a twinge of something very like remorse when at last he bows her out and away.

Being alone he remembers his useless letter to Andromeda and intending to destroy it, thrusts hand into the pocket of his dressing robe and finds there his handkerchief and nothing more,—begins a languid search for it, wearies and thinking of Andromeda, forgets all about it. . . .

It is about now that Mr. Standish, this indefatigable friend, having no better fortune with flowers, yet indomitable as ever, demands word with the Duchess herself in my lord's name, is admitted to her dominating presence and there pleads his lordship's woeful plight to such effect that this small, potent lady knits her brow and gazes wide-eyed on vacancy, like a musing Sibyl, nods her arrogant head like chiefest of the remorseless Fates, giggles suddenly, like a schoolgirl and beckoning Mr. Standish near, bestows such counsel that he giggles also,—and returns jubilant to find my lord sunk in a gloom deeper than ever.

"Well, Harry?" his lordship demands, hopelessly.

"Ex-ceeding well!" nods Mr. Standish, at his jauntiest. "The Duchess and I have arranged it all! Three nights hence you will elope—but from—her Grace's house!"

"Ay, I know that!" growls Sam. "But—what o' me and——"

"You, m'dear f'low, will drive away—not in your own but in one of her Grace's carriages and with four relays o' horses on the road. You should arrive at th' chiefest inn at Wrybourne in time for breakfast. . . . And there you will find happiness."

"Is there such a thing?" groans Sam. "But what the devil—why all this confounded mystery, this——"

"M'dear, old lord, no mystery, no! At eleven precisely, three nights hence, you step into her Grace's carriage and——"

"But why hers? What the——"

"That's all I can tell you. Now curse me if y' feel so inclined but—ha, thank heaven, there's the supper bell! C'on old f'low, let's peck and sip—do us both good——"

CHAPTER XI

HOW THEY FARED—HOMEWARDS

RAIN, and a wind that raves in angry gusts, the clocks chiming eleven—and my lord, guided by Mr. Standish, reaches the shelter of a dim seen gateway, hears a sound of hoofs and wheels, sees in the rain-lashed darkness the loom of a carriage that stops and is helped up into its black interior; then the door slams, hoofs clatter, wheels grind and away rumbles this vehicle.

My lord has not travelled very far when he raises his voice above rumble and clatter and hiss of wind-driven rain, to say—far more pleasantly than he feels:

"Well, Rowena, we're off! But—what a night for us! How are you feeling?" But instead of the sweet voice expected, all he hears is rumble and clatter and rush of wind.

Surprised and startled, he tries again:

"Rowena, you're here, of course,—but where are you?" Still nothing to hear save the rumble and rush of their going. So my lord reaches out his one serviceable hand . . . touches velvet, feels beneath this a firm, round arm that snatches itself from his contact.

"Good Lord!" he exclaims. "Surely you're not—afraid of me, Rowena?"

"No!" answers a voice, richly sweet though bitterly scornful. "Oh no, she would probably be in your arms,—but I would rather be lying out in the mud and rain!"

"Well . . . now . . . damme!" gasps Sam, hardly believing his ears. "What the—how—Andromeda! What in the world are you doing here?"

"It seems your lordship has entered the wrong carriage!"

"Oh no, madam, no!" says my lord, "it is only too perfectly evident that you are kidnapping me."

"Lord Wrybourne, bid your coachman turn and drive me back at once, or you will compel me to—to scream."

"Madam, you would merely waste your precious breath, for my coachmen never heed women's screams, indeed they usually drive faster. So, instead, pray inform me what astounding and happy chance brings you within reach of my arms——"

"Never dare to touch me again!"

"Oh, but I must,—yes, my lady, you shall lie—cradled upon my bosom, unless you explain how and why you are here."

"Because of your lying message."

"But I sent you no message, and my letter you refused——"

"Yet I received your deceitful note—here it is."

"May I have it?"

"Yes, pray take the loathsome thing!" In the darkness this paper is given and taken by fingers that shrink from each other's touch.

"And now, madam," says my lord, slipping this into his pocket, "since it is too dark for reading, pray tell me what is written—the words of this message."

"Oh, no," sighs she, wearily, "you know all its cruel falsity."

"However, madam, I beg you'll tell me—or know the hideous shame of my embrace."

"Anything rather than—that!" she retorts. "This deceitful note, so far as I recall, says: 'If you would see him in life and before the end, go at once to Mrs. Leet's cottage at Wrybourne'."

"Ha!" exclaims my lord. "So at once you set out—and in this storm! I wonder why?"

"Because I believed he was my clean, pure-hearted Sam—instead of this—this false, hateful profligate and brutal duellist Lord Wrybourne."

"Madam, now you astonish me! For here are you even now, kidnapping this same unfortunate, misunderstood gentleman who fondly imagined he was eloping with a lady beautiful as yourself,—though her silky tresses are a glorious gold instead of—merely black."

"Oh, how incredibly vile to so parade her shame and your own! I beg you will say no more—for her wretched sake."

"So be it, madam. Though 'pon my soul, I'm greatly wondering where she can have got to. I should be carrying her south and indeed thought I was. Why aren't I? Where is she? There's something vastly wrong somewhere. The question is—what?"

"No, my lord, the question is—why! Why are you not upon your death-bed in Mrs. Leet's cottage?"

"Oh, lady! Are you reproaching, blaming me for daring to be alive to retort upon you instead of lying dead, a poor object for your gracious pity and all-too-late endearments?"

"No, my lord, I blame myself for believing there ever was a Sam."

"Then, madam, is my so detested, libertine lordship to understand that you truly loved this Sam fellow?"

"God knows I did."

"Then why a God's name, did you make a football of his poor simple heart? How could you let him go out to fight for his life with scorn in your eyes, upon your lips and anger in your heart? Madam, I await your answer." Instead, she turns on him to demand, breathlessly:

"Oh . . . how dare you . . . affront me with such questions? You . . . whose name is the subject of such infamous gossip . . . duellist, gambler, base seducer—how dare you speak to, much less question me? Drive back, my lord, drive back and in my place take up that poor, frail creature you expected, this miserable girl who is so unwise ever to trust herself to such as you! Go back and if in you is one spark of honour,—cloak her shame with marriage."

For some while after this wild tirade, no word is uttered; even after cobbled streets have given place to the open road and their going smoother and less noisy, my lord remains speechless.

And so, once again, out of the darkness nearby this fiercely scornful voice lashed him:

"Do I then plead your wanton's cause in vain? Why do you not return and take her to your arms? Is it because your lordship is already wearied, sated, and seek newer prey? Well, here am I—alone and at your mercy, but——"

"Yes, madam, you are certainly alone, but alas—I have only one arm to serve me. Wherefore you may know yourself, for the time at least, safe from my brutality. But, my lady, being now in the dark and unable to feast my wicked eyes on your enticing beauty, I can the better appreciate and realize the acid venom of your tongue, the hidden cruelty of you that, perched upon your pinnacle of chastity, can so condemn and vilify your sister woman. Ah, the Lord protect me, ay, and especially all unfortunate she creatures, from the merciless rage of a virtuous woman!"

"While your lordship takes breath, may I suggest once more that you turn back and exchange me for your——"

"Don't say 'wanton' again!"

"Sir, I shall say precisely as I will . . . but now, because," here her voice falters, "because of what I once . . . believed you to be . . . I beg you will order the carriage to turn back or . . . suffer me to alight."

"A light?" he repeats. "Happy thought!" And fumbling in the darkness he finds the check-string at last, pulls it and the carriage jolts to a halt. Then the door opens on wind-swept blackness and a voice enquires:

"Yes, m'lord?"

"Why are we driving without lights?"

"Wind do blow 'em out, sir."

"Have we no lamp in the carriage?"

"Yes, m'lord."

"Then light it."

"I be reekin' wet, m'lord."

"No matter,—light it." In comes a rain-scattering shape and, after some to-do, the lamp is lit and seems quite dazzling.

"How far to the first stage?"

"Matter o' five mile, m'lord."

"Then lock both doors!"

"Yes, m'lord!"

Now as they drive on again, the flickering light showing that beloved face and form, my lord keeps his eyes averted as he says:

"Madam, as I have been compelled to hear your reproaches, you shall now hear me—are you listening?" he demands, for she has turned, hiding her face in the deep shade of her bonnet.

"Yes, since I must! But why weary me and shame yourself with more lies?"

"Ah, what venom!" sighs my lord. "Should you ever wed, your spouse is to be pitied. However, you with poisonous tongue have defamed a sweet and lovely lady, called her wanton, not that you know this for truth but merely because of rumour that I love her——"

"Can you—dare you deny it?"

"Certainly I can—and do!'"

"Oh, insufferable! I tell you Lady Marwood boasts how you love her daughter, Rowena herself admits it! And to-night——"

"To-night, madam, I should have eloped with her that she might wed the man she loves, my friend Harry Standish. A promising scheme which you have wrecked very completely. And why? Be pleased to inform me."

Now at this, Andromeda turns to look at him with such fury of passionate contempt as for the moment seems beyond utterance, yet when she contrives to speak it is in quite passionless tone:

"Lord Wrybourne, being a Scrope, shameless evil is part of your heritage——"

"Too true!" he sighs.

"So now to spare myself the shame of hearing you perjure yourself any longer, I will show evidence of your base deception,—words written and signed by you!" And from the bosom of her cloak she draws a letter and tosses it contemptuously upon the seat beside him;—taking this up, my lord sees it is superscribed: To The One, and as contemptuously tosses it back, saying:

"This is the letter poor Sam wrote to Andromeda——"

"Oh, no!" she retorts, bitterly. "This is the letter my Lord of Wrybourne sent to the woman for whom he fought, risked his life, and maimed her then acknowledged lover!"

"Then pray how did you come by it?"

"Lady Marwood's French maid delivered it to me—by mistake, of course!"

"And you kept it for proof of my lordship's infidelity! Yet, madam, I tell you again—that letter was written to you by poor, grievous, woeful, wounded Sam pleading your mercy,—the letter that merciless, hard-hearted you returned —it is the same letter poor, desperate Sam, heart-broken by your cruelty, rammed into his pocket and lost while listening to the Marwood Mama who must have found or taken it under a misapprehension, believing 'The Only One' to be her daughter—no pray do not interrupt! Finding her mistake this 'Darling Mama' gave it to the right and Only One, either to help or hurt her——"

"Oh, why plague me with this absurd rigmarole, all these audacious, wicked——"

"Don't say 'lies'!" he warned her. "Instead, tell me—did you show this letter to the Duchess—did you?"

"Yes, I did and——"

"Then God bless her nimble wits! Ah, what a woman! For you are her riposte, her counter-stroke to 'Darling Mama', yes—you! For by her contrivance here you are, despite yourself and your silly, cruel doubts,—within reach of my arms—no,—my arm!" So saying he rose and seated himself beside her and so near that she drew away, shrinking further into her corner, saying as she did so:

"My lord—no—I beg——"

"Oh damme!" exclaimed Sam, scowling. "Andromeda, don't be such a fool." Now though his voice was harsh and face grim, she sighed deeply and her whole quivering body relaxed because instead of cynical, smiling, gently-spoken aristocrat here beside her was gruff sailorman.

"Now, woman," he growled, "you're going to hear God's truth and, believing it, come into my arms—no, arm, and lie here on my heart where you belong,—ay, and shed a tear or so, that I may kiss 'em away,—or—call me 'liar' again, but—for the last time on this earth. So—are you listening?"

"Yes!" she answered, looking into these grey eyes of his that were always too steadfast for deceit. "Tell me—Sam!"

And so, beginning with his arrival in London, tell her he did and with such minute detail that they lost count of time, nor heeded how often where or when they stopped at the various stages to change horses.

"Now," he demanded, when at last this very protracted narration was ended, "are you going to pipe your lovely eye with regret for your loss o' faith and cruel treatment of poor Sam? Are you going to cuddle up to me close as possible and confound my arm! Are you going to give me that lovely beloved mouth that is quivering already, or——" Andromeda, swift and passionate in her remorse, did all he bade. . . . Lips to lips and breast to breast she clung to him, though tenderly careful of his slung arm, her coquettish bonnet back-thrown upon loosened strings that she might see him the better.

"Oh," sighed she, at length, removing her bonnet altogether, "thank God the detestable earl is gone and my Sam come back to me."

"Madam," says my lord, "it is but right you should know and fully apprehend that both you and your Sam are now and henceforth my lordship's own particular property."

"Indeed, my lord," she answers, almost shyly, "I can well believe it and do own it gladly—when I am safe on the breast of my Sam."

Thus, stage by stage, southward they journeyed through the rushing darkness, yet now about them was a radiance not of the flickering lamp, but a glory all their own. And when at last he bade her try to sleep, she pillowed her head upon his breast and with a sigh of happy weariness, obeyed.

As for Sam, looking down upon this beloved head, this splendid woman that he knew at last was all his own—and remembering how and why,—he called down fervent benedictions upon the little Duchess and presently slumbered also. . . . He awoke to find his head softly pillowed (a fragrant pillow this that slowly, gently rose and fell) and the golden eyes of Andromeda looking down upon him in a radiant dawn.

"You slept," she murmured, "like a baby. And sometimes you are very like a child. Now lie still and hear me tell my Lord of Wrybourne it is the sailor, just Sam that I so truly love——"

"Which, madam, is a marvel!"

"And because I love only Sam, my lord must woo and win me for himself—for Sam's sake."

"This, my lady Witchery, shall be my lordship's persistent and joyous endeavour. Though I am astonished that you, a lady born and bred can stoop to bless such rough, clumsy fellow. So I desire to know how and why—your Loveliness can possibly love this graceless Sam?"

"At first, my lord, just because he was Sam, and later because he is so very much more than I ever dreamed,—so wise and generous that he could give back half his fortune, so magnanimous that he could even free his avowed enemy from prison and allow him the chance of new life and happiness, and—yes—such a man that he could out-wit and out-fight the merciless wretch everyone believed quite invincible! These, my lord, are a few reasons why I love—only Sam. I shall find many others later which I will mention to your lordship. And now, Sam dear, where are you taking this woman of yours?"

"First to Grannyanne's cottage, according to that mysterious note—'if you would see him in life' and so on. I'm still wondering who wrote it."

"I guess that Godmother of mine, all things considered."

"Ha, the Duchess again! So I guess, and God bless her! She's a grand person, ay, and so is Grannyanne, you've learned to know her lately, haven't you?"

"So well that I understand why Sam is so fond of her."

"And what of your Uncle Arthur?"

"Godmother has commanded him to paint her portrait."

"Splendid! And when it's done, she won't allow him to destroy it—not she! It may do him a power o' good, let's hope so. . . . Listen,—there's Wrybourne church-clock striking eight! Soon we shall be kissing Grannyanne and having breakfast with my shipmate Ned and his Kate at Willowmead where we shall bring to,—anchor, d'ye see, till our wedding day. That day of days when you will glorify Sam into your husband—learn him something of your own gracious dignity and gentleness. And then, Andromeda, with you always within hail o' me——"

"With my 'acid tongue', Sam dear!"

"Ay, to be sure, your sweetly acid little tongue to rake me fore and aft with shattering broadside when needed, or bring me up with a round turn if I'm in shoal water with social rocks in my lee! Ah, but—then my Andromeda, we together, you and I, will steer such course that soon or late, this cursed name of Scrope shall come to be honoured and someday, maybe—even loved."

"It will be, my dear one,—oh, it shall be!"

"Why then, if . . . Oh, Andromeda, if we should be so blest . . . children, d'ye see, my dearest, we should leave them something worthy—to live and strive for."

"A heritage truly honourable, my Sam, a heritage noble as my own sailorman,—to endure long after us, I pray God, clean, strong and true as Old England itself. Oh, lovely thought!"

"And yonder," said Sam, drawing her arm closer about him, "yonder is Wrybourne Church where, soon as maybe, a sailorman will be spliced to his lass,—so now, my lady, pray kiss your lord, to seal the blessed compact."

Thus, in this new day, through a world all green and fragrant after last night's storm,—now, with rumble of wheel and thud of hoof, they turned into that familiar, shady lane in time to hear, sweet as any piping bird, Jane's high, clear voice upraised in her favourite song:

"In Scarlitt town where I was borned
There was a fair maid dwellin'
Made every lad cry lack a day
Her name was Bar-bree Alling . . ."

Then rose the deep, joyous barking of a dog.

"And there," said Andromeda, sitting up to adjust her cloak, smooth frills and furbelows and tie on her plumed bonnet, "there is our welcome home!"

"Ay, 'home'!" repeated Sam. "The dearest word in any language, and with you in it, Andromeda, the loveliest, the holiest, the most——" But here, with murmur rather like a sob, Andromeda kissed him.